KINGDOM OF A
THOUSAND
DAYS

He was like some small, rare species
come to roost in the Kingdom of the Zulus,
his red hair and blue eyes a mark of his rarity.

ISABELLA BLESZYNSKI

To my grandfather, William Macpherson, master seafarer and story teller,
who showed me how to find my way by the stars.

Also to my grandmother, Jessie Dubh Macpherson,
who had her own tales to tell.

Earthly power does not last forever
Neither do the men, black or white
Who imagine they hold it in their grasp.
Zululand 1828

Prologue

1825. *The north-east of Scotland,*

Mid-February, and the frost had been cruel for a week or more. The sky was drained of colour; the farms and crofts huddled low against the snow-blasted Buchan landscape. The pony and trap carrying Charlie and his father lurched and jolted over the icy, rutted roads between Fraserburgh and Aberdeen, his tin trunk and sea bag rattling and louping about on top.

The dull weight of the parting from his mother and the familiar world of his childhood was lodged somewhere between his throat and the pit of his stomach. His eyes felt tight-stretched and gritty, as if he hadn't slept for a week.

The way his mother had gripped him to her at the last had rattled him no end, as had the muted sobbing of his sisters Rebecca and Isabella. Trying to blink away his own tears, he'd been grateful for the pressure of his father's hand on his shoulder and the gentle, but firm way he'd said to his wife, 'It's time for us to be away, Charlotte...the ship'll no wait for us, lass.'

As the horse and trap rounded the end of Commerce Street, leaving the forlorn little family group behind, Charlie shot a sideways glance at his

father. He noted the tightly clenched jaw and the film of sweat on his brow
with some alarm.

'Women's tears,' Francis Maclean muttered, 'if I had to choose between
them or dealing with a South Seas hurricane, I'll give you no prizes as to
which I'd choose, boy. Taking your leave of them is aye the same, pure
bloody murder.'

A moment's silence and then he added, 'Of course, ye maun have sympathy with them, too – the poor mothers having to wave their wee chicks
farewell lang before their time to leave the nest.' He sighed. 'But it's the
way of the world, Charlie, there's no getting away from it.'

Shooting a sideways glance at the bent head of his nine-year-old son
and noting the tell-tale flush on his face, he added gruffly, 'And, in case
ye're wondering – it's no' any better for fathers either, I have to tell you.'

At noon, the pony and trap stopped at a farmhouse standing by the
roadside, an open house for travellers. The farmer's wife bustled in with a
steaming pot of stew, two lassies behind her carrying blue and white
tureens of potatoes, kale and mashed turnip. Afterwards, a huge plum duff
was edged on to the table.

'Load up,' his father said, his blue eyes crinkling at the edges. 'This
could well be the last of a woman's good cooking you'll see for a twelve
month or more.' Stricken, his nine-year-old son looked at him over the top
of the plate, a spoonful of dumpling halfway to his mouth. Francis
Maclean hastened to reassure him.

'No, no, Charlie, don't you fret. Many a fine cook we had aboard ship.
Some will turn out a plum duff every bit as good as this one. Just you wait
and see.'

Outside, Charlie's breath turned into puffs of mist in the bitter cold. He
stood watching the driver of the trap break the ice in the stone trough so
the pony could get a drink before having the nosebag of oats fitted over its
head.

Nearby, drops of icy dew outlined the intricate threads of a spider's
web, while strands of sheep's wool caught on the wire fence stood out in
peaks, stiff and bleached white by the frost.

He stamped his feet and blew on his fingers, the cold nipping at his nose and cheeks. Thrusting his hands into his pockets for warmth, he looked out over the countryside. Frost rimed the fields with silver and the air was sharp and smoky as if someone had lit a pipe nearby. Suddenly, the sullen, grey-beaten sky opened up to allow shafts of sunlight through, turning the wintry landscape into a thing of beauty.

As a curlew cried sharply somewhere over the fields, the boy turned his head in its direction. Crows were wheeling high among the leafless trees and the sharp smell of horse dung and the tang of fresh-chopped turnips were keen in his nose.

A wave of homesickness filled him. Suddenly, leaving on a ship for the Americas or Africa didn't seem such a good idea: they were too far away, too unknown, out there on the edge of the world...

A hand on his shoulder told him it was time to go. 'Don't dwell on things too long,' Francis Maclean said, softly. 'Better to think of what's ahead of ye, there's a lad. Buchan'll aye be here, Charlie.'

He'd arrived with the dawn in August of the year of 1815. He did not arrive so early in the day, however, that his father, Captain Francis Maclean, along with his close friend, John Dalrymple, a shipbuilder and prominent man in the town, felt they should forego a dram or two to celebrate his birth.

The family had come to the town some eight years earlier. This was entirely due to his mother, Charlotte. After faithfully following her husband from port to port along the south coast of England, having babies in each of them, she had finally and firmly put her foot down and insisted on staying in one place. Luckily, she'd had her own way, and now Charlie, or Charles Rawden Maclean, to give him his full name, was the third of her family to be born there.

The town of Fraserburgh lay in the ancient earldom of Buchan, a land of granite, squat dour farms, of wind-stunted trees and lowering skies, out on the exposed shoulder of the north-east of Scotland. Bounded by the North Sea, it was a place as hard as the stones that lay below its soil, one that could break the backs and the hearts of those who were foolhardy enough, or thrawn enough, to till its soil or fish its seas.

Being August, it was the height of the herring season and the town was full to capacity. Fraserburgh had long since earned itself a name for its excellence of herring curing, and exported barrels of the silvery fish to many countries, including the sugar plantations of the West Indies where it formed part of the staple diet of the slave workforce. At this time of year, every spare room, attic and bothy was packed to overflowing with workers, for demand was high.

As he was growing up, the harbour formed a perennial source of interest to Charlie and his friends. Exciting to see the great sailing ships coming in on the tide; intriguing to hear the babble of tongues, Gaelic, the native Doric, Dutch, French and German, with the clanging of bells and the hammering of the coopers ringing out over a melee of boats, men, fisher lassies and predatory seabirds.

The rage and the roar and the smell of the sea were part of the life of the local community. The dread and the pull of it both attracted and yet put the fear of God into them, though they could no more resist its wild call and boundless freedom, than bees could honey. His old friend and story-teller, Sandy, was fond of reminding him of it.

'It's no wonder we folk of the sea are a restless kind at heart,' the old fisherman would say. 'We're nae born for the fireside, and though we might well curse it, the sea is where we belong, and what we must bend ourselves to… aye, boy, to follow the stars, the tides, and the will of the Lord.'

Then he would tease him, his faded blue eyes shining with humour. 'After all, who are you, my bonnie lad? You're of the clan Maclean from the Western Isles: so where else would you go but to the sea? It's in your blood, and that's all there is to it.'

The subject of Charlie's future had been raised when his father came home on leave in November of the previous year.

'It'll soon be time for you to begin your apprenticeship,' he'd said, 'it'll have to be the Mercantile Marine since there's no possibility of you being taken on in the Royal Navy.'

Surveying the boy over the top of his newspaper, he went on, 'The country's been in a parlous state since the end of Napoleon's war. 1815, the same year you were born – though I expect you know that already, since I've mentioned it a few times. Experienced officers like myself have nearly all been pensioned off – till we get to the next war, of course,' he added, with a touch of cynicism.

He cleared his throat. 'The man I'm going to put in charge of you is well known to me. Lieutenant James King's a fine man, and a God-fearing Presbyterian, at that. He's from Halifax in Nova Scotia.'

Seeing the look of apprehension crossing his son's face, his blue eyes lit up in humorous self-defence. 'Och, now, Charlie, would I put you aboard with a Holy Willie, eh? Never fear, he's a good man and one that can take a laugh.'

And so it was decided. At the end of February, he would board Lieutenant King's brig the *Mary*. Outward bound on a trade run, they would sail first to South America and then across the South Atlantic to the Cape of Good Hope where the Lieutenant had business to attend to.

The Cape of Good Hope… the Americas!

His heart pounding with excitement, Charlie had run like a hare all the way down to the fisher town of Broadsea, racing round the gable-end of Sandy's cottage and in through the door in a whirl of snowflakes to tell the old man his news.

It ran like wildfire around the town. Soon, every lad he met knew about it and, as he was to find out, the news had also travelled to the school dominie, Mr Woodman.

Out with his friends, running with a terrier or two at their heels, he carried on much as before, daring the gale-ridden seas that came spewing and crashing over the harbour wall, braving the depths of the mysterious Wine Tower or scouting round Warld's End, the historic house where it was said the Jacobite rebellion of 1745 had been planned.

Many a time he came home like a drowned rat with his boots full of sand and sea-water, hoping to escape up the back stairs before anyone spotted him. As often as not, luck was against him, for his mother had devilish sharp ears and missed nothing.

One thing he did notice, though. Before, he would have had a skelped arse for the ruination of his clothes, now he just got the telling-off that came with it. And that told him, plain as plain, that he had acquired a new status in his mother's eyes. These days, she would hesitate before aiming a slap at the backside of an officer apprentice about to go off to the Americas and then Africa…well, that was Charlie's way of thinking, anyway.

On his very last day at school, the dominie had risen from behind his high desk, cleared his throat, and fixed him with a look in his eye that was very different from its usual disciplinary glint. At the sight of it, cold finality settled in Charlie's stomach like so much ballast. If old Woodie was in a friendly mood, it really was the end.

As Mr Woodman rubbed his hands together, the sound rasped in the sudden hush that had fallen over the classroom. The smouldering peat in the fireplace settled in the grate with a crackle and spit. Hitching up the faded scholar's gown on to his shoulders, he announced gruffly, 'You'll all have heard of the great adventure that Charles Maclean will be setting out on in the bye and bye. I'm sure you'll want to join with me in wishing him good fortune and safe voyage.'

Once out of the school door, Charlie had followed his deepest instincts and bolted like a hare all the way down to the harbour. Buffeted by the ice-laden nor'easter tearing in off the Firth, and soaked by the spray coming in over the sea wall, he'd thought his heart would burst.

His school days were over. No more running down to Sandy's; no more seeing Ginger Tamac, the cat, with its paws tucked neatly below it, casting a winking eye at him as he appeared in the doorway; no more reading the adventures of Daniel Defoe to his young brother, Henry, no more…

Mind you, looking back on it, Charlie wondered if Sandy had been so sure of his calling at all, especially when he'd finally stood before him, all stiff in his new clothes with his red hair braided behind into a pigtail, and his sea-bag and tin trunk packed and waiting for him at home in Commerce Street.

Bound for the far-away southern oceans and the land of Africa, and all the time trying hard not to look what he really was, a lad of only nine years and six months of age.

Sandy's pipe had wobbled between his clenched teeth as he'd bade him farewell at the cottage door. A look of dread had crossed the old story teller's face, a sudden shine and fierceness filling his faded blue eyes, both for the missing of him from his place at his elbow – but most of all, for the fear of the wrath of the cruel sea.

It was one thing to tell a boy about the sea and its moods, to cover over the hardships and dangers with blithe sailors' songs and tales of adventure from the safety of the hearth with the firelight gleaming on brass and Ginger Tamac purring fit to burst – it was quite another to think of him far from home, and with only the grace of the Almighty to keep him from its pitiless ways.

'Mind you say your prayers, now,' was all the old man could say. His work-worn hand gripped Charlie's shoulder as if unwilling to let him go from the safety of his fireside. 'An' may the good Lord keep you safe, boy…'

Not long after the Southampton-bound vessel set sail from Aberdeen and passed the Girdleness light, Charlie became aware of the sea-dog lurking below the exterior of the tall, red-haired man who was his father.

Seeing him framed against a backdrop of plunging decks and whipping sails, Charlie realised that the smile on his father's wind-chapped face was one of exhilaration, even of joy. Suddenly, he understood that for all its trials, dangers and unpredictability, Captain Francis Maclean loved the sea, loved the restless ocean in the very heart and bones of him; all of its comings and goings, the sight and sound and smell of it, the cold nor' easters, the taste of salt on his chapped lips and the wild, open skies above his head.

The purpose of their journey also became clear. It was no less than a symbolic handing over of his son to the great sailing ships and oceans of the world, an introduction to the mistress he would be bound to for the rest of his life. This was his birthright, his heritage and his destiny, things they both now shared. He had done the same with Charlie's elder brothers, Francis and Alexander, sharing the last precious days of boyhood with them before the tall ships and the tides had borne them away.

Painfully, Charlie swallowed the lump in his throat. The words of Sandy, the old *sennachie,* came spinning out of the snow-flecked ocean, bringing tears to his eyes.

'Folk like us are nae born for the fireside, Charlie – and though we might curse it at times, the sea is where we belong, and what we must bend ourselves to – aye, boy, to follow the stars, the tides, and the will of the Lord.'

On the night before they docked at Southampton, Charlie and his father stood out on deck in the bitter cold looking up at the icy stars suspended in the winter blackness above them.

'Keep a weather eye open for the Southern Cross when you get below the Line, Charlie,' Francis Maclean said. 'It'll be a constant for you, the same as the North Star, Polaris. ' Holding his nine-year old son tightly against him, his voice was suddenly gruff as he spoke. 'Remember to keep your eyes on the stars, lad. They can be a comfort in hard times.'

They stood for a long time under the glittering northern skies, Charlie's face pressed against the brass buttons of his father's Navy greatcoat, smelling the smell of home on him, while the winds and the tides carried them ever nearer to the parting of the ways.

As he stepped on to the gangway of the *Mary*, his boots rang hollow on the ridged boards. As he made his way up towards the open deck, his canvas sea-bag bumped against his back, the edge of a tin cup digging into him. His father strode on ahead, bearing the blue-painted sea-kist on his shoulder. On it, he had carefully printed Charlie's details, the white lettering standing out clean and proud against the fresh blue.

C. R. MACLEAN
FRASERBURGH, SCOTLAND

As Charlie struggled on behind, a stray thought hit him. I wonder where my feet will hit the ground next? Will it be South America, St Helena – or even Cape Town? His mouth went dry with the thought of it.

At the end of the gangway, the rails of the brig stood deserted in the cold morning air. The thud of booted feet on the deck made his heart jump. A booming voice hailed them. 'Welcome aboard! Francis, old man, it's been a long time.'

What immediately struck Charlie was the odd twang in the man's speech. Then he remembered that his new captain came from Nova Scotia, far away across the North Atlantic. Glancing up, he found himself looking into a pair of startling, deep blue eyes with a pair of dark eyebrows quirking good-naturedly above them.

Lieutenant James Saunders King, his new captain, was tall, a few years younger than his father, with a broad streak of silver running through his shock of black hair. Stocky of build, he was wrapped up against the cold in an old naval greatcoat, an incongruous red and yellow striped muffler looped around his neck.

A hand fell on his shoulder, and James King said with a grin, 'So this is Charlie. A grand name, fit for a king.' His laughter boomed out over the bare, wind-scoured harbour.

'Och, still at it, James, I see,' said Francis Maclean, gripping his old friend's hand. 'Aye one for the Cause, eh? It's a wonder ye're no sporting the Jacobite white cockade into the bargain – just to show the world where your allegiances really lie!'

James King struck a dramatic pose, hand on heart, 'No need for out-ward show, Francis. Keep it close to the heart, that's my motto.'

Another hearty laugh, a slap or two on their backs and then they were whisked away into the pleasant fug of the Master's quarters, Charlie's sea kist and bags stowed away below decks.

For the next two or three days, that's how it was; Charlie watching his father and his old friend re-live their war-time experiences, himself listening to it all, already missing his father though he was still in front of him.

They made their farewells an hour or so before the *Mary* was due to sail. Even though he'd said to his father that it was all right and not to wait in the cold, Charlie's heart lifted when he caught sight of him standing on the pier, bareheaded in the smoky grey dawn, his red hair forming a visible link between them.

Francis Maclean raised his hand in a last salute. Then, easing his naval cap back on to his head, he thrust his hands into his pockets, turned and began to walk away down the cobbled pier.

As he watched his father's tall figure disappear among the bustle of dray carts and scurrying humanity, a wave of dislocation and shock ran through Charlie.

Clutching the ship's rail, he pushed down the awful need to call him back, to say he didn't want to be a mariner after all, and that he wanted to go home with him, back to the Broch, back to all that was familiar… and oh, so dear.

'Well now, Heelander,' a voice drawled at his shoulder. 'Whatever it is ye're thinking, it's far too late for it.'

The voice had a Scot's burr, much like his own, but spiced with a flavour he couldn't identify. Later on, he would discover that that it came from the Caribbean island of Jamaica.

Stung by the casual, yet burning truth behind the words, a flicker of annoyance crossed Charlie's face. Whirling around, he found himself looking into a pair of mocking blue eyes. Set in a brown, tanned face, they were offset by a shock of blonde, almost white hair, tied back in a sailor's pigtail with a length of tarry twine.

A flash of gold in the youth's earlobe caught his eye, as did the blue and red rose tattooed on the back of his right hand. About sixteen, he was clad in assorted layers of old, patched jackets with a long blue muffler wound round his neck, his brown legs bare below the ragged work trews, feet thrust into a pair of unlaced boots.

Reaching into the depths of his many layers of clothing, the youth produced a battered tin whistle and a silver and red mouth organ. With a flourish, he raised the whistle to his lips.

'Ta-ra!' After giving him a tootle or two on the whistle, he followed it with a few bars of a sea shanty on the mouth organ. Bestowing on Charlie the impudent grin that would soon become so familiar to him, the exotic stranger punched him gently on the shoulder.

'We're bunk-mates, by the way,' he said. 'Apart from the common herd, that's us. Just you follow Ned Cameron and he'll not see you wrong.'

That particular piece of advice was one Charlie would have cause to hotly debate in the future. As he was soon to find out, his new shipmate could be as tricky as a ferret in a paper bag, with a carefree disregard for anyone's rules but his own.

His blue eyes held Charlie's for a moment in a curiously sympathetic gaze, then he said, 'What ever's on your mind, Heelander, I have to tell ye, all that's past is jist that – done an' dusted with. So it looks like here's where the rest o' your life begins.'

With that, he turned away and headed below decks. After hesitating for a moment or two, Charlie followed him.

All in all, he was pleased with his new life at sea. Was it not fine to have as a bunk mate a lad who wore a gold earring and looked like a Viking pirate, and sometimes to breakfast on cake and raisin bread instead of the usual bowl of parritch?

Added to which, he had made another friend, one unlike any he had ever had before. He was the best and the biggest of all the ship's dogs, and they liked each other fine from the very start. The first time Charlie clapped eyes on him was not long after the ship set sail from Southampton.

The sails were as hard as iron, ice-coated and crackling with frost, snapping against the ropes and rigging. Charlie shivered as he'd watched the men disappear up into the scurrying snowflakes, scrambling aloft to set the sails in readiness for the *Mary* hitting the open seas.

Just then, a movement along the deck caught his eye. He turned his head to see what it was. A dog was standing by the rail. Its massive brown head was raised to sniff the air, ears lifting and ruffling in the bone-chilling wind, the furred, stout legs braced to take the swell of the icy deck.

To Charlie, it looked for all the world like one of the Sheltie ponies he'd seen being led ashore off the Kirkwall boat on to the Fraserburgh pier. In all his born days, he had never seen anything like him . . .

As if aware that someone was watching him, the dog turned its great shaggy head in his direction. A pair of brown eyes set deep in pouched sockets peered at him through the whirling snowflakes. Then a look of glee came into the starry, roguish eyes, a look that said, plain as plain, 'Now here's a boy to my liking, one for a bit of fun!'

The dog ambled towards him, mouth quirked sideways in what looked like a grin. Up close, it was massive, its head level with Charlie's chest, which meant that his ears and the side of his face came well within licking distance, so that he was forced to stagger back against the rail under the friendly onslaught.

First officer, Hatton, came forward to ruffle the hound's shaggy head.

'Well, lad, I see you've made the acquaintance of our Rover. Great tub o' lard he is, but worth his weight in gold. The Captain brought him all the way from his home port of Halifax – that's in Nova Scotia.'

Charlie stared at the first officer, indignation rising in him. *Rover?* he thought – for pity's sake, that's no name for such a magnificent brute! 'Rover' was a feckless kind of word, the sort you would use for any old mongrel. In any case, it was too… English. Aye, that was it. After all, the dog came from Nova Scotia, which as everyone knew means 'New Scotland.'

So, right there and then, Charlie gave him a new name, one in his own Gaelic tongue. *Dileas,* meaning 'the faithful one'. Now there was a name fit for a fine beast, he thought, both in the Gaelic and the English too. But it would just be between the two of us, for now, he warned his new friend, who rewarded him with another wide grin.

Lieutenant King appeared by the companionway. A smile crossed his face when he saw his youngest crewmember and the massive dog standing close together.

Seeing it was his first voyage as his officer apprentice, Charlie attempted to stand to attention in the way his father had taught him, but what with the cant of the deck on one hand and the weight of the dog leaning against him on the other, he struggled to stay upright.

The Lieutenant, if he'd noticed any breach of sea-going etiquette, drew no attention to it and came forward to pat the dog's broad head. 'New-foundlands like this good old boy are much prized, you know,' he explained. 'They're powerful swimmers. Their layers of fat and muscle and thick coats mean they can survive even the coldest of waters, and for long spells, at that. Many a seafarer has owed their lives to them.'

Smiling, he ordered the dog to lie down on the deck, which it did with great obedience. Lifting up a large front paw, King showed Charlie the flaps of webbed skin between the toes.

'Imagine that,' Charlie said, amazed to see such a thing. 'Fancy a dog having feet like a frog!' Both King and first officer Hatton joined in the laughter.

The word 'frog' set him thinking. This was the time of year he and his friends usually went out looking for tadpoles and young frogs in the ponds and burns outwith the town – only this time they would be going without him…

He pushed away the treacherous memories. Och, he told himself, frogs are just frogs. Dileas is better than any amount of tadpoles.

Little did he know then, how soon afterwards he would be grateful for the dog's webbed feet and what he had been told about the breed known as Newfoundlands.

There was no sparing anyone from certain duties, and Charlie was there to learn. *'All hands aloft!'* The command meant what it said.

He had been up in the yards before, with no mishap other than a few barked knuckles and a skinned toe or two. This time, however, when the *Mary* was somewhere off the Azores, his bare feet must have slipped on an oily rung or he'd misjudged the distance, for down he went, grabbing frantically at the rigging to try to save himself from falling.

Too late; gravity and the cant and sway of the ship dislodged him completely. The burn of the rope on the palms of his hands, a jolt of panic, his heart hammering in his mouth, then there was nothing but space and a sick feeling in his belly. He fell like a stone, and went on falling, the air rushing past him, his feet twisting over his head. Somebody was yelling and screaming and he realised it was himself.

The sea rushed up and hit him with a smack that knocked the breath from his body. Then he was falling again, going down, down, into the warm green saltiness, the waters closing over his head. It was followed by a rushing and pressure in his ears then a deep silence. Gradually, he became aware of the world of water in which he was suspended, floating, spiralling downwards.

Charlie discovered that his eyes were open and he could see. His long red hair had come loose from its pigtail and was floating like tendrils of weeds around his face, his hands like pale fish in front of him.

He looked up and saw a layer of light far above. Floundering, striking out with his arms and legs, his mouth tightly shut, he struggled up towards it. Even as his head broke the surface, he was yelling, taking in great gulps of air. Salt water rushed into his mouth. Coughing and spluttering, salt stinging his eyes, he felt himself begin to go down again.

Charlie had never learned to swim. For all their talk of the sea and its dangers, very few of the local people along the north-east coast could swim, which was a queer enough thing when you think of it, because most of them were seafarers and constantly at its mercy. Struggling against the downward pull, desperately trying to remember what real swimmers might do, he made strong paddling movements with his hands and feet.

Buoyed up by the salty water, he somehow managed to tread water and keep himself afloat. Pushing the hair back off his face, he took in deep gulps of air. As he retched up dribbles of sea water, his throat burned with the sting of raw salt.

How long would it take the vessel to come about and find him?

The glare of the sun bouncing off the sea was blinding. He squeezed his eyes shut and saw black spots dancing behind his closed lids. The heat drilled through his sodden shirt, skewering him with red-hot needles as he bobbed about in the swell like a cork.

When he rose on the crest of the next wave, he looked for a sight of the brig's tall masts. But there was nothing, only the dip and swell of the ocean and the sapphire blue bowl of the sky above. No ship, no long-boat…

Wild fear took hold of him and shook him like a rat. Growing up, he'd listened to tales of mariners falling like a stone from the shrouds, or being washed out over the rail in heavy seas, drunk, sober or playing the fool – some even throwing themselves over the rail in despair when the harshness of life got too much for them.

Even if the man overboard was lucky enough to be spotted, it was virtually impossible to slow a vessel down fast enough, let alone turn her round. By the time the anchor was let out and a boat launched, it was usually too late to save the poor devil – even if they could locate him among the swelling waves and troughs.

His boy's heart quailed. Now he knew why most seafarers chose not to learn to swim. 'Better to let the sea take you,' he heard a gruff voice say, 'better than swimming around in circles till your strength gives out, waiting, hoping and praying for the rescue that never comes.'

The swell lifted him and bore him up on its crest and then down into the next green trough. *How long should I wait,* he thought… *how long before I let the sea take me?* A quiver of distaste ran through him.

And…and what if they come looking for me just as the waters are closing over my head, what would I do then? Revulsion was replaced by a shaky sense of defiance. *Sandy – what would Sandy be telling me if he was here now?*

He'd never tired of hearing the story of how the old story teller had miraculously been on hand, one blustery March morning, to save him from falling off the pier and likely drowning when he'd been no more than three years old.

A sudden image of a pair of piercing blue eyes came flooding back to him; eyes that held the long hard stare of a man used to squinting at far horizons and scanning the skies for signs of bad weather or approaching squalls.

The eyebrows above them were fierce and sculpted, great swooping wings of peppered grey that tapered out to silver points before curling back in on themselves. They dominated his face, giving him the look of a hooded and wise old eagle.

He had told Charlie that they had been blown into that shape by the nor'easters, the winds that were a constant on that part of the Scottish coast. And for years and years, until he was about eight years old or so, Charlie had believed him.

And it was to that image that the nine-year-old now clung. What would Sandy be telling him now?

'*Let go, boy, dinna struggle…it's just the way of the sea claiming its own. Ye kent fine the risk…*'

Or would it be: '*Och, tae hell wi' trumpin' your end afore its time, Charlie Maclean. Stick in there an' pray like buggery somebody saw ye fall.*'

Charlie coughed up some more water then tried to hold on to the face of the man who had once saved him from the sea. *Save me now, Sandy…*

Due to his father's frequent absence on naval duties, the fisherman came to be his mentor, historian and fellow adventurer. There was no witch, mermaid or kelpie that he hadn't seen or heard of: no sung or unsung hero or heroine belonging to Scotland's past whose story he did not know.

Picts, Celts and Vikings paraded through Sandy's tales in all their wild glory, catching at Charlie's imagination and colouring his dreams; Robert the Bruce and William Wallace; Mary, Queen of Scots; Edward and Charles and the long line of ill-fated Stuarts. The legions of kings and queens buried on St. Columba's holy isle of Iona were no strangers to him, nor were the Covenanters, the Norse Shetlanders, or the wild cattle reivers of the Highlands travelling down through the high mountain passes with their long-horned shaggy beasts to the markets in the south.

Stay with me, Sandy... he repeated, over and over again. As *long as you're here, all's not lost –*

On the crest of the next wave, he raised his head, his red-rimmed eyes desperately scanning the rolling waves of the endless Atlantic. No masts, no ship, no Sandy, the image gone, only the empty ocean and the crystal blue of sky, an empty sky –

What he did see though, was something arrowing its way towards him. There was no mistaking the singular determination in the brown head's unwavering approach, its unerring aim. Thinking it was some kind of sea beast, a shark or some other denizen of the deep coming for him, Charlie yelled out, his voice hoarse with terror. Frantically, he kicked and thrashed, frothing up the water, hoping to drive it away.

A deep, rolling sound carried across the water. His scalp prickled. *Could it be? Could it really be –*

As he rose on the swell of the next wave, he saw it clearly. The Newfoundland, its big head bobbing up and down, strong legs paddling strongly as it closed the distance between them.

Charlie sprang half out of the water in excitement, yelling fit to burst.

'Dileas! Dileas! Here, dog!' Floundering, he went down again, the water closing over his head. In desperation, he pushed himself upwards again, determination in every kick. His head broke the surface, his mouth wide open and gasping for air.

If he were to swear an oath at any time then or since, he could honestly have said that the dog was smiling as it came alongside him. Treading water, it larruped him fiercely with its tongue, all the while growling low down in its throat.

Charlie threw his arms around the animal's neck and held on to him for dear life. 'Good boy, good dog...'

With the wet dog smell in his nose and the heat from its great body warming him, Charlie felt the hot flood of tears spill down his face. After a bit, he stopped sobbing and began to kick out froglike, trying to help the dog so he didn't drag him down.

Dileas started to paddle back the way he'd come, giving out a loud woof from time to time, the boy holding on to the ruff around his neck and paddling alongside. Despair began to edge in again. *Will we be able to find the brig though? What if they haven't noticed we're missing?*

First, a round of frantic barking, then the creak of oars and men's voices echoing over the water. The dog changed direction and headed towards them. As boy and dog rose on the next crest, Charlie spotted a man standing up in the bows of a longboat, shading his eyes against the glare, staring out over the water.

'Here we are!' Over here, over here!' he croaked.

Dileas gave a deep woof and began to swim strongly towards the boat. Then hands were lifting Charlie bodily out of the water, heaving him arse over elbow into the bottom of the boat.

A circle of sweating faces peered anxiously down at him. The first thing he noticed were the scuffed, ruby red carpet slippers belonging to Aloysius Biddle, the bo'sun, which he'd recently taken to wearing because of his bunions. Ned was also there, the sunlight glittering on his gold earring.

'My stars, boy,' Biddle croaked, blinking down at him. 'Ain't you the lucky one?' Sweat dripped off the end of his bulbous nose. 'If it wasn't for that there hound o' yours, we wouldna' have missed ye till suppertime.'

Ned butted in. 'Pay him no heed, Heelander. I saw you take the drop, but by the time I shinned down, you were gone. Never fear, though, the dog spotted your red shirt in the water and went over the side, goin' hell for leather after ye.'

As the seamen bent their backs and rowed to where the brig swung at anchor, the dog swimming alongside, a great cheer went up from the crew lining the rail.

Nicholls, a burly fellow built like an ox, came down on a rope to help the men in the longboat. Charlie was hoisted aboard and dumped on the deck like a prime catch of fish. Stripped of his wet clothes and wrapped in a blanket, he was led off to the galley where Cookie plied him with hot gruel and a dram of grog mixed with boiling water and a spoonful of molasses.

A great fuss was made of the dog for saving Charlie's life. To get it back on board, they had to bring the animal up in a kind of net cradle made out of rope, much jesting going on about its weight.

Ned, playing the fool as ever, pretended to be broken backed, staggering around bent double, carrying it to extremes as he did most things.

If the dog hadn't heard him yelling as he fell from the rigging, or hadn't spotted his red shirt in the water, he would have been lost – but then, Charlie knew better than anyone what his fate would have been.

Nicholls had the last word. With a dead-pan expression, his lined, grey-stubbled face set as if in stone, he grunted, 'Better the sea, lad, than goin' straight down on to the deck. That would do more than knock the breath out of your carcase, I can tell ye.'

After hawking the baccy juice from his throat, he aimed a long, messy spit over the rail. Then he added in the same sombre tone, 'Not only that, Jack me lad – yours truly would've probably had the job o' sluicing down the deck after what was left of ye was put over the side weighed down in canvas.'

But his left eye closed slowly in a huge wink as he said it.

The dog was not the only one to have acquired a new name. Charlie's own name had also changed. Almost as soon as the brig cleared the Solent, he became part of the sea-going fraternity, the brotherhood he would belong to for the rest of his life. In keeping with time-honoured tradition, his past life and land-rooted identity was laid aside. And like many who had gone to sea before him, he came to be known as just 'Jack' or 'Jack, boy.'

Not that Charlie had any problem with this. He knew who he was, Charles Rawden Maclean from Fraserburgh, no matter what anyone else called him. Any other name he collected along the way was just part of where he happened to be at the moment.

Part One

One

September 1825. Cape Town, South Africa.

After endless weeks at sea crossing the South Atlantic, enduring scudding winds and mountainous seas or periods of dead calm and listless, burning air, how grand a thing it was to come at last into the cool grandeur of the Cape of Good Hope.

'Will ye just look at that!' Ned yelled in his ear. Beyond the rail of the *Mary,* Cape Town harbour was packed with ships, the flags and pennants of many nations fluttering at their mastheads. The quayside was abuzz with noise and colour, the cries of the Malay water sellers and merchants vying with the rattle of carts and rolling of barrels across the cobbles.

Excited, Ned pointed out the neat white houses and lush gardens scattered around the bay and the lower foothills of the majestic flat-topped mountain dominating the city. 'Now that's what I call a town, better than Kingston, Jamaica any day!'

Signs of the southern spring were everywhere. A faint dusting of green covered the hillsides, fields and gardens while flowers seemed to be bursting out of every nook and cranny. They gazed open-mouthed at the flat-topped mountain as the spill of dramatic clouds spiralled down from the heights, obscuring the plateau.

'Got its "tablecloth" on today, Jack,' Hatton, the first officer said, as he came up behind them. 'Legend has it there's an old African god up there who keeps the clouds on the boil if he gets a bit mad with what's going on down below.'

As if on cue, the scene before them changed. Clouds began to roll swiftly down the hillside, reducing the colourful panorama of the city and harbour to shades of grey and black.

'I spoke too soon,' Hatton laughed. Handing the boy the ship's glass, he said, 'Have a look, Jack, an' see if you can spot the old fella-me-lad up there who's calling the squall down on our heads.'

Through the powerful eye of the telescope everything was magnified tenfold. Whitewashed houses leapt into his line of vision, along with mansions with red tiled roofs, some with horses and carriages at their doors and winding driveways leading down through vineyards and orchards.

Jack swept the glass up to where the jagged crags of stone and the writhing mists began, then higher still, scanning the grey towers and outcrops of rock. Suddenly, a crag loomed out of the swirling mists, so close he could see the textures of the stone and the tufts of grass and lichens clinging to it.

For a second or two, he could have sworn a face looked back at him, one that was stern and forbidding, a warning in the black eyes that seemed to bore into his.

A stifled gasp shot from him and he almost dropped the telescope.

Ned hissed in his ear. 'What's the matter, Heelander? Seen one of them old gods Hatton was on about, did ye?' Grabbing the telescope, he aimed it at the upper slopes.

After scanning the shifting mists and finding nothing, he grunted, 'Too much Heeland superstition, that's your trouble, Charlie boy!'

A day or two later, Ned came up behind him and looked over his shoulder at the sketch of the waterfront he had pinned to his drawing board. 'The captain got bad news today, I think,' he sniffed, casting a critical eye over Jack's artwork. 'He seemed very agitated when he came back aboard.'

Jack went on drawing. 'What kind of bad news, then?'

'The usual kind is my guess,' Ned retorted. 'He fair threw himself up the gangplank, his heels sparking off the boards, shouting out for Hatton sour-like as he went. Then he barged into the Master's cabin and slammed the door near off its hinges. Shortly after, Hatton was seen to go in.'

Jack looked up expectantly, waiting for the next instalment. When none was forthcoming, he asked mildly, 'Is that all, then? Did ye not manage to hear what was being said?'

Ned Cameron shot him a look salted with varying shades of intolerance. 'My lugs don't stretch that far, Heelander.'

An hour or so later, when the cabin door finally opened, anyone who was passing – which in this case just happened to be Ned – could see a mess of maps and accounts ledgers spread on the table and the Master's cabin thick with cigar smoke and worry.

According to Aloysius Biddle, the bo'sun, who also had ears in many places, the captain's business partner, Lieutenant Francis Farewell, had gone missing. The last heard of him had been a year ago when he'd sailed north with a party of potential investors. But that wasn't all.

Apparently, their supply ship, the Julia, had also disappeared. Port records showed that she'd made the trip back to Cape Town with members of the original party, leaving the Lieutenant and a few others behind in Zululand. After making a quick turn around, the vessel had set off north again with fresh supplies. And that had been the last anyone had seen or heard of her.

The more experienced among the crew of the *Mary* shook their heads. It would hardly be the first time a vessel had disappeared along the treacherous Wild Coast of south east Africa. Even if there were survivors, what hope would there be for mariners unlucky enough to be shipwrecked somewhere along the miles of savage, unexplored coastline?

The following morning, King gathered the crew together. It was clear he'd had a restless night, for it showed in the shadows beneath his eyes and the haggard look around the gills.

'I need to find out what's happened to Lieutenant Farewell,' he said. 'Dead or alive, I need to know, as does his young wife here in Cape Town. She might well be a widow and not know it yet, poor thing.'

A rumble of agreement laced with sympathy ran round the crew. No stranger to them, this tale of lost ships and new widows.

King ran a hand through his unruly black hair. 'There's too much at stake here to sit on our arses and do nothing or wait for news that may never come. It's not only men's lives, but also time, money…aye, and promises given in good faith.'

His eyes travelled round his crew. 'And that includes those I made to yourselves, in that you'd have your bounties if you decided to pitch in with me on this venture, even knowing it might be some time before any profit might be realised.'

Jack listened to the men talking. Ships' masters often followed up lucrative trade deals under their own cognisance. Seafarers' wages were notoriously low, so any chance of bringing some extra silver into their pockets was usually enthusiastically supported.

And he knew from the crew's gossip that this arrangement had seemed a golden opportunity, too good to miss, even if it did entail sailing into new, untested waters – aye, and biding their time till the profits began to come in. Already they'd scored some extra bounty from the trading done in South America, Cape Verdi and St Helena. Good berths were hard to come by, these days, as were good captains.

James King was a sober and God-fearing man. Although he was a teetotaller, he didn't grudge them a bit of carousing ashore and was always on time with their tot of grog. Not a man handy with fist, boot or cat-o'-nine-tails, he had long since earned their respect.

One of them raised the question, 'So what if nothing's been heard of them for a twelvemonth or more? The sea's aye a fickle mistress, even at the best of times.'

'Lord knows, anything could have happened to delay her,' someone else chipped in. 'A broken mast or rudder, sickness, or being beached and not able to get afloat again.'

No need to be unduly pessimistic then, about either the vessel or Lieutenant Farewell's party. No point in sitting in harbour, wasting time, either. What else could they do except go looking for the captain's partner and the lost ship?

By explaining to the crew that they would be sailing into uncharted areas of the south east coast of Africa, King had given them the story straight enough before they'd signed on at either Southampton or on the other side of the Atlantic.

He and his partner were convinced that the venture they had in mind would provide a very lucrative living for those with enough grit and dermination to seize the opportunity. Apart from ivory, which would form their main source of income, an abundance of fine timber was at hand, the land was fertile and well watered and the place was teeming with game.

As mariners, their remit would be to sail between the bay itself, the port of Algoa Bay and Cape Town, delivering goods to be sold at auction before making the return trip carrying fresh supplies and trade goods for the purpose of bartering with the natives.

That was what King had told them. Basically, it was all true. But he hadn't been entirely honest with them, either.

What he had failed to mention was that the ruler of the country they would be entering was a warrior king who happened to have a reputation for savagery unsurpassed anywhere in Africa.

Undoubtedly, he would also be someone who would take great exception to anyone trying to take what was rightfully his, whether goods, chattels or the tusks of the great herds of elephants that roamed his territory.

And now there was something else James King didn't dare tell his crew. Yesterday, when he'd called on Lieutenant Farewell's wife, Elizabeth, to pay his respects, the news she had disclosed to him had forced a return to the *Mary* in somewhat of a hurry.

Apparently, Johannes Petersen, her stepfather, along with twenty-six other investors, had gone north with Farewell in the July of the previous year to assess the trading prospects of the bay and the surrounding area. In fact, a camp had already been set up there, with artisans contracted to construct a stone jetty in preparation for the loading and unloading of goods.

On hearing this, King had to choke down his anger. How dare Farewell go ahead and enter Zululand without making any effort to contact him – especially with such a large number of potential investors in tow! No message had been sent to London to bring him up to date with his plans. As an equal partner, it was the least that Farewell could have done. With a sinking feeling, James King had difficulty in hiding his displeasure and anxiety from Elizabeth Farewell.

But there was more. Apparently, Petersen, now also a major partner, accompanied by the investors – about whom King also knew nothing – had returned post haste to Cape Town in a state of great agitation, after only a few weeks away.

According to her stepfather, who had returned an angry and disillusioned man, not only had he witnessed the horrific executions the warrior king carried out on his people, but he had also been subjected to personal acts of humiliation and cruelty.

On one occasion, he had been forced, on pain of death, to swallow copious quantities of medicines known for their laxative properties. The resulting misery had nearly killed him.

After the *Julia's* failure to return, Petersen had spread rumours around Cape Town that the warrior king, in all likelihood, had appropriated the vessel and slaughtered the remaining white men, including his son-in-law, Lieutenant Francis Farewell.

James King wisely kept his mouth shut. As a man with considerable experience of sea, ships and other inexplicable twists of fate, he suspected there could well be other reasons why the *Julia* had failed to return, or why no news of Farewell had been received.

Fifteen months was a long time, of course. But, given the nature of the wilderness into which they'd ventured, anything could have happened – or very little, depending on one's point of view.

As he paced the Master's cabin, King decided that nothing would be gained by publicly querying Petersen's opinions. It would only fuel more gossip and draw attention to the fact that, not only had the other half of Farewell's partnership arrived in Cape Town, but their grand plan had run into deep difficulties. But that was not all.

The name on the ownership papers of the brig *Mary* might well read '*James Saunders King, Esq.*' but the hard truth of it was that he'd committed a considerable amount of his mother's money, as well as that belonging to other investors, to its purchase. In short, every penny he had in the world was tied up in the success of the joint contract he had entered into with Lieutenant Farewell.

So, come hell or high water, the brig *Mary,* her captain, and every last soul aboard would set sail on the morning tide, and head north to Zululand, and the last known place where Lieutenant Francis Farewell had been seen alive.

Two

Ten days later. The bay of eThekwini

The night was velvet, warm and alive with rustles and whispers. Hosts of insects whirred and chattered while bullfrogs ballooned their cheeks and sounded mating horns from among the reeds and floating lily pads.

In ink-shaded spill of moonlight, a leopard crouched to lap at the water's edge; emerald of eye, a slip of tongue just visible between its incisors and curled lip. Some distance away, an elephant tribe was at play in the shallows, quicksilver ebbing and flowing over their bodies. The old bull reared out of the water, squirted a spray of water over his back and surveyed his herd of matriarchs and youngsters with yawning pleasure.

A watchful baboon paused in the shadows near the water's edge. Teeth bared in silent concentration, its desire for water was tempered by caution as a pair of hump-backed hyena sidled by. Now was the time when predators stalked the night and all soft and fragile things feared the darkness.

High up on the forested headland, a tall man wrapped in a cloak of monkey skins sat cross-legged and unmoving below the pine trees. The cat-like creature at his side kept watchful guard, its whiskers quivering, alert to every sound.

Seemingly impervious to the dangers lurking on the forested heights, the man appeared to be lost in the beauty of the night. With his eyes fixed on the cloudless sky, he rocked to and fro, his lips moving in a soundless chant.

Hypnotic in its silver beauty, the full moon was destined to sail on till morning, its great lunar seas and oceans dark craters on its surface. Mirrored in the waters of the lagoon below, lustrous chips of stellar fire echoed the grandeur of the heavens.

After he had finished praying, the man gathered his cloak around him, settled down among the drifts of pine needles and closed his eyes. His feline companion took up her position beside him and purred softly in her throat.

Far below, the arms of the lagoon held its scattered islands in a loose and loving embrace, while sentinels of birds stood with their heads tucked beneath their wings. Beyond the headland, the Indian Ocean washed along the beaches with a sweet and rhythmic sound.

Some hours later, the moon slipped serenely behind the wooded cape. In the east, a faint blush began to appear on the rim of the world. As it arched slowly upwards, pushing back the night, a flock of crab plovers swooped like silent ghosts over the drowned depths of the ocean, while somewhere among the bamboo thickets along the shore, a bird began a warbling song. A new day had begun.

Up on the headland, the man stirred, then lay for a few moments looking up into the red-streaked morning sky. Casting aside his cloak, he rose to his feet, the long plaits of hair swinging over his shoulders. Beside him, the animal stretched and yawned, showing its sharp white incisors.

The man walked over to the edge of the clearing and drew back the overhanging branches. As he looked out over the lagoon, a smile lit up his face. Although he was still young, Langani was one of the most powerful diviners in the land, and very different from others of his kind.

He had known of the imminent arrival of the white men's vessel long before his human eyes had spotted it in the late afternoon of the previous

day. Now it lay moored well beyond the rocks and treacherous sandbanks
that concealed the entrance to the lagoon.

His teeth showed in a secretive smile. So, Kingi, the man with the silver
streaks in his hair has returned to eThekwini. The signs in the smoke and
in the throwing of the bones had indicated that it would be so. *At the time
of the next full moon, they will come...*

And so they had. Not only the leader, James King, was aboard the vessel anchored beyond the headland, but so was the boy with the hair like
fire and the eyes as blue as the skies, just as Langani had known he would
be. After a long year of waiting, all the *isangoma* wanted was to be able to
see him in the flesh as he stepped ashore on to the sands of eThekwini.

Langani knew that Kingi, the leader, would be cautious and bide his time.
When the tide and the winds were right, he would try to breach the formidable barriers of sand and rocks protecting the entrance to the bay of eThekwini.

The diviner pondered on all the reasons why the man had returned to
Zululand at this particular time. A frown crossed his handsome features.
Ah, yes, he searches for those he fears lost. In his mind's eye, he could see
the man Farewell, as sly as the fox, so full of arrogant pride now that Shaka
had unexpectedly presented him with the bay of eThekwini and land
surrounding it to rule as he wished.

He directed his attention back to the dark haired man aboard the ship,
the one known as Kingi. When he saw the faint ring of darkness hovering
around him, he closed his eyes in sorrow. *Aii, he does not yet know the
truth of what awaits him here.*

'This time, *umlungu*,' he whispered, 'you are here to stay. And although
they do not know it yet, some of those accompanying you will also never
leave the land of the Zulus.'

Several hours later, Lieutenant James King flung a string of curses into the
wild, grey skies and struck the rail of the *Mary* with a clenched fist. The
keening wind plucked at his sodden naval jacket with vicious fingers,
chilling him to the bone.

Hearing the thump of Hatton's feet on the deck behind him, he swung
round. The first officer joined him at the rail, his face a clear barometer as
to the seriousness of their situation.

'Where in the hell did this spring from?' he muttered, wiping spray from his face. 'It's the nature of the Wild Coast,' King answered wearily. 'Two years ago, it turned out just the same. One minute calm, the next, like the end of the world had arrived.'

Just after sunrise, he had ordered one of the longboats lowered, his plan being to go ashore with a few men to see if they could find any trace of his missing partner or those who had gone with him. Realising it might take a few days or more to make a thorough search of the bay, he'd stowed aboard sufficient tents, food and a decent stock of firearms, powder and shot.

Around mid-morning, however, while they were still trying to find a way in through the high ridges of pitted sandbanks, the wind had begun to rise, the thin keening echoing over the water, a haunting sound that seemed to dim the brightness of the day.

Within a short time, black, threatening clouds had swept in, churning the water into a boiling frenzy and threatening to scupper the longboat. Cursing their ill luck, King had reluctantly given the order to head back to the ship. But, after managing to turn the longboat around, what he'd seen had made his heart sink.

Clearly, the *Mary* herself was in danger. The anchors he'd put down earlier were slowly dragging, their hold weakened by the strengthening winds and strong running tides. Pulling on the oars like madmen, the crew had managed to reach the brig and scramble aboard without damage either to the brig or the longboat. Only then, did the full realisation of what was happening strike home.

The truth was that vessel was now too close to the jagged rocks at the foot of the headland to allow them to turn round and head back out to the open sea with any degree of safety.

Standing at the rail, icy fear ran down King's back. Born and bred in Nova Scotia, not only had he lived through the storms and icy seas of the North Atlantic, but had also survived years of naval bombardment and running sea-battles during the Napoleonic wars.

Fear was no stranger to him, and he had learned early in life that it came in many guises. He shot a quick glance along the deck.

Apart from first officer Hatton, there was seventeen-year-old Nathaniel Isaacs, his sallow face stark with anguish. The youth was a reluctant sailor who'd fled his uncle's business in St. Helena and run off to sea. Next to him was the irrepressible Ned Cameron, his features bearing their customary stamp of cheerful rebelliousness, only this time tinged with deep reserve.

And then there was the boy called Jack. Not long turned ten, the lad was the son of his old friend, Captain Francis MacLean, a man who had also lived through his fair share of naval battles and sudden storms.

The slight, red-haired boy was clinging for dear life to the huge New-foundland dog James King had brought with him from Nova Scotia. The boy and the dog had been virtually inseparable ever since the Newfound-land had saved the boy's life.

Clad in a faded blue work-shirt and trousers, the lad's face was white with distress. With a wrench, King noted the pathos of the child's bare legs protruding from the cut-down seaman's trews. The captain of the *Mary* drew in a sharp breath, his thoughts in turmoil.

Dear God, keep the boy safe – don't let the sea take him. I promised his father...

When he spoke, his voice was gruff, sharper than he intended. 'Get yourself and Able Seaman Rover below decks, lad. Look lively, now! Off to the galley and lay him out some ship's biscuits.' Forcing a smile to his lips, he added, 'And get something for yourself, of course. Stay safe, boy.'

He watched the boy and the dog traverse the heaving deck until they'd disappeared safely below. Relieved, James King turned back to the urgent business in hand.

The barrier of glittering surf and millrace of swirling water was, if any-thing, even more terrifying than the last time he'd looked into its gaping maw. It was hard to believe that beyond the sinister devil's cauldron and the forested bluff lay a beautiful bay, calm waters and safe anchorage.

King cursed his bad luck. Out there somewhere was the answer to the fate of his missing partner and the men who had gone ashore with him a year and a half ago. For a split second, he debated the wisdom of his decision to come looking for them at all, but quickly thrust it aside. What was done was done...

Hunched at the rail, the captain and his first officer surveyed the scene. King's voice boomed out. 'We're like sitting ducks at a shoot, Hatton. All we can do is to head her in and pray like buggery we live to tell the tale.'

'God help us, but I don't see we have any other choice,' Hatton yelled back. King's mind raced as he tried to calculate their chances of survival.

The tide was still high, with enough draught of water below the keel to clear the sandbanks – a narrow fit, as close as a seagull's fart, but it *was* just possible. Very soon, the tide would turn and the level of the water swirling over the ripples of hard-packed sand would fall. Then there would be no chance at all.

King glowered at the storm-lashed seas, his thoughts bleak. Unbelievable! Yet here I am, back facing the same predicament as we did two years ago aboard the *Julia*. He pulled himself up sharply. The longer I hesitate, the higher our chances of coming to grief. Thrusting away his doubts, he replaced them with the cooler logic of his professional training.

Head her straight in, the same as Garrett had done last time. Both ship and men had survived, hadn't they? By the grace of God and Garrett's steady hands, the little vessel had been literally swept in over the sand bars with a whisker to spare. But the *Julia* had been a smaller, lighter vessel. Can I do it with the *Mary*, a far larger ship?

He drew in a deep breath. There was no more time. It was now or never. He roared out the orders. Over the bar it was. Better a flying chance than no chance at all…

Up on the headland, the wind howled and spat, whipping the *isangoma's* long plaits around his head, the cloak billowing out around his lean body.

This wasn't the first time Langani had looked down from the headland and seen a vessel in acute danger. The only difference was that last time he alone had been responsible for conjuring up the storm threatening its survival. Not that the destruction of either the ship or the men aboard had been his primary intention. In using his powers to summon up the elements, he had merely sought to deter the strangers from entering Zululand, by forcing them to abandon their plans and turn away.

This time, he had played no part whatsoever in the storm currently whipping up a fury out in the wider ocean. The treacherous winds and currents of the Wild Coast were solely responsible for the vessel's present predicament. This time, his only interest in the ship had been to see exactly who stepped ashore on to the sands of eThekwini.

Langani already knew that one of them would be the *abelungu* known as Kingi. And the boy with the hair like fire? Ah, now that was something else again. The boy was the real reason he was here, for he wanted to see him in the flesh and to know that what he had foreseen in his dreaming had come true. The last thing he would have wanted was to endanger the vessel that had travelled across the world to bring the boy safely to the land of the Zulus.

For the last year or more, he had watched a small orb of light dance and jink across the dappled ceiling of the rocky pool below the waterfall near his home. Knowing what, and *who*, the joyful globe of light represented, it had been no hardship for the diviner to travel many miles to watch the ship arrive.

The young boy from the cold lands across the sea had some vital connection to the Lord of the World, King Shaka, but how, why, or even when it would come about, was still unclear to the diviner.

Langani's attention swung back to the ship. When he saw that it had turned to face the dangerous sandbanks blocking the entrance to the lagoon, his heart sank. The boy was aboard. Nothing must happen to him…

The young diviner stared at the ship being buffeted about by sea and wind. James King had been aboard the first ship, the one he had been tempted to sweep to destruction – surely he would have remembered how to ride the waters as before and come safely into the bay?

The hard reality of their present situation hit him. 'I doubt you knew just how close to death you came last time,' he said aloud. 'In spite of your great skills, man of the sea, it was mainly my intervention that saved you. It was no wish of mine to see you dead, only to stop you coming to my land.'

This time, it was even more serious. Aboard the vessel was the young boy, the one he had seen during his 'times of dreaming,' the human embodiment of what the glowing orb had represented. The first time he set eyes on him, the boy had been a *toto* of only two or three years old, in grave danger of falling into the cold sea lying below his uncertain feet. The next occasion had been more recent, when the ocean had sought to claim him for a second time, not long after the beginning of his long journey to get here.

Langani shuddered at the memory of the boy, alone and adrift on the great waters with no other human being within sight or sound of him. Once again, he had been rescued – this time not by a passing storyteller, as he had been on the first occasion, but by a dog that could swim like a fish and who also loved the boy. Aiii, it had been a wondrous thing to behold, the love of a beast for a human.

And now once again, for a third time, the sea was threatening to destroy the ship that had crossed the oceans of the world to bring him safely to Zululand. Angry now, the diviner closed his eyes. *Cha! The sea will not have you, not now...*

As he concentrated all of his powers on the business at hand, his lips began to move, shaping the powerful words that were needed at this time. In spite of the buffeting winds, beads of sweat began to stand out on his brow and trickle down the side of his face. With the wind streaming around him, tearing at his clothes and hair with increasing strength, he began to rock to and fro.

After a time, he cupped his hands and began to blow softly into them. Then he opened his long fingers and allowed what was captured within them to fly off into the raging winds.

Aboard the brig, King gave the order to lift the anchors. The *Mary* scudded forward, her bows plunging deep into the terrifying millrace. From the depths of his soul, he prayed that the vagaries of wind and tide would allow him to navigate her into the safe haven that lay beyond the terrifying walls of water and treacherous tongues of sand.

The brig rolled and pitched, yawing dangerously. Sea-water rushed hissing over the decks sweeping away anything not tied down. The air was cold and salty, the tang of ozone and seaweed in its breath.

'Steady, man! Steady as you go, now... easy, easy.' King's voice was cool and measured, his eyes fixed on the helmsman. *'Hard a port! Keep her steady, meet her, meet her!'*

Out of nowhere, a gigantic wave came rolling in fast. It struck the brig amidships, sending her lurching into the abyss. The next breaker, coming in close behind, swept the *Mary* up on to its crest as effortlessly if she was a child's paper boat.

With a sickening crash that grated all the way down to her keel, the brig plunged down, her starboard side hitting the blunt snout of a sand bank. Veering off course, she staggered and lurched like a drunken man.

Shouts of pain mingled with curses and prayers. Men lost their footing and desperately tried to hold on to anything solid.

Below decks, the air was sour with the stench of chicken manure. With the help of the red haired boy, the cook and one of the sail-makers struggled to prevent the coops of squawking poultry from being thrown about. From the galley came the crash of pots and breaking crockery.

Tied to an iron ring in the overhead beams, the ship's dogs barked furiously, straining to free themselves. A pair of white goats bleated piteously, their cleft hooves skittering along the deck, while two small pigs and a pregnant sow squealed in alarm.

'All's right. Now she goes! Steady, lads – '

King had a brief glimpse of what lay beyond the turbulent millrace. The glint of smooth gunmetal water caused his heart to lift. An illogical thought surged through him. If only the brig could lift clean out of the water and fly over the sandbanks, they would be safe...

The faint hope was stillborn. With a sickening crash, a towering wall of foam-streaked water struck the *Mary* broadsides. She shuddered, wavered off course then struck the sandbanks with a vicious crack. A second bone-shaking crash followed, and then another.

Hatton was thrown up hard against the companionway steps, his shoulder taking the brunt of the collision. His face turned white with pain. King yelled 'Are you all right, Hatton?'

Before the first officer could reply, a groaning cry was wrenched from the brig's stressed and ripped timbers. Water crashed over her in a tumble of sails, rigging and cordage, broken masts, yards and spars, the rudder swinging uselessly in its casing. Water began to seep in silent swirls through the planking below the water line.

A terrified plea rang out over the tumult. '*Lord, save us all –* '

It was cut short, snatched away by the wind. Then another voice sang out, the Devon burr loud and clear. 'Never mind thy prayers, lad, keep them till later. Just lend a hand now, sharp like, with this 'ere rope...then when I do tell 'ee, pull on it like buggery!'

The clouds scudded lower. The whole world turned grey, the sea and sky a mass of sound and fury. As darkness began to fall, they all knew that there was no chance of saving the ship.

As for saving themselves, aye, well, there was the rub – now they were at the mercy of the winds and cruel waters on one of Africa's most deadly shores and only the Almighty could tell if any of them would survive.

That night, fifteen men, a boy and a dog clung to the channels and deadlights on the broadside of the vessel. There was no moon to give them hope and light the blackness of the abyss. Even the stars had gone out, drowned by the heavy spray and driving rain.

Heavy seas broke against the hull; hammer blows and cracks of doom echoing all the way down to her keel. The huge Newfoundland stayed close to Jack, James King's young apprentice, the heat of its body helping to comfort him. When the vessel was thrown on its beam end around midnight, and the noise of the storm and the boy's fear grew too great, the hound growled into the teeth of the gale and pressed closer to him. On either side of them, the captain and the first officer were silent and past talking; trying to stay alive, for theirs was the ultimate responsibility for both the crew and the ship.

Wavering between a fitful doze that might have lasted an hour or just seconds, the ten-year-old knew, just knew, that somewhere below, green tentacles glowing with phosphorus were reaching out to pluck him down.

Jack, whose name had been Charlie before his indoctrination into the life of a sea-going sailor some eight months before, would have been hard put to express the depths of his feelings at that particular moment.

We're done for, he thought, his teeth chattering with cold. We're either going to be drowned, eaten by sharks – or swept ashore and killed by yon black men the bo'sun was telling us about.

He wasn't sure at that moment which would be worse. The thought of the last possibility made him shiver with fear. He had read *Robinson Crusoe* from cover to cover more than once and knew the story was a true one, based on an account of the author Alexander Selkirk's own experiences.

All of it terrified him, the sea and howling winds, the numbing cold and the grinding of the brig in her death throes. Out there somewhere was the alien land of Africa, like a beast ready to swallow them up; the folk of it black as the night that surrounded them, wild, savage and heathen, far from the knowledge of God's mercy – or so Aloysius Biddle, the bo'sun, had said.

With a shudder, he buried his face in the dog's matted pelt and held on to him for dear life. A jet of spray hit the hull, a dull boom that echoed all the way down to the keel. The obscenities spat out of the mouths of desperate men only served to rouse the boy for a moment or two before taking shelter once more in what was comforting to him.

His father and mother, his sisters, and brothers, Alexander and Francis, presently on the high seas somewhere off the China coast... would he ever see them again?

Moaning in his sleep, he wound his fingers tighter into the ruff around the dog's neck. Dileas, the faithful, whined and larruped the side of his face with his rough tongue.

A trickle of hot fluid between the boy's legs caused him to stir. When he realised that he'd wet himself, he flinched in shock. A muttered protest escaped from between his pinched blue lips. The Newfoundland dog with the Gaelic name whined deep in his barrel chest and beat his tail against the hull in sympathy.

Out of the darkest time of the night, a voice rose clear above the storm. Someone was singing. James King lifted his head, straining to identify the voice. He had heard the song before. Suffused with warmth, colour and irrepressible cheek, it contained the soft lilt of the West Indies.

'*M'donkey walks, m'donkey talks…m'donkey eats with a knife an' fawk… m'donkey drinks, m'donkey eats…m'donkey sleeps between the sheets …*'

Ned Cameron, for it could be no other, went on singing, each verse more bawdy than the last. A weak voice groaned, 'Trust you, Cameron.'

King felt the beginnings of a smile tug at his mouth. Other voices began to join in, faltering at first then growing stronger, each man taking strength from those around him.

As if it were to be their last and sweetest song, the crew sang on, in defiance of the sea and their precarious hold on life. One melody blended into another, one refrain to the next. From sea-shanties and songs of home, daft

ditties of roistering and sweethearts left behind, all the way to the mariners'
hymns of old, prayers to their God to save them from the cruel seas.

The singing came to an end as naturally as it had begun, with the voice
of sixteen-year-old Ned Cameron. When it was finished, he bent his head,
his blonde hair plastered to his skull, and muttered, 'Amen, boys, amen.'

King stretched out a hand and gripped Ned's shoulder. 'God keep you,
lads, one and all.' he said. 'Now, start praying…'

In spite of his appeal for his men's prayers, however, King's own state of
mind made it impossible for him to focus on the Almighty, let alone ask
for His help. Now that the worst had happened, the full reality of his
situation returned to taunt him. With his limbs cramped and chilled and
his body and mind wracked with stress, his thoughts began to drift.

A few days ago, after enjoying a fine supper and a glass of Cape 'smoke'
with Hatton, the two men had gone out on deck to enjoy their cigars.
Inevitably, the talk had turned to the business venture he and Farewell had
set in motion two years earlier.

The sea had been calm that night. With the moon sailing serenely
above them and the ocean dancing with pin point gleams of light, the
night had seemed almost magical.

Standing at the rail with Hatton, he'd joked about how he and Farewell
had spent six back-breaking months risking their necks to hell and back
along the coast lying off their port bow, taking the longboat in death-
defying rides in over the pounding surf to try to find a sheltered anchorage
so they could begin the great, grand plan they'd dreamed up – the one that
would make them rich.

Another huge wave hit the stricken brig, sending gouts of spray over the
shattered timbers of the hull. King, shuddering with cold and remorse,
groaned aloud.

Just because he'd escaped the jaws of death in the *Julia* on the last trip,
he'd secretly hoped that the Wild Coast would spare him a second time.
Bloody stupid of me…

He frowned. Now that the end seemed near, other matters began to
bother him. When he'd stood with Hatton on deck in the moonlight that

night, he'd been pretty niggardly with the details he'd given him about the venture.

Instinctively, he glanced sideways to where the first officer lay spread-eagled on the hull, his sandy hair matted and eyes black holes in a pallid face.

'Forgive me, Hatton,' he mumbled, 'but I couldn't risk telling you of my suspicions concerning Farewell. Without any hard evidence, I only had his father-in-law's account and what Elizabeth Farewell had told me, to go on. If the crew'd got wind of it, they might have decided to jump ship.'

He drifted away for a moment or two. 'Twenty years in Britannia's Royal Navy taught me to button my lip and keep my fears to myself. Bred in the bone, Hatton, bred in the bone. You should know that. Command can be a lonely place.'

As his concentration faded, the desire to sleep was overwhelming. Grimly, he fought against it. 'Something else I didn't mention,' he muttered. 'The African king whose territory we're hell bent on entering? Well, just let's say his reputation ain't exactly the sweetest. It's possible he'll turn out to be a greater danger to us than all the wild seas and storms put together.'

How could he tell him about Farewell's father-in-law, Johannes Petersen, who had described in such lurid detail the brutal treatment he claimed to have suffered at the hands of the Zulu king? A spurt of rage shot through James King. *Damn you to hell, you blithering old fool...*

The existence of a black man powerful enough to dominate thousands of square miles of south east Africa was what both he and Farewell had gone to great pains to play down. That the fabulous tusks of ivory were to be found in his private hunting grounds was something they'd never intended for public consumption. What the eye didn't see...

He shot a glance at the first officer hunched in agony against the oak timbers. 'Not that I didn't trust you,' he muttered, 'but if word of this had leaked out!' A spasm of pain ran through King's cramped legs.

Ivory – the damned ivory was at the root of it all. Gritting his teeth, he swore. 'Farewell, you bastard, if you hadn't gone ashore at Delagoa – if you hadn't clapped eyes on those damned elephant tusks – and if we hadn't met up in Rio, and I hadn't become as smitten as you were with the idea, then it wouldn't have come to this, drowning within sight of land –'

A fit of coughing stopped him, but only for a moment. 'And damn you to blazes also, Farewell, for going north and bringing your own private investors in on our arrangement, while I'm in London trying to raise money and cajoling the Sea Lords into supporting our venture.'

The heat of rage ebbed away. His physical resources nearly at an end, the abscess of accumulated doubt, suspicion and humiliation that had been eating away at him finally erupted.

Leaning sideways, he spewed into the sea. The sound of his retching was muffled by the roaring turmoil of water, the sour smell of vomit snatched away by the south-east winds.

Only then, scoured and emptied of both bitterness and hope, was James King able to mumble his prayers for the safety of those who had trusted him to lead the way into the unknown.

Up on the Bluff, the young diviner sat cross-legged and very still, his long grey monkey skin cloak wrapped around him, the fire he'd lit creating a fragile gleam of light and warmth in the howling darkness.

If anyone had been watching, they would have noticed that the flames rising from his fire did not flicker or tremble and that the resinous sparks were not scattered by the winds but flew straight and true up into the stormy night.

Within the circle of firelight, there were no howling winds, angry seas or driving spray; only calm, peace and warmth, as Langani continued to pray, with the young female cheetah keeping watch beside him.

Somehow, the crew of the *Mary* were spared. The sun rose out of its watery grave, a red and angry eye poking blindly through the ragged clouds scudding overhead.

A grudging light illuminated the scene, one that forced Jack's heart into his boots. He shuddered, unable to tear his eyes away from the silent shapes of the sandbanks. Grey and pitiless, they were like a pack of ancient beasts come sloughing out of the deeps, ready to grind them to dust or drag them down below.

Spreadeagled on the hull beside him were Hatton and King. 'Are you all right, lad?' Hatton croaked, lifting his head. His grey eyes were streaked red with fatigue and the effects of salt water, the hand reaching out to him bleached grey and lifeless.

Jack nodded, his lips too frozen to form words. When he glanced at his own hands, he saw they were no better than Hatton's, cramped in a death grip on the collar round the dog's neck. The first officer eased the wrinkled cravat away from his neck. Thick reddish stubble glinting on his chin, his grey eyes twinkled as he tried to jolly the boy's spirits along.

'You've done well, Jack,' he said, raising his voice above the roaring of the sea. 'What with falling from the rigging, being rescued by a dog, and now a shipwrecked mariner – not bad for a maiden voyage, eh?' His broad, honest face crinkled up in humour. 'Nobody can say you're not worthy of the name o' mariner now.'

King leaned over, and added quietly. 'Your father would be proud of you, Charlie. Carried through like a true blue Maclean. I'd expect no less from someone carrying the blood of sea-warriors in his veins.'

His blue eyes were strained, his face sallow and exhausted below the tan. Jack felt sorry for the man who was his captain. In spite of all his efforts to save the *Mary*, in the end the sea had been stronger.

Dileas showed his great canines in yawning approval, his wet tail thumping against the bulkhead. King patted the dog's head. 'You too, boy, you did a good night's work.'

Turning to Jack, he added with a weary smile 'Did I ever tell you this dog's worth his weight in gold?'

Some time later, Jack managed to inch his way further up the upturned hull and peered over the top. Between the rise and fall of the fearful swell, he caught brief glimpses of smooth, windswept beaches and trees bending and tossing on the looming headland.

An endless confusion of masts, yards and sails, cordage and splintered spars swept this way and that. Relics of their floating home went bobbing past. Here, a rocking chair, Cookie's pride and joy, an upended table from the officers' cabins; Ned's second-best concertina, its music forever stilled; an upended chicken coop, brown feathers stuck to the spars. As they watched, it dipped beyond the hull and disappeared.

The carcase of a dog, a fine red setter taken aboard at St Helena, suddenly disappeared below the surface as if plucked down by an invisible hand. Jack turned his head away, cold dread clutching at him.

Just then, he heard an angry cackling and clucking break out. A rooster came strutting along the keel, followed by a gaggle of squawking, damp-feathered hens. Cocking a fierce yellow eye at the men pinned to the hull, the rooster threw back its head and let out a crowing that would have wakened the dead, its bright red comb quivering in indignation. A wavering cheer broke out from the exhausted crewmen.

King braced himself against the swell, his eyes black holes of weariness as he addressed his exhausted crew. 'The night's over and all souls are accounted for. We're not out of danger yet, but God willing, we'll make it ashore.' At that point, his voice caught in his throat and he could say no more.

Heads bowed, he and his crew mumbled their prayers through numb lips, the wind carrying their voices towards the unknown land that lay waiting for them beyond the pitted sandbanks and turbulent waters.

Three

Couped out of the jollyboat into the tumbling surf, Jack went under, yelling as he went. With a roaring in his ears and blinded by the sting of salt water, he felt himself being dragged down by the undertow. His knees and elbows were scraped raw as the current took hold of him and sought to drag him back out to sea.

The Newfoundland was quick to the rescue. Grabbing him by the neck of his shirt, its strong teeth nipping the skin, it dragged him clear then dumped him unceremoniously at the water's edge amongst a soup of seaweed, pebbles and debris from the upturned boat. Gasping and spluttering, salt water dribbling from his nose, Jack lay sprawled on the wet sand, his hair plastered flat to his head.

'Not drowned are ye, lad?' one of the sailors asked, rolling a plug of tobacco around in his mouth. Jack shook his head, and coughed some more. Crawling on his hands and knees away from the water's edge, he found a patch of dry sand, and fell face down on it. After he got his breath back, he sat up and had a look around.

A crate full of damp hens was bobbing up and down at the water's edge, beating their wings against the sides of the coop, while a second was upended close by, its occupants squawking fit to burst. A litter of boxes were in danger of being drawn back out to sea or smashed open and their contents spoiled. Sailors jumped in after them, dragging then clear, swearing and erupting into guffaws of laughter, while the ship's dogs ran about, barking madly and getting in the men's way.

The bo'sun, Aloysius Biddle, swore a blue streak as chickens set about pecking his fingers as he was trying to rescue their crate. 'Avast that, ye feathered bastids!' he snarled, 'else I'll let ye all fuckin' drown.'

Ned appeared with a squealing piglet tucked below each arm. 'Drunk again, Heelander?' he said, with his usual impudent grin, 'we'll have to put a watch on the grog from now on, hey?'

Jack's lips refused to move. Shivering, he drew his knees up to his chin, the scrapes on his knees and elbows stinging like fire.

'You just stay where you are,' Ned said, tying a length of twine around a leg of each of the protesting porkers. 'Keep an eye on these two an' I'll bring the chickens and put them by you. We're goin' back to the wreck to ferry the rest o' the crew ashore and whatever else we can salvage. Keep your peepers open till we get back.'

After he'd tied the pigs to a tangle of tree roots nearby, Ned put his hands on his hips and looked down at him anxiously. Trickles of sea-water dribbled on to the sand from his sodden clothes and hair. 'You'll be ship-shape till then, Heelander? We'll not be long.'

Frozen to the bone, he could only nod. A quick wave and Ned was off, jogging back down the beach towards the longboat, sand spurting up from his heels, his bedraggled pigtail thudding against his shoulder blades.

Jack wiped his nose on the tails of his shirt. They were no drier than any other bit of him, but they were all he had. Stripping off his shirt, then his trews, he spread them out to dry on a fallen tree. His hands and feet were sorry-looking things, bleached and wrinkled by the salt water, the scrapes and cuts plum-coloured and blue round the edges.

Nearby, the piglets were burrowing down into the sand, grunting and snuffling as they hollowed out a space for themselves. A few minutes later, they appeared to be asleep, curled up together, their white-lashed eyelids tightly closed, flat snouts quivering.

As Jack sat watching them, something Aloysius Biddle had once told him leapt into his mind. *Pigs is very clever beasts...*

The bo'sun, being a keen observer of both human and animal behaviour, was very likely right, he thought. So he set about scraping a hollow for himself in the dry sand. Burrowing into it, he curled himself into a tight ball, naked except for his drawers.

After a bit, the earth's residual warmth began to spread through him. The chill lifted, and gradually his teeth stopped chattering. Dileas, finished with his rescue work, dropped down beside him, spraying him with drops of sea water.

Without warning, the sun broke out from behind the clouds and flooded the beach with sunshine. The dog rolled over on to his back, grunting and squirming in pleasure, tongue lolling out of the side of his mouth.

Jack emerged from the hollow and squinted around. The ship's dogs were scuttling around, exploring their new territory, sniffing and lifting their legs on everything in sight. The chickens in the coops seemed reconciled to their new surroundings, confining themselves to an anxious clucking from time to time.

The lagoon was a palette of turquoise, greens and blues, the longboat a black dot against water that shimmered and rippled over white sands. The click and groan of the oars in the rowlocks drifted faintly back to him.

As wisps of steam coiled gently up from the ground, the air smelled of pungent earth and the tang of salt. A deep silence hung over everything. All Jack could hear were bird noises, the roar of the ocean beyond the reef and the hiss of waves on the beach. On the far side of the bay, stray shafts of sunlight lit up patches of woodland, turning green to gold.

Revived by the hot sunlight, Jack got to his feet. Here he was, a real Robinson Crusoe, shipwrecked on the shores of Africa, with only a Newfoundland dog, a pair of sleeping pigs and a coop or two of chickens for company.

Just then, his foot came up against something hard. Looking down, he saw that he'd stepped on some interesting shells half-buried in the sand. Squatting down, he prised them loose then laid them out to get a better look.

The largest of the shells fitted into the palm of his hand. Brushing the rough grains of sand away, he turned it round between his fingers, and examined it closely. The inside was pale pink and delicate with a sheen of mother of pearl, the outside a pale, speckled brown, full of interesting twirls and ridges.

The smallest shell caught his eye. It was tiny, roughly the size of his thumbnail, a miniature replica of its larger brothers. Jack's lips curled in a smile. Picking it up, he blew into its curled ear once or twice to clear away the grains of sand. A few moments later, a sudden change in his immediate vicinity made him glance up and look around.

Fifty yards away, the figure of a tall black man began to materialise out of the wavering sunlight and seemed to flow upwards on the waves of heat rising from the sand.

Squinting against the harsh light, Jack got to his feet, still clutching the shells. The man stood unmoving, his bronze skin gleaming in the noonday sun. Jack stared, mesmerised, at the long plaits of hair rippling over his shoulders like coils of snakes. The man had seen him, all right. No mistaking the stillness of the muscular body and the intensity of the dark eyes watching him.

A flicker of movement caught Jack's attention. Another shape seemed to be emerging from the shimmering heatwaves, something sleek and cat-like. Hairs stood up along the back of his neck when he realised what it was. With long rangy legs, a small neat head and spotted pelt, the amber eyes of the creature were fierce and direct as they fixed on him.

A rumble of sound from the huge dog at his side distracted him, and his eyes flicked sideways. No need for alarm. Dileas' tail was waving lazily from side to side and apart from his cocked ears, the dog was showing no signs of hostility towards the newcomers. But by the time Jack looked back, both man and animal had disappeared, and only the shifting heat waves, the long curve of the beach and the glittering waters of the lagoon remained.

He dropped to his knees in the sand, his mind in a whirl. Where had the man come from? One minute he was there, the next he'd gone. Who was he, and why did he have a wild beast with him?

While he was struggling to understand what he'd just seen, a delicate movement on the sand a few yards away caught his eye. To his amazement, a patch of pale blue began to dissolve gently before rising up and moving towards him. Startled, he scrambled to his feet and stepped back, only to find that it had followed him and was fanning out in a cloud around his head.

It was then he realised that the hovering mass of blue was made up of hundreds of butterflies. Not only were they of varying sizes, they were also of differing shades, their delicate wings creating a never-ending kaleidoscope of colours ranging from the palest of blues to deep shades of violet.

When he moved, so did they, dipping down then rising again, coming closer then fluttering out of reach. Their delicate wings brushed his face and settled on his wet hair, before lifting again to alight somewhere else.

He was in the centre of the cloud, at the heart of the game. Holding his breath, almost afraid to move, he slowly raised his arms. Hundreds of butterflies fluttered over him, tickling him with their delicate feet and wings, as if tasting the strange half-naked creature that had entered their domain. Gently, they paraded over his face, eyes and ears leaving no inch of him untouched.

Then, as if at a pre-arranged signal, they lifted their gossamer bodies into the air and began to move away. Jack stood very still, not daring to breathe.

His sisters, Charlotte, Isabella and Rebecca shot into his mind. Oh, if only you could've been here, he thought, how much you'd have enjoyed this. And you'd have been much sweeter-tasting than your brother, that's for sure!

As if reading his mind, the smudge of blue hovered in the air for a brief moment before moving away to find whatever it was that butterflies seek.

Once they'd gone, Jack sank down on his knees and searched for the shells. He stared at the delicate whorls and stripes for a long time, wondering whether or not he should blow into the tiny one's ear again, just to see if anything else might happen. Thinking better of it, he carefully stowed them away in the pocket of his sodden trews. Some other time...

The spot for their makeshift camp had been well chosen. It lay in a natural clearing, sheltered from the wind coming off the sea by a mass of dense bamboo, yet not far from a source of fresh drinking water. Rough shelters had been erected out of spars, sails and wreckage from the brig. Huge piles of driftwood, fallen branches and logs were in place, ready to keep the fires going.

All the crew had managed to salvage that day was safely stored below canvas. As soon as it was light, diving would start up again in the flooded holds. Those who could swim would go below to rescue whatever they could before the tides changed or another storm blew up. James King cast a speculative eye around his battered, weary crew.

'Tomorrow, all hands to make an account of how you stand as far as sea chests, personals, and general booty go. Those that have will be handing out to those that haven't, if you get my drift.'

Raising his eyebrows in a sardonic grin, he said, 'No need to lower our standards just because of a small hitch like a shipwreck, huh?'

Jack looked at his clothes steaming by the fire. They consisted of a pair of duck trousers, a tattered shirt and a pair of boots stuffed with grass to dry them out.

The fine, blue-painted sea kist on which his father had carefully painted his name hadn't been recovered yet, but maybe tomorrow it would turn up. In his sea bag were three pairs of trews, four shirts and a weskit, a cold weather jacket, one knitted Guernsey, two pairs of summer drawers and a spare pair of boots.

Even before he'd finished eating his supper, his eyelids felt as heavy as lead. 'Best get some sleep, boy,' King said, noticing the boy's pinched face. 'It's been a hellish long day – an' who knows what tomorrow might bring.'

Yawning, Jack wrapped himself in a blanket smelling of bilge water and pillowed his head on the sea bag that held all his worldly goods.

Less than a hundred yards away, the waters of the lagoon lapped gently against the sandy beach. Beyond the rim of firelight lay the African night, black as pitch and filled with the crick and buzz of insects. The smell of wood smoke and the heady fumes of rum filled the air, the low drone of men's voices barely audible above the crackling of the fires.

Drawing the blanket up round his head to keep the insects away, Jack thought about the tall black man and the wild beast that had risen from the shimmering sands in much the same way as the clouds of blue butterflies had done before melting away into the sunlight.

He yawned again and turned on to his side. Afterwards, he'd looked for traces of the mysterious man and his animal, just to see if they'd been real, and he'd not imagined it. The man's footprints weren't interesting at all, just long and regular, much like everyone else's.

But those of the cat-like animal were a different thing altogether. The paw prints clearly showed that they were just like those belonging to a dog, and nothing like a cat's pads at all. So what kind of a beast was it? He was still wondering when he fell asleep.

He could never remember which came first, the howling of the dogs, the snarling of a wild animal, or the awful, long drawn-out scream that followed.

Dizzy with exhaustion and lack of sleep, their mouths suddenly dry as bones, men struggled out of their blankets. The dogs were up and baying, hair standing up in angry ridges along their backs. Someone cried out, in a voice rigid with shock, 'The bastard's got Higgins... snatched away in front of our noses, by God!'

Men cursed as they ran about in their drawers to see what could be done. Hatton came by, pushing his shirt into his trousers as he ran, while Nat Isaacs loomed out of the shadows at the back of the tent, his eyes burned-out coals in an ashen face.

Animals circled in the shadows, their eyes gleaming red in the firelight, the stench of rotting meat revolting. Jack's eyes followed them, hypnotised by the sight of their sinister humped backs and cringing prowl. Bursts of fiendish cackling broke out. Someone muttered: 'Holy Mary, what in the hell's that?'

Something heavy was being dragged through the undergrowth. They could all hear it; a snapping of twigs, the snarling cough of a great beast, a low moaning like an animal in pain. Suddenly, the air was full of the acrid smell of gunpowder as a volley of shots rang out.

Nat Isaacs bent over and spewed the remains of his supper into the sand. Struggling to keep a hold on the Newfoundland, Jack could only listen in horror to the muffled, inhuman sounds coming from the darkness.

Norton pushed past him, struggling to load his musket. 'These sons o' Satan are havin' themselves a laugh at our expense. Let's see how you like a dose o' lead up your arse, mateys.'

The night dissolved into a bedlam of noise and frantic activity. The humid night air was full of smoke, the stench of cordite and the sharp crack of gunfire. In the darkness beyond the circle of light, animals snarled and whined in pain as bullets found their mark. Men burst through the clouds of acrid smoke, yelling like banshees as they reloaded and kept on firing.

'More wood on the fires!' shouted King, snatching up a blazing piece of wood. 'Try and keep the ring tight,' he urged, 'don't let any of these bastards through, or we're done for.'

Ned thrust a burning stick into Jack's hand. 'Let's give 'em a singed arse or two, Heelander!' Sparks flew in an arc round him as he whirled a fiery branch round his head. With his blonde hair spilling round his shoulders, the gold in his ear glinting in the firelight, it seemed to Jack that the only thing missing as far as Ned was concerned was the horned helmet and metal-studded targe of his Viking ancestors.

Dileas tore out of Jack's grip and threw himself with the other dogs out onto the rim of the firelight. The boldest in the pack lunged out into the darkness, snarling and snapping at the lurking hyenas and jackals.

A patch of thinning smoke ahead suddenly cleared. Looming out of the smoky haze was a beast like a demon straight from hell. The sloping haunches, hunched back and glint in the huge dog hyena's eyes had Jack rooted to the spot. But what really filled him with horror were the animal's jaws. They were enormous, powerful, and agape, thin threads of saliva spooling from them.

For a split second, boy and animal faced each another, Jack with the burning stick in his hand, the hyena undecided whether to sidle away or defy the fire and drag him down.

Without warning, the Newfoundland forced its way past Jack, knocking him down. Teeth bared, fangs snapping at the beast's throat, the dog's unexpected attack knocked the hyena off balance. Rolling over on the ground, it cowered off into the scrub, snarling as it went.

Jack picked himself up. Trembling with fear and sheer relief, he fended off Dileas' fussing and whining.

'Hey, boy, that's some dog you've got,' Hatton commented. 'He's really the captain's dog, you know,' Jack answered defensively.

Hatton grinned and patted Dileas' head. 'Is that a fact, lad? I'm damn' sure he's in no doubt as to where his loyalty lies.'

The rest of the night was spent in an uneasy truce. The men of the wrecked brig fell into a superficial doze, jerking awake at any suspicious sound, while the ship's dogs growled and snapped fitfully in their sleep.

Dawn found them weary, stinking of wood smoke and covered in insect bites, their eyes bloodshot and smarting and with throats that were dry and cracking from inhaling smoke.

Beyond the circle of smouldering campfires lay the bodies of several dead hyenas. Some had been killed outright, while others had crawled away into the thickets to die. Turning the carcases over, the men poked them with sticks to examine them.

'Them jaws would put the frighteners on anybody,' Ned commented, 'rip a man's arm right off, they could.'

'Never mind your fuckin' arm,' the burly mate Thompson snarled, 'your balls would be a mite tastier and nearer to hand.'

If there was ever a trace found of poor Higgins, Jack never heard it mentioned, at least not in his presence. In the days and weeks that followed, a sudden picture of the dead man would come back to him. Sam Higgins, the light from the lamp in the galley catching the gleam of gold in his ear and the slash of red in the kerchief knotted around his throat.

And every time it did, he would ask himself the same question. 'Just how is God going to find poor Higgins come Judgment Day?'

'Time's of the essence,' King declared the following morning, his face grey with exhaustion after the night's battle. 'We can't risk another storm tearing the guts out of what's left of the brig. Everything must be stripped from her – and by that, I mean every last piece of timber, ripped canvas, nails and screws, crooked or straight. We're going to need every single piece of salvage, let me tell you.'

Swivelling a pair of red-rimmed eyes around men stinking of woodsmoke and gunpowder, he added, 'But, first, everybody get themselves off for ablutions and a change of togs.'

A quick glance at his fire-blackened clothing and dirt-ingrained hands produced a rueful chuckle. 'Don't want to start off the day looking like chewed-up pieces of dog shit now, do we?'

From his secluded place below the trees up on the bluff, the young diviner's eyes anxiously scanned the distant figures scurrying around on the beach below. Noise carried at night and he had lain awake on the headland listening to the boom of their weapons and the howling of dogs as they'd fought off the scavengers.

At the entrance to the bay, the pitiless early morning sun played over the broken mass of timbers and shredded sails that had once been a fine vessel. A small boat was plying its way from it towards the knot of figures waiting on the shore.

Langani gave a visible sigh of relief when he spotted the small figure among the men dragging objects from the boat and piling them up on the sands. Seeing the boy at close quarters as he had done the day before, he had been struck by just how slight and pale-skinned he had been, and how bright and extraordinary the mass of hair tumbling around his shoulders.

The diviner smiled. Like me, you prefer to grow your hair long. Brave too…

In his mind's eye, he saw again the boy's small head bobbing in the vastness of the great ocean and the courage with which he'd faced death; of how he had risen to his feet to face him on the sands, with no trace of fear, only surprise, even when he saw the cheetah. Curious – and clever too, he thought with a smile, searching for footprints in the sand to make sure we were flesh and blood and not spirits come to haunt him.

Sympathy for the boy welled up in him. How could the father of such boy send him far from his home and his people, to brave the frightening waters and wander among strange nations?

Resigning himself to what he knew must be the truth, he whispered, 'Aiii, I know… because it is his destiny. One must walk where the gods decide, no other path than that. Who should know it better than I?'

The diviner looked out to where the broken vessel lay on the sandbanks. Today, the ocean was peaceful, a raging lion turned into a lamb, no fury, no lashing of tail or growling roar.

A sense of relief washed over him. Everyone had survived, including the boy. He was here at last in the land of the Zulus, just as he had known he would be, one day. The mischievous golden orb, which had danced across the roof of the sunlit pool in his sanctuary for the past months, was now present in the flesh.

Unlikely as it seemed, this was what had happened. And what would come in the days ahead? As always, the answer lay in the hands of the gods.

Four

During the backbreaking days that followed, every object large or small was systematically looted from the pitiful bones of the *Mary*. Luckily, the weather held. Day after day, the sun shone out of cloudless blue skies and the sea was as calm as a millpond. King and Hatton pushed the men without let-up or mercy from the first streaks of dawn to the last glimmers of daylight.

The best divers went in pairs down into the flooded hulk to save anything useful before it rotted or was scoured out by the tides, while the rest of the crew plied ceaselessly between the wreck and the shore. Soon, the beach was littered with huge piles of canvas, rigging, ropes, anchors, chains, battered sea kists, clothing, crockery, tools, kegs of whisky and rum, boxes of sodden trading supplies – even clothing and odd boots and shoes.

The Newfoundland was in its element. Its thick pelt and webbed feet meant it could stay in the water for long periods, helping the men rescue items which had floated away. It also kept a watchful eye open for their safety. More than once, a diver coming up for air, exhausted after a lengthy spell below, was glad to hold on to the dog's powerful body and be helped to safety.

It was the seventh day after the storm. The sea was calm, only a light breeze moving across the waters of the lagoon. The longboat was making its way back from the wreck towing the laden jollyboat behind it.

Its load included two six-pound carronades and the gaudy carved figurehead that had once graced the bows of the *Mary*. Standing in the bows, its nose pointing into the breeze was Dileas, the Newfoundland dog, its coat sleek after the day's work. The water swished cleanly around the bows and the clink of rowlocks and the splash of oars were gentle in the last rays of sunlight.

Suddenly, one of the sailors pointed ashore. 'Ahoy ahead, captain! On the beach, to port… natives, appear to be waving somethin' - a tattered rag o' some sort.'

The oars were shipped, the boat steadied. King clambered forward and put the glass to his eye. 'By all that's holy!' he said, in disbelief. 'The 'tattered rag' they're waving, gentlemen, appears to be no less than the Union flag!'

He lowered the glass, slowly. A British flag – tattered or otherwise, could only have come into their possession through Farewell or someone in his party. Whether they had been alive or dead at the time was another question altogether.

A woman stood at the front of the group. Her blue cotton dress was clean and matched the spotted bandana covering her head. Gold earrings neatly encircled her long ear lobes and the glow of the fading sun accentuated the warm brown of her skin.

In her hands she held a tattered Union flag, its colours faded by years of years of exposure to tropical sun and wind.

The boat grated against the shore. As the sailors jumped out to secure it, wails and screeches rose from the natives milling about behind her.

One of the sailors swore. 'It's the fuckin' gilded lady what's settin' 'em orf,' he said in exasperation, jerking a thumb at the long golden tresses and voluptuous bosoms of the carved figurehead lashed across the jollyboat's stern.

Impervious to the terrified wailing, the woman waited in silence while King and Hatton waded through the surf towards her. When she smiled, her teeth were even and white in a generous mouth.

'Welcome, *meneers*, I em Rachel.' The voice was deep and earthy, the accent unmistakably Cape Dutch. 'I em watching your ship break and come looking for you.'

Peering over her shoulder was an old woman clad in a leather apron, one arm badly scarred from shoulder to wrist. She glanced up from beneath lowered brows, stroking her damaged arm as if to comfort it, while her beady eyes appraised the newcomers.

Pushing in behind her was a handful of half-naked natives of both sexes, some with small children clinging to them. Standing slightly apart was a tall white youth with a musket slung over his shoulder, and a cat-skin cap pulled down over his brow.

King introduced himself and his first officer. 'Rachel,' he said, with a smile.' You've taken us by surprise. You aren't quite what we expected to find here.'

When the Newfoundland nosed his way forward to sniff at Rachel's bare feet, the natives clustered behind her shrieked in fear. Tail wagging, oblivious to the fuss, the dog licked her hand. On seeing this, the tribes-men set up a fresh burst of wailing.

The tall lad took a few steps towards them. About eighteen years old, he had fair freckled skin and a badly peeling nose. Leaning on his long-barrelled musket, his grey eyes stared out at them unblinking from beneath the cat-skin cap. His breeches were ragged, carelessly slashed off at the knee, his shirt bleached to a dirty grey.

Rachel nudged him forward. She spoke slowly and carefully, as if she had been practicing what to say. 'This one is Tom –Thomas Halstead, *meneer.* His father came with Mr Farewell, but went back to the Cape on the small ship. Together, we must look after everything until the men return.'

On hearing Farewell's name, King was stunned for a moment, staring at her, until he finally found the words. 'Farewell's alive then?'

Rachel's dark eyes held a hint of amusement as she answered. 'Alive? *Ja*, of course, is very much living.' Recovering his equilibrium, King asked, 'You mentioned others, other men. Who would they be?'

He shushed for silence to allow Rachel to speak. 'Mr Farewell and John Cane, gone many days now –'

Brows drawn together in a frown, as if searching for words, she hesitated.

'Hunting?' King prompted, 'perhaps they've gone hunting?'

Rachel shook her head. 'No, they were called away.'

'Called away?' echoed King, 'why were they called away, and by whom, may I ask?'

The answer, when it came, brought a rumble of disbelief from the listening sailors. 'They were called away to *fight*?' James King's voice cracked in disbelief. 'What d' you mean? Who called them to fight – and to fight whom?'

In the dense thickets beyond the beach, a squall of angry monkey noises broke out amid screeches of frustrated territorial ambitions and a crashing of branches.

Rachel shook her head, confused by the questions. 'Shaka... what other could it be? They have gone to help him fight.'

A rustle of emotion emanated from the natives, followed another round of wailing. *Shaka*...the name obviously disturbed them. Inwardly, King groaned. *Shaka, the barbarian King, already on the scene...how in hell am I going to explain him away now?*

Flicking a glance around the crew, his eyes met those of the mate, Thompson. The man raised his eyebrows, a mixture of malice and curiosity in his flat, stone-coloured eyes. Aware of the latent question in the hostile glance, angry colour rose in King's face. Ruthlessly, he quashed the desire to strike out at something – or someone. When he spoke, it was with barely controlled rage.

'So Farewell has made contact with the Zulu king, then? But what in the devil is he doing getting involved in fighting for him? '

Rachel shrugged her shoulders. 'This is Shaka's land. What he says all must do.' The eyes that looked back at King were dark and sad. 'You have much to learn, *meneer*.'

A shaft of shimmering, red-gold light lanced out and lit up the bluff, gilding the tree-clad heights and casting the deeper parts into shadow.

King reluctantly decided it was time they returned to camp. The sun would soon be down. When he asked Rachel where they lived, she waved a hand towards the other side of the lagoon. As she turned to leave, James King caught her gently by the arm, and indicated the trailing Union flag.

'Where did you get it?' he asked, trying not to sound accusing. Rachel smiled, unperturbed by any suggestion of impropriety.

'The place where I live is Fort Farewell.' Holding the tattered ensign above her head, she laughed throatily. 'Mr Farewell keep it high up on...a...'

'Flag pole?' King supplied, in total disbelief.

'*Ja,*' Rachel replied, nodding. 'Flag pole, this is the word I did not have. Every morning the flag go up, every night it come down.'

The only sound was the crick-crick of insects in the amber light and the slow lap of water against the shore.

'Good God,' Hatton muttered, sarcastically. 'Taking it a bit far, isn't he? I mean to say – naming a Fort after himself *and* hoisting the colours morning, noon and night. I wonder if he does a musket volley at sunset as well?'

King gave no reply, merely stared at the woman's departing back. Once she was out of earshot, Hatton cleared his throat and said, 'I think you've been keeping a few things a shade too close to your chest, captain. So let me ask you...who the hell is this King Shaka? Just what kind of trouble can we expect from him?'

Fixing his cool grey eyes on the man who was his captain, he straightened his shoulders and demanded. 'And why wasn't I, as first officer, let in on the secret? My life's also been on the line, as well as the crew's.'

King shot him a look of undisguised misery. Then he turned on his heel and set off back to the longboat. 'Now's not the time, Hatton,' he said, shooting a warning glance at the mate, Thompson. 'Later, I'll discuss it with you later.'

Close to midnight, the darkness was silvered by the crescent of a rising moon, traceries of phosphorus ebbing and flowing on the tide washing along the shore. Most of the crew had retired for the night, safe behind the newly built high fences. Some of the ship's dogs prowled around the perimeter while others slept by the fire, paws twitching, occasionally waking to snap at insects.

King and Hatton, having elected to take first watch, were seated on upturned boxes by the fire, loaded muskets at hand. Hatton, irked by having to wait till they were alone, raised the same questions he had at sunset.

'Just who is this man Shaka, anyway?' he asked, 'and why does he seem to be leadin' your man Farewell by the nose?' James King sighed and pinched the bridge of his nose in weariness.

'Since I don't know what's been going on here as regards Farewell, I can only tell you what I know of the Zulu king, because that's who Shaka is. All second, third or even fourth hand accounts, of course, but they seem to tie in pretty well with each other.'

'Where and when did you first hear about him?' asked Hatton, his curiosity aroused. 'I take it you've known for some time he might prove a problem?'

'Almost from the start,' King replied, in a sincere effort at honesty. 'Farewell told me after I met him in South America. That was when the stories of Shaka came to light, his fearsome reputation – '

'Which is?' Hatton demanded; his voice gruff with impatience.

King met his eyes squarely across the fire. 'All hearsay, of course, but it seems –'

His words were drowned out by the sound of frantic barking and snarling. Hyenas and wild dogs, maddened by the tantalising odours of the livestock inside, were trying to find a way in, while the ship's dogs responded in kind.

Rolled up in his blanket with only the top of his head showing, Jack awoke with a jump. The night was dark and savage, full of strange noises, hordes of biting insects and snarling wild animals.

Around him, men's exhausted voices threw curses into the night, their dark shapes silhouetted against the fires as they loaded their firearms.

'Black as a witch's bloomers out there,' he heard Aldred Williams say as he stared gloomily out into the pitch darkness

'An odd remark for such an upstanding young married man to make,' retorted John Evans with the striped satin waistcoat, who, according to Biddle, had been a minister of religion, a Methodist, before running off to sea, because of a mix-up concerning his relationship with one of his parishioners.

'Not if he's a Welsh taffy,' replied Nicholls with unholy glee, aiming a stream of saliva into the crackling fire. 'I bet them buggers is up to all sorts in them valleys o' theirs.'

It only took a few musket cracks to send the scavengers fleeing out of range. Gradually, the hubbub died down, and order was restored. Men stumbled back to their makeshift beds, grumbling and coughing. Soon, all was quiet again. Hatton threw more branches on the fire to keep the blaze going.

Jack lay awake, watching the leap of the flames and the upward drift of golden sparks. Over and above the night sounds and the crackling of burning wood, he became conscious of the low rumble of men's voices nearby.

The captain and Hatton were still on watch. Judging by their voices, something serious was being discussed. Curiosity getting the better of him, he pulled the blanket around himself and rolled closer to hear what was being said.

Hatton's voice was credulous as he asked, 'Are you sure it's not a case of superstitious natives getting carried away with things? To believe this Shaka's a god, able to see and hear all they do – isn't that carryin' things a bit too far? And what's all that about his palace being ringed round with huge elephant tusks? Do you think he's that powerful, or rich?'

Jack waited in the shadows, almost afraid to breathe.

'Don't know about being rich, but do I think he's that powerful?' King repeated. 'Yes, I do, Hatton. Remember, this is a man who's conquered nearly every tribe to the north, south, east, and west of him. And his influence stretches even further than that. Apparently, he's strong as a bull and extremely clever. His warriors are well-trained and disciplined, and can run for days through all kinds of terrain – which is why they're well-nigh unconquerable.'

He leaned over to light another cheroot from a burning stick plucked from the blaze. 'Let me tell you, Hatton – even though very few of them have actually set eyes on him, Shaka of the Zulus scares the hell out of the Portuguese. Their trading in ivory is all done through a series of interme-diaries, rarely face to face. Believe me, they're not the sort to exaggerate, or play down what this man's reputed to have done. Or what he *is*.'

'I take it that how he *punishes* his people aren't exaggerations either?' Hatton asked in a voice as dry as a bone.

'You mean the killings?' Charlie stared at the sparks flying up into the night sky. An odd, sick feeling started in his belly.

'Hearsay again,' answered King, poking the fire. 'But, yes, skewered up the arse, set up on a bamboo pole, then left to rot, to die of starvation, loss of blood or until predators nose them out – that would be a fair account of what happens to those who run seriously foul of Shaka of the Zulus.'

Saliva flooded Charlie's mouth. Screwing his eyes shut, he prayed he wasn't going to retch or spew up his supper and alert the Captain to the fact he was eavesdropping.

'But that particular punishment's reserved only for the worst offenders, mind,' King added, with some sarcasm. 'He has other ways of disposing of people who offend him.'

A snort of disbelief came from Hatton. 'Well, now,' he said, with some sarcasm, 'I'm right glad to hear that – it relieves my mind no end! So what other form do his punishments take?'

King's North American drawl became more noticeable as he went on.

'He doesn't believe in short term measures, Hatton. No flogging or cat 'o' nine tails, no keel-hauling, no hanging, drawing or quartering, no cutting hands off, no stocks, no prisons – none of our more civilised ways. Apart from the skewering, straight death's his way, carried out by slayers, men specially trained for the job. One snap of the neck and it's over – unless you're unlucky enough to get the other kind.'

Images of cannibal feasts on Crusoe's desert island flooded Jack's mind. A long silence followed. When Hatton next spoke, there was weariness in his voice. 'Good God Almighty! Just answer me straight! How much trouble d' you think this man is going to be to us?'

King shrugged his shoulders and fixed his first officer with the stare of a man who had just lost a ship and most of his prospects.

'Only time will tell,' he said, 'if he sees us as a threat, or thinks we've got nothing to bargain with, he might just kill us and be done with it. Who knows?'

Suddenly, Jack didn't want to hear any more. Rolling back to where he had started out, he pulled the blanket over his head, curled into a ball and stuffed his fingers in his ears.

Out beyond the makeshift barricades, the predators resumed their pacing and prowling, while the flickering flames of the shipwrecked sailors remained the only signs of life in the immense blackness of the bay called eThekwini.

Five

After losing another of the ship's dogs to prowling leopards, King decided it was time to build a more permanent camp, one with high fences and stout wooden gates.

'Not only are these nightly hyena fights bad for morale, they're also very costly. At this rate,' King said, 'we'll run out of powder and shot, and damn quick at that. Then where will we be, gentlemen? Marooned and defenceless – and that's not an option I intend to contemplate.'

Jack was greatly relieved to hear him say it. The captain would see to it that they wouldn't have to face the dreaded Zulu king undefended.

The sun stood directly overhead, a baleful eye peering through a haze of molten grey. Heat rose in waves off the shimmering sands. The glare was white-hot and blinding, the humidity high, draining their energy and resolve.

Exhausted, the men lay sprawled in the shade, smoking quietly or dozing with their hats over their eyes. They had been hard at it since sunrise, clearing the bush and driving in stakes to mark out the site of their new camp. Now they were taking a well-earned rest.

A squad of amaTuli tribesmen had been helping them with the back-breaking work. Timid people, they'd taken to putting in an appearance every morning and evening, drawn by the aroma of roasting meat and fish being prepared in the camp. In exchange for their labour, they were given food, enough to feed themselves and their families.

Suddenly, Biddle, the bo'sun, stopped drinking the coal-black brew he called tea, the chipped enamel pannikin halfway to his mouth. Cocking a hand to his ear, he muttered. 'Singin'... I hear singin', bugger me lugs, if I don't!'

Grabbing Jack by the arm, he asked, 'D'ye hear it, Jack? Gawd! Tell me it ain't the angels come for us, boy – 'cos I ain't ready!'

Fifteen pairs of eyes swivelled to the forested slopes beyond the half-cleared site. Now they could all hear it – the rise and fall of rhythmic chanting, accompanied by a babble of voices and the unmistakable shuffle of feet, many feet, scrambling down the maze of paths threading the hillsides.

'Ye're right, Biddle,' said Nichols, the thin caulker with a cast in one eye, 'Only it ain't angels, sounds more like the hordes from hell.'

Jack saw Hatton slip quietly away with Thompson. He guessed they'd be heading to where they'd stacked half a dozen muskets that morning. He shot a glance at Ned Cameron who shrugged his shoulders expressively.

Suddenly, the amaTuli workers took to their heels and high-tailed it into the bush. 'Oh, gawd,' moaned Biddle, eyeing the fleeing tribesmen, 'the rats is desertin' the ship! Always the first to know, ain't they?'

Thompson and Hatton were back, handing out muskets. Jack's heart was in his mouth as he looked down at the small axe in his hand. Ned armed himself with a heavy stick and swished it a few times around his head to try it out. As he motioned his crew to spread out into the under-growth and lie low, a trickle of sweat ran down King's face and a muscle ticked along his clenched jaw.

Moments later, they caught sight of the first of those coming towards them through the trees. There were at least thirty young men there, strong, and muscular, their skins gleaming with oil and sweat. Assured and confident, these young bucks looked very different from the timid amaTuli labourers. As they spread out through the trees, the sun glinted dully off the tips of well-sharpened spears.

In sharp contrast, the flood of people stumbling down the hillside be-hind them looked weak and half-starved. There were men and women, mothers with babies on their backs, children of all ages trailing at their heels, wailing in tiredness. Hollow-eyed, limping and footsore, some were stark naked, while others were clad in remnants of tattered animal skins.

'Who in the hell are these people comin' on behind?' Ned whispered. 'I hope it ain't what it looks like.' Jack shot him a questioning look.

'Slavers,' the youth muttered. Hatton turned his head sharply, his eyes raking Ned's face. 'Is that what you think this is?'

Ned shrugged his shoulders. 'Dunno for sure. One lot armed and well fed, the other poor bastards, thin as sticks. No neck-irons or restraints, though.'

Another group of armed men came scrambling down the hillside. 'With any luck, they'll pass by,' Ned muttered, 'we've no chance of taking them on, anyway, too many of 'em.'

Jack's palms were slippery with sweat, the small axe growing heavier by the moment. They pressed further back into the undergrowth and crouched down, out of sight.

Without warning, the chanting petered out. Only the wailing of exhausted children broke the sudden hush. 'They've spotted our workings,' Ned breathed, nodding towards the piles of stripped timber, bundles of thatch and patches of cleared-back bush.

A moment of acute hiatus followed. In the noonday heat, the buzzing of insects sounded abnormally loud, almost deafening. Then King, Hatton and a group of sailors stepped out of the thicket, loaded muskets at the ready. The rest of the crew gripped their hoes, axes and hammers and prepared for the worst.

At the sight of the armed white men barring the path, screams of fear rose from the exhausted women and children. The reactions of the others were totally different. In a flash, they had moved forward, their short spears at the ready.

Just as confrontation seemed unavoidable, Hatton stopped dead in his tracks, his eyes fixed on something behind the advancing spears.

'Well, well, what have we here, then?' he muttered. All eyes swivelled to a point beyond the armed stand off. In an instant, the atmosphere changed to one of wary indecision.

The two scarecrows sauntering along the path towards them were barely recognisable as white men. The taller of the two was clad in a tattered blanket that barely covered his buttocks. Bearded, his long, sun-streaked hair and dark skin gave him the air of a derelict prophet.

'Good Gawd!' Biddle croaked, the hammer falling loosely to his side. 'It's a white man, one of us.' 'Amen to that,' responded Eldred Williams, the young Welshman.

Perched at a rakish angle on the man's head was a broad-brimmed straw hat. The crown, having long since come unstuck, clung to the main body of the hat and flapped with every step. A mass of floating black and white ostrich plumes woven into the band of the hat topped it off.

Jack's eyes dropped to the man's feet. His homemade sandals were crudely fashioned from strips of leather and fastened with thongs wound round his muscular, sunburned legs. Slung over his shoulder was a long-barrelled firearm.

Scuttling along beside him was a second scarecrow. Smaller in stature, the outfit he wore was equally eccentric. A pair of thin, bony legs poked through slits in the ragged trousers flapping about his knees like a skirt. His tattered sailor's tunic was several sizes too large for him; one sleeve rolled up, the other somewhere around his finger ends. On his head, he wore a cat-skin cap with the tail dangling over one ear.

A few steps nearer and the reason for his shambling walk became clear. Only the strips of leather bound round his broken boots prevented them from total collapse. Oblivious to the presence of a score of armed strangers barring his way, he kept on singing in a fine tenor voice, the stick in his hand keeping in time with the melody.

King lowered his musket. 'Who are you – or *what* the hell are you, I should perhaps ask? Mummers dressed for a play, or citizens of King George?'

Just then, the deserting amaTuli burst out of the bush in a raucous gang and ran round the two men, whooping and laughing.

'*Mbuyazi... Mbuyazi!*' they yodelled, jinking around the two ragged figures. '*Ohlo...Ohlo!*' Judging by their reception, the two men were neither strangers nor slavers.

The eccentric leader of the multitude strode up to King, his hand held out in welcome, a broad beam splitting his bearded face.

Jack stared at the man in disbelief. Robinson Crusoe himself, straight out of the pages of Daniel Defoe! The scarecrow swept off his straw hat in a flourish of black and white ostrich feathers, bowing low in exaggerated courtesy.

'Afternoon, gents,' he crowed, 'Henry Fynn, at your service – also known hereabouts as Mbuyasi, the finch.' Nodding towards his ragged companion, he said, 'An' this here's the one they're callin' Ohlo.'

Not to be outdone, the second man stepped forward. Bringing his disintegrating boots together in a military snap, he doffed his cat-skin cap and spoke out in an accent that was pure Yorkshire.

'How do! Ogle be the name, gents, Henry to me friends.' He finished off his introduction with a trill of high, warbling notes, sending the amaTuli wild.

'Well, I'll be damned,' King shouted above the hullaballoo. 'Where in the hell did you two spring from?'

Half an hour later, after the straggling columns had been led off to find food and shelter, Fynn turned to King and said, 'You were asking me something, I believe, before we were interrupted?'

'So I was,' replied King, still bemused at the turn of events. 'So I'll say it again. Just where in the devil did you two spring from?'

Fynn propped himself up with his back against a tree. Stretching out his long legs with a sigh of relief, he said, 'Me and Ogle here have been away for a couple of months, down in amaPondo territory, two hundred miles or so south of here.'

'And the poor devils with you? Where are you taking them, if I might ask?'

The wary questions came from the first officer. King flicked a glance in Hatton's direction and noted the first officer's tight lips. Obviously, he was still taking Ned's suspicions about slavery seriously.

'Here. End of the journey,' replied Fynn, narrowing his eyes against the sunlight. 'Last time we came back, there was even more of 'em with us.'

King stared at him, unwilling to put his suspicions into words.

Henry Fynn hooted with laughter. 'Let me say, first and foremost, my business is ivory, with a bit o' trading thrown in. It's just that I find it hard to turn away poor devils who've got nothing but starvation to look forward to... just in case you were thinkin' Ogle an' me were into black-birding, that is.'

His hazel eyes were fixed on Hatton as he added, 'Shaka himself's given his blessing to their bein' here. A year or so since, his *impis* over-ran their people, drove off cattle, destroyed their crops, those they didn't kill were left destitute.'

He looked through the trees to where the lagoon shimmered in the sunlight. 'Not that pity for them motivates the man, o' course, but I managed to put forward a pretty good case on their behalf. There are thousands like them back there, scavenging for what they can find...even eating each other, I've heard tell, if things get too bad.'

In the deathly silence that followed, the high shrilling of cicadas sounded very loud. King's mind was reeling. If what Fynn said was true then, *ergo,* it meant that the man sitting before him had already met the legendary warrior King.

Careful, careful... his inner voice urged. Don't show too much interest in the Zulu king – not yet, anyway. Better to wait till you get Fynn alone.

Changing the subject, he asked, 'How old are you, Henry?'

Fynn laughed, showing a set of very white teeth. 'Twenty or so, at the last count, I reckon.' Reaching into his pack, he brought out a pipe and proceeded to stuff it with strands of tobacco from one of the pouches around his neck.

King was silent. There's so much I need to ask this man who's just dropped in out of the blue like a wandering wind – especially about Shaka of the Zulus.

Jack watched in fascination as Fynn used two pieces of stick and a few wisps of dried grass to raise a tiny flame to light his pipe. King decided to probe for more news of Farewell.

'How did you fall in with Farewell, if you don't mind my asking?'

'Signed on with him at the Cape,' Fynn replied, puffing away at his pipe. 'The way it was put to me, a tidy sum could be made in a short time, six months or so, maybe. Since I'd nothing to put in the pot, manager of trading transactions was to be my title – and my responsibility. Ogle there came aboard at Algoa Bay. Me, I'd been looking for a way to get north ever since I took a trip to Delagoa a few years back.'

'Delagoa?' exclaimed King, raising his eyebrows. 'You didn't happen to meet Farewell there, did you?'

Fynn grinned. 'No, but as it turned out we saw something there that pricked our curiosity – as well as our business instincts, you might say.'

'The ivory,' stated James King, baldly. Fynn nodded. 'Aye, gold, too, though I haven't seen a sign of that – not yet, leastwise.'

King was thoughtful for a moment, recalling the heavy bundles on the heads of the men coming down the hillside. 'Ivory – I take it that was the main reason for your recent expedition down the Wild Coast?'

Fynn poked a finger through a hole in the crown of his straw hat. 'Hit it square on the head,' he said, with a grin. 'Truth be known, though, I'm also partial to a bit of a wander. Ever since I left London, I like nothing better than a good stretch of the legs through wild country.'

He squinted through pipe smoke at the former captain of the *Mary*. 'It's no secret who's the law around here, and who controls everything. Hunting any animal of note in the kingdom of the amaZulu is the sole prerogative of the king – especially the big cats, leopard, lion and cheetah – and the elephant, of course. They're all under his protection. He's their natural and spiritual guardian. *Izilozi Nkosi, Lord of the Beasts.*'

King's blue eyes pinned him down. 'So what you're saying is that you carry on with your trade well out of his sight?'

Fynn's bearded face split into an amiable grin. 'Well, now, Captain, the answer to your question is both yes and no. It's doubtful, see, if anything or anybody is ever "out of his sight" as you put it. The Zulu king's got eyes and ears everywhere, and in places you'd least expect. You'd do well to remember that.'

Tapping the side of his nose with a grimy forefinger, he winked. 'Yes, I mostly hunt away from Zulu territory. My plan was to find a likely spot near the coast where a small vessel could drop anchor, pick up the tusks, take 'em to the Cape, sell 'em, then drop off some more trade goods. I did have an arrangement, but I fear something's gone wrong.'

He sighed, scattering bits of glowing tobacco about his person. 'The vessel in question didn't show, even though I waited long past the time we'd arranged. In the end, I had no option but to bring the tusks back here with me.'

A sudden bolt of awareness shot through King. He leaned forward. 'The *Julia,*' he asked, 'you weren't waiting for the *Julia* to pick up the ivory, were you?'

Curiosity flared in Fynn's hazel eyes. King met his glance squarely.

'It's not good news, Henry. I'm sorry to tell you, but she's feared lost with all hands. I heard about it at the Cape. Not a sight of her – or her crew.'

Fynn's face fell. Rubbing a hand over his face, he stared at the ground, and said softly, 'Garrett was a good man.' After a bit, he sighed. 'Another man's also missing. Maybe you knew him. Joe Powell.'

Now it was King's turn to groan. 'Joe, a rock of a man, fought alongside him during Boney's war. What in God's name happened?'

Fynn drew heavily on his pipe. 'He took off with another fella, trying to get to Delagoa Bay overland, last year around August time, I think.'

'Another unmarked grave along the way, then,' said King softly.

His thoughts turned to poor Higgins, turned into carrion by a leopard; Garret and his crew, lost somewhere along the thousand miles to the Cape... and now Joe Powell, last resting place unknown.

After a long pause, King said, 'A question, Henry, if you'd be so good. Just who are the natives with you, the ones who handle those damn spears like they know how to use 'em?'

Fynn's teeth showed in a flash of humour. 'No mystery, there, Captain. They're Zulus, Shaka's warriors.'

A jolt of shock followed this announcement. Eventually, King asked, 'And what of Farewell, what's been happening here?'

'Farewell?' Fynn replied, taking the pipe from his mouth. 'Grapevine has it he and John Cane have been summoned by Shaka to help the man do what he does best.'

Bemused, King asked, 'And what might that be?'

Fynn roared with laughter. 'Waging war, of course – what else? Don't tell me you came all this way without knowing a little somethin' about the man?'

Somewhat miffed, King lost patience with the way things were going. 'Time for riddles later, Fynn,' he snapped. 'Now, tell me – where in the hell exactly *is* Farewell, and what is his involvement with the Zulu king?'

As it neared midnight, the flames of the huge bonfire threw flickering shadows over the men sprawled around it. In the half-darkness, some of the people who had followed Fynn home for over two hundred miles sat huddled together, intrigued by the presence of so many white men.

Jack was enjoying himself hugely. Fynn was a great storyteller. As time went on, the Cape brandy the captain had broken out of the ship's supplies was making him even more eloquent.

Intrigued by his long sun-streaked hair, the braids of elephant hair around his wrists and the beaded ring he wore on his big toe, Jack could hardly take his eyes off Henry Fynn.

The man the amaTuli called Mbuyasi was in the throes of describing the magnificence of the starry nights, the spectacular sunrises and sunsets he and Ogle had experienced during their sorties into the wilderness of the Wild Coast.

'More breathtaking than any artist could portray,' he said to his captive audience. 'Stars hanging so low, a man can grow dizzy just lookin' at them.

Some nights, the moonlight is as clear as day, it's so bright you can watch the hunters on the prowl an' see the elephants cavort an' play in the rivers.'

He spoke of the grey silent shapes of the herds of elephants, and the way they would appear out of nowhere, drifting out of the trees when a man wasn't looking. Jack was spellbound as Fynn told how they could uproot trees and trample a man into the dust, or break him like a twig if they got aroused, or smelled their scent on the wind. But they were the most caring of beasts to their young, he said, their tribe sharing the upbringing of all the calves.

At that moment, he was in full flow, describing with relish how Ogle had been bitten on the backside by a huge black spider as he squatted to relieve himself in the bush.

'Well, damn me,' Fynn said, 'did not that blessed thing stick to poor old Ogle's arse like a limpet. Took a great likin' to it, if truth be told... though for the life of me, I can't see why, since that part o' poor old Ogle is just about as unappealing as the rest of him.' Henry Ogle, not to be outdone, sprang to his feet, offering to undo his breeches to show the scars.

From beyond the firelight, came a flash of teeth as the watchful audience joined in the fun. The exact meaning of Fynn's words might have escaped them, but Ogle's miming told the whole story.

'What happened next then, Fynn?' roared out Nicholls from across the fire.' How did ye dispatch the beast?'

'Aye, Fynn, tell us the rest!' The demand was unanimous.

Ogle broke in. '*I* should be tellin' it. It was *my* spider, after all!' Ned whipped in as quick as a flash. 'Aye, matey…and it was *your* arse, as well.'

Pandemonium broke out with opposing sides in noisy conflict. Fynn stepped in and neatly brought the fracas under control, lowering his voice so they had to stop their racket to hear what happened next.

'In the end, we had to rush him down to the water's edge, lively like. No amount of threatening and poking could get the beast to let go. So, applying all my medical skill to the problem…'

Ogle, breeches around his ankles, took centre stage again, miming his waddle down to the water's edge, with the black spider still adhering to his posterior.

'So, applying all my medical skills to the problem,' Fynn repeated, solemn as a judge, 'I came up with the solution.'

'Tell us! Tell us!' came the chant. Fynn paused in the firelight, waiting till he had his audience in the palm of his hand. ' We had to stick poor old Ogle's arse, spider an' all into the cold, cold briny till one or the other fell off!'

'A stubborn bugger, though…' Ogle whipped in, rubbing his buttock 'A whole hour it took. Even when he was stone cold dead, he was still hangin' on like grim death – might be bits of 'im still there, for all I know!'

As midnight drew near, the mood changed. Beyond the high fences topped with bamboo stakes, the dark shapes of predators flitted in and out of the shadows. An owl hooted eerily nearby, and as if in answer, jackals and wild dogs howled in unison. Although his eyes were gritty with lack of sleep, Jack was determined not to miss anything. He stole a quick look around.

Most of the sailors were spark out, the effects of the fire, the grog and weeks of hard labour taking their toll. Even Ned was asleep, snoring gently, his head pillowed on his pack, his ear-ring glinting in the firelight.

A few yards away, King sat quietly smoking a battered Dutch cheroot, his long legs stretched out in front him. Facing him was Henry Fynn, his pipe clenched between his teeth.

'Tell me how you came to meet the Zulu King,' King asked, bluntly.

A sudden alertness came into play between the two men. Jack's eyes snapped open, the sick feeling oozing back into his belly.

'For days, all we saw of the amaTuli were their blessed footprints in the sand,' Fynn said, 'poor devils, terrified of their own shadows. Had to chase old Mahamba there up the beach and lay him out flat, being he was the only one I could catch, him being the oldest and the slowest.'

The wiry, grey-haired Mahamba flashed him a crooked smile from across the fire. Fynn idly scratched his bare knee then shot a glance at King.

'In the end, though, you could say the Zulus and me ran into one another. Literally. Everything that happened afterwards was because of that chance encounter on the sands.'

The irrepressible Fynn chuckled. Leaning forward, he threw a few more logs on to the fire. Flames leapt into the air, crackling and throwing out sparks.

'Shortly after we arrived, I set out north with old Mahamba, Frederick and Jantyi Michael, my trackers, to have a look-see. I decided to keep to the beach, well away from the thickets. At least on open sands a man can see what's coming a good distance away – or so I thought!'

Shaking his shaggy head, his eyes twinkled in amusement. 'The trouble was, Captain, things didn't quite turn out like that. After a bit, I stopped for a bit of a rest. An' then I just happened to cast a glance back the way we'd come…'

His voice tailed away. Clearing his throat, he fiddled with the glowing shreds of tobacco in the blackened pipe bowl. In the silence, Jack became acutely aware of everything around him; the breeze rustling in from the sea, the crescent moon half-veiled by thin drifts of cloud, and the humped figures of sleeping men.

'Like a black tide, they were,' Fynn said, soberly, 'stretching back for as far as the eye could see. Marching out of the sea-haze, wave after wave of them like a column of soldier ants I once saw on the frontier, marching like nothing on God's earth could ever stop them.'

Up on the wooded heights, an owl hooted, an eerie reminder of the wilderness lying beyond the circle of firelight. Jack let his breath out slowly.

'I tell you true,' Fynn went on. 'Frozen to the spot I was, my arse fixed to the ground. Thousands upon thousands of 'em, head feathers streaming in the wind, the army of the Zulus flowing back for as far as the eye could see, looking as if they could march for all eternity.'

The silence was palpable, intense. Jack was as wide-awake as he'd ever been in his life.

'Nearer still,' said Fynn, 'and I could hear the clink of their weapons, the shuffle and slap of their feet on the wet sand. Then the front ranks stopped dead in their tracks. A long hiss told me we'd been spotted.'

'Good God!' said King. 'What did you do, then?'

'Thought bloody fast!' Fynn retorted with some passion, before directing a stream of tobacco juice into the flames.

Jack was speechless; overawed by everything Fynn had told them. And, as far as the man himself went – why, here was Robinson Crusoe himself, come back to life, a full-blown hero straight from the pages of a storybook.

Scratching an insect bite on his leg, he thought, Pity Ned slept through it all. He'll be spitting feathers when I tell him what he's missed.

Fynn's adventures weren't all he'd overheard and understood, though. Oh, no, not by a long shot. What he also witnessed was James King's explosion of disbelief when Fynn finally told him the whereabouts of his missing partner, Lieutenant Francis Farewell – and what he was involved in.

Bewilderment and anger had burst through James King's composure like a rip tide. 'He's doing what! In God's name, what is is he thinking of? We were expressly forbidden by the Cape authorities to take sides in any native rough stuff.'

Beyond the firelight, inquisitive eyes watched every move. A murmur rose from the watchers as they debated the possible source of the white man's anger.

Fynn waited calmly while King gave vent to his misgivings. 'With all due respect, Captain,' he said, 'you're not at the Cape now. No Colony rules here, no Navy regulations either. This is Zululand, Shaka's country – his kingdom, where his law is absolute. Farewell and Cane had no choice whatsoever. Take my word for it.'

King was only slightly mollified. 'I take it you're speaking from personal experience?'

Fynn nodded. 'Too true, Captain. It was John Cane and myself last time. If I hadn't taken myself off down south, I'd be out there with them right now.'

King felt the hairs stir on the back of his neck. Briefly, he thought of the mass of pinprick fires they'd seen from the deck of the *Salisbury* when they'd anchored off the coast some two years earlier. Farewell had been right. Clearly, what they'd seen had been the massed Zulu army camping for the night; a sight burned into his memory.

The thought that the same Lieutenant Francis Farewell, late of His Majesty's Royal Navy, decorated with honours for bravery in battle, might be out there marauding with the same savages, was either an exaggeration – or the beginnings of a nightmare.

The crescent moon had long since disappeared behind the headland and only the blaze of starlight and the luminous glow of phosphorescence from the lagoon illuminated the darkness. Dawn was still a few hours away.

Fynn sniffed the cool air drifting up from the bay. Padding over to the fire, he stirred up the embers, added some dried grass and twigs to the small darts of flame then rooted about for a spill of wood to light his pipe.

All the talk of running into the Zulu army the year before had stirred up memories of what his chance meeting with them had set in motion.

Deciding to follow the streams of warriors heading north, back to Shaka's stronghold, had led to his meeting with various chiefs, including Shaka's uncle. Then there had been the old dying woman whose life he had saved, earning him the accolade of having the power to bring back the dead – the sole factor he believed had been responsible for Shaka's invitation to kwaBulawayo and the earning of his ultimate respect.

No wonder it was hard to sleep. Tilting his head back, he gazed up into the sky. The sheer impact of the stars strewn across the night skies never ceased to be a source of wonder, no matter how often he saw them. His nose wrinkled in humour. Like everything else in Africa, they're vivid, full of colour and vibrancy of spirit.

Fynn's eyes were hooded as he recalled the high, round breasts of the girl called Langazana, and her musky smell.

In your arms, at the end of a rifle barrel, or at your throat, Africa's creations leave an indelible impression on you…one way or the other.

Then he smiled his mad Irish smile, and bent his head back so that his vision was full to overflowing with the startling beauty of the heavens.

*

A few nights later, Jack awoke in the dead of night, to find him gone. His legs were still cramped from the dog's weight, so he couldn't be far away. Untangling himself from the blanket, he whispered softly, 'Dileas – here, boy…'

The night was full of the whine of mosquitoes and the chirping of cicadas and tree frogs. Nearby, a man snored, while another mumbled in his sleep as he turned over on the hard ground

Halfway to his feet, Jack called him again. Somewhere close an animal, probably one of the goats, rustled among its dried grass bedding. A hen clucked softly, the flap of feathers soft in the dust. The night air was cool and sweet, the earth warm beneath his feet.

From the fireside came the clink of a tin mug as one of the men on watch poured some coffee. Fergus, the black and white collie, padded up and thrust a damp nose into his hand.

He spoke softly. 'Where is he, Fergie, boy…where's Dileas, then?' The collie's wagging tail told him nothing.

Then, out of the deep silence, he heard a low, coughing sound followed by a rumbling growl of defiance. His heart leapt into his mouth, sending the blood drumming in his ears. A frenzied snarling broke out, punctuated by deep-throated growls. As soon as he heard it, he knew. *Dileas was out there…and so was something else…*

Jack broke into a run, yelling at the top of his voice. The men on watch leapt to their feet, hands reaching for their loaded, primed weapons. Within a silence that shrivelled him to the core, his heart was beating like that of a rabbit caught in a snare. A long wailing cry of an animal in agony filled the air, a sound of hurt, pain and fear, then a pitiful snuffling and whining.

The collie put its head back and howled, a low mournful cry of despair, sparking off the other dogs. Men came stumbling out of their blankets, the air blue with oaths. He rushed headlong towards the barred gates, his feet barely touching the ground. He didn't need to be told that his dog was out there...or that it was in trouble.

'Hold on there, Jack!' A strong pair of arms caught him up bodily and swung him off his feet. 'And where might ye be thinkin' of going, now?'

He kicked and struggled, tearing frantically at John Hatton's restraining arms, desperate to find out where his dog was fighting for his life. 'Let me go!' he screamed, 'Dileas is out there. A leopard's got him. I need to help him!'

The terrifying sounds out in the pitch black night filled his head and turned his knees to water. 'Damn it to hell an' back!' Someone cursed close by, as guns fired into the darkness.

A voice muttered. 'Poor brute, I doubt he's done for.'

'Jack.' Hatton spoke close to his ear, his voice gruff with compassion.

'There's a good lad, now. If I do let you go, promise me you'll not be doing anything foolish. If your dog be fighting to protect us, he wouldn't want you to get in his way, would he now?'

Wordless in the face of such logic, Jack could only shake his head, vomit acid and sour in his throat. Hatton released him, slowly, his eyes wary in the firelight.

The guns stopped. In the terrifying silence that followed, even the cricking of the insects was stilled. Jack stood alone on an island of bitter dread, echoes of the gunfire continuing to thud in his head and in his heart.

When at last he lifted his head, he knew. The truth was written across John Hatton's face, and the man couldn't hide it.

For the rest of the night, he stared dried-eyed into the darkness and watched the showers of sparks flying up like golden bees into the night. He knew that the eyes of prowling hyenas would be glinting out there in the darkness as they padded to and fro, attracted by the smell of blood.

Dileas' blood...

The dog had been his faithful companion ever since they'd first set eyes on each other, the bond between them instant and loving. It had jumped overboard and saved his life after he'd taken a tumble out of the rigging off the Azores. Without its quick reactions after spotting his shirt in the water, he would not be alive to tell the tale.

Dileas was gone. The great Newfoundland hound had come all the way from Nova Scotia, had crossed half the oceans in the world, only to die in Africa. Raw grief stuck in his throat. He wouldn't cry, for it wouldn't do for a mariner to show his tears ... but his boy's heart broke all the same.

In the morning, Hatton sought him out and said, in that quiet way of his: 'We'll show 'em, Jack. Just you wait.' His ruddy face was grim for the boy in his loss, but determined all the same.

He took Jack to see what he had rigged up. As he knelt down to show him how it would work, he could see that some of the first officer's fingernails were torn and bleeding after his efforts.

Tears flooded Jack's eyes as he realised how much time and thought Hatton had put into his plan to avenge Dileas and poor Higgins.

But it wasn't only a boy's sharp loss that had to be avenged. A man had also been lost, his body torn and dismembered, like so much carrion. Poor Higgins. All Jack could really remember about him was that he was a man who used to laugh a lot and wore a bright red kerchief round his neck.

John Hatton had made several cages out of bamboo, and intended to place them at different places around the perimeter of the camp. They were open only at the front. Inside each was lodged a musket, its stock firmly fixed into the ground, the muzzle elevated at an angle, double charged with powder and ball.

A piece of bloody meat had been salted below the raised muzzle. A cord had been attached to the bait, which in turn passed round the butt of the musket, then secured to the trigger.

Bending over his devilish contraptions, the first officer said softly, 'It's my strong intention, lad, to blow the face clean off any beast that gets too close, on this, or any other night.'

Nightly, he got his wish. Gradually, there were fewer predators who dared show their face – at least within their circle of firelight. In the weeks that followed, each morning several hyenas were found with their jaws shattered. Hard experience proved that it needed three or four balls of lead either to kill or seriously injure one of them.

Occasionally, they followed tracks of blood to where the wounded beasts had crawled into thickets of thorn bush. Once or twice, they came upon some who were cornered and wounded, and to spare their suffering, they riddled them with shot. But nothing could bring Jack's dog, no matter how many marauders had their heads blown off.

He still dreamed of him. For a long time afterwards, he would wake in the dead of night, thinking he could feel the heat and weight of the Newfoundland lying across his feet. Then, with his heart pounding against his ribs in cold fear, he would hear over and again the terrifying snarling of both dog and leopard, and the long wailing cry as the great heart of his dog, Dileas the faithful, stopped beating.

Slowly, Jack began to learn the ways of Africa; frequently it was cruel beyond words, ruthless in its natural aggression. Even in the beautiful bay, life was hard and dangerous. All of them, including himself, would need as much skill and cunning as the wild beasts if they were to survive it.

Six

Dawn broke slowly, the tip of the hazy red sun inching above the horizon. As light began to spread across the lagoon, the mists shrouding the scattered islands began to lift.

Someone came running past the hut where Ned and Jack were sleeping. Bare feet drummed on the ground and a voice called out for James King. Beyond the gates, the amaTuli workers began to ululate, a high, shrilling sound, eerie in the early dawn.

Yawning, Jack stuck his head out of the blanket. 'What's all the commotion about?' Ned raised himself on an elbow, bleary eyed. Drawing aside the goatskin flap covering the doorway, he peered out. 'Who in the hell is *that?*'

A man in ragged black trousers and a faded shirt was strolling into the camp, a long hunting rifle slung casually over his shoulder. Peering over his shoulder, Jack had a quick impression of shoulders the width of a barn door and hands the size of hams. A bluff red face peered out from under the conical straw hat jammed down on his head.

'John Cane, has to be, by the size of him,' Ned replied, answering his own question. He shrewdly eyed up the newcomer. 'Carpenter by trade, came up from the Cape with Farewell. Now maybe we'll hear more about what's going on.'

Some time later, Farewell rode in through the gates of the compound. Mounted on a chestnut stallion, he was followed by a surge of whooping amaTuli tribesmen. James King scarcely recognised him.

The former elegant naval officer had disappeared, and in his place stood a tall, rangy man, his skin burned the colour of teak, his blond hair bleached almost white, his finely-trimmed beard and moustache streaked with silver.

The well-cut dark naval jackets, fine linen stock and slim-fitting breeches of old had been replaced by a faded shirt and a tattered waistcoat of what had once been silver brocade followed by a pair of baggy trousers and ancient, though well-polished boots. As far as King was concerned, only the gold-rimmed monocle was recognisable as belonging to Francis Farewell, the dashing naval lieutenant of old.

Slapping dust from his clothes, Farewell handed the reins of the stallion to one of the native trackers, rattling out instructions as to the care of the animal. Sweeping off his battered hat, he drew the sleeve of his shirt across his brow. Only then did he acknowledge King's presence.

'James, old chap!' he shouted, striding towards him. 'Glad to see you, old fellow.'

'What d'ye think?' Ned asked, as they stood watching the captain and his partner engage in a series of routine courtesies. 'Will this partner o' his take some o' the load off the capn's back – or maybe put more on it?'

Jack looked up, surprised by his tone of voice. 'Is it no' a good thing that the two have met up at last?'

Ned shrugged his shoulders and eyed the two men suspiciously. 'See all that palaver? You mark my words, things are no' what they seem. I smell a rat, Heelander. It'll no' work out – and the cap'n will likely come off worst.'

Later that day, at Farewell's insistence, the partners set out on horseback for his homestead on the other side of the lagoon. Being Sunday, a day of rest, some of the crew had set out earlier on foot, following the track that wound round the bay.

As the horses bearing Farewell and King cantered up the winding path leading to the homestead, women and children came running to greet them from the neat gardens surrounding the compound.

Beyond that lay a gently undulating valley rimmed by soft wooded hills, with peaceful land stretching into the hazy distance. It was dotted here and there by clumps of stately trees, as gentle and elegant as the parkland around a squire's country house.

Herds of roebuck and fallow deer were grazing, cropping the sweet grasses, tails twitching. One or two idly raised their heads to watch, mouths chewing placidly. Most of them cast little more than a cursory glance in their direction, before bending their heads to graze once more.

Fort Farewell turned out to be a ramshackle, mud-coloured sprawl of low-roofed buildings surrounded by a high fence topped with sharp-tipped bamboo poles. At each corner of the enclosure circular turrets had been erected; each of them graced by a platform with a waist-high barricade. Obviously they had been constructed to serve as lookout points.

The main house stood in the middle of the square. Built roughly in European style, it was constructed of traditional wattle and daub and topped by a neatly bound thatched roof. Four or five smaller buildings were clustered to the rear.

Apart from a pair of half-assembled ships' guns lying among the long grass, by far the most memorable thing about the Fort was its flagpole. Leaning drunkenly to one side in the middle of the overgrown square, a faded red, white and blue Union flag hung limply from it.

Once through the gates, Farewell dismounted then took down his rifle, pack and rolled-up blanket. Stiff-legged, King swung down from the saddle.

After the horses were led away, steam rising from their glossy coats, Farewell turned to King. With an exaggerated flourish, he announced,

'Here it is, then, James, Fort Farewell, home sweet home.' Taking him by the arm, he indicated that they should step inside the main house.

Coming up behind the two men with Ned and Aldred Williams in tow, it was impossible for Jack not to overhear what was being said.

King's voice was strained as he shook his arm free of Farewell's grip. Clearly, the trouble Ned had anticipated was already beginning to bubble to the surface.

'If what I've been hearing is true about you taking part in the Zulu king's wars, Farewell,' King snapped, 'you must have taken leave of your senses.'

With a sharp glance in their direction, Farewell pushed open the creaking door of the main house. 'I don't know yet what it is you've heard, old chap but do let's get inside before we begin chinwagging within earshot of the lower ranks.'

As King barged his way past him, Farewell pulled the door shut behind them with a creaking snap.

Ned cocked a knowing blue eye in Jack's direction. 'D'ye hear that, Heelander? Was Ned not right? All's not well between yon two.'

He hesitated for a moment, eyeing the closed door as if deciding whether or not to put his ear to it. Jack whipped in quickly and dragged him away.

'What if either of them sticks his head out, Ned?' he hissed, 'what excuse would ye give, then? "Oh, pardon me, Captain, I was only passing by – sorry if my lug was just a wee bit close to your door?"'

Ned sighed, and fixed him with a weary blue eye. 'You should have taken up the pulpit for a livin' instead o' the sea, Heelander.'

Behind the hastily closed door of Farewell's wattle and daub house, Ned's instincts were in danger of being proved right. A battle of wills was being played out between the two partners.

'Before we get involved in the intricacies of Zululand politics, James,' Farewell was insisting. 'There are a few things you should know –'

'You're damn right there, Farewell.' cut in King, glaring at him. Irritably, he ran his fingers through his shock of black hair. 'Not a dicky bird from you in over a year, in spite of the fact that I kept you abreast of what was happening in London. Dammit, man, I had to come all the way to the Cape to find out that you were already in Zululand – along with a brand new set of investors and partners.'

Farewell produced a dusty bottle and two glasses. Pouring a stiff tot of brandy into each, he held one out. King knocked it aside.

'You know damn well I rarely taste the stuff,' he snarled. Ignoring his outburst, Farewell neatly drained the contents of his own glass in one long, hard swallow.

King snapped, 'It was only when I called on your wife, Elizabeth, that I heard the full story. How you'd changed your backers to Thompson and

Company, and appointed your own bloody father-in-law, Johannes Petersen as chief partner. Obviously, you were planning to leave me out in the cold.'

The smell of spilled brandy was overpowering in the heat. Undaunted, Farewell poured himself another three fingers of the fiery liquor. King went on, 'I also learned how nearly all your investors had withdrawn their funds after Petersen came running home with tales of Zulu brutality spilling out of him.'

He was openly shouting now, not caring a whit who heard him.

'Then like a fool, I came up here looking for you to see if you were dead or alive. Damn nearly lost my men's lives as well as the ship. And what's the next thing I hear? Not only that you're alive and well, but off giving the Zulu king a hand in fighting his latest war!'

Farewell said nothing, his face a study of sheer indifference as he swirled the brandy around the balloon-shaped glass. King clenched his fists, struggling to keep control of his temper.

'I hardly thought a man of your experience would be stupid enough to get involved in native skirmishes,' he said, stiffly. 'Under no circumstances were we supposed to take up arms against anyone, other than in self-defence. For you to aid and abet any native group, Shaka's or otherwise, is plain stupidity.'

A flood of rage and bitterness rose in him. 'Dammit, man, what were you thinking? Did it never occur to you that you might be endangering other people's lives?'

In his agitation, he failed to notice the red flush rising in Farewell's face. The Lieutenant slammed the glass down hard, sending dust motes floating up into the ray of sunlight filtering through a window.

'Hold on, James,' he insisted, 'before you say any more, let me tell you some things you may find of interest.' King glared at him, refusing to be mollified.

'First of all,' said the former naval lieutenant, 'you have absolutely no idea of how *delicate* things are here, as regards what we will do, or won't do. We're not on the poop deck of one of King George's warships now, old boy. Secondly, we're standing in what's going to become His Britannic Majesty's latest acquisition – the colony of Natal.'

He gestured to the faded red, white and blue flag hanging limply from the lop-sided flagpole. The angry flush receded from King's face, leaving it pale and weary.

Farewell raised his hand in a dismissive gesture. 'Before you say anything else, there's something else you need to know.' His cold blue eyes raked his partner's face while he delivered the fatal blow.

'I have in my possession a copy of a land grant made by Shaka, signed, sealed and delivered. And you're looking at the sole beneficiary – me, Lieutenant Francis George Farewell.'

Screwing the gold-rimmed monocle into his eye, he surveyed his partner as he would an insect, his eyes shining in triumph.

'So you see, James old boy, it's a *fait accompli,* as they say. The day I arrived back here with the necessary parchment in my hand, I simply raised the jolly old flag. As the place is now mine, I can do what I like with it.'

King's heart sank like a stone. He listened in silence as Farewell laid out his bald statement of intent.

'*My* company, that is, F.G. Farewell and Co. has the *sole* right to trade here – and anywhere else in Zululand. I should tell you now that I fully intend it to stay that way.'

James King held himself stiffly erect, refusing to rise to the bait. Although he felt as if a ton of ballast was lodged in the pit of his stomach, his eyes were steady as he spoke, his voice measured and calm.

'Farewell, I'll want to read over the supposed "missive of purchase." Say, after supper tonight?'

The deep sarcasm in his voice caused a flood of colour to rise to Farewell's face. 'Naturally, old boy,' he said, smoothly. 'By now, a copy should be lodged with the Land Registry at Cape Town. I handed it to Garrett, along with my instructions, before he sailed south in the *Julia.*'

Farewell stared down his long finely chiselled nose at his one-time partner. King felt his knuckles crack with the strain of keeping his fists under control. All it needs now is for him to take that damn eyeglass and screw it back into his eye, he thought. If he does, I'll hit him such a smack in the mouth his teeth'll be halfway down his throat before he knows it…

Outwardly, his stare met Farewell's squarely. His deep blue eyes glittered with secret amusement, while behind them a towering anger stoked his resolve to beat his former partner at his own game, no matter the cost.

Later on that day, after skimming through the carefully worded legal document, bile rose into King's throat. Hands shaking, he contemplated ripping up the pages of vellum and scattering them to the four winds.

Instead, he tilted the document towards the candlelight to read it through carefully a second time. The formal words penned in Farewell's familiar, slanting hand swam into focus.

King wryly acknowledged Farewell's foresight and attention to detail. You cold-hearted son of a bitch, he thought. Who else but you would have made sure to have a supply of good quality vellum and sealing wax to hand just in case a few title deeds needed to be drafted?

Sweat beaded his forehead as he read on. Even though he held the proof in his hand, King still couldn't come to terms with Farewell's duplicity. Suppressing a groan, he began to scan the final part of the document.

Printed at the foot of the last page was Shaka's name and those of his witnesses. Looking closer, he saw that a wavering cross was scrawled below each of them. King peered at the names, curiosity overcoming his disgust. *Mbikwana... Msika... Mbopha.*

He stared at the large sprawling X below Shaka's name, noting the strong, clean lines of the strokes. Yes, strength and power, he thought, his senses reeling, the undeniable attributes of a warrior king.

James King drew in his breath sharply. *But did you really understand what exactly it was you were signing over to Farewell – and how he intends to use it? Somehow, I doubt it.*

Something else struck him forcibly. It appeared that the King's interpreter, someone called Hlambamanzi, had also witnessed the signing of the damning piece of parchment.

King frowned. Just who was this Hlambamanzi? If he was acting as interpreter between Shaka and Farewell as was stated, it followed that he must understand English. Indeed, to translate even the basics of Farewell's land treaty, the man's understanding of the language must have been more than just rudimentary. Bearing in mind that his translation would also have had to pass muster with the Zulu king, it was clear this man, Hlambamanzi, the interpreter, was someone to look out for.

When he looked at the date on the final page, and saw the actual date of signing, his heart sank. *In the year of Our Lord, August 7th 1824...*

Fynn had told him that the *Antelope* had brought him north in early July of last year. That meant it had taken Francis George Farewell just a little over a month to achieve an absolute miracle, namely, having persuaded the warrior king to willingly hand over such a prize.

The land grant had not only gave him the bay known as eThekwini, but also the land for a hundred miles around it, with twenty-five miles of sea coast to the north and south thrown in for good measure. It was almost unthinkable.

King began to pace to and fro. Now that he'd read the damn thing from end to end, he realised that the situation was far worse than he'd suspected.

Farewell, by both word and deed, had betrayed him – all the way down to the keel of the wrecked *Mary.* Sweat trickling down his back, waves of frustration and anger rolled over him in waves. Then he stopped dead in his tracks.

Hold on though, something didn't quite ring true... Impatiently, his eyes scanned the parchment again, searching for the actual date of signing.

August 7th 1824. His mind raced. Only four short weeks in between Fynn and his artisans landing on Zululand's shores to be followed some two or three weeks later by Farewell and his investors –

King lost the thread of his thoughts, but quickly regained it. What in the devil had happened in such a short time to prompt the Zulu monarch to hand over a sizeable piece of land to a white man he barely knew?

He snorted in disbelief. Nothing, but nothing of what they'd heard regarding the warrior King's reputation in any way suggested that he would be *that* welcoming to strangers, white strangers, at that – who had so recently breached the shores of his kingdom.

Yes, god dammit... Farewell did have a certain air about him, one of superiority and an unspoken assumption that he could get what he wanted just by demanding it- but, no way, no way, could he imagine a man like Shaka Zulu being unduly impressed by such an attitude – and especially not in the kingdom he ruled with such ferocity.

No, King swore, I'm not swallowing it, Farewell. And by God, I'm going to find out just how you did it! In his mind's eye, he could see the face of the man who would know the truth of how it had come about. Fynn, Henry Fynn, the first white man to clap eyes on the Zulu army. *Next time I see him...*

The brief moment of euphoria didn't last. All too soon, hard reality swept back over him. Not only were he and his crew marooned on the shores of Zululand, far beyond regular shipping lanes with no reasonable way of returning to the Cape, but they were also reduced to being unwelcome guests in the personal fiefdom of the man who had betrayed him.

However, a small nugget of comfort still remained. If what Farewell said was true, he had entrusted a duplicate of the original land grant to Garret, the captain of the *Julia* before he set off back to the Cape.

But what Farewell didn't yet know was that the vessel had been reported missing, suspected to have gone down with all hands somewhere along the notorious Wild Coast – *along with a copy of the Land Grant signed by Shaka himself!*

In spite of the gravity of the situation, King's spirits began to rise. As he resumed his slow pacing, he tried to clarify his thoughts. Zululand was not British territory. In fact, the country had nothing whatsoever to do with either the Cape Colony's Land Registry, the Governor himself, or even the authorities at the Cape.

So, on that premise, exactly what legality could such a land grant really have – even if the remaining copy were ever to find its way south?

James King smiled to himself and felt considerably better. It would give him more than a little pleasure to play that trump card when the time came.

After returning the document to Farewell the next morning, King paused at the doorway. 'Yesterday you said you had three things of interest to tell me. You've informed me of two of them,' he said, with heavy sarcasm, 'so what was the third?'

Farewell looked away before replying. 'Shaka is expecting you and your senior crew to proceed to kwaBulawayo forthwith.' King steeled himself to show no reaction to the news. He simply nodded.

'Very good, we'll set out for Shaka's place within the next day or so – I trust you'll supply the necessary native guides.' Below his calm exterior, his heart was racing as he went in search of his horse, keen to get way. A string of possibilities were already taking shape in his mind.

If Farewell had managed to manipulate Shaka into giving away a prime piece of coastline, a natural sheltered harbour and land for a hundred miles around it – if he played his cards right, what further concessions might he himself be able to wrest from the warrior King?

As he rode out of the derelict gates of Fort Farewell, James King's head was up and his shoulders were squared. The game was on.

Next morning, he assembled the crew at the area of cleared bush he'd ordered to be marked out by bamboo stakes.

He announced briskly, 'I hope you'll realise what I'm going to say next is for our own good. It's our only chance of survival, in fact. To turn bad luck into something better must be our sole priority. A fighting chance is what we need.'

His eyes travelled round the apprehensive faces of his crew. 'Gentle-men, the clearing you're standing in will become our boatyard. It'll be called Townsend Boatyard after Lord James Townsend, my patron at the Admiralty. In short, I intend to build a replacement for the *Mary* and sail back to the Cape.'

A moment's stunned silence was followed by a babble of voices. King ordered them to pipe down. Biddle, the bo'sun, spoke first. 'Beggin' your pardon, Cap'n, but a sea-goin' vessel needs a draughtsman and boat builder to do a proper job.'

King indicated his first officer. 'Mr Hatton here is just the man,' he said, 'and a fully qualified one, at that. He'll do the needful, lay down the plans, draw them to scale, supervise it every step of the way.'

The red-faced Thompson, ever the "sea lawyer" grunted, 'An' who's goin' to act as chippies, sawin', hammerin' an' suchlike? Don't recollect ever signing up as a chippie, me.'

'As to that,' King said, coolly, 'we'll all have to learn new trades – either that, or start walking. The Cape's a thousand miles, or more away, Algoa Bay several hundred. You might make it in a year or so, if you don't get picked off first by wild beasts or some of the tribesmen Fynn was telling us about the other night.'

The silence deepened. Every man Jack of them remembered the harrowing tales of shipwrecked survivors of vessels like the *Grosvenor* or the *Sao Jao* who had come to grief along the barbarous Wild Coast.

King cleared his throat. 'I'm not saying it'll be easy. We're mariners, we all know that. It's just that we'll have to learn new tricks for a spell.'

He gave Thompson a cold, hard look. 'I don't have to lay it out, do I? Our survival depends on it. Bar a ship putting in here in the near future, what else can we do? We can't just sit here and rot, gentlemen.'

As his eyes raked round the circle of faces, his voice had a steely edge to it. 'Those that don't agree, feel free to start making their own plans. I'll not have layabouts sitting around causing trouble and living off the fruits of other men's labours. Anyone wants to leave, go with my blessing – but it'll have to be by Shanks' pony, so think on before you come to any decision.'

As the men began to disperse, muttering, he interrupted them. 'One more thing, gentlemen – it appears some of us have been invited to attend a soiree, a very special one.'

'A soiree, is it?' said Thompson suspiciously, 'an' who's gonna hold such a thing around here, I'd like to know?'

'Aye, an' just who's been invited to this 'ere soiree, then?'

'That's easy,' answered King, straight-faced. 'His Majesty, King Shaka himself has done the bidding. Who's going? That'll be me, Hatton, and senior crew – and that includes you, Thompson.'

Pointing to the blanket of heat haze across the lagoon, he added, 'Day after tomorrow, boots on, ready for a hundred and fifty mile spot of walking – in that direction.' Turning on his heel, he walked away with Hatton, sand spurting beneath his boots.

After they'd gone, Ned wiped his brow with his shirt tail. 'Well now, Heelander,' he said, 'that would seem to be that. We're castaways, marooned, official like. So we'd best get on with it.'

A few days later, the camp had a hollow, empty ring to it. The remainder of the crew at the boat yard were busy with the tasks Hatton had assigned them to complete before his return.

Even though it was still early in the day, haze shimmered on the horizon, blurring the line where the sky met the land. Jack wondered how bo'sun Biddle's feet were holding up on the long walk to the Zulu King's lair.

He eyed the toes of his boots with a critical eye. They were beginning to fall apart, the seams splitting, curling in the heat. Taking them off, he knotted the frayed laces and hung them around his neck.

The man called Shaka seemed to be looming larger and larger in the scheme of things, Jack thought, gloomily. Ever since he'd overheard King telling Hatton about the terrible punishments Shaka handed out, he'd tried hard not to think about it.

In his heart, he knew it was only a matter of time until the King of the Zulus demanded to see the rest of them. Even as they'd stood watching the red dust settle along the empty track after King and the others had gone, Ned Cameron had summed up the situation pretty well.

'As sure as eggs is eggs, Heelander, it'll be our turn next. See if I'm no right.'

As usual, Ned was dead to rights. When the party returned a few weeks later, King told the remaining crew to prepare for the long trek to kwaBulawayo. The Zulu king had demanded to meet all those who had come to his shores – with no exceptions.

Seven

The Place of Dreaming

Langani's hands stilled among the young watermelon plants he was tending. Lifting his head, he sniffed the air cautiously. After a few moments, although his fingers continued with the delicate work of securing the first of the season's new green shoots, his mind was elsewhere.

There it is again, he thought, that unmistakable odour of dissent and betrayal, thin, dark and almost silent, uncoiling and spreading its tentacles.

For over a year now, he had known of Farewell's treachery and what his intentions were as regards his partner, the man known to the native people as Kingi. After he'd discovered that Shaka had made a gift of the bay of eThekwini to Farewell, a man with the instincts of a feral wolf, the diviner realised that the strife he had been dreading, even before the actual arrival of the first of the white men, had already begun.

The unfortunate destruction of King's ship meant that he and his men had no way of leaving the shores of Zululand under their own volition. The seeds of betrayal had been planted and there was no way of knowing what their eventual flowering would bring forth.

Langani sighed, and brushed soil from his hands. If only humans were as predictable as plants, he thought. Straightening his back, he cast a glance at the horizon.

From up in the high place where he had made his home, he could look out over miles of bush. Apart from a few twists of smoke rising up from small scattered villages in its depths, he could see nothing unusual, only the violet and blue haze of a day that was ending and the odd bird making its way home.

To a man like Langani, skilled in interpreting glimpses of the invisible, the unseeable and the mysterious, his instincts told him that the apparent tranquillity was deceptive, masking the hidden forces that were out there, waiting for the right time to wreak their havoc. The sound of tinkling water attracted his attention, and a smile lifted the corners of his mouth.

The small waterfall that provided his drinking water had its source high up among the rocky crags or even somewhere deep within the mountain itself. Over time it had carved out a deep hollow in the rock below, forming a pool that was rarely empty. Sheltered by a rocky overhang that protected it from the direct heat of the sun, the water gathered in it always remained cool.

Squatting down, Langani bent over and looked into the still waters. As he did so, a draft of cool air brushed against him. On the face of it, the pool looked unremarkable. He could see nothing more than still, translucent water with the odd fleck of grass or leaf floating on the surface.

Dipping his fingers into it, he stirred it gently, watching the ripples flow out towards the rocky edges. It was here he had received the first mysterious intimations concerning the men destined to find their way to Zululand in the fullness of time.

This time, there were no brilliant-winged dragonflies to mesmerise him and draw him in with their glowing colours; no fragments of floating leaf or twigs, no small pulsing lights representing the souls of those who would later be revealed to him.

As time went by, he had identified and accounted for each of the major players in what he foresaw coming to pass within the kingdom of the Zulus.

Farewell, King, Henry Fynn, and the Xhosa, Jakot – all of them drawn here through the sometimes tortuous pathways set in motion by various shifts of fate. Now, they were all in one place – here, in Zululand, and close to Shaka, the warrior King of the Zulus.

Langani's eyes flicked to the lichen-covered overhang jutting out above the water. Over the past months, he had watched, bemused, as a small, playful golden orb of light had danced and jinked its way across it, sometimes hovering over the surface of the water, as if admiring its reflection, before dodging up onto the roof again.

Although it, too, was another of the mysterious manifestations, his instincts had told him that it was very different from the others. There had been nothing dark or secretive about it, no taint of dissent or treachery, only the youthful energy of a child with innocence at its core – but no ordinary child, either.

He smiled. The presence was no longer there; no more need for it to be confined to the rock pool. The life force it had represented was now here in Zululand, in the flesh. And Langani had seen him with his own eyes.

On the day the boy had been swept ashore, after the destruction of the white men's vessel, he had stood within a few yards of him, so close he could see the marks of fatigue and stress written plain across the frailty of his child-like body.

Now the boy of the sea people, with the hair like fire and the eyes as blue as the sky, was about to embark on a journey that would shape him for the rest of his life.

There was nothing he, Langani, could do to change it, for the die had been cast a long time ago by other powers, far older and stronger than his own. What the end might be, he did not know, but he vowed that he would do his best for the boy and to see he came to no harm.

Eight

It had looked so easy when they'd first set out. 'Just a long walk up the beach,' John Hatton had said. So, for the first hour or two, Jack had managed fine. After that, it was a different story.

The sand, which was soft and deep as well as being devilish hot, sank over his ankles with every step. Spray off the surf compounded the effects of the blistering sun and every inch of his tender, exposed skin was suffering. Tiny particles of salt had found their way into the cracks in his lips, chafing his sunburned flesh.

Ahead, all he could see was another endless curve of blinding white sands, the high sand dunes and impenetrable thickets fringing the coast distorted by shimmering waves of heat.

Jack began to falter then fall behind. Even having Ned to jolly him along didn't help. The sounds of the sea and the screaming of the sea birds overhead faded, the world tilted, and he felt himself falling into a hot, sick place. His knees buckled and he collapsed face down on the sand, his hat rolling away in the wind.

When he next opened his eyes, his head was pounding and his tongue felt as if it were glued to the roof of his mouth. All he could see was a forest of strong black legs and wide, splayed feet. A language full of strange, click sounds rose and fell around him.

Painfully, he squinted upwards. A ring of faces looked down at him, the eyes fierce and direct, but with no threat in them. The hands that lifted him up were black and very strong. While one man propped him up, then wiped the sand from his mouth and face, another trickled some water between his bleeding, cracked lips.

Hatton's worried face wove into sight, his sandy hair whipping about his face, Ned close behind. From a long way off, Jack heard him say, 'This dratted heat and wind – it's too much for you, boy. Maybe best you return to camp. D'you reckon you could manage it back on your own, though?'

Jack threw a terrified glance back the way they'd come. The endless beach stretched for miles behind them, empty and desolate under the blistering sun. Tears pricked his eyes as the hard facts suddenly loomed stark before him.

Fear fluttered in his chest. If he had to travel alone back across the burning sands, what would happen if he fell down again? It might be dark by the time he reached the bay. How would he find his way to the camp? With a shiver, he remembered the savage darkness and the terrifying sounds that haunted it after nightfall.

The young Zulu who had given him water smiled, displaying a set of strong white teeth. Dropping down on one knee, he gestured for Jack to climb up on his back. Strong hands picked him up and settled him on his shoulders, so that his bloodied feet dangled down on to the fellow's broad chest.

And so they set off again, with Jack perched on the young warrior's shoulders, master of all he surveyed.

An hour or so later, he thought it very likely he was going to spew again. The feeling in his belly was the same as the time he'd eaten too many wee green apples.

A stiff breeze blew off the ocean, peppering his exposed flesh with stinging particles of sand. His face was peeling badly, his nose especially, and his feet, already scraped raw by the rough sand, were oozing blood.

But that wasn't really what was worrying him. The primary source of his concern were the floating black and white ostrich feathers in the headband of the young Zulu on whose shoulders he was being carried. His head throbbed. What if he accidentally dislodged them?

In his mind's eye he saw the headdress tumbling along the water's edge, its feathers broken and bedraggled. Taking liberties with King Shaka's warriors was a worry, and no mistake.

The dull throbbing behind his left eye grew worse. His belly rumbled and sourness rushed up into his throat. Leaning sideways, he retched into the sand, narrowly missing the young Zulu's broad feet.

Waves of dizziness swept over him, and he felt himself begin to fall, spinning and spiralling, back down into the dark place where he'd been before. For the second time that day, Jack found himself on his hands and knees in the sand, spewing up the last of his breakfast.

The same kindly fellows wiped his face and mouth and gave him some more water. One of them ran down the beach after his hat and put it back on his head, while his benefactor motioned for him to climb up again, smiling broadly.

This time, Jack found himself with his face pressed against the young Zulu's shoulder blades. Holding on to him like a limpet, he rode comfortably over the sands while somewhere above, the young warrior's ostrich feathers fluttered in the wind, safely out of harm's way.

Mile after mile, they stepped it out over the crucible of burning sands, lulled by the cries of sea birds and the ceaseless roar of the ocean. Soon, they came to the mouth of a broad river.

'The Umgheni,' said Hatton, eyeing the turgid flow of brown water, as it wound sluggishly round the bleached tree trunks, boulders and other debris littering the watercourse.

The Zulu clambered down the steep bank, with Jack clinging on to him. Picking his way over the slippery, weed-coated boulders, the water barely reached his waist. John Hatton waded alongside, his musket held above his head.

'Lucky the rains haven't started,' he said. 'Otherwise, we'd never get across this easily.' The water level had fallen since the last time he'd come this way a few weeks earlier. 'I hope to God the weather holds till we get back,' he said, 'otherwise we'll be in trouble.'

Fifty yards away, several scaly grey shapes detached themselves from the sand banks and slithered into the water. The surreptitious movements of the reptiles caught Jack's eye, and he eyed the V-shaped ripples heading their way. The sight of the blunt snouts, predatory eyes, and sinister ripples spreading across the sluggish waters put the wind up him. Silently, he willed the man carrying him to hurry. But mercifully, by the time they managed to clamber up the bank on the other side, the crocodiles were still yards away.

He slid off the Zulu's back, hobbled into a spot of shade beneath the trees and lowered himself down on to the ground. Beside him, the Zulu reached into a small bag round his neck, took out some dark strips of dried meat. Offering him a few pieces, he urged him to eat.

Jack edged a piece into his mouth. Ned leaned over and helped himself. 'Wild pig, probably, or deer meat,' he said, with a grin. 'Beef jerky, we call it back in Jamaica.'

After they'd drank some water, the young Zulu lay back and threw an arm across his face to keep the sun out of his eyes. Jack darted a surreptitious sideways glance at him. His skin was not black at all, as he'd expected, but more of a burnished bronze. Apart from a kind of amulet strung around his neck, his only item of clothing was a short breechcloth made from soft deerskin.

Above their heads, the leaves rustled gently, the pound of the surf against the shore muted to a distant roar. Only the trickling of the river, the lazy drone of a passing bee and crickets chirping in the long grass disturbed the silence.

Jack yawned and closed his eyes. His belly gave a loud rumble. Breakfast seemed a long time ago. Slowly, he began to drift away.

Later on in the afternoon, they left the sands behind and turned inland. Just as the sun was setting, a cluster of beehive huts came into sight. Several dogs rushed out, darting in to sniff at them, hair standing up on their backs.

'The chief will give us food and shelter for the night,' Hatton said, taking a swipe at the nose of an over-enthusiastic village dog. 'He knows we're coming.'

After a good night's sleep on full bellies, they set off again at sunrise. When the young Zulu offered to carry him on his back again, Jack shook his head, pride preventing him from giving in to his sore feet, but he stayed behind with his new friend whose name was Viyasi.

A little way from the village, they topped the rise of a hill. Ned whistled. 'My Lord, Heelander, now that's what I call a sight for sore eyes.'

Early morning light flooded the valley lying below. Meadows sprinkled with flowers stretched into the distance while groves of flat-topped trees promised shade in the heat of the day. Beyond that were miles of rolling grasslands that folded into the ridge of hazy, blue mountains on the horizon.

Every so often, they stopped to drink at one of the many streams winding their way over the plains. 'This is more like it, fresh runnin' water all the way,' said the ship's cook, mopping his face and neck.

Suddenly, Ned stood up and cocked his head to one side. 'Listen!' he said. 'What is it?' asked Hatton, reaching for his musket.

'Nix,' Ned replied with a grin, spreading his arms out wide. 'Have you ever felt a place so still, quiet like? Not a soul to be seen, not a dicky bird. Uncanny, I'd say.'

The first officer relaxed. 'Cameron, my lad,' he said, softly, 'Wait till we go on a bit further, then you'll see maybe see why.'

Jack pricked up his ears. What had Mr Hatton seen last time he'd passed this way? He'd need to keep his eyes open and be sure not to miss it, whatever it was.

Each day the pattern of their lives was dictated by the rising and setting of the sun. In the mornings, the sky was invariably clear and blue, but by noon, it grew hazy and stifling, the heat rising in waves off the hard-baked earth.

At dawn and sunset, the world was illuminated by fierce orange and reds filtering through layers of clouds, the wisped tails of cirrus indicating high winds far above the earth.

'Not that different from life aboard ship,' Hatton commented, gesturing around him. Instead of being surrounded by the green, endless swell of the ocean, they were adrift in a sea of tawny grasses that rippled in long, sweeping waves for as far as the eye could see, rustling and singing as it went.

A few miles further on, Ned stopped to rummage in his pack. Pulling out a long, thin flute, he said, 'Feel like a bit o' music, Heelander?'

Jack nodded. He'd watched Cane, the carpenter, carving the flute out of a length of bamboo. Sure enough, there was his signature, a deer's head, etched near the mouthpiece.

Ned warbled a scale or two to tune it in. After a few more runs, he struck up one of the old sea shanties the men used to sing during the long crossings to and from South America. The reedy notes of the flute floated out into the silent land, carrying the haunting melody to the men trudging over the plains.

> 'Oh, Shanandoah, I long to see you
> A —a-way, you rolling river…'

The Zulus in front of them stopped dead in their tracks. Captivated by the bitter sweet melody, they quickly located Ned and his flute as its source. Laughing and chattering, they then began to join in, their deep bass voices adding a flow of harmonies to the reedy notes of the flute.

> Oh, Shanandoah, I love your daughter
> A-away, you rolling river,
> 'Tis ten long years since last I saw her…
> But away I'm bound to go, 'cross the wide Missouri.

Ned was in his element as he and the Zulus created an impromptu symphony, a fusion of Africa and the far Americas. With his head cocked to the side and the shock of sun-bleached hair loose around his shoulders, his nimble fingers teased the poignant melody out of the flute's thin reed.

To Jack, at that moment, he was more than just Ned, his shipmate, his friend from Jamaica. He was the captain of the dance, a magical piper in ragged trousers and flapping shirt, leading Zulu and seafarer alike through the lush, rolling hills of Zululand, and ever closer to the stronghold of King Shaka.

Apart from the occasional shrill cry of birds and the rustling of the grass as it marked the passage of the wind, the silence was deep, profound.

Jack twisted round to see if anything was happening further down the line. To his disappointment, nothing had changed.

Hatton was out in front with his musket looped casually over his shoulder, water bottle around his neck and dark patches of sweat showing through his shirt. The Zulu *induna* walking beside him was tireless, oblivious to the heat, his muscular legs and dusty, wide-splayed feet easily keeping pace with the first officer. Ned's bent head showed he was lost in his own thoughts, the others strung out behind him.

The only thing of interest was some tall, lichen-studded rock formations about a hundred yards away. Jack decided to go and have a look. Maybe I'll climb up on top, see what I can see from there, he thought.

Wandering out from the main group, he made his way towards the rocks, the long grass swishing round his ankles. White lilies with long, trumpet-like waxen petals were scattered like stars among the long grass, their pouting stamens heavy with pollen.

Jack wound his way among the clumps of flowers, the exotic fragrance heady on the still, hot air. When something rolled away under his foot, he glanced down to see what it was.

The object he'd disturbed had come to rest against a low outcrop of brownish stone. As smooth as a sea pebble, the round shape gleamed dully up at him. Nestling against the rock, half-hidden in the grass, there was something curiously familiar about it.

Squatting down, he rolled it over. Jagged eyeholes, gaping jaws and a perfect set of teeth grinned up at him. With a yelp, he snatched his hand away as if he'd been stung by a nest of hornets. As the skull rolled sideways, a long-legged centipede inched its way out of one of the empty eye sockets and squirmed away into the grass.

Jack leapt to his feet and wiped his hand on the seat of his trews, his face screwed up in horror. Frantically, he searched for Ned and the others. The line of men was on the skyline, almost over the rise. In a moment or two, they'd be out of sight. He took to his heels and ran.

Swerving to avoid an outcrop of rock, his feet became tangled in the long grass. He tripped and began to fall. Instinctively, he put out a hand to steady himself. A pile of rocks clattered and rattled and fragments of grey shale tumbled loose. He let out a strangled yell. The broken shards he'd taken for weathered rocks were splintered human bones. Stained green with mould and bleached dry and brittle by the heat of many summers, they were still recognisable as human.

Everything stood out in gruesome detail. The long tapering fingers and toes still attached by remnants of hardened gristle; the long curve of shoulder and hip bones; spinal cords, rib cages, ghastly in their curved symmetry; skulls, large and small, grinning inanely up into the shining innocence of the oh-so-blue sky.

Over the years, the fragile white lilies had flourished amongst the remains of what had once been people, men, women and children. Tendrils of green leaves had sprung up to support the delicacy of the flowers, adding pathos to what remained of the human beings left where they'd fallen.

Jack's breath rattled in his throat.

The loose pile of bones gave another sigh, as if the thin ice of winter winds had just passed over them. Two small skulls rolled out. Nudging one another gently, they finally came to rest a few inches from his bare feet.

An agonised glance showed broken teeth and gaping holes in the smooth white bone. He stared at them, unable to tear his eyes away.

Then he turned and fled through the clumps of fragrant white lilies, trampling and crushing the delicate blooms. Sobs and gasps burst from him as he tried to flee from what lay behind. Running headlong through the grass with his hair flying around him, his blistered feet forgotten, he began to yell out, his voice shrill with panic.

'Ned! N-e-ed! Wait for me!'

Unseeing, he cannoned straight into Hatton and Fire, one of Fynn's Xhosa interpreters, who had turned back to look for him. Hardly able to speak, he could only point back in the direction he'd come and stutter out what he'd found.

Hatton grunted wearily and swept off his hat. Wiping his forehead with a handkerchief, he said, 'I'm surprised you hadn't noticed anything before now lad. This whole place is littered with bones.'

Jack stared up at him, still trying to catch his breath. So this was what he'd meant earlier. The officer pointed back the way they'd come. 'See there, Jack. It must have been one almighty battle. Look yonder…'

From the rise, he could make out the dull gleam of weathered bones strewn across the plains. Fire ran his finger across his throat. 'Shaka, peoples all gone now.'

Only silence, broken by the raucous crying of crows, the sighing of the wind and the shadows of the fish eagles moving like ghosts across the empty landscape.

Hatton put a hand on his shoulder. 'Don't take on, Jack. It could be there was nobody left to bury them. Maybe they don't bury their dead like we do– it's just their way. Dare say our country would look the same if we laid our dead out with only God's good sky above them.'

Jack had a sudden memory then, of the old cemetery at Fraserburgh, with the steely north winds raging round the braes and the gravestones standing in serried ranks under a rain-swept sky. their lettering cut into the red granite.

Remembering Sandy's stories, though, Jack knew that in his own native land there were also those who weren't neatly arranged in tidy cemeteries: drowned sailors, the abandoned and murdered and those killed in battle.

Scotland had plenty of its own dead, lying where they had fallen, in unhallowed ground – Highlanders and Lowlanders alike, dead from killing the English, or each other – unknown and forgotten, buried below the heather or in peat bogs. And the bodies wouldn't be all of men either…

In this foreign land, on whose shores they'd been cast, there was poor Higgins, and his grand dog, *Dileas*, the faithful – not under the soil or above it, but part of the living flesh of the savagely beautiful leopards that had killed them, now part of eternal Africa.

When they reached the top of the rise, he turned and looked back. The two small skulls of the children who had died out there were hidden by the waving grass, the waxen beauty of the lilies their only marker.

Jack was sad as he turned to face the mountains ahead. The valley of the Umhlatuze River lay on the other side. That was where they would find kwaBulawayo, the seat of Shaka's power.

As he fell into step with the others, the thought of actually have to enter the place where Shaka lived made the familiar knot of anxiety begin to worm away at him.

They struck camp in late afternoon. The mountains that had beckoned them like a talisman were no longer blue or distant. They were close now, very close, and all that stood between them and kwaBulawayo. The full moon was only two days away, the Zulu *induna* told them.

The plains were no longer deserted. Groups of tribesmen headed for kwaBulawayo began to overtake them, slowing down to stare at them as they loped on past.

It was breathtakingly beautiful that night, deceptively so. Camp-fires twinkled like fireflies in the night. Snatches of song, men's laughter, and the throb of drums drifted across to where Hatton's party were camped.

Wrapped in his blanket, Jack lay with his hands behind his head staring up at the dark bulk of the mountains, rendered even more mysterious by the silvery moonlight. 'I hope there's no leopards up there,' he said to the blanket-shrouded hump beside him. Getting no answer, he saw that Ned was already asleep, his mouth open, snoring gently.

Leopards weren't Jack's main worry, though. On the other side of the mountain lived a man more dangerous than any leopard. A lump rose in his throat as his mother's face drifted into his mind. How far away home was, how far away his family. A wild dog howled at the moon, a sound of such loneliness it made his scalp prickle. Others responded, bound by a common need to reach out to others of their kind.

The sight of the Zulu sentries was re-assuring. Hatton, Nicols and Isaacs would also take turns in keeping the fires alight, their muskets loaded and primed, ready for anything. Around them the African night hummed and vibrated with insect life. Beyond the circle of firelight, the eternal cycle of life and death was being played out on the plains of Africa, just as it had since the dawn of time.

Jack yawned, and wrapped the blanket closer about him. He kept his eyes on a winking, bright star hanging low in the sky until his lids drooped and sleep claimed him.

Next morning, hundreds of men overtook them as they headed for the trails that led up and over the mountain. Calling ahead to each other, they slowed down to get a better look at the straggling group of white men and Zulus, their faces registering incredulity as they passed by.

When they finally reached the forested slopes of the Nkwalini hills, a cool green silence reached out to wrap them in a peaceful embrace. A timeless quality seemed to pervade the forest.

Although Jack had never been in a cathedral, he thought it might be pretty much the same as this, another world, one of shade and stillness.

The higher they climbed, the cooler the air became. Now and again, the forest cleared to reward them with stunning views of the plains below. Once over the summit, a feeling of euphoria began to sweep through them, Zulu and sailors alike.

Picking their way between the twisted roots and stones the descent into the valley quickly turned into a race. The air vibrated with voices, hoots of laughter and catcalls ringing out as someone lost their footing and went slithering and bumping on their backsides down the needle-strewn slopes.

The lower down the hillsides they came, the more they were caught up in the mood of the moment. Sailors and Zulus alike came whirling down through the trees in a shower of twigs, pine needles and dust, yelling and whooping until they were finally decanted into the broad valley through which the Umhlatuze River flowed.

Blinking in the glow of the setting sun, all Jack could do was stand and stare at what lay before them.

For as far as the eye could see, campfires were strewn over the valley, their tiny flames winking like stars in the fading light. A babble of voices rose like the prayers of holy men from the crowds of people camping there. The throb of drums added their rhythmic beat to the sense of anticipation running like wildfire through the valley.

Lines of women wound in and out of the crowds, bearing gourds and covered platters of food on their heads, while scores of children jinked about, laughing and chattering. Herds of cattle added their strident bellowing to the general hubbub, while herd boys caked with dust ran on ahead, small black figures in a sea of heaving flanks and tossing horns.

Very quickly, the group of white men and their guides became a small island in the vast stream of humanity flowing round them. Open-mouthed, Jack stared around him. After endless days of walking beneath vast, empty skies with only herds of animals for company, to be suddenly surrounded by so many people was overwhelming.

Hatton broke the silence. 'Was it you, Ned, who asked me what kwaBulawayo was like?' He gestured upwards. 'Well, lad, there it is. See for yourself.'

The massive, oval-shaped settlement was sprawled on the hillside like a great tawny beast. At its widest point it must have been well over a mile in diameter and more than a mile and a half in length. Intricately woven stout fences ran round its entire perimeter. At the lower end, a pair of huge gates lay open to admit clusters of people both entering and leaving.

A host of campfires studded the hillsides on either side. Wraiths of smoke hung veil-like above the scene, tiny flames flickering and shifting within it. To Jack, it seemed like a living, breathing entity, dominating everyone within range.

The sun sank slowly behind the hill, leaving only the afterglow behind. The valley was transformed into a vast bowl of winking lights. The citadel crouched above them, its brooding darkness intensified by the hubbub of voices rising out of the gathering dusk.

Their Zulu escorts stirred restlessly, impatient to move on.

'Nothing for it, then, lads,' Hatton said quietly, hitching up his rifle. 'At least we got here in time for the full moon.'

A tingle of excitement ran down Jack's back. Ahead of them loomed the massive gates of kwaBulawayo. At least thirty feet high, sets of huge elephant tusks had been embedded into the ground on either side of the carved hardwood posts.

An arch made from intricately woven thatch spanned the space be-tween the massive gateposts. On it were arrayed the curled horns of water buffalo; elephant skulls with the tusks still joined to the jawbones, also those of lion and leopard, with their fangs bared in a final snarl.

Jack's flare of excitement waned. As he cast an anxious glance back down the hill, panic began to lick at him. Behind them, the blue evening shadows whispered in from the darkening land, barring any chance of escape.

With his heart thudding against his ribs, he stepped over the threshold, the macabre arch poised like the sword of Damocles above his head.

Ahead of them lay the huge oval-shaped concourse that formed the heart of kwaBulawayo. Beyond the fences to their left lay a huge sprawl of huts. Clustered together like beehives in a giant hive, they formed one of the main residential areas, while a mile or so away on the other side of the settlement, the distant twinkling of cooking fires served to remind them of the vastness of the place.

When the Zulu *induna* rattled off a string of click sounds, Fire, the interpreter, gestured for them to stay where they were. 'Here we wait,' he said. 'Someone will come.'

Hatton let his pack slide to the ground with a groan of relief, while Jack scuffed his feet in the dust, and had a look around.

Beyond the fences, the lazy flickering of cooking fires threw long shadows against the outlines of the beehive huts. The comforting sounds of women's laughter, the sleepy cry of a child and the clatter of pots could be heard, creating a sense of normality.

Jack sniffed the night air. Over and above the wood smoke and dust, there was something else, a familiar aroma, and one that made his mouth water.

Beef! he thought, *roasting beef!* Last time he'd eaten had been at sunrise, a long time ago now. 'I'm starving, Ned,' he said, 'd'you think they might give us some?'

He would never know what Ned's answer might have been, because a hiss from Fire alerted them to a couple of men heading their way. As the interpreter went forward to greet them, his smile of welcome was reassuring.

Exceptionally tall, the elder of the two men stood head and shoulders above everyone else. A man of authority, Jack thought, eyeing the leopardskin cape and elaborate feathered head-dress.

The other man was much younger and dressed in a tailed kilt with strands of brightly coloured beads wound around his neck and wrists, a cloud of red and black feathers on his brow. He exchanged greetings with Fire in a language Jack could only suppose was Xhosa. The he came forward to meet them, smiling as he did so.

'Welcome to kwaBulawayo,' the man responded in passable English. Intrigued, Jack stared at him, amused at hearing his own language coming from the lips of this exotic stranger. Bowing courteously, the fellow indicated the tall, dignified Zulu at his side then introduced him. 'Please. This is Chief Sotobe of the Sibiya.'

The chief was distinguished by the peppering of silver in his hair and neatly trimmed beard, his eyes alert, missing nothing. They swept over the group of sailors, a look of astonishment in them as they rested on Jack.

Hatton stepped forward and held out his hand in greeting. Sotobe glanced at him with a small smile of recognition and then looked down at the first officer's outstretched hand. Shifting the long carved staff he was carrying into his left hand, he placed his right into that of Hatton and clasped it.

The first officer spoke softly to the interpreter. 'Tell the chief that this is one of our oldest customs. We hold out the right hand to show it holds no weapon and that we come as friends, not enemies.'

The Xhosa's handsome face was still and watchful as he replied. 'But how is a man to know what the u*mlungu* might hold in the hand that is hidden? One could live to regret such trust.'

'Very true,' Hatton replied, his cool grey eyes studying the interpreter. In answer to the subtle jibe in the man's comment, he brought his left hand forward and laid it on top of the pair of clasped hands in a double grip. 'This is to show there is only friendship, nothing else in the hands.'

The interpreter translated for Chief Sotobe, his face expressionless. The chief smiled and let his hand drop away from Hatton's.

'King Shaka bids you welcome. You have come a long way, so first you must eat and rest. The Nkosi will see you in the morning. I shall come for you when it is time.'

After exchanging a few words with Fire, the chief turned and left them, with a pleasant nod. The Xhosa interpreter's smile was wolfish in the firelight, as he introduced himself.

'My name Is Jakot – Jakot Msimbithi,' he said. 'Here I am known as *Hlambamanzi*, the swimmer.'

Hatton spoke quietly. 'Yes, I know who you are. This was the last place Lieutenant King expected to find you.'

The interpreter nodded. '*Yebo,* after the ship left without me, I was indeed lucky to find my way here.' He looked around. 'Kingi is not with you? Does he not wish to return with you this time?'

Jack looked quickly at Hatton and then at the man called Jakot.

'Oh-ho,' Ned muttered in his ear, 'now, which ship left him behind, and how does he know the captain?'

The Xhosa's smile was open and untroubled as he gestured up the slope. 'Now, if you are ready, I will take you to your place for sleeping.'

The moon was rising from behind the hills. It was almost full, the valleys and craters on its surface clearly visible. The world was drenched in its silver glow, the stars reduced to twinkling pinpoints of light in the cloudless skies.

'I don't think I've ever seen a moon as big as that,' Jack whispered as he gazed at it, mesmerised. 'What are ye whisperin' for, Heelander?' quipped Ned. 'There's only ourselves here – an' them, of course.'

He jerked a thumb towards the posts of *mopani* wood silhouetted against the sky. Hundreds of cattle stood motionless inside the enclosures, moonlight glinting off their horns. Poking their muzzles through the stakes, they snuffled curiously, showing the whites of their eyes.

Jakot pointed up the hill. 'Here is where King Shaka lives. You must never go there unless you are asked.' Jack stared at the high fences standing ghostlike in the moonlight. What might a man like him be doing on such a beautiful night? he wondered.

The Xhosa stopped outside a large beehive hut and gestured for them to go inside. Judging by the scuffle of reluctant feet, the original occupants had only recently been told to vacate it.

Cookie gave him a nudge. 'All aboard then, Jack,' he said, impatiently. 'Me feet are worn down to the uppers.'

Too tired to argue, Jack slipped off his pack and crawled inside the hut. It was warm and dark, still sweaty from the bodies of the previous occupants, and illuminated only by the embers of the dying fire outside.

He felt his way inside on his hands and knees. The floor was hard and smooth, made of a kind of packed clay smelling of grass, or hay. A central pole rose out of it, and disappeared up into the rafters. Jack chose a spot facing the door and got out his blanket.

Half an hour later, the interpreters Jakot and Fire returned. A delicious smell of food wafted after them. Jack's mouth started to water.

Three women followed, carrying baskets on their heads. Uncovered, they revealed a wooden platter of beef, bowls of steaming maize porridge, several loaves of flat bread, a gourd of beer and earthenware jugs of water.

'My stars,' said Cookie, eyeing the food. 'They've done us proud, an' no mistake.'

No one wasted further time on words. Sitting around the fire, they wolfed into the food, slaking their thirst with beer. Afterwards, John Hatton and the men sat talking and smoking, drinking the last of the sorghum beer.

Yawning, and with his belly pleasantly full, Jack crawled back into the hut, wrapped himself in his blanket and promptly fell asleep.

Some time later, he woke up. Sounds, much like the scratching of harvest mice on stubble, filtered through the doorway. Cautiously, he opened one eye. Several dark figures were bending down to peer inside. Someone, or something, bumped against the framework of the hut, accompanied by much giggling and laughing.

Pulling the blanket over his head, Jack turned over and went back to sleep.

Nine

J akot returned at sunrise, coughing discreetly at the doorway. Jack crawled
outside in his under drawers, blinking and yawning in the early sunlight.
After the sweaty warmth of the hut, the morning air was sharp and clean with
drifts of mist still wreathing around the tops of the surrounding bee-hive huts.

'*Sakubona*,' Jakot greeted him. 'Did you sleep well?'

Rubbing his eyes, Jack mumbled a reply. From inside the hut came the
sound of coughing and clearing of throats as the others stirred to life. Two
women appeared with several tall earthenware pots of water. Placing them
beside the doorway, they silently withdrew.

'Water for washing, or for drinking, whatever you like,' Jakot announced, with a broad smile. 'And these for cleaning the teeth,' he added,
pointing to several bunches of twigs with sharpened points.

As the morning sun lit up the Xhosa's face, Jack stared at him in fascination. A slice of roughly two-thirds of the deep brown iris of his left eye
was different from the other part. It seemed as if a tawny section, full of
swirling green and brown flecks had been spirited into it. It was a golden
eye, a feral eye, belonging more to a lion than a man.

If the interpreter noticed him staring, he said nothing, only withdrew
with a nod, as silently as he had come.

Jack let his breath out slowly. An eye like that only added to the air of mystery that seemed to surround Jakot, the Xhosa interpreter.

The group of sailors sat in the shade waiting for Shaka's summons. Ned was dressed in a red-and-black checked shirt and a pair of black trews, the frayed edges tucked into his boots, Jack in what he had manage to salvage of his formal naval dress uniform; a dark blue frock coat, swallow-tailed at the back, along with a pair of cream-coloured pantaloons, his long red hair neatly plaited behind in sailor fashion.

Jakot appeared. Clad in a kilt of grey fur tails, with a cape of soft deer-skin draped over his shoulders, on his head he wore a circlet of padded otter skin sporting bunches of curling white feathers.

The interpreter made an expansive gesture towards the groups of warriors who had turned out in full array, ready for the coming celebrations. 'This time is called *Umkhosi*, the time of first fruits. Nothing, no corn, fruits or vegetable can be picked before this time. It can be very *hard* on the people.'

He hesitated, as if undecided about what to say. 'Why so?' queried Hatton. Jakot chose his words carefully. 'People, especially children, are often hungry at this time. Sometimes they pick some food to eat – without waiting for the king to say it is time.'

'And then?'

The interpreter shrugged his shoulders. 'They not live long enough to join in any more eating.' His brief words spoke volumes about how life was arranged in the kingdom of the Zulus.

Suddenly, a drone of voices filtered down from the other side of the high fences. A ripple of excitement ran through the ranks of squatting warriors. The hair rose along Jack's arms. It was as if a surge of immense energy was gathering momentum, drawing everyone into its wake, like fiery particles in the tail of a shooting star. The court of King Shaka was in progress.

'*Yebo, Baba... yebo, Baba...*'

Jakot chanted the refrain mockingly below his breath. 'It is always what they say, these peoples. Whatever Shaka says or does, when he smiles or dances, when he roars like lion, even when he is killing them, it is what they always say. *Yebo, Baba...yes, father.*'

From beyond the divide, there was only silence. In the deep hush, the lazy shirring of crickets and the shuffling of bare feet seemed muted. Then out of the stillness came a voice, a deep male voice that carried out to the waiting crowds beyond the gates.

Jack's head jerked up. There was absolutely no doubt in his mind that it belonged to the King of the Zulus. He shot a glance sideways at the interpreter. Jakot's golden eye was alert and fierce, much like that of a hunting animal.

The royal guards stepped aside to let Chief Sothobe through. He came hurrying towards them, the profusion of feathers in his head dress making him look even taller than he had on the night before. His eyes were bright and courteous as he addressed them. Jakot translated the formal greetings. 'The chief hopes you slept well. Soon, the king will call for you to come.'

As Jakot turned to look after Chief Sotobe's departing figure, the cape draped over his shoulders parted to expose a section of his smooth, muscled back.

For the third time that day, Jack stared at the Xhosa, dumbfounded. From the man's shoulder blades down, long curved weals and raised lines of scar tissue criss-crossed the tender skin of his back.

A sharp hiss and a muffled curse told him he wasn't the only one who had noticed. 'By God, the poor bastard's been lashed!' The muttered exclamation was gruff, though not unfeeling.

When the interpreter turned round again, the cape slipped back into place, concealing what lay beneath it. Almost simultaneously, the droning responses stopped abruptly.

Warriors rose to their feet in a flurry of feathers and animal skins. Court messengers came hurrying through the gates, calling out impatiently.

'*Nango umlungu bo! Now the white men! This way, this way!*'

'Here we go then, boys,' Hatton said. 'All ship shape?' Fixing a stern grey eye on Ned, he remarked, 'Cameron, lad. A warning shot across the bows. Desist from any tomfoolery. This is the wrong place for it.'

As they followed Jakot in through the gates leading to Shaka's meeting place, Ned's eye caught Jack's and closed in an unrepentant wink.

The right-hand corner of the large square was dominated by a huge fig tree. In the dappled shade below its spreading branches, a half-naked man was reclining on a series of coiled straw mats. Prostrated on the ground before him were row upon row of bobbing heads, a virtual sea of colourful plumes and feathers trembling in the hot sunlight.

Leading the way, Jakot could be heard muttering, *'Head down! Not look, please, this way, this way!'*

Jack stared open-mouthed at the powerful body of the man dominating the proceedings. Transfixed by the gleaming black flesh, the absolute stillness of the massive body and the virtual army of warriors lying face down in the dust before him, he was unable to tear his eyes away.

Just then, the man on the dais looked up. The slight, red-haired boy and the Zulu king stared at one another for a long moment, their eyes locked across the distance. Nudged none too gently from behind, Jack was forced to look away. Knees trembling, hanging on to Ned's shirt-tails, he followed the others to where Jakot was urging them to sit down.

Without warning, the voice of the man on the dais boomed out in an explosion of anger and pent-up rage. Around them, men babbled and moaned in fear and pressed themselves into the ground, their proud feathers fluttering in the dust like wounded birds.

'Christ!' muttered Ned. Jack stumbled and barked his shins on something hard, the sharp pain going to his stomach like a knife. Hatton hissed a warning. 'Keep your lip buttoned, for God's sake.'

Jakot turned an anxious, sweating face in their direction. While the voice of the Zulu king continued to storm and roar, the group of sailors scrambled awkwardly into place. Shortly afterwards, the sound of a blow rang out, followed by a high-pitched scream of agony. A long, low moan tailed off abruptly into a rattling sigh.

Jack gripped his throbbing shin. At first, he thought he might be going to spew, but then realised it wasn't that kind of feeling at all.

It was much worse...

As young as he was, one thing he had never been able to swallow was the way that some folk tried to grind others down. To deprive someone of their worth and bring them low, either by using harsh words or a bigger fist, tended to bring out a hot rage in him.

So now, when he least expected it, that devilish awkward quirk in his nature rose up to confound him, like a cunning fox biding its time. His father had warned him, more than once, about the Maclean temper.

'For long ages past, we Highlanders have been famous for it,' he'd said, 'Even the Romans acknowledged the fact. "*Furor Celtica*" they called it – "*the rage of the Celts.*"'

Francis Maclean had chuckled at that, then added, 'You'll rarely get a chance to ignore it, Charlie, for it'll lie as thrawn and hard in the gullet as any bone, until you either hawk it up, or swallow it whole. Either way, it's aye a tricky business.'

Jack, who was still a Maclean, no matter what kind of sea name or any other he answered to, felt the familiar rush of blood to the head.

It must have been seeing grown men cowering like daisies in a field that had set it off. A glimpse of the proud, kilted warriors, their poor feathered heads humbled in the dust like slaughtered birds had forced his sense of injustice to the fore. He fidgeted uneasily, trying to keep it under control.

Hatton hissed in his ear. 'For Lord's sake, Jack, stop movin' about…ants got at you have they?'

He shook his head. Pressing his knees together, jiggling them in agitation, his thoughts ran wild. Ned glanced suspiciously at him, 'Ye don't want to piss, do ye, Heelander? For ye can't – and that's all there is about it!'

He squeezed his eyes shut, remembering the last time the red fox had flared up. Last year, it had been… Three lads, older and bigger than he was – Jeems Soutar, Willie Mackenzie and Dan Campbell – had spread out across the lane, barring his way, taunting him, thinking that maybe he'd turn and slink away. *I saw them, they saw me…*

There had been no time for niceties or diplomacy. In the end, the bloody nose, the torn shirt and the skelp from his mother had been well worth it. The red fox had served him well, and he'd had the satisfaction of knowing it would do his reputation among the other lads in the town no harm at all.

Sometimes, it wasn't about the actual *winning* of a fight – oh no, it wasn't about that at all. It was that you'd stood up to whatever it was that was aggravating or threatening you…

Jack took a quick look around. The interpreters, Fire and Jakot, were squatting with their heads bent, Jakot's fingers nervously toying with the beads around his wrists, while the sailors were withdrawn and grim, their eyes fixed on the ground.

Glancing at the warriors prostrated on the dusty ground, another unacceptable thought leapt into his mind. What if this king, this Shaka, also expected them to lie face down in the dirt before him – what then? The familiar prickling started up again on the back of his neck.

No! I'll not go on my knees for you, Zulu king…or any other kind of king!

So now, the Charlie Maclean of old was caught between two very powerful forces. On one hand, there was the king of the Zulus – and on the other, the God of the Old Testament.

Born and raised in that north east part of Scotland, the threat of retribution, just or otherwise, came at you from all sides – from the Kirk, from the schoolhouse – and from your elders and betters. The list of *'Thou shalt nots…'* was impressive and all encompassing, leaving little room for misinterpretation. And it was laid on folk from an early age.

On the one hand, there was the fear of retribution, while on the other, the promise of forgiveness – though the balance, it had to be said, usually weighed heavily on the side of the stern Old Testament God.

'His wrath is in the thunder and the lightning, the roaring of the seas and great winds. He sees all, hears all… nay, nothing can escape Him, not even the unspoken secrets of the heart.'

The God that the Reverend Cumming conjured up from the pulpit every Sabbath was a fearsome one, right enough, Jack thought, as tried to move his cramped legs. And, what was more, he greatly doubted that the same stern old God would allow himself to be mocked – not even by what the King of the Zulus might demand as his right.

'Thou shalt have no other God before me, for I am a jealous God. Thou shalt not bow down and worship graven idols or false images…'

There it was. The message was clear.

Jack wasn't quite sure whether the Zulu king could be classed as a "graven idol" or "false image." It didn't really matter, though. All he knew was that he wasn't going to fall on the ground before him…and that was all there was about it! But he had more than that to contend with. The Almighty was only part of the problem. *'Bow the knee to none but thy Maker…'*

This injunction was loosely connected to the Almighty, but also to the thrawn sense of self-worth passed down to every Highlander along with his mother's milk. Francis Maclean had reminded him of it more than once.

'Often, it was all our people had to arm themselves with against a cold and hostile world, Charlie,' he'd said, 'it was all that stood between them and defeat, starvation and despair. It was what drove them to pick up their courage, and hurl it back in the face of an enemy, temporal or spiritual – whether it was laird, clan chief or any other kind of ruler that demanded too high a price for their loyalty.'

So now, he hadn't just one problem but two – both of which involved the Zulu king and the One who was even higher than Shaka.

Jack, who was still Charles Maclean from Fraserburgh, no matter which name he was currently known by, mulled it over while the voice of the Zulu king continued to rage above his head.

How could he arrange things to give Shaka the respect that was his due, and not offend him, and yet allow his knee – and possibly his thrawn Maclean neck, as well – to remain unbowed?

He came then to another awkward thing. It concerned the nudity of His Majesty. From the swift glimpse he'd had of him earlier, Jack thought it likely that he was stark naked. Now, while he'd seen enough men's bare backsides and balls since taking up seafaring for any false modesty, it was quite another thing to view the private parts of a king, even by accident.

Sweat burst out on his forehead. *What'll happen if I'm no sufficiently in command of my eyes to stop them wandering where they shouldn't be?*

While Shaka continued to rage from the shade of the fig tree, he deliberated his options, his face turned as red as a turkey cock with effort.

'Ye're not going to spew are ye, Jack?" queried Ned, glancing sideways at him. He shook his head, and looked down at his knees, the ones that weren't, under any circumstances, going to bend for the Zulu king.

Suddenly, the ranting stopped. The warriors scrambled on to their feet. Bowing and shuffling, they backed out of Shaka's presence with a rustle of feathers and scuffling of bare feet.

Jakot hissed out an urgent plea for them to get ready. A sickening lurch in Jack's belly told him it was time. As the interpreters began to usher them forward, curious looks were cast in their direction. Paint-daubed faces peered at the group of white men, taking in their bearded faces, outlandish clothes and the oddity of their pale, sunburned skins.

By this time, his brain was a jumble of emotion; defiance mixed with terror. Below his fork-tailed dark blue jacket, trickles of sweat ran down his back, but he kept his head up, and his back straight, determined not to bend his knees an inch, no matter what.

Forward they moved, ever nearer to the looming presence of the Zulu king. In that moment, the waves of heat rising up from the sun-baked earth before the dais seemed overpowering, suffocating, a fact which, rather than weakening his resolve, only added to the fluttering knot of defiance that was his rapidly-beating heart. Any minute now…

To his immense relief, however, just as he thought the moment of truth had arrived, everyone followed Hatton's example and quickly sat down cross-legged on the ground, with himself at the front. A period of shuffling and re-arranging themselves followed, while Jakot hovered, watching them anxiously.

They were no sooner settled, than a sudden vile stench made Jack look up. Inches away, two black eyes with large, dilated pupils stared into his. The face was neither young nor old, for its skin was as smooth and unlined as an egg and as grey as the underside of a toadstool. Pulled over the creature's head was the death mask of a leopard.

Jack stared in horror at the dried blood congealed around the snarling incisors, the long dried up, opaque eyes and the stunted whiskers curling back on either side of the gaping mouth. In an incongruous attempt at gaiety, tufts of brightly coloured feathers adorned the dead animal's head.

It shuffled closer. The dead beast's mask swung from side to side, the whiff of putrid flesh nauseating as the engorged black eyes continued to stare into his. When a blood-red tongue flickered out of the mouth, a strangled yell burst out of the ten-year-old. It turned into a loud retch, rapidly followed by another.

Saliva dribbling from his mouth, Jack leaned forward and spewed on to the ground. Mortified, he clapped his hand over his mouth. Next to him, he felt Ned's body shaking with laughter.

No one moved. No one spoke. Scarlet faced, he squeezed his eyes tight shut and waited for the sky to fall in on him.

A swift movement somewhere above his head was followed by a loud thump; a thin whining; and the sound of something heavy being dragged away. By the time he dared to open his eyes, he saw that the creature had disappeared, leaving only the whiff of corruption behind.

'Jesus!' swore Cookie below his breath, fanning the space in front of his nose. 'Worse than old sea boots, that!'

The voice somewhere above him boomed out a command. Jakot inched forward on his knees, his head bent respectfully. Fire stayed behind, squatting on his heels, in charge of the boxes of gifts for the King.

Minutes dragged by, with only the lazy drone of insects and the rustle of the leaves on the fig tree. Then the voice spoke again. Jakot began to translate, while Hatton answered.

'You are the *umlungu* who came in the vessel, the *umkumbe*? You are King George's people?'

'Yes, we are the people of King George.'

'King-i promised to send me some medicines. Do you have them with you?'

'We do.' John Hatton motioned to Fire who crawled forward to present the boxes. 'Lieutenant King sends you his best wishes.'

One of the royal servants opened a box or two under Shaka's impatient eye. Hatton was then beckoned forward to explain about the contents and what they could do. The medicines seemed to be of great interest to Shaka and Jack could tell by the purring in his voice that he was pleased with them.

After they were examined to his satisfaction, he waved both servants and boxes away. Jakot whispered, 'He likes very much the things of the white men, especially your medicines.'

As he leaned back to speak to him, the strands of scarlet beads coiled round his wrists slipped, and for the second time that day Jack caught sight of the deep scars gouged into the interpreter's flesh.

A moment later the deep voice boomed out again. After a few moments, Jack realised that the Zulu king was addressing him personally. A large forefinger waggled at him, demanding that he come closer.

Ignoring Jakot's urgent request to do so on his knees, it was with a sense of disbelief that Jack rose to his feet, carefully avoided the puddle of vomit and took a step forward. With more than a hint of impatience, Shaka crooked an inperious finger at him as he bade him come closer.

'*No eyes! No eyes! Look down!*' Jakot's agonised whispers passed clean over his head.

Trying to hold every thrawn nerve in his ten-year-old body in check, Jack took two or three more paces forward. Then he lifted his head and looked into the face of the most feared man in Africa. The ragged hiss of Jakot's indrawn breath told him he was on dangerous ground.

For the second time that day, the warrior King and the red-haired boy regarded each other in silence. The hair began to stir along Jack's arms.

In the bright sunlight, Shaka's eyes appeared black, a flickering intensity and intelligence in their depths. His face was very masculine with a flared nose and full lips, a lightly trimmed beard adding to the strong line of the jaw, a broad neck rising out of a pair of massive shoulders.

High on his cheekbone, below the left eye, was a crescent-shaped scar. As Jack's eyes lingered on it, he wondered briefly who had dared come close enough to such a man to be able to wound him. So this was the storm cloud, the man people feared and ran from in terror, the one who had small children killed and their bones left out on the plains among the lilies.

He hadn't expected the warrior king to be handsome, but as far as Jack could tell, he was. He hadn't expected him to be that young, either. The tight muscles in his arms and legs stood out like thick cords, evidence of his superb fitness, his belly flat and ridged. Catching a glimpse of a dark bush of pubic hair, he looked away hastily.

Shaka raised a hand to swipe away a fly then wagged a finger at Jakot to translate. All the time, his eyes lingered on the mane of russet hair tumbling around the boy's face.

As if in a dream, Jack carried out all he was asked to do. Turning round to let him see the pigtail hanging down his back, he loosened his hair as Shaka bid him, shook it out and spun round and round, making it fly around his shoulders. The squatting warriors laughed and clapped their hands in wonder.

After that he took off his jacket, folded it carefully and laid it on the ground. Then, for the next ten minutes or so, he jumped, leaped and ran, turned cartwheels and stood on his hands with his feet in the air.

When he could do no more, he threw caution to the wind and collapsed on to his back, his face red with effort. Above his head, the sky was very blue, only a thin drift of cloud passing over the sun. Around him, the rise and fall of voices sounded like water trickling over stones.

'*This little umlungu is a very clever fellow...*'

'*Yebo Baba...*'

'*He is very quick....*'

'He has hair like fire- such a wonder!'

'*Yebo, yebo. Baba!*'

A wave of murmured responses, an ebb tide of clicking sounds, as the chiefs and plumed warriors agreed with Shaka's compliments.

Jack sat up, the sweat dripping off the end of his nose.

Shaka leaned down, a smile lurking at the corners of his mouth. Jakot inched forward attentively.

'You are very brave for one so young,' the Zulu king said, addressing the boy directly. 'To have come so far across the waters shows you have a strong heart.'

Shaka and Jack looked at each other again. Around them lay a deep silence. In the fig tree, a pair of yellow finches hopped from branch to branch, singing their hearts out.

Then the king of the Zulus added thoughtfully, 'But I do not know what use you would be in a battle, or for building an *umkumbe*, either.'

Jack saw a flicker of humour in the black eyes, but was mollified to realise it wasn't of the unkind sort at all. Shaka switched his attention back to Hatton.

'Does umGeorge have as many warriors as the King of the Zulus?'

'Many times more,' answered Hatton, after Jakot translated.

'Then umGeorge will be the great king of the whites, and I shall rule the black people. It is good.'

The great head turned to look at Jakot, his voice stern again. 'Is it not so, Hlambamanzi? This would be a good thing, would it not?'

Jakot bobbed his head and muttered a suitable reply. Shaka looked down at Jack once more and smiled. Then, with a wave of the hand which encompassed them all, he announced. 'I give you into the care of Chief Sotobe. He will see to it that you have all you wish to eat and drink.'

Jakot inched his way over to where Jack was sitting, indicating that he should move back with the others. Their audience with Shaka was over.

A few hours later, it all began with no preamble, no fanfare. One moment the ceremonial area was empty, only the high buzz of the excited crowds dinning in their ears, the next, wave upon wave of warriors came pouring into the huge parade ground.

In the lead were the Royal bodyguards, the Fasimba, a massed phalanx of white shields rippling like the crests of billows on the ocean, their black head plumes and snowy white cow-tails at knee and elbow a symphony of contrasting colours.

On and on they came, unstoppable, invincible. *Zhee… zhee… zhee …*

The deep throaty sound of challenge, the pound and stamp of bare feet on the hard-packed earth and the beating of assegai handles on shields made the hairs stir on the nape of Jack's neck. His eyes swivelled to the tall man at their head. Dominating the massed elite of the Zulu military was Shaka, the warrior king.

'*Gawd!*' said a voice. The single word said it all.

He was taller than expected – but then, he had never seen him standing up before. During their visit, he had been very formal and had remained seated.

The single, blue crane feather in the circlet of leopard skin around his forehead added another foot or so to his already impressive height, the leopardskin cape around his shoulders denoting his royal status. A kilt of leopard tails hung almost to his knees. Fringes of carefully combed, creamy cow-tails cascaded from his upper arms to the wrists and from knee to ankle.

Shaka, the ruler of the People of the Heavens was, at one and the same time, human physical perfection fused into a terrifying image of violence and terror.

A trickle of sweat ran down Jack's forehead. No wonder James King was reluctant to bring what he'd heard of him out in the open, he thought. No bloody wonder he'd kept him a secret…

As a foil to the stark black and white of the Fasimba, the other massed ranks of the Zulu army poured into the arena, bringing bright splashes of colour with them.

Stepping out, high and proud, each line of men moved as one. With a flutter of bright, coloured feathers, tossing of horned heads and animals tails, they acted out the glory of their battle triumphs, each regiment distinguished by shields of different colours; pure black, black on white, tan on black, golden brown speckled with grey.

Here was Dingane, next in line to Shaka, with his half-brothers, Mhlangana, and the young boy, Mpande, followed by Shaka's senior commanders, Ngomane, Mgobozi and Mdlaka and the full range of tribal chiefs.

A high piercing ululating began to sweep like wildfire round the great oval, the shrilling voices of the Zulu women as savage and compelling as the masculine power on display.

Now the rhythm grew fast and wild. The warriors leaped high in the air, stabbing and thrusting at imaginary enemies, while behind it all was ordered sequence and iron discipline, advancing, retreating … but always winning, Shaka the dominant figure, lithe as a great cat, the flash of scarlet feathers brilliant and bloody at his temples.

The wild and terrifying spectacle was a celebration of armed might, militant warfare transferred into exultant dance. Back and fore it raged, ebbing and flowing while thousands of feet stamped and pounded in unison, the very air vibrating with their energy. When the dance came to its inevitable climax, the drumbeats slowed, and a sigh like a ripple of wind ran through the crowds.

Just then Ned got to his feet and whistled, loudly. 'My stars, will you just look at *that!* '

Hundreds of young women were pouring into the arena. Bare breasted and clad in short skirts, clouds of feathers waved around their heads, while brightly coloured fringes of beads fell to their waists and were coiled round their wrists and ankles.

Ned grinned down at Jack. 'You're a shade too young for this, Heelander, but I guess it's never too soon to learn. Get an eyeful of those little beauties!'

'Just watch it, Cameron!' Hatton warned, mindful of the effect so much female flesh was having on his crew, especially the volatile seventeen-year-old Ned Cameron. More girls, two perhaps three hundred came running in, their naked breasts bouncing as they came.

'*Umtwane Nkosi,* the king's women, his '*sisters*' – at least that's what he calls them!' hissed Jakot, his eyes full of mischief.

Their petticoats were decorated with tiny brass balls that glittered and sparkled in the sun, the black and red feathers on their heads fluttering with every movement. Loops of beads and strings of tiny brass balls circled their heads and dangled from their ears, wrists and ankles. Streaming down through the ranks of warriors, the women fanned out on either side of Shaka, to form the centrepiece of the display.

Dust hung above the dancers, peppery and red-gold in the bright sunlight, the rhythm of the pounding drums running like a fever through it, high and fast. A spiral of shrill ululating rose then broke off as suddenly as it had begun.

Jack leaned forward, wondering what was going to happen next.

While the men fanned out to enclose the king, the women of the *seraglio* encircled their *Nkosi* in a ring of soft flesh and exotic adornments.

Ned poked him in the ribs 'Quick! Shin up after me, Heelander,' he said, indicating the tree behind them. 'We'll get a rare view from up there.'

A moment or two later, they were perched in a fork of the tree, half-hidden by the foliage. From his position, Jack could see beyond the hills all the way to the far horizon. Shrouded by a band of blue haze, it lay shimmering in the heat, stretching into infinity. Ned tugged at his coat. 'Come on, Heelander. Ye're missing all the fun!'

This was a different dance altogether. Like the first, it was a celebration – but of something totally different. It was a thing of joy, a celebration of the rhythms of life, the warriors of Shaka's armies paying homage to the beautiful young women of their tribe. It was wild and grand, full of primitive splendour – and as old as the hills.

The silence, when it came, was abrupt. 'What's happening?' he whispered to Ned. 'Wheesht!' was Ned's response.

The ranks of warriors and comely girls folded gracefully into the dust. A light wind moved across the face of kwaBulawayo, ruffling the feathers and ox-hair fringes of the dancers strewn on the ground.

As if caught in the web of silence Shaka stood poised; a figure of great and terrifying beauty. The breeze stirred the fringes of cowtails on his outstretched arms, and ruffled the tip of the blue crane feather on his head dress.

Pivoting round, first he embraced the whole enclave in a gesture of defiance, then the fine warriors and maidens lying prone in the dust around him. Sweat coursing down his body, the warrior king ran forward for a few paces then, taking a gigantic leap, sprang high into the air, before landing lithe as a cat in a graceful crouch, the tips of his fingers touching the ground on either side of him.

A great sigh rippled through the crowds. Slowly, he straightened up. Then, the man who was their King, their Lord of the World, their Nkosi, began to dance.

This time it was no celebration of war or fertility, for it was different from all that had gone before. This time, Shaka was dancing for himself alone. Exultant and powerful, a prince at the peak of his powers; he was tender and passionate, fierce and cruel, gentle and moving, in turn.

Jack held his breath. Who else could have such a stage on which to perform? Who else could command such an audience?

The massive crowd watched with baited breath while a cast of thousands lay strewn in the dust around him, like so many discarded dolls.

If I live to be a hundred, Jack thought, I'll never forget today.

This was a day where he'd come face to face with the man who was not only the terror of southern Africa, but also a man who could laugh with the sheer joy of life as he danced for his people below the vast blue skies of his kingdom.

That night, the valley and hillsides were ablaze with fires. The vast oval settlement rang with laughter, singing, and the throbbing of drums.

Chief Sothobe had ordered fifty oxen to be slaughtered for the feast, and scores of cooks had been sweating all day over the roasting pits. The smell of the delicious juices made Jack realise how hungry he was.

Huge wooden platters of corn porridge and various relishes had been prepared to go with it, and the women brought pitchers of beer to swallow it down. Round the fires, there was lively talk and outbursts of song.

Jack fell asleep in the middle of it all, with a piece of beef halfway to his mouth. In the morning, he had no recollection of how he'd even got to bed.

'Just dropped off the perch you did,' Cookie said. 'Same as an old linnet my Ma once had. One minute, singin' its little heart out, next thing… gorn, feet turned up in the bottom o' the cage.'

Ten

Jack had never seen anyone die before, so he had no idea what to expect.

Up till then, the atmosphere had been light and festive with the sailors in fine fettle as they watched the king of the Zulus perform his morning ablutions while waiting for their second audience with him.

It didn't last long. One flick of Shaka's finger was all that it took, both to sign the death warrant of two of his people and to flood Jack's soul with the terror of him all over again.

As two burly men wielding heavy wooden clubs pushed their way forward, a moan of fear ran through the crowd. Jakot's face changed to a mask of grey and his voice stuck in his throat as he tried to say something.

Hatton made a grab at Jack, intending to shield him from witnessing what was about to happen. 'Don't look, lad!' he muttered. 'Keep your head down!'

Too late – the slayers' clubs connected with the victims' heads in a series of dull thuds and cracking of bones, blood spattering in a wide arc around them. As the bodies sagged to the ground, still twitching, muffled blasphemies issued from Hatton's mouth.

Afterwards, they had no choice but to sit and wait while Shaka finished preening himself, choosing each item of dress while the smell of blood hung thick and coppery in the air. The victims lay in crumpled heaps where they had fallen, mute testimony to the seriousness of defying tribal law – or Shaka's law – whichever applied at that moment.

Jack stared in horrid fascination at the pools of grey brain matter trickling from the dead men's skulls. Nervously, he shot a glance sideways at the others.

Ned's blue eyes were vacant, all emotion drained from them. Hatton was staring at the ground, a mask of stoic control, betrayed only by the tiny pulse hammering on his jawline. With shoulders slumped and heads bent, the others had their eyes fixed to a point somewhere around their feet. Jack closed his eyes and squeezed them tight in an effort to stop the tears.

While the sightless eyes of the dead stared up into the lustrous blue of the sky, bluebottles began to buzz and settle on the corpses. Shaka's brows drew together in a frown. A flick of his fingers brought the slayers back.

When Jack next opened his eyes, all that was left were long smears of red on the iron-hard ground. In no time at all, the sun had dried them to a dull brown.

For the next day or two, Shaka no longer played the ruthless judge and tyrant.

He gave out many indulgences, and could be seen joking and laughing with his chiefs and courtiers, beaming at the sailors, endlessly generous and concerned for their welfare.

The next few days were spent lazing in the shade and being entertained by dancers and shows of military prowess. Every night, they drank and feasted, while the People of the Heavens danced and sang far into the night.

KwaBulawayo, ablaze with hundreds of fires and torches, looked like a city under siege, with a vast army camped out below the stars for as far as the eye could see.

The time of the full moon passed. On the fifth night, it rose much later, and when it did, it was no longer perfectly round. From now on, its light and influence would be on the wane.

As Hatton surveyed it thoughtfully, his eyes followed the drift of thin clouds passing over its surface. 'It's almost time to go, boys,' he said. 'We've a ship to build, best we get back and settle down to it. Then, with any luck, some day there'll be a mornin' tide waiting to take us home.'

A rustle of agreement followed. 'Tomorrow,' he added, decisively,'we'll leave tomorrow. I'll tell Shaka we need to start back before the rains set in.'

Laughter and singing drifted up from the concourse. Jack looked down into the vast bowl full of twinkling fires and lingering woodsmoke. Their visit had been exciting, and terrifying, all at the same time.

Tomorrow, though, they would set out on the long journey back to the bay. In his mind's eye, he could see the vast plains, the herds of animals and the gleaming of the network of streams criss-crossing the land until they came down to the sea again.

After that, there would be the Umgheni River and soon after that they would see the misty lagoon of eThekwini where the hippos sported and the flamingoes and herons stood like soldiers on the rocky islands. Home – or the nearest to one he had at the moment.

'A bad omen, that,' McCoy said, gloomily, scanning the dawn sky. With the waning of the moon, a queer atmosphere seemed to hang over everything. The sun had sullenly refused to rise that morning, and when Jack crawled out of the hut, it was into a different world.

KwaBulawayo was like an island marooned in a sea of mist. The tops of the beehive huts were shrouded in drifts of grey that moved and shifted eerily. Gone were the colour and gaiety, the dancers, the pounding rhythms and the peppery smell of heat and dust. The great oval lay deserted, with only the faint cawing of crows to disturb the echoing stillness.

Jack shivered, and went back into the hut, still warm from the heat of their bodies. 'According to Jakot, the rains are late,' Hatton said, rubbing his hands together, 'one more reason to set off afore the rivers rise. I'll beard Shaka this very hour and tell him we'll be leaving tomorrow.'

As if on cue, a shaft of sunlight broke through the clouds and lit up the hillside across the river. 'Hey,' said Ned, ' that's a good omen.'

Jack popped his head out to look at the magnificent rainbow arched over the valley, brilliant against the dark green of the forested hills. It hung there shimmering, its beginning and its end lost in the shifting mists.

By late afternoon, when Hatton still hadn't returned, they knew something was wrong. The day hadn't improved with age; it was still cool, damp and grey.

'A dog's day,' Ned said, 'an' good riddance to it. Shove some more wood on the fire, somebody.' Nichols did the needful, and they huddled round the spluttering flames, glad of the warmth and light.

'Mebbe we should start to pack up?' McCoy posed the question to no one in particular. Thompson stared out beyond the firelight into the gathering murk, while Nat Isaacs went on writing in his journal, as he did every day.

Nobody spoke. It was as if they were trying not to think of what might be delaying Hatton. The silence lengthened. When at last the first officer appeared darkness had fallen, the flickering flames their only light.

Hatton looked utterly defeated. His face was drawn and pale, his eyes red-rimmed and sunk into his head with exhaustion.

He said nothing, just stared into the fire. At length, he cleared his throat, and ran his fingers distractedly through his sandy beard. His words, when they came, were flat and drained. He glanced over at Jack, anguish written stark across his face.

Something in the way he was looking at him made Jack's heart plummet to his boots. Hatton said softly, 'There's no easy way I can break this news, Jack, my boy.' His voice wavered. 'All God's good day I pleaded with him, over and over, but to no end. Jakot tried, too, but he refused to listen.'

Ned was on his feet, his eyes sparking fire. 'What's any of this got to do with Heelander?'

Hatton beckoned Jack over. Putting an arm around his shoulder, in a voice raw with emotion, he asked, 'Tell me, Jack...do you believe that John Hatton, first officer o' the *Mary*, has been a loyal and true friend to you since you've been with us?'

He nodded dumbly, wondering what was coming next.

'A man you could trust on a high rigging and an officer you could raise a salute in respect to?' Hatton's voice was reduced to a croak.

Jack's eyes clung to the man's ruddy face, one that was ridged with sorrow. He nodded again. Hatton's grip on his shoulder tightened. 'As God's my judge, I've done and said all I can, in this moment of crisis.'

Ned roared out. 'An' what bloody 'moment o' crisis' might that be, Mr. Hatton?'

Hatton kept his hold on Jack. 'It's just... Shaka won't take no for an answer, on this matter. On all else he was the voice of reason. We can go tomorrow, back to the bay...'

Ned butted in, his eyes like chips of ice. 'There ye are then, that's all right.'

'Ye don't understand, Cameron,' Hatton said, 'we'll be allowed to go, but Shaka's adamant the lad stays here – with him.'

He shook his head, his eyes full of anguish as he looked at Jack. 'I don't know how long he means to keep you, boy. And that's the honest truth. He wouldn't be drawn on it, no matter what I said.'

Jack, frozen to the heart, stood on the edge of an abyss. '*No! No... no... no... o!!*'

He backed away into the shadows, the long wailing cry of anguish torn out of him. For a moment, he stood exposed on the edge of the firelight like a small trapped animal, his face pale and childlike.

A circle of shocked, bearded faces turned in his direction. All he heard, as he turned and ran, were the blasphemies and shouts of protest issuing from the sailors' mouths.

Although he knew they were vented on his behalf, that's all they were...just sounds, empty, powerless noises. In his heart he knew that none of them, not even Hatton, had the power to change anything. Not here in the stronghold of kwaBulawayo, Shaka's domain.

Sobs and great trembling shivers of fear tore at him as he ran mindlessly into the darkness, his only thought to escape what lay both behind and in front of him. In truth they were one and the same thing, the demon-like presence of the man known as Shaka.

Feet came thudding up behind him, voices shouting his name, but he was small and quick and easily dodged away, his thoughts chaotic, desperate as he fled. *What does he want with me? I'll be his prisoner... how will I live, how will I pass my days?*

Stumbling through the dark maze of huts, he called out for his father, his mother, and for Sandy, to come and take him home.

Tall shadows loomed up, barring his path. Eyes gleamed in the darkness and the smell of musky bodies was close. Panicking at the touch of the hands reaching out for him, he slapped them away, swerving out of reach. A hiss of spilled water and a clatter as pots were overturned; yells of alarm, searing heat as fire scorched his legs, making him cry out.

Recklessly, he dodged and weaved in and out of the firelight, knowing that even if he managed to reach the heavy gates and pull them open, all he would find would be pitch-black darkness and the savage African night.

When Jack cannoned head on into someone, he was no figment of imagination, created out of smoke and darkness. The body he came up against was all too solid; its fierce grip on him uncompromising.

Wildly, he lashed out, pitting his boy's strength against it. It was only when he heard his name being called that he stopped struggling.

The golden segment in the man's eye immediately identified him as the interpreter, Jakot, also known as Hlambamanzi, the swimmer. People jostled around them, hemming them in. Jakot put a finger to his lips. 'Best walk slowly in this pit of snakes, little friend,' he said, softly.

Keeping a hand on his shoulder, he propelled him forward, shielding him from the crowd as they went. Thoroughly dejected, and knowing he had little choice, Jack allowed himself to be guided through a twisting maze of passageways. Finally, the interpreter stopped outside a large hut and indicated that he should enter. Reluctantly, Jack bent down and crawled inside.

Two women were sitting on rush mats by the small fire burning in the centre, the smoke curling upwards towards a gap in the thatch. Between them lay the sleeping body of a child, curled on its side, a small thumb tucked into its mouth. The women looked up, shock registering on their faces at the sight of his pale face, unruly mass of red hair and the terror in his blue eyes.

'My wife, Nontonella and her sister,' said Jakot, softly. The woman called Nontonella got up and moved towards him, making clucking noises of sympathy. At her shy touch, a wave of mixed relief and tiredness passed through him.

After Jack managed to eat some of the food she gave him, he went to sit outside by the fire with Shaka's interpreter to listen carefully to what Jakot had to tell him about life in kwaBulawayo.

The first thing he learned was that name kwaBulawayo meant '*the place of killing*' which didn't surprise him at all, considering that he'd witnessed some of Shaka's deadly justice only yesterday. After they had finished their *indaba*, Jack went inside and lay down on the sleeping mat Jakot's wife had laid out for him.

Comforted by their closeness, the smoky warmth of their bodies and the peaceful breathing of the baby, he fell into a deep and dreamless sleep.

In the ragged light of dawn, Jack stood with a heart like lead, his fists clenched in the pockets of his trews so that nobody would see the trembling in them. To watch his shipmates preparing to go away without him was pain enough. He prayed they would go quickly. Jakot stood a few feet away from him with his arms folded across his chest, his face inscrutable in the morning light.

One of the sailors had just lashed out at Jakot in frustration, calling Shaka and all black men savage niggers and *kaffirs* until Hatton threatened to give him a thrashing. The first officer stood by, red-eyed with fatigue, Ned with a face like a poker, while the others were silent and withdrawn, saying nothing.

'Jack, my boy,' the first officer said, as he tried to put as good a face on it as he could. 'If I had the power –'

'Mister Hatton, sir, I know very well that you do not. It's just...' The words stuck in his throat. 'It's a terrible long road back to the bay... but I'll find my way, you see if I don't.'

'That's the spirit, lad,' the first officer said. Drawing a battered, leather-bound Bible from the inside pocket of his jacket, he pressed it into the boy's hand. 'I've had this a long time, Jack. My parents gave it to me when I was about your age. Keep it by you, boy.'

With Hatton's Bible clutched in his hand, Jack stood and watched the first officer and the remaining crew pass down through the huge arena and then below the high, arched gates leading down into the valley.

At the last moment, his friend, Ned Cameron, turned and touched his fingers to his forehead in salute, as did others in the crew. A final wave of the hand and then he was gone, along with the others.

Eleven

J ack stood in the middle of the empty hut and regarded his worldly possessions. Two blankets, neatly folded, one grey striped with blue, the other green-checked. The only clothes he owned formed another pile; a jacket, three pairs of trews, four shirts, three pairs of under-drawers and one of Betsy's hand-knitted Guernseys.

His best shirt, pantaloons and dark blue jacket were laid out separately. When Jakot came to deliver him up to Shaka, he would dress as befitted a sea-going Maclean.

Only two things remained. The first was an ivory comb given to him by Fynn. Jack ran his fingers over the smooth surface, tracing the design seared into the beautifully carved object.

The second was the King James Bible Hatton had pressed into his hand as he was making his farewell. Jack picked it up and looked at it. The leather cover was faded by years of sun and spotted with damp.

Opening it, he peered at the faded writing on the fly leaf, and saw that it had been given to John Hatton by his parents when he'd left home to join the Royal Navy. He looked at the date. *1810*.

Five years before he'd even been born. Napoleon's war had been raging then and would continue for another five years. The first officer had been ten years old, the same age as he was now, when he'd joined the Navy and gone off to war.

The sudden rush of tears to his eyes unnerved him. Closing the Bible, he stowed it away with his other things, then lay down on the sleeping mat to wait for Jakot.

The man called Hlambamanzi sat smoking in the shade of a nearby hut. The boy would need to be alone for a while. Perhaps he would even cry.

Jakot had never seen a white person weep, and had no way of knowing whether they ever did. He shook his head in disbelief. This unexpected twist of events was disturbing. What did Shaka want with the boy? And what was it about white men that he could never be free of them?

It wasn't the first time time he'd asked himself the same question and he suspected it wouldn't be the last. Squatting in the shade, he pondered on the strange ebb and flow of his own fortunes.

Here, once again, was this seemingly unbreakable link between himself and the *umlungu*. He clicked his tongue in a flash of impatience. No matter how hard he tried, he could never quite escape them. Not even the stronghold of Shaka of the Zulus was safe from their influence, it seemed.

Picking up a stick, he began to draw in the dust. The strands of red and green beads on his wrist slipped, revealing the ridges of scar tissue, a constant reminder of Rademeyer, the Boer farmer who had put them there.

Idly, he allowed his thoughts to wander. On one hand, if he'd had no tales to tell of the white men, he would have had nothing to bargain with after finding his way into Shaka's kingdom. But then again, if it wasn't for the cursed Boers, the whole cycle of events which had conspired to lead him here would never have happened.

Since arriving in kwaBulawayo, he'd put all his energies into making a good life for himself with the Zulus, but the moment he'd heard that a white man and two yellow-skinned natives had been spotted near the Umgheni River, Jakot had steeled himself against the knowledge that, sooner or later, it was inevitable they would find their way to Shaka's court.

Consequently, he'd almost laughed out loud at the look of astonishment on Farewell's face when he'd stepped forward, dressed in his tribal finery, to greet them in his new, important role as Shaka's interpreter.

Jakot shrugged his shoulders. He bore them no grudge…with the exception of the dog, Thompson, who'd threatened to have him sent back to Robben Island, even after he had saved him from drowning in the waters off the sands of St. Lucia.

Not wishing to stir up any further memories of the St Lucia incident, he got up and padded over to the doorway of the hut to see how the boy was faring.

He was asleep, his face turned away from the light, his red hair gleaming in the sunshine streaming in through the doorway. Jakot sighed in resignation. Another *umlungu* who would have to be catered for –

The boy stirred and burrowed under the blanket like a small animal. Jakot glanced at the frailty of the pale foot sticking out from below the coarse grey blanket.

It reminded him of Majoze, the young Xhosa boy from his village who had d been captured by the Boers at the same time as himself. A surge of pity stirred in him. The boy would be about the same age as Majoze was when he died, or rather, when the Boers had roped him to the saddle of a horse then run him to death.

Jakot thrust the ugly images away. This white child has the same fragile look about him, he thought. Not for the first time, Jakot felt a strong surge of dislike for the ways of the white man.

Truly, what kind of people were they? To send a child like this far from home was cruel enough, but to abandon him to the whims of the dark gods and spirits of the waters that howled and wailed in the darkness of a strange land was beyond human understanding.

The boy had shown great courage last night, and again this morning, when he'd shown his mettle and stood firm, not shedding a tear or making it difficult for the men to leave.

Jakot began to argue with his inner self. Even so, he is not my concern. I already do much for the white men, seeing to their needs, talking with them for Shaka…

Out of the past, Majoze's face swam into view. Twisted and fearful in death, with the tears still wet on his cheeks, his young eyes stared fixedly up into the endless blue skies above him.

Jakot Msimbithi closed his eyes in resignation. *All right, all right, Majoze my friend…I will do my best for him.*

Watching the sleeping boy, he thought how delicate the paths were that each of them would have to tread in the future. There were those in high places, close to the heart of the Zulu court, who nursed deep and bitter hatred for the mighty Shaka. Rumour had it that he had given the white men land – a great deal of land. Not to mention cattle and oxen, as well as corn and tusks of ivory.

The threat would also be levied on those perceived to be favoured by the King – for example, a man like himself, a Xhosa, who now had a kraal of his own, with fat cattle, a wife and a fine son.

The boy tossed in his sleep, his eyelids flickering rapidly. 'Best to walk slowly, carefully, my friend – just like Hlambamanzi,' Jakot whispered below his breath.

Jack woke feverish and confused, unsure of where he was. The sunlight had gone and the inside of the hut was shrouded in shadow.

'It is time,' Jakot said from the doorway. As if in a dream, Jack rose from the sleeping mat. His fingers shook as he dressed himself in his trews and blue jacket. As he got ready, he could hear his father's voice say, 'Ship-shape and best foot forward, Charlie, there's a lad.'

Placing the ivory comb and Hatton's Bible in the top of his pack, he moved to the doorway and stepped outside.

The sky was overcast; grey and sultry with heat, drained of colour. Even the birds seemed to have stopped singing. Abject loneliness struck the boy like a knife, and he shivered in spite of the heat.

Jakot stared at him anxiously as they walked towards the high gates separating the general concourse from the royal residences.

'All will be well,' he said, by way of reassurance. ' You will not be alone, Shaka will allow me to stay with you.'

Jack blinked rapidly to stop the tears welling up. This man was the only person he could talk to now, the only one who spoke his language. Without him, how would he understand what was going on? How would he know what to do and what Shaka's intentions were?

The gates leading to the royal residences loomed ahead. The young soldiers stood aside to let them pass through, their curious eyes flicking over him, lingering on his hair.

Small things began to stand out in sharp detail. The pierced earlobe of one of the guards, an intricate little horn cleverly arranged as a snuff-holder; a lizard that turned blue as it scuttled up into a tree; a small, brown spider hiding in the folds of the woven fence.

The ground shifted below his feet. Sickness rose in his throat. A queer shaking began to run through his body, something beyond his control.

The wide square is empty. No dais under the spreading fig tree in the corner, no buzz of voices rising and falling in patient rhythm, no waiting audience.

A bead of sweat runs down the side of his face. He stumbles, although there is nothing on the ground to trip over. He and Jakot come at last to a group of imposing huts. Weathered by sun and wind into a smooth silvery grey, the thatch is thick and falls neatly over the high-dome. The arched doorway is high enough to allow even the tallest man to pass through without bending his head. It is beautifully adorned with plaited bundles of reeds and the horns and skulls of animals.

He catches sight of a dark figure moving inside. His body seems to be floating, and he can hardly feel the ground beneath his feet. As he stumbles forward, words from his childhood float into his mind to keep him company and give him courage until it is time for him to be delivered up.

Our Father, Who art in heaven… Hallowed be Thy Name… Ar n-Athair a ta air neamh …

Jack is sitting with his brothers and sisters round the oval mahogany table in the parlour, dressed in his Sabbath best. No escape for him today. No matter how much he might long for the freedom of the braes and the beaches, he knows it is not to be.

It is Sunday, the Lord's Day. No harbour or boats, no running with his friends, no Bowser the terrier with his straight-up ear, cocking a bandy leg at every gatepost …only the stiffness of new clothes and best behaviour.

Thigeadh do rioghachd Deanar… Thy Kingdom come…
Thy Will be done on earth… do thoil air antalamh…. as it is in Heaven…

He and Jakot are only a few feet away from the great doorway. So close, he can see the massive middle posts that hold up the vaulted roof, the soft glow of light and the lurking shadows.

His hands tighten their grip on his pack. It carries all he has in the world. *It's not all I am in the world, though…my name is Charles Maclean, and that is who I am.*

From somewhere far away, a warning rumble of thunder rolls in above his head. Flashes of lightning illuminate the darkened interior. Inside, the man is waiting for him.

At the doorway, Jakot tries to pull him to his knees. He refuses, shakes his head. Words in a language Jakot does not know tumble from his lips.

Ach saor sinn o olc… Deliver us from evil. For Thine is the Kingdom, the Power and the Glory… An cumhachd a ghloir…

Jakot is afraid. Jack can feel his fear. His own fear is two-fold, for he has the terror of losing his immortal soul and also the retribution of the earthly King, so close now.

Swaying on his feet, he looks across at the man in the carved chair. He cannot see his face clearly or read what is in his eyes. He looks like God sitting on the throne of the world. Like all gods, he has the power to strike them down.

His lips move, the words pouring out of him, feverish, disjointed

Bow thy knee to none but thy Maker… Thou shall have no other gods before Me.

Jakot pulls frantically at his jacket to remind him he must get to his knees. Their fate hangs in the balance. He knows it, now.

But, wait! He hears another voice. It belongs to the minister, Reverend Cumming, and it is thundering out of the pulpit in the kirk as it does every Sabbath.

'Render unto Caesar the things which are Caesar's…and unto God that which are God's.'

A great swell of relief sweeps over him. So, it is the heart and soul and what's in them that matters; not what we sometimes have to do to survive, and for the sake of other folk…

His knees begin to buckle. *Gu siorruidh… Amen.*

Jakot's ragged breathing slows down. The floor of the chamber is dark and glossy. The soft lights reflected on it waver towards him.

The man in the chair rises out of the shadows and towers over him, a colossus of dark flesh. Through the roaring in his ears, and the burning chills running through his body, he hears him calling out a name.

'*Jackabo…*'

Time passes. Jack does not know what day it is or even where he is. The air is fresh and cool and he is glad to be outside. He hears a familiar sound, and cocks an ear to listen. His face lights up.

A flute! There is only one person who plays a flute like that!

His stomach lurches. Hope floods through him. *Ned, you've come back for me.* The thin warbling notes are coming from somewhere down in the body of the great kraal. His eyes search frantically for his friend, Ned, thinking he would catch sight of his mane of blond hair and the flash of gold in his ear.

He tries to ignore the ringing in his ears and the pounding in his head. It has been with him since yesterday…*or was it the day before, or the one before that?*

The earth is hot and dusty beneath his bare feet. He wants to lie down and sleep. *I can't…I have to watch out for Ned, or I'll miss him.*

The flute stops. In the silence, all he can hear is the twitter of the black and white birds on the *mopani* stakes of the cattle enclosure. A croak bursts from his dry throat. He turns round and round in useless circles, looking for the flute player.

There it is again.…

Jack runs on wobbling legs down through the empty arena. The massive gates lie open, beyond them, green hillsides, mimosa trees and the glint of water. Frantically, he follows the haunting melody, ignoring the stares of the black men going about their business.

'Ned!' he calls out. 'Wait for me, Ned! It's Jack…I'm coming.'

The reedy warbling is coming from just up ahead. Near one of the huts, two men are sitting with their backs to him. When they hear his voice they scramble to their feet in surprise. One of them has a bamboo flute in his hand.

No-o-o-o!

Jack's long cry of denial splits the air, stopping the smile of recognition on the Zulu's face and drowning out his words of greeting.

His heart dives in disappointment. Grabbing the flute out of the man's hand, he turns and runs back the way he has come. As he passes below the great arch, the wide horns and skulls gaze sightlessly down at him, the gaping eye sockets cold and remote.

At the foot of the hill, the glint of water beckons him on. His throat hurts, his head hurts, his bones ache, but he rushes on.

If I run fast enough, I can catch up with them. Up and over the mountain, down through the forest and out onto the plains… I know the way. The sun on my left in the morning and on my right at sunset. Wait for me, Ned!

Just ahead, Ned's flute is trilling merrily. *"Oh Shanandoah, I long to see you…"*

All he has to do is follow the music. Cracking and plaintive, his child's voice joins in the bittersweet melody of the old sailors' song.

"Far away I'm bound to go… across the wide Missouri."

Ahead, he sees a small valley, a hillside. And men, there are men, some standing, some lying down, white men by the looks of them.

'Wait for me!' He cries out of a throat like dust, and holds up the long thin flute to let them see it. *'It's me, it's Jack… it's Heelander.'*

He scrambles up the hill on his hands and knees. As he gets closer, he notices that the men are very thin, as if they've been hungry a long time. *Almost there now…*

The face that peers down at him is like no other he's ever seen…

No, he thinks. *I've met him before… down on the plains.* His eye and nose holes are black and gaping, his teeth bared in a hideous grin.

The thin man doesn't see him, though, just goes on grinning, his arms gently swinging in the breeze. Jack's shaking dislodges him from the stake.

The sharpened point of the stake that is holding him up is dark brown where it sticks out through the bones of the rib cage. The smell of trampled grass is sweet, but it fails to mask the smell of the man impaled on the bamboo stakes, or the rest of the ghastly regiment.

Jack cries out in terror. Not all are bone and dust, picked clean by the birds and jackals. Some have tatters and scraps of bloody flesh still holding them together while others have dark flaps of scalp and hair still clinging to the smooth white skulls.

The terrible hill of Golgotha, the place of the skull.

Jack hears the soft flap of wings. It comes closer. The red scrawny necks, the hooded eyes and the strong, curved beaks of the birds terrify him. They move towards him – a sideways shuffling and flapping, intent clear in their cruel eyes.

He rises, tries to run, but the fever has sapped his strength. The winged ones begin to fight over him, flapping and scrabbling. The world is suddenly red and full of pain. Jack hears screams, hoarse, guttering squawks, then the sound of men shouting.

Now other voices reach him, women's voices, soft and soothing. Cool water soothes him and gentle hands ease away the pain.

He struggles to rise. The terrible wings flutter closer. Jack is afraid, and he cries out for his mother. A man's voice comes now, patiently calling his name.

'*Jackabo…*'

Strong hands cradle his head and ease a sip of liquid between his lips. A face swims in and out of focus. The crescent-shaped scar on the man's cheekbone is familiar… but who he is, Jack ca not remember.

Then his name and identity slip away from him along with the last of the smoky light.

Part Two

Twelve

Jackabo, as he now seemed to be called, lay drifting in and out of sleep, not knowing whether it was night or day. The darkness was as black as the inside of a chimney and reeked with the smell of soot. Once or twice he thought that goblins were lurking in it, and he woke up screaming for his mother, his voice trailing away as his strength gave out.

Some time later, his eyelids flickered and he moved his head. Through half-open eyes, he saw two women close by. One was pouring water into an earthenware bowl, while the other fanned the air with a broad palm leaf. Beyond the doorway he could see nothing, only a dark arc of night sky.

Without warning, the women suddenly abandoned their tasks, sank to their knees and bowed their heads to the ground. A rush of alarm at this move sent waves of dizziness shafting through him.

A man moved into the half-circle of shaded light. Side-stepping the women, he moved towards him, coming closer with every step. Jackabo's breath was trapped in his throat. Panic rose in him. In the dusky light, the height and power of the man's muscled body was overwhelming. Vainly, he struggled to lift his head.

The touch of the man's hand was firm and warm: the strong fingers surprisingly gentle as they drew the hair back off his face and wiped away the beads of sweat. Petrified, he willed himself to stay still.

A soft yet sharp command, then a rustle as one of the women came forward bearing the bowl of water. The sprinkling of cool water on his brow forced his eyes to flicker open. To his horror, he found himself looking directly into the eyes of the man who was the king of the Zulus.

A flare of curiosity stirred in their depths. For some reason, the tiny gold flecks in the irises reminded Jackabo of the water marigolds eddying in the currents of peaty water flowing through the burns of his homeland.

He opened his mouth to relay this piece of information, but no sound came out, only a scraping whisper. His gaze slid to the crescent-shaped scar on the man's cheekbone and lingered on the ragged edges of the tear in the smooth, brown flesh. He became conscious of a hand on his arm. He turned his head to look at it. The hairs on the back of the wrist were fine and black against deeply bronzed skin, the nails broad, square and neatly trimmed, the palm almost as pale pink as his own.

In spite of himself, his eyes closed and he drifted away.

The next time he woke, he found himself flat on his back and clear-headed, only the creaking of the thatch and the crick-crick of grasshoppers to disturb the stillness.

Drawn by the chirping of small birds, he squinted over at the patch of sunlight by the doorway. All he could see was a pile of rolled-up sleeping mats and several earthenware pots. Trying to lift his head only made it ache. The world spun in dizzy circles around him, forcing him to lie still.

He stared up at the crossbeams above his head. The massive poles supporting them were covered in webs of coloured beads. Woven in intricate designs, they spoke of endless patience and nimble fingers. Even the inner walls were covered in finely executed, flat-plaited woven reeds.

A surge of fear made his head pound with anxiety. *Where am I?* A subdued hum of voices caught his attention, and his eyes swivelled back to the patch of sunlight. The sound of women's voices and a quick, throaty bubble of laughter showed him all was well in the mysterious world beyond the doorway.

The air smelled of woodsmoke mixed with an oddly familiar odour. Half-way through a painful yawn, he realised what it was. Beeswax! It was what his mother used at home to polish the furniture.

Is that no a strange thing... he thought drowsily, just as sleep claimed him again... that someone in Shaka's house polishes his furniture just like my mother does in hers?

The face of the woman looking down at him was dark and round. Through half-closed eyes, he noticed the faint lines etched round her eyes and mouth and the threads of silver sprinkled through her cap of woolly hair. Her ears were large and fleshy and the long lobes had holes pierced in them.

A movement by the door caught his eye and he stared over the woman's shoulder to see what it was. A man stood framed in the great archway. The light from the flickering, smoky lamps lit up one side of his face, leaving the other in shadow, enough for Jackabo to see the scar high on the cheekbone. Even in the dim light, the bulk of his shoulders was unmistakable.

Shaka. His heart sank.

The woman turned away to exchange a few words with him, then rose to her feet. The set of her back, so straight and proud, spoke volumes, as did the angle of her head. A toss here, a lift there...

To Jackabo, it indicated an unbending will and plenty of straight talking. It was only when he stole another look at her that he realised who she was.

Her strong, handsome face bore the same stamp as the king of the Zulus, her whole demeanour an echo of his. As he watched through half-closed eyes, he saw the Nkosikazi of Zululand raise a forefinger and wag it from side to side as she addressed her son ... *tick-tock, tick-tock.*

It was clear the all-powerful Shaka wasn't getting his own way. In this instance, he was no match for the woman he called Mame. Jackabo, being not unfamiliar with the ways of mothers, felt a sudden flash of sympathy for him. Even kings, it seemed, no matter how powerful, still had mothers to contend with...

When Shaka jabbed a finger in his direction, he realised that he had become the focus of their argument. Fear grabbed at him. *What were they saying? Why was he so angry?*

He screwed his eyes shut, hoping that neither of them saw that he was awake and watching them. After a few minutes, he dared a quick look in their direction, long enough to see Shaka's mother making a brief gesture in his direction followed by a wave of the hand, as if to indicate somewhere distant. A jolt of shock shot through him.

If she takes me away, how will Hatton and the captain know where to find me? Even if I escaped, he thought wildly, *how would I find my way back to the bay?*

A sudden movement swept such thoughts from his mind. Shaka was bearing down on him, his oiled skin gleaming in the glow of the tapers. Lithe as a cat, the Queen Mother stepped in front of him, barring his way, her hands thrust out to protect the boy behind her. The set of her head, with its silvery threads of hair knotted into neat plaited rows, was formidable.

Her son's face was hard, closed off and set into rigid lines of disapproval. The warrior King seized his mother by the wrists. For a moment, it looked as if he was about to thrust her out of the way, and none too gently at that.

No!

Jackabo disentangled himself from the covers and lurched upright. Waves of dizziness hit him. The ground heaved below his feet like the deck of a ship in a storm. Fever-stricken or not, he felt the red fox rise in him, untamed as ever. He cast wildly around for something to use as a weapon, but found nothing.

Blue eyes blazing out of a pinched, white face, he yelled, 'Get away! Get away from me, d'ye hear, the pair of ye!'

The sound of his voice came as a shock.. Shrill and high-pitched, it seemed to echo inside his head. 'I'm not going anywhere with ye, lady! You've no right to take me away!'

Astonished by the sight of the *umlungu* child rising out of his sickbed with his puny fists clenched, ready to fight, the king of the Zulus and his mother stood rooted to the spot, staring at him. Squaring up to the most feared man in Africa seemed to the boy, at that moment, to be the most natural thing in the world. His freedom was threatened, therefore he would fight like the cornered wee beastie he was.

A moment of truth had arrived for Charles Rawden Maclean. What rose to the surface in his ten-year-old heart was the same spirit that had infused the breast of every beleaguered Maclean down through the centuries when faced with danger or the curtailing of his liberty.

One more for Hector, and let the devil take the rest!

In spite of the lightness in his head and the heat rising up in waves from his body, the fists stayed up. Wavering, his knees were beginning to shake, threatening to give way beneath him. Worse than that, the hard, empty bubble of a hiccup was starting to gather in his gullet. It was only a matter of time before it came to the surface.

Desperately, Jackabo sucked in a deep breath, hoping to drive the bloody thing back down. He had made a stand, and there was no going back. A trickle of sweat dripped off the end of his nose.

Shaka pushed past his mother and came towards him, his hands held out reassuringly, his voice low and soothing. But the red fox was rampant now, beyond warning, beyond caution. He glared defiantly at the warrior king and forced down another painful gulp of air.

'I'm no' going anywhere, dammit! You've no right to keep me here. Ye're naught but a... a...'

Words failed him. He thrashed around looking for a suitable epithet that would shock them. '*Ye're naught but a pair o'... dirty heathens!*'

There! He had said his piece. He teetered among his crumpled bedding, a bantam cockerel with ruffled red feathers, ready to take flight, or fight to the death.

His success was short-lived, however. He read the warning flash of anger in the man's eyes. As Shaka skewered him with his gaze, cold reality flooded through him. Eyes watering, Jackabo stared back at him, determined not to look away.

Then it happened. He had no way of stopping it. A bloody great hiccup exploded, knocking the breath from him. His sweating face turned scarlet, and water flooded his eyes. He tried to hold his defiant stance, but his fevered sense of invincibility was waning fast. Another hiccup tore out of him and then another. His knees wobbled. Staggering back, he sat down abruptly.

A grudging smile crept into the pair of black eyes watching him. The woman stepped forward, crooning, holding her hands out to him. Jack saw only kindness in her eyes and felt a flush of shame for calling her names.

It's no' their fault they're heathens, he thought. But still, they've no right to keep folk against their will, or take them away to places unknown.

Jackabo allowed Shaka's mother to press him back down on to the blankets. She folded them more comfortably under his head, and stroked the hair off his brow. 'Eh, Jackabo,' she said, patting him with a large hand. She shot a meaningful look at her son indicating that he should leave.

Shaka paused at the doorway. Looking back through the smoky half-light to where the boy was being comforted by his mother, Nandi, the man who was king of the Zulus mockingly laid his clenched fist over his heart in the universal warrior's gesture of salute and farewell.

A final glance of the dark, brooding eyes and then he was gone, the echo of his laughter floating back to them out of the darkness beyond the arched doorway.

The Great She-Elephant had advised Shaka that her homestead in emKindini was more suited to the small *umlungu's* health than his larger, more military centre of kwaBulawayo. At least, that was how Jakot told it.

Jackabo, knowing better, said nothing. On that score, the king of the Zulus had been well and truly trounced by his mother. When he asked Jakot if he would be coming with him, the golden segment in the interpreter's eye glowed irritably.

'*Cha!*' he said, fingering the beads around his wrists. 'I must remain here. My duties to the Nkosi, you understand.' He thought for a moment, then said, 'Eh, Jackabo, this woman is truly worthy of the name "*Ndlovukazi, the Great She-Elephant*"

The look in his eyes was one of pure mischief, as leaned forward and nudged Jackabo in the ribs. '*Yebo,* she has a big mouth… and an even bigger arse!'

A day or two later, the straggling retinue began to move down through the ceremonial ground of kwaBulawayo. Flanked by her bodyguards, the magnificent figure of Nandi, Nkosikazi of all Zululand strode imperiously at its head.

Below the cloak of fine deerskin, she wore a length of scarlet cotton draped around her ample shoulders and a skirt of otter tails falling to calf length. Following in her wake was a gaggle of swathed females, personal servants and assorted bearers with bundles on their heads.

At the tail end were small boys commandeered to tend the prize white cattle Shaka had chosen for her from the Royal herds. Somewhere in the middle of it all was Jackabo. Since Nandi had refused to allow him to walk all the way to emKindini, her personal fiefdom, he once again found himself being portered on the broad back of one of her personal guards.

Just as they were about to pass through the gates, he caught sight of a blur of black and white ostrich plumes sidling in his direction.

The Queen Mother frowned, an impatient 'Tch!' clicking out from between her white teeth. Jackabo shot her a pleading glance. A softening in her dark eyes and the twitch of a scarlet-clad shoulder gave Jakot permission to approach. Sliding down off the fellow's back, he went to meet the Xhosa.

'Eh, Jackabo,' the Xhosa said, softly, drawing him aside so no one could hear. 'I came to wish you a good journey. Also, I should tell you – that in spite of the size of her arse – this woman means you no harm.'

Jackabo's eyes met his in a silent exchange of laughter. Jakot leaned closer and whispered in his ear, 'Some call her Mother of the Nation, while others say she is a she-devil. I will pray that for you, she is the first – and not the second.'

Having delivered his message, he closed one eye in a wink. '*Sala kahle,* Jackabo. Stay well.'

As he touched Jackabo's shoulder lightly in farewell, the strands of plaited beads slipped, revealing the puckered scars on his wrist. Instinctively, Jackabo's's fingers tightened on Jakot's in clumsy sympathy.

'I see you, Jakot,' he said, tears stinging his eyes. '*Hamba gahle,* stay well.'

By the time they had completed their journey, the first pale stars were twinkling in the sky. Shortly afterwards, with dusk falling softly around them, Jackabo entered another centre of power, that of emKindini, the domain of Nandi, the mother of Shaka Zulu.

Once inside the gates, she dispatched her servants and bodyguards into the nether regions of the great kraal. They scurried away, pursued by a spate of instructions. Free at last after hours of clinging on to the back of the stalwart fellow who had transported him piggy-back during the long journey, Jackabo took a few tottering paces on his own, feeling lightheaded and dizzy.

Beaming, Nandi threw an arm round his shoulders, crushing his head against one of her voluptuous breasts. Like a newborn calf clinging to its dam, he was shepherded through the doorway of the huge ceremonial beehive hut rearing out of the dusky light. Inside, it seemed several shades darker. Blinking, Jackabo cast a bewildered glance around him, but could make out very little.

A sharp hiss of indrawn breath alerted him to the fact that they weren't alone. Rustling, whispering and the warm smell of musky sweat and excited breathing leaped out at him from the darkness.

He stared into the gloom, blinking like an owl. The soft glow of wax tapers threw flickering shadows on to the walls and the domed thatch above his head. Details began to swim out of the half-light. The opalescent gleam of teeth and eyes, the curve of bare shoulders and soft cheeks, full breasts with dark protruding nipples –

A giggle erupted out of the smoky darkness, quickly smothered by the Queen Mother's withering glare. Jackabo sagged against her, his head pounding, still dizzy and light-headed. *Girls! Oh, God – there must be hundreds of them!*

Then, out of the the gentle clicks of the Zulu tongue flowing over his head, he heard his name – once, then several times more.

'Jackabo… '

The warm, smoky night was suddenly full of the high, rushing chatter of voices. A press of women's bodies came forward and hemmed them in. Hands reached out to touch him, but were quickly snatched away after hissed warnings from the matriarch. The proximity of so much half-naked female flesh began to overpower him. For once, he was glad to be 'under the wing' of the mistress of the house.

His feelings of gratitude were to be short-lived, however. Her introduction at an end, Nandi released him from her protective grip. Wagging her finger, she let loose another round of instructions.

Beaming, she twirled a forefinger at him, indicating the doorway, letting him know she was leaving. Another twirl of the finger, Jackabo took to mean that she would return. When, it was hard to say…

Before he could protest, she had turned her scarlet-clad back on him and bustled towards the doorway, the mass of women's bodies obediently parting to let her through. A moment later, the humming night had swallowed her up.

A long silence followed. Ten-year old Jackabo and the women of Shaka's *seraglio* surveyed each other for a long moment. Frantically, his eyes darted around, looking for a way of escape. Too late, his path to the doorway was blocked. Daniel in his den of lions could not have felt more surrounded or outnumbered than he was at that moment.

It took Shaka's "sisters" a few more minutes to realise they now had him all to themselves. Like a small pale moth captured by a stronger and infinitely more exotic species, Jackabo was at their mercy. As they jostled, pushed and wrestled for the right to claim him, waves of tigerish energy flowed off them. Thinking they were about to do him a serious injury, he let out a skirl that echoed up into the rafters.

The girls fell back and looked fearfully at the doorway. Pressing fingers to their lips, giggling, shushing and swearing him to silence, they came to their senses. Then with only a little shoving and nipping for good measure, four clear winners were declared.

A path to the doorway cleared as if by magic. Jackabo's exultant captors bore him through it and off into the night. Above his head, the stars were a blaze of light, dazzling after the smoky shadows, the night air sharp and clean.

Wedged in between his captors, his pack gripped tightly against his chest, Jackabo's feet hardly touched the ground, as they raced this way and that through a maze of huts, hissing over their shoulders at the pack of giggling women trailing after them.

He was bundled inside a doorway, his head bumping against the framework. The four girls pushed in behind him and the goatskin flap covering the doorway was pulled down. Breathlessly, they waited until the pattering of bare feet had passed by.

A small fire was burning in the centre of the hut, its dull red embers still glowing among the ash. Woven sleeping mats stood rolled up by the far wall, along with some covered earthenware jars.

Once the fire had been stirred up and more wood added, the ring of four closed in around him, light glinting off their brass armlets, necklets and strings of beads. The youngest didn't seem much older than he was. Her face was soft and round, her hair plaited in intricate patterns, while strands of scarlet beads hung down between her budding breasts.

Her soft full-lipped mouth parted in a smile. Jack thought she had the longest eyelashes he'd ever seen in his whole life…and the whitest teeth.

'*Yack-a-bo.*' His name sounded strange on her lips. Catching his hand, she pressed it against her naked breast. Mortified, blushing to the roots of his hair, he tried to pull it away.

'Si-bon-gile,' she announced, emphasising each syllable with a flourish, as she pinioned his fingers in an unbreakable grip. 'Sibongile,' Jackabo repeated, sweating profusely. Not to be outdone, the other three flocked round, demanding attention.

The tallest girl had a gap between her front teeth. Loosening his hair from the pigtail, she began to tease at it. When she got too rough, he pushed her away. Fingers fumbled at the buttons of his shirt. As they wrestled each other to relieve him of it, the material stretched and threatened to tear.

The boldest, a plump girl with hair teased out in stiff spirals around her head, made a grab at the waistband of his trousers, trying to peer down the gap. Temper flaring, he shoved her away none too gently.

'Mind your own business, madam! And get your fingers off my trews!'

She pouted, then flounced. Far from being intimidated, the other three burst into shrieks of laughter and lay on their backs, kicking their legs in the air.

Two of them disappeared into the darkness while the remaining pair laid out some sleeping mats, poured water into a large earthenware bowl then placed a small dish of fatty unguent beside it. Maize porridge with meat and a tasty relish, followed by bread and curds appeared out of the darkness with surprising speed. He was fed to bursting point, his captors taking turns in placing carefully selected morsels of food into his mouth.

After they'd eaten, Jackabo had no choice but to face the inevitable. All he could do was screw his eyes shut and submit to the liberties they took with his person. With much giggling, they stripped him of every stitch of clothing. Then they proceeded to bathe him, pat him dry and comb out his hair with a wooden comb.

Sleep brought him no privacy, either. After he'd been nudged, poked into place and patted down to their satisfaction, all four of them fell asleep with a minimum of whispering and fidgeting.

Bedded down like the runt among a litter of puppies with two buxom girls on either side of him, Jackabo's stomach gurgled all night, full to overflowing with the bounty of emKindini.

He lay awake for a long time, afraid to move in case he woke them. Cautiously, he removed the arm of the spiky-haired one from around his neck.

What a day it had been! Already, kwaBulawayo seemed a long way away – another kingdom, in fact.

As time went by, Jack found a name for his mischievous minders. The Four Maries. He'd learned a song at school about Mary Stuart, Queen of Scots, who was beheaded by her cousin, Elizabeth Tudor of England.

> 'Yestere'en the Queen had four Maries,
> The nicht she'll hae but three.
> There was Marie Beaton, and Marie Seaton…
> And Marie Carmichael, and me…'

Sibongile was Marie One, and she was his favourite. Marie Two was Nokukhanya, *the bright one*; Bhekisisa, *the cautious*, was MarieThree and Nhlahla, *good luck*, the spiky-haired one became Marie Four.

Almost at once, Jackabo began to pick up some of the language, although his attempts to master the perverse click sounds had his teachers dissolving into giggles of laughter. Shaka's mother, however, had not had Jackabo taken to her private residence to abandon him to the young women of her son's *isigodlo*.

Oh, no. As he was to find out, Nandi was even more of a tiger than all the others put together. When she set her mind to something, there was no stopping her. So, in between feeding him honey cakes and fruits, and combing and plaiting his long red hair, she set about teaching him her language.

She had a very expressive face. Sometimes, when she was beating some unfortunate servant with the knobbed stick she kept at hand for the purpose, Jackabo found the likeness between mother and son almost frightening. But her rages never lasted. Moments later, her handsome face would be wreathed in smiles.

'Eh, they are a bad people, Jackabo,' she would say, with a '*tch*' and a shake of her head. 'If I didn't beat them from time to time, they would run over my head and then kill me.'

Late one afternoon, Jackabo stood watching the herd boys bring in the last of the cattle, a few scrawny dogs nipping at their heels. The sun was sinking and soon it would be getting dark.

Days tended to flow into one another in emKindini and soon the weeks began to follow the same pattern until he was no longer sure how long he had been there. Yet, all that day, he'd had a feeling that something special was in the air, a sense of excitement that he couldn't quite explain.

Whistling, he set off for his favourite place, the old fig tree growing hard up against the fence at the rear of the royal homestead. Once up there, perched with his back against the trunk, hidden among the glossy leaves, no one could see him. From his hiding place, he was able to look out over the valley and spy out anything interesting.

One day, he'd spotted smoke from a forest fire drifting on the wind in the shape of a huge question mark that hung in the air for a long time. Another time, he'd seen a pride of hunting lions stalking a herd of impala, and had nearly fallen out of the tree while yelling out to the deer to run for the hills.

Just then, an animal snarled, and a pair of eyes glowed green fire for an instant before blending back into the twilight. Minutes later, there was a blur of ghostly wings as a horned owl swooped silently down on an unsuspecting small creature somewhere in the long grass.

But today it was the luminous star hanging low in the sky that caught his attention. Jackabo's eyes scanned the darkening sky for Venus, the evening star. Sibongile had taught him the Zulu name for it, *Komotsho*.

But this wasn't *Komotsho*. This star's light was icy and brilliant with a blue spit of fire in its heart. Not a cold thing, though, only stronger and more powerful than the others.

Someone called his name once, then again. It would be one of the four Maries, calling him to supper. He ignored the call. The feeling of there being something special in the air returned, as if reminding him of something he'd mislaid, something he couldn't quite remember. Parting the leaves of the fig tree, he looked up at the star again. Was it his imagination or was it even brighter than before?

He stared at it for a long time, lost in thought. Now more than one voice was calling out for him, a hint of anxiety clear in the sounds. A twinge of guilt hit him. It would be the Maries, wondering where he was, worried for him.

As he started to shin down the tree, something startling sprang into his mind, a sudden realisation that made him lose concentration, forcing him to slither down the last few feet, skinning his knees in the process.

Christmas! It was Christmas! What else could the star mean?

The power of what it represented clutched at him, the thought of home like a knife in his heart. He could see his family in the lamplit room behind the shuttered windows, the town lying in the pitch-black of winter, the familiar streets frosted with snow –

Dashing tears away with the back of his hand, he began to run, suddenly anxious to be with those who were looking for him, calling out for him, here in this place, so far from home.

No, Mother... Dada, I'm not lost. It's Christmas... and I'm to dine with friends tonight.

While the star hung motionless in the African night, its brilliant light finding its way into every nook and cranny of emKindini, Charles Maclean –also known as Jackabo – sent his silent words out into the night, willing them to carry all the way home to Fraserburgh.

Thirteen

Ahundred and fifty miles away, the party of sailors led by first officer Hatton stepped wearily off the windswept sands and trudged into the comparative safety of the bay known as eThekwini.

It took them another hour or so to reach Townsend camp on the other side of the lagoon. James King was pacing up and down, waiting for them. His eyes raked over the sand blasted, weather-beaten remnants of his crew.

Hatton stepped forward and met his eyes squarely, neither apologetic nor fearful. King looked over the rank and file for the third time, searching for the small figure he expected to appear. 'Where is he – where's the boy?'

The first officer swung his pack wearily off his shoulders. 'As far as I know, Lieutenant, he's fit and well. He was all right the last time I saw him.'

He hesitated for a long moment then straightened his shoulders in an almost defiant gesture. 'The truth is, Shaka wouldn't allow him to come back with us.'

'Good God!' King exploded. Ned burst out, 'Wee Heelander was mighty upset, I can tell you – no' that he said anythin' for he's a tough little bugger below the skin, but I could tell he was feared to death.'

Hatton ran a hand through his sandy hair. 'I did my best to talk Shaka out of it, tried every way, every excuse. God help me, but I even threatened him with King George! But there was no budging him.'

King groaned, 'I'll have to go back myself then, and see if he'll listen to me. There's nothing else for it. I owe it to the boy's father.'

He rubbed a hand over his bearded face. 'My God, what if Shaka never lets him go? How in the hell will I explain that to Francis Maclean?'

Two days later, a group of amaTuli fishermen, while out with their nets at first light, looked up to see a vessel with tall masts looming out of the morning mists. With a rattle of chains, it lowered its anchors and rode the gentle swell, the rays of the sun gilding its masts and furled sails.

Although they had never seen a ship before, the simple fishermen had no difficulty in recognising the sleek lines and rows of gun-ports of the British man-o'-war as being something of great menace from a world they knew nothing about. Dropping everything, they rushed to Townsend camp to raise the alarm.

When he eventually heard the news of exactly why the vessel was moored outside the entrance to the bay, Fynn swore, 'By all that's holy! A Royal Navy gunship, no less, dispatched on the say-so of the Governor to transport our war hero back to Cape Town!'

'Aye, and anybody else that likes to go with him,' added Ogle, hitching up his tattered trousers. 'How about it, Fynn, fancy a stroll up Adderley Street?'

Henry Fynn grinned. 'Not bloody likely, Ogle me old mate, too much goin' on here.'

'Me neither,' Ogle said, reaching inside his shirt to scratch his chest. 'This is more my style o' livin', thanks all the same.'

'Be mighty interesting to find out just *who's* goin' to step aboard her, though,' Fynn added, thoughtfully. 'Wanna place a wager on which of these fuckers turns yellow, an' runs, Ohlo?'

Three days later

King's blue eyes glittered as he stood watching the forested headland slip away in the wake of the Royal Navy gunship, HMS *Standfast*.

Pacing aft, he lifted his face to the freshening breeze. By God, he thought, it's good to feel a deck beneath my feet again, especially one belonging to His Brittanic Majesty. How long has it been? With a shock, he realised it had been over ten years since he'd left active service shortly after Bonaparte's defeat at Trafalgar. When the long, agonising war had eventually ended, the Royal Navy had pensioned off most of its personnel on wartime service.

Catching a glimpse of an immaculately attired officer on the bridge, King glanced down at his own water marked naval jacket and cracked shoes, all he owned that had survived the wreck.

He straightened his shoulders and patted down his crumpled lapels. Not quite up to the standards expected from His Majesty's Royal Navy, eh?

Well, all that would soon change. Instinctively, he touched the leather pouch concealed below his shirt. Ten gold sovereigns, all he had left in the world. Closing his eyes, he deliberately focused on something different.

Cape Town. A vision of cobbled streets, elegant carriages, fragrant women in silk gowns and parasols and the starched collars and frock coats of prosperous businessmen flashed into his mind. Perhaps a few of them could be persuaded to help me out of my difficulties, he thought, with a touch of irony.

King looked away to the darkening horizon. No sign of the high wooded bluff now, only the bruised outline of the coastline slipping away on the starboard bow. He continued to stare sightlessly into the dusk.

A great deal had been left behind in Zululand, tangible and otherwise. The gaunt wreck of the *Mary*, for one; most of his trade goods either at the bottom of the ocean or watermarked and spoiled. Less visible was the bitter humiliation of Farewell's betrayal.

Apart from that there were the men he had made pledges to. Poor Higgins, mauled to death by a leopard on his first night ashore, the boy Charlie gone, vanished into the lair of the Zulu King –

A stab of remorse hit him below the breastbone. The decision to take this unexpected opportunity to get to the Cape hadn't been an easy one. On one hand, by taking up this totally unexpected opportunity of a passage south, there was a fair chance he'd be able to drum up some financial support for his lost ship and assist his crew to get out of Zululand – while on the other, his conscience dictated that his priority should have been in trying to free his young apprentice officer from the clutches of the Zulu warrior king.

A memory returned to haunt him then: that of a a snow-laden sky, a tossing deck and a boy's lively blue eyes watching a Newfoundland dog roll over on to its back to show him its webbed feet.

Jack. Only his real name wasn't Jack, it was Charles Maclean. And if that weren't enough, his father was an old friend, Captain Francis Maclean, also a veteran of Bonaparte's war, a man to whom he, James King, had made a solemn pledge. '*Look after my boy.*' They had been the last words Maclean had said to him at Southampton.

Riven by a double sense of failure, his head sank on to his chest. Dear God, he agonised, I wonder where the boy is tonight – and what his chances of survival are in that den of savages?

When King next raised his head, the sea birds had disappeared. All that remained was the dull red afterglow of the dying sun, the shadows of the gathering night, and the alien land slipping away to starboard.

Fourteen

Nightfall found Shaka in a restless, brooding mood. Drawing the leopard skin cloak around his shoulders, he stepped out into the starlight and let the cool night air wash over him.

Earlier on that day, he had held an *indaba* with some of his commanders. Urgent military matters were discussed: in particular, the impending clashes involving the Ndwandwe, the arch enemy of the Zulus.

He frowned. High on the list were the reports on the improved fitness levels of his regiments. Recently, this had been a source of great disquiet to him. Knowing that some of his warriors were not at the peak of physical fitness had angered him greatly. Inactivity and boredom was the scourge of any army.

Shaka shrugged his shoulders irritably beneath the leopard skin cloak.

If young men had no enemy to take their spleen out on, very soon they would start to butt horns with each other and start to brood about women – or the lack of them. His virgin soldiers needed to be kept away from sexual temptation, except for the rare times it was allowed; in the aftermath of a successful campaign, for example, age-old tribal laws having condoned such a practice for centuries. For the rest of the time, their skills had to be honed and sharpened before being pitted against the enemy, to either live or die on the field of battle.

Aware of the tension in his neck and shoulders, Shaka thrust matters of state away and began a slow promenade around the inner square, determined to enjoy the air.

To him, evening was the haunting peppery smell of dust and sun-baked earth, the acrid smell of crackling firewood and the taste of *tswala* beer. Ah, but morning! The first hours of the day were lightsome times, dancing with energy and smelling of fresh cow dung and dew-laden grass.

Beyond the high fences lay the women's quarters, the *isigodlo*. The high notes of a young girl singing and the sounds of two women quarrelling brought a smile to his lips. Silently, he moved on through the ceremonial square and neared the high gates leading to the general concourse below.

On catching sight of him, the Fasimba guards snapped to attention.

My fine young lions, he thought, with a surge of pride. Acknowledging their salute, he walked on for a while before stopping to look out over his citadel.

Hundreds of cooking fires twinkled and flared in the darkness below, a pall of aromatic wood smoke wreathing above them. Somewhere, a child cried and a woman's voice shushed it quiet. Down by the river, a pack of wild dogs set up a frantic yip-yipping, while others of their kind answered them from a long way away.

Shaka tilted back his head and looked up into the night sky. It was as if the rains of the last months had washed the stars clean and burnished them to perfection.

This year, torrential storms had made all but the highest ground sodden and waterlogged. Villages had been flooded, some swept away, with many lives lost. Thousands of cattle had to be moved to higher ground and new enclosures built to contain them. As a result, military training had to be postponed. Only his elite warriors remained on full alert while the other regiments were released to help the people cope with the floods. But what delayed my own army, he mused, also hindered my enemies.

Recently though, several other things had happened to complicate matters. First, the rains had stopped as abruptly as they'd begun. That had been followed by the sudden death of his stepfather, Mbeya. A period of mourning had to be arranged, putting back his plans yet again. Then, to compound matters further, a surprise visitor had walked in through the gates of kwaBulawayo with a urgent message for Shaka.

The brother of Sikhunyana, Zwide's elder son, and the present chief of the Ndwandwe, had come to seek refuge with his father's most deadly enemy. As a bargaining tool, he carried vital information concerning Sikhunyana's plans to avenge their father, Zwide, who had fled several years ago after suffering a massive defeat at the hands of Shaka and his *impis*.

Zwide, that treacherous dog...

Unconsciously, Shaka rubbed the thin ridge of scar tissue on his side. Fortunately, the assassin's blade had gone clean through between the ribs. *Aiii,* he could still taste the blood in his mouth and feel the sudden sharp pain of it. Luckily, the white man, Fynn, had been there to bind his wound and apply the salves that had saved his life. Unfortunately, the killer had managed to escape, otherwise he would have been spitted like an ox and left to die a slow death.

Cursing Sikhunyana, he said aloud, 'I was denied the personal pleasure of killing your sire, Zwide, only because he ran away like a dog with its tail between his legs.'

A grim smile played round his lips. 'However, as you well know, I wasn't totally cheated. Apart from ridding the world of five of your brothers, I also captured a prize of another sort, your grand-mother, Ntombazi, the witch.'

Ntombazi, who had entrapped and murdered the mighty King Dingiswayo, the man to whom Shaka owed a great debt as regards his present position, had suffered a terrible death, involving the bone-grinding jaws of a dog hyena. It had been a just penalty for her treachery and the morbid habit of keeping the skulls of her victims on display in a hut set aside for just that purpose.

'Most of all, though,' Shaka added with some satisfaction, 'I had her killed for daring to defy the King of the Zulus.'

Abruptly, the situation changed. Ever alert to the possibility of sudden attack, Shaka's keen senses told him he was no longer alone. The balmy evening air was no longer benign, but charged with sudden urgency and a hint of danger.

Allowing the leopardskin cloak to fall from his shoulders, he kicked it aside then dropped into a half-crouch, ready for combat. Even unarmed,

Shaka of the Zulus was a formidable opponent, more than capable of killing a man with his bare hands if he had to.

Only this time, there was no indrawn hiss of killer's breath, no glint of metal in the starlight, only a rustling sound, much like the wind passing through the long grass during the dry season.

Part of the shadows seemed to flow towards him. A faint odour of earth and herbs reached his nostrils. Out of the starlit darkness came a whisper, more a grating sigh than a human voice. The hair at the base of Shaka's skull prickled.

'Bayete! Mighty King of the World, slayer of witches, Langani greets you.'

Shaka let his breath out slowly. The diviner's choice of words was very telling, sinister even, particularly as the witch Ntombazi had been uppermost in his mind a moment or two ago.

'A curse on your whole tribe,' Shaka muttered below his breath. 'Dead or alive, Ntombazi, the procurer of heads, and Nobela, the witch-sniffer were a thorn in my flesh, like all those of their kind.'

A grey wraith seemed to detach itself from the shadows and move a little closer. This time, the voice was light and humourous. 'Tell me, great king, do you still consider Langani to be "one of their kind"? Last time we met, I believe you thought otherwise of me.'

Shaka said, dryly, 'Have a care, Langani. Few have risen from the shadows so close to Shaka of the Zulus and lived to tell of it. I have no need of a slayer to dispose of trespassers.'

The voice answered, smooth as silk, 'It is a truth known to all, mighty warrior king, Lord of the World. Who would dare stand against you, man to man? After showing you some of the powers at my command last time we met, surely you know I would only use them against the dark powers that seek to do harm to either our people – or our land?'

Shaka's keen ears picked up a faint sound in the background, one that seemed separate from the hum and chirp of insects. His nostrils flared as he caught a drift of a musky catlike odour and a riffle of noise that sounded suspiciously like the soft purring of a cat. For a brief moment, he thought he saw a flash of animal eyes in the dusk, but that was all.

The diviner spoke again. 'Shaka has no need to watch the shadows when Langani is at hand. I am your eyes and can part the mists of time on your behalf.'

As if on cue, a glowing star streaked through the heavens, a shower of sparks following in its wake. Shaka's scalp tightened. The last thing he needed was another intimation of impending danger from the young diviner. The last time he had issued him a warning had been just before the assassin's attempt on his life.

A brief image of the diviner, as he had been on that occasion, flashed before his eyes: a ghost in a cloak of grey monkey fur standing squarely in the middle of the path in the forest while streams of fire crackled from his fingertips, setting trees alight and making flames spurt from the undergrowth.

Shaka stared into the patch of shadow. There had been something else there, too, that last time, only a glimpse, a faint one – that of a cat-like animal pressed against Langani's legs, its eyes glinting in the light of the flames.

The form below the fig tree wavered then solidified, revealing a tall, sinuous body and long coils of plaited hair falling over the shoulders. Shaka's lips twitched in a smile.

The hair, oh, yes, the hair, how could he forget it? The first time he and Langani had met, years ago now, he had been a youth of fourteen or fifteen, and the *isangoma* a child of only three or four.

They had encountered one another during the terrifying storm that had broken out in the aftermath of his blatant defiance of his father, the former king. The young boy with the mass of curling hair falling to his shoulders had been alone, laughing and dancing in the face of the thunder and lightning.

The hint of a smile touched Shaka's mouth, as he remembered how he had hoisted the defiant little boy up on to his shoulders, then danced with him, while the rain poured down, and the ferocious lightning storm roared and raged above their heads.

Enough! Narrowing his eyes, Shaka picked up from where Langani had mockingly offered his services. 'If ever I have need of your skills, man of magic,' he responded, 'I will bear you in mind. Now depart, for I have much to think of. Before long, I may well find the enemy at my gates.'

As the shifting form below the tree stilled, Shaka heard the whispered words of the man who was the interpreter of the spirits. 'What you say is true, great king. But the real enemy is already within your gates – or should I say, already within your kingdom.'

A faint sigh as the wind lifted the diviner's words and bore them away into the sultry night. Shaka bristled. 'You do not know everything, diviner,' he said, scornfully. 'I know only too well who walks within my land. So I will tell you once again. I have no need to fear a handful of white men. Neither does the kingdom of the Zulus.'

He took a step forward as if to bodily challenge the *isangoma*. Langani came out of the shadows to meet him, his face partly concealed by the hood of the cloak.

Pulling it back, so that his face was clearly visible, he said quietly, 'You do not understand what it is I am telling you. I already know that the one called Fynn saved your life after the Ndwandwe assassin plunged his knife into your body. Did I not warn you then that you were in grave danger? You should have listened to me, Nkosi.'

Langani shook his head and went on. 'It is what follows after the white men that I fear. It will not happen in a moment, perhaps not for some years, but it will come. I have sensed it many times, although I cannot yet see its true face.'

But I will, he silently added. Before Shaka could reply, Langani said quickly, 'The *umlungu* boy, with the bright hair, what are your plans for him?'

Startled by the abrupt change of topic, Shaka was caught off-guard by the seemingly casual question. 'Plans? Why must I have plans for him? He will stay with me and live in the house of the king of the Zulus.'

'And will he be safe – in your house?' asked Langani.'

Shaka's laughter rang out. He spread his hands wide in a gesture of largesse. 'Have a care, Langani! You dare to ask me if the *umlungu* child will be safe in the heart of my kingdom, in the house of the King?'

Clapping his hands in great good humour, he said, 'Tell me, *isangoma*, my brother dancer of the storm – where else in this kingdom would he be safer than with me, the Lord of the World?'

Receiving no response, Shaka looked to where the man in the grey cloak had been standing moments before. But both the inky patch of darkness and the presence within it had disappeared. All that was left was a small breath of night air moving among the branches of the tree. And along with it, came a whisper, faint, but clear enough to reach the ears of the Zulu king.

'*You should make very sure of that, Nkosi, for the boy will become very important to you.*'

The warrior king shook his head, bemused by the diviner's sudden disappearance and the cryptic words left behind to hang on the wind.

'Like you, Langani, I have never believed in chance,' he muttered, 'so it was not by accident we met that first time – nor even on the second occasion, though I gave it no thought at the time. Nothing has changed. Once again, it was not by accident that you rose from the ground before me tonight. Nor was your talk of the boy mere coincidence.'

As he drew his cloak about him and prepared to retrace his steps, he muttered, 'The only thing is – who is directing our meetings? Is it you, Langani, man of magic – or some other power?'

As he set out walking, another thought struck him. And why does the *umlungu* child interest you so, brother dancer? What do you know about him that I do not?

Fifteen

Even before Jackabo and Jakot, the Xhosa interpreter, walked in through the gates of kwaBulawayo, they knew something serious was afoot.

For the last few miles, they'd been aware of the drums beating out an insistent message and had been overtaken by large groups of heavily-armed warriors running fast towards Shaka's citadel. Even though it was common knowledge that open warfare between the Zulu and the Ndwandwe armies was imminent, there seemed to be a new urgency in the frantic drumming and the loping strides of the young warriors running to join their comrades in kwaBulawayo.

Had something happened? Was Sikunyana within sight of kwaBulawayo?

Once inside the citadel, their fears were intensified. A mixture of exhilaration and fear ran through the vast centre like tongues of fire, darting from one group to the other. Jakot grabbed someone passing and demanded to know what was happening. The man rattled out a spate of Zulu, too fast for Jackabo to understand.

'The Nkosi has put out a call to the *amakhanda*,' Jakot explained pursing his lips. 'All the regiments must report here by tonight, or at first light at the latest. It is not known how close the Ndwandwe forces are.'

The golden sliver in his eye glowed in the sunlight. 'Aiii, this is not good, Jackabo. If it is to be war, then Jakot too will have to fight.'

After dark, sitting by the fire and listening to the hubbub of voices, Jackabo was able to piece together small nuggets of information. Now the rains were over, the enemy was on the move. There was no more time for delay. The Zulus must be ready. The drums had been beating since first light, passing on their message throughout the length and breadth of the kingdom.

In spite of himself, Jackabo felt a stir of excitement. He remembered what Sandy had told him about what used to happen throughout the Highlands of Scotland when trouble came.

Men would run through the night bearing fiery crosses to warn the inhabitants of the remote clachans and scattered crofts that trouble was heading their way. *The enemy is coming! Prepare for war!* All across the land, the blazing crosses would be set alight on hilltops, while weapons hidden in barns or secreted below the thatch would be recovered, ready for whatever might come.

Over the centuries in his native Scotland, the enemy could have been the Danes, other Highlanders, as clan fought clan, or the Hanoverian dragoons and their mercenary forces. During the Jacobite rebellions, the face of your enemy would largely depend on who you were and what you believed in. Sandy had summed it up pretty well when he'd declared: 'Highlander or Lowlander, Jacobite or Hanoverian, each man knew the face of his enemy.'

Listening to the pounding of the Zulu war drums, Jackabo reckoned the warning would still be the same, though, whether delivered in Gaelic, English or Zulu.

'*The enemy is at hand. Ayi hlome, to arms!*'

Gazing into the fire, Jackabo's thoughts drifted from the rumours of imminent war to his own struggles to survive. Since returning from the gentler world of Nandi's emKindini and his life among the women and girls of the *seraglio*, his life had not been entirely without risk.

During the first weeks and months of his life in the largely military establishment of kwaBulawayo, and armed only with the rudiments of the language, he had poured every instinct into survival. Like a small animal turned in on itself, they were sharpened, telling him who to trust, and who to avoid.

No matter where he went, it was impossible for him to be overlooked. He was like some small, rare species of creature come to roost in the house of the King, his blue eyes and red hair a mark of his rarity. News of him had spread fast. This was not to be wondered at, for who else, apart from the mighty Shaka, had the power to draw rare creatures and objects to himself for his amusement?

Quickly, he was also reminded that Shaka's citadel was a place where men died on a regular basis. Sentence of death was often carried out very often for no other reason than someone sneezing or farting at the wrong time.

He glanced across the fire to where Jakot was deep in discussion with one of the elders. His face was carved into lines of severity with no trace of his usual humour and quick-witted repartee. Obviously, he was concerned about might happen to his wife, Nontonella, and their child if Shaka called on him to join in the armed struggle.

Jackabo was still very wary of Shaka's motives for detaining him in kwaBulawayo. More than once he'd asked Jakot about it: 'If he says I'm too young to fight and not strong enough to build a boat – then what does he want me for?'

The Xhosa didn't have an answer to offer. 'Who knows what is in the mind of such a man?' he would say, shrugging his shoulders. 'Kings do not have to have a reason. In any case, Shaka of the Zulus is not as other men.'

And the two of them would end up staring into the fire, pondering on the enigma that was the Zulu monarch.

A hundred and fifty miles away in eThekwini, Henry Fynn lay sprawled in a makeshift chair in the long, narrow hut set aside for meetings. His long, sun-bleached hair was tied back by a thin strip of ox-hide, while his straw hat with the flapping crown was thrown carelessly on to the table in front of him.

He cast a lazy brown eye around the room. Most of the others were present, including Farewell. Casting a glance at Henry Ogle, Fynn bared his teeth in a grin. '*Ohlo*. How've you been, man?' The Yorkshireman lifted a lazy forefinger in acknowledgement.

There's another one who can never go home again, Fynn thought, eyeing his friend with a grin. Yorkshire isn't big enough to hold a man like Ohlo any more. Once Africa puts its mark on you, there's no going back. An' I should know.

His eyes moved to the man at the head of the table. Lieutenant Francis George Farewell, RN. Now, this one's another kettle of fish.

The man he secretly referred to as 'the Governor' still remained, in essence, the steely-eyed naval officer he'd always been. His trousers and shirt were much mended, but spotlessly clean, his beard and moustaches neatly trimmed.

Fynn's eyes travelled to the elegant, gold-rimmed eyeglass screwed into the man's right eye. Gossip among the men had it that he even wore it in bed. Probably true, he thought – unless he's had a special pocket made for it in his night-shirt!

While watching him unobtrusively, he tried to puzzle out something that had been intriguing him for a while. Take Farewell's wife, for example. Pretty woman by all accounts, and not long married, prevails on the Cape Governor, Lord Charles Somerset, to send a British warship all the way to Zululand to bring her husband home. But when the damn ship sails into the bay – does the man see fit to even go aboard? Not a bit of it.

Fynn shifted his bony buttocks on the hard chair. But then, come to think of it, nobody else had made any move to run back to the Cape, either – except for Lieutenant James King of course. Naturally, he had declined to confide in anyone how he was going to find his way back to his crew – or even if he intended to return at all.

John Hatton, the first officer, would certainly know. But Fynn knew the quiet, sandy-haired man would never breach his captain's confidences. No, the answer to his questions lay with the man whose piercing blue eyes were impatiently raking the room as he waited to begin the meeting.

Shaka, an ever-astute judge of character, had coined the perfect name for him. *Febana ka ma-jo-ji,* King George's man.

Farewell coughed discreetly. 'Gentlemen,' he said, addressing the group of sailors lounging around the doorway, 'I'm about to open the meeting. Please be seated, you're making the place look untidy.'

Only after the last man had scuffled into a seat and settled himself, did he begin. Adjusting his eyeglass, he glanced around the table.

'As I'm sure you all know, this meeting has been called to decide what response we're to make concerning the recent demands made by King Shaka.'

Two days ago, Shaka's runners had delivered an urgent message. Direct and unequivocal, it was no less than a call to arms. Zululand was under threat once again from the Ndwandwe, this time led by Sikhunyana, Zwide's heir apparent. The white chiefs of eThekwini must rally their men and help the Zulu army to defend it.

A stir of agitation ran round the table. Farewell cleared his throat.

'As you might know, rumours of impending war have been circulating for the last month or two. One part at least, is true. Sikhunyana had indeed mobilised the Ndwandwe, but was thwarted by this season's unusually heavy rains. Accordingly, the same reasons have prevented the Zulu forces from getting into battle mode.'

The gold rim of his eyeglass flashed as he looked around the room.

'Now the rains are over, the drums talk of regiments being recalled, and warriors being doctored for battle by the *izinyanga*.'

Fynn stirred uneasily. That wasn't quite true. Due to the death of his stepfather, Mbeya, Shaka was currently in mourning. Out of deference, family commitments and respect for the dead man's spirit, he had decided to wait until the following full moon before launching an attack.

'Gentlemen,' Farewell went on, 'we're more than familiar with this sort of request.' He stared hard at the sailors. 'Mr Cane, Mr Fynn and I were prevailed on to support him last time – but only after much protest, I may add.'

Cane nodded, the chair creaking dangerously beneath his massive frame. Fynn caught his eye. The two men stared at each other, remembering how it had been. The frightening moonlight raids they'd been caught up in still returned in the dead of night to haunt them. Neither of them would forget the raw power and aggression of those they ran with, and the ruthless discipline that bound them to Shaka.

'This time, however,' Farewell went on, raising his pale eyebrows, 'Shaka expects all of us, without exception, to turn out –'

A rumbling of angry voices interrupted him. Thompson jumped to his feet, snarling, 'Now, look here – I never signed up to fight no wars, not for King George, nor for any other black son-of-a-bitch Satan that comes along!'

For once, everyone agreed with him. A long, low growl of dissent followed his outburst.

'Yaay…'

Farewell raised his voice above the hubbub. His tone was brusque, bringing them back to the harsh realities of their current situation. 'This is getting us nowhere. We have even fewer choices than we did last time. The problem remains the same. Do we fight?'

He cast a quick eye round the table. Some shook their heads vigorously, while others avoided his eyes or looked the other way. Farewell was remorseless.

'Come, gentlemen – do we refuse to comply with Shaka's requests, ignore him? Or, as we did last time, ask for a few volunteers in the hope of appeasing him?'

Placing the tips of his fingers on each side of the open ledger in front of him on the table, he said briskly, 'Time's running out. I'll need a show of hands. Also bear in mind that if we refuse to comply with Shaka's demands, the consequences might be severe –'

Thompson, looking as if he was about to explode, stood up, took off one of his tattered seaboots and banged it loudly on the table. A sudden hush fell. Every eye in the room was on him.

'With all due respect, ye've left somethin' out, sir.' Raising his voice in a passable imitation of Farewell's clipped accent, he bellowed out, "And if not, my good fellows, you run the exceedin' good chance o' bein' skewered up the arse by yon black savage what calls hisself a king!"

With that, he launched himself through the door and slammed it shut behind him. The meeting dissolved into bedlam.

Later that night, Jackabo chose his moment carefully then asked Jakot the question that had been intriguing him for some time. 'What does *umnyama* mean?' The words dropped into the insect-filled night with the force of a cannon ball.

The golden sliver in Jakot's eye glowed uncannily, and he stared at Jackabo for a long moment, his face inscrutable in the firelight.

'You have an uncommon nose for a small *umlungu*,' he answered, pulling a sliver of wood from the fire to light his pipe. 'Are all the children of the white men as you? Or are you a wizard that flies to the secrets of the Zulu like a bee to honey?'

Jackabo grinned at him. Once the pipe was puffing to his satisfaction, Jakot asked: 'Tell me how you came to hear this word?'

'Viyasi,' the boy said, mentioning one of the young warriors who had befriended him on the outward journey to meet Shaka. 'Viyasi told me about *umnyama*. I could tell by the way he spoke that it's no' a good thing.'

'*Yebo*, this is true,' the interpreter said. 'When war comes, so does death. Men will die. It is the nature of things. Also, when the worlds of humans and spirits are too close, *umnyama* is often present.'

Tiny jets of flame spurted from the burning logs. 'The evil sucks away the spirits of brave men,' Jakot went on, 'so that they lose their will to fight. *Umnyama* is to be greatly feared.' He looked at Jackabo sternly. 'Do you understand?'

The boy nodded. Something secretive and deep in Jakot's eyes made him suddenly aware of the shadows lurking in the darkness beyond the circle of firelight.

After a bit, he prodded him for more information. 'So, what kind of *muthi* do you take to keep safe from *umnyama*? Is there magic in it?'

Jakot laughed. 'Eh, Jackabo, the secrets of the *izinyanga* are not known to me. Even if they were, I would never tell you.' Suddenly, his humour died away. His eyes were hard, serious now. Tapping him on the knee, he said 'Listen to what I say.'

Jackabo gave him his full attention. 'You are clever for one so young, as full of curiosity as a small monkey... this is good, because you learn quickly.'

The boy watched the Xhosa's long fingers tap strands of tobacco into his pipe. That used to be one of Sandy's ploys, he thought. When you need to do some quick thinking, fiddle with the pipe, buy yourself some time.

'It is just, sometimes...' The interpreter's words tailed away. A lifetime of being told off by exasperated folk had made its mark on Jackabo. 'I know, I know,' he said, unrepentant to the end, 'I ask too many questions.'

Humour filtered back into Jakot's eyes. 'You see, what I have said is true, you have understood everything.'

Leaning closer, he said quietly, *'Be very careful* where you put your nose, especially about matters such as you have mentioned. Not everyone takes kindly to noses being where they shouldn't be, especially *umlungu* noses. Boy, I think you often forget you are not a Zulu.'

The Great Hut was full of queer shadows. Even the lizards and scuttling insects in the thatched roof seemed unusually subdued. Shaka's brooding presence dominated the gathering. His oiled body gleamed, reminding Fynn of a cobra coiled in long grass, fascinating, but capable of striking at speed, its bite deadly and usually fatal.

Fynn was sitting cross-legged with an elbow casually propped on each knee, Jakot in his usual position, halfway between one camp and the other.

Farewell looked as if he was nailed upright to the mast of one of his ships. His hair, bleached by the sun to a pale gold, matched the epaulettes on his shoulders, while the formal hat with its braided peaks lay stiffly across his knees.

When he spoke, Shaka's voice was curt and controlled. Jakot began to translate, faltering over some of the words. Shaka made an irritable gesture, and flashed him a dark look. Jakot hurriedly moved on.

'When a king goes to war, those in his kingdom must follow. Are you familiar with this?' Farewell nodded. 'I have heard it is your custom.'

Shaka demanded, 'Is it not your custom to follow umGeorge? Surely, he expects his people to follow him on the field of battle?' His eyes glittered as he waited for Jakot to translate.

The Lieutenant replied. 'King George has many generals to lead his armies. Not every man in the kingdom must follow him to war. Also, he has many kinds of warriors. As you know, I am one of his sea warriors, as are most of the men at eThekwini. We never fight on land. It is not our purpose.'

Shaka stared at him long and hard, before waving a dismissive hand.

'*Yebo*, I know of this. But you are not with umGeorge now. You are in the land of the Zulus. And I ask you again – where are the men and the weapons I asked you to bring with you? Where is Kingi? I gave orders for him to come.'

When he stood up, it was with the smooth, effortless ease of the striking cobra he so resembled. Jakot moved into a squatting position, poised as if for flight.

'You know I could have all of you killed – every last one of you?' The voice was no longer gentle or deceptive. 'Jo-Ji could send every one of his soldiers to find you, but no one would say where you went, or even if you had ever come to the land of the Zulus at all. Is this not so?'

Jakot translated; his voice tense with strain. With characteristic coolness, Farewell ignored Shaka's threat of annihilation and replied calmly, 'It is as I said before. We are forbidden to take up arms against people who have done us no harm, or to involve ourselves in the wars of others.'

Suddenly, Shaka's patience came to an end. He jabbed a finger at Farewell. 'No! It is for none of these reasons, *Febana ka ma jo-ji*. It is because you are a coward!' A flick of the hand followed. 'If you will not fight then you will have no need of your weapons.'

Jackabo's glance darted to where the muskets stood propped beside the doorway. On Shaka's command, Jakot swiftly rose to his feet and gathered them up.

Fynn spoke then, addressing Shaka in a burst of rapid, but fluent Zulu. Whatever he said was enough to change the prevailing mood. Shaka slowly sat down again and motioned for Jakot to return the muskets.

It appeared that some kind of compromise had been reached.

Outside, the night air was cold and sharp with the spice of old, burned-out embers. 'Whew!' Fynn said, relieved to be back in the fresh air.

Farewell polished his eyeglass thoughtfully with a handkerchief then placed it carefully back in his breast pocket. 'Thank you, Henry,' he said, easing the monocle back into place. 'Not the roasting we could have had, if you pardon the pun. Would you say we've got away with it?'

Fynn snorted. 'Don't fool yourself, Lieutenant. Look yonder.'

He pointed to the blood-tinged moon rising out of the dark bulk of the Nkwalini hills. They gazed at it in silence. Down below in the valley, a pack of wild dogs snarled and howled.

Fynn gestured towards the rising moon. 'What you see there, gentle-men, is Shaka's timepiece. I reckon we only have two or three days left before it's full – then, it'll be time for action.'

His teeth gleamed in the dusky light. 'If it's any consolation, Shaka hinted he only wants us along for support. Though what in the name o' Harry he thinks a few whites an' a handful of assorted natives can do to affect the outcome of what promises to be a bloody business, God only knows.'

Farewell pursed his lips. 'Moral support, my arse,' he said, scathingly. 'Let me tell you something, Henry – a man who scares the hell out of half of Africa does not need a few sailors, a former surgeon's assistant and a carpenter to bolster up either his courage, or his reputation. So what the hell is he after?'

Sixteen

A goat bleated plaintively somewhere below, and a woman's voice hushed it, as if it were a fretting child. Jackabo cocked open a sleepy eye.

Beyond the goatskin flap, he could just make out the first streaks of dawn colouring the sky. Soon, kwaBulawayo would be stirring; men coughing and hawking, babies crying, the shrill crowing of roosters heralding in the new day – but not yet. Yawning, he ducked down again and closed his eyes. After a bit, he turned over on to his back and lay there, listening.

Outside, there was only the cawing of pied crows in the cattle enclosures, beyond that an unnerving silence. Frowning, Jackabo pushed aside his blanket. Crawling on his hands and knees over to the doorway, he lifted the flap and peered out.

The sun was a misty red ball floating on a band of violet haze. The air was sharp and smoky, with a tang of frost in it. Within kwaBulawayo, though, not even the roosters were crowing.

A twinge of unease gripped him. Shivering, he backed inside then hastily drew on trews and a shirt, fumbling his arms into the sleeves. Slipping on an old plaid weskit of Ned's, he went out into the chill morning air to see what was going on, pushing his shirt-tails into his trousers as he went.

As he made his way towards the royal residences, the contours of Shaka's Great Hut loomed out of the writhing mists, the massive thatch gilded by the first rays of watery sunlight. No sign of life in or around it, no stir of movement either, in the servants' quarters. Somewhere inside the *isigodlo*, a woman wept softly. A burst of quarrelling voices drowned out the sound of the pitiful sobbing.

The Fasimba guards were no longer at their posts. Instead, a group of older men wearing the *isicoco,* the head-rings denoting their marital status, was sitting around a small fire, nodding and talking softly. That told him all he needed to know. There was no doubt about it. Shaka had gone, and so presumably had his personal servants – and his regiments.

Squeezing past the guards, Jackabo ran to the brow of the hill and looked down. Not everyone had deserted kwaBulawayo, though.

At the lower end of the settlement, he saw that the gates stood wide open and a huge knot of people were jostling and pushing their way through. The faint sounds of women's voices, the shouting of herd boys and the lowing of cattle beyond the gates told Jackabo what he already suspected. Shaka and his warriors had gone to war and his people were getting ready to follow him.

He raced back through the gates as if the devil was at his heels. Ten minutes later, with a few pieces of extra clothing and essentials stuffed into his knapsack, and a blanket rolled on top, he came whooping down through the great oval arena to join those moving out through the gates, speeding on their way to join in Shaka's war.

'Now, where d'ye suppose the boy's off to at such a lick?' Fynn asked as he spied Jackabo racing down through the empty parade ground.

Without waiting for an answer, he turned to Farewell. 'How in the hell did Shaka manage to up and off into the night with his whole army, with nobody hearing so much as a fart?'

'Damned if I know, Henry.' Farewell responded as he bent to pick up his bedroll. 'But he's had a good three or four hour start, I'd say.'

Fynn squatted down to *indaba* with the guides who were waiting to accompany them. They gestured north. 'Army split up, taking different routes,' he said, as he hoisted the long-barrelled musket over his shoulder. 'We'll head for esiKlebeni, the old Senzangakhona kraal, we might catch up with them there.'

A few old men came out to watch them leave. Only dead cooking fires, empty huts, the elderly and the very young were left behind as keepers of kwaBulawayo.

'Whatever else you may say about Shaka,' Fynn remarked, 'he knows what he's about. The control he has over his people is absolute. It has to be, to move 'em about like mice in the night.'

In his mind's eye, he could see them: Shaka's warriors, doctored up and primed to kill, moving down through the valley in the light of the full moon, fanning out along the hillsides, their spies already ranging out in front, signals and hidden messages echoing eerily back to the main force.

'Night or day, it's all the same to them.' Fynn said, as he swung himself up into the saddle. 'The Zulus are unstoppable – like the tides, or the phases of the moon.'

From his position out on the flank of the vast human flood coming up behind the Zulu army, Jackabo could see little more than the bobbing heads or shuffling feet of those directly in front of him

The snaking entity, which made up Shaka's secondary force, was comprised of the sisters, mothers, and younger brothers of the regiments, its progress marked by clouds of red dust.

The women's regiments were out in force. Fresh food and beer, bread, corn and vegetables, enough to last the first days of the campaign were being carried in huge woven baskets on their heads.

After the food ran out, many would turn back, especially those with young children, although some would follow the army to the bitter end. *Udibi* boys ran to and fro, caught up in the excitement of the moment. The eldest were responsible for the cattle, the youngest for carrying sleeping mats, head-rests, pipes and other comforts the warriors might need at the end of each day.

In spite of the numbers, this was no haphazard gaggle of camp followers: it was an organised, disciplined force, kept in order by the eagle-eyed matriarchs, the indomitable Zulu women who had followed their men into battle before and who had no doubt also treated their wounds or watched them die.

Already, some of the younger children were showing signs of distress. Several items of the baggage they were trying to carry were too heavy or awkward and their small legs had to work twice as hard to keep up with their elders.

Jackabo squatted in the dust by two of the fallen. They were about six years old, he reckoned, the small one even younger. Except for the string of beads around their bellies, they were stark naked, the chubby look of babyhood still on their faces. They stared at him open-mouthed, snot and tears glistening on their cheeks.

'*Sanibona,*' he said, in greeting. '*Unjani*? How are you?'

The lips of the small one quivered. His tear-filled eyes flashed a panic-stricken look at his brother, confused by the sudden appearance of this strange, pale-skinned boy. 'Come, little brothers, I will walk with you.' Jackabo said, gathering up their burdens.

They stood watching him solemnly, their feet and legs covered in reddish powdery dust. Jackabo moved off, whistling. Moments later, he heard the patter of feet come running up behind him and grinned to himself.

Later on, the clouds dispersed, revealing clear blue skies. Jackabo sniffed the air. For the past few days, there had been a different feel to it. The grass had turned a tawny gold, and dry leaves were rustling and drifting across the ground. Flocks of birds flew overhead, heading north, a sense of urgency in their beating wings.

A group of young girls passed by, giggling and chattering as they came. One of them made a grab at his hair, her eyes darting with mischief.

Jackabo stuck his tongue out at her. Shrieking with laughter, they squeezed as much fun out of him as they could before their mothers scolded them back into line.

The glare of the sun was blinding. The landscape was flat and dry, only dust and stunted bush for as far as the eye could see. The little ones were exhausted, and Jackabo's arms and shoulders ached from carrying their

packs as well as his own. His stomach rumbled, and he remembered he
hadn't eaten since last night.

'Jackabo! Hau, Jackabo!'

Surprised to hear his name being called, he stepped to one side, closely
followed by his two small shadows and gratefully slipped the packs off his
shoulders. A tall boy appeared at his elbow. Dust sprinkled his hair and
clung to his feet and legs. He was bare footed, a folded blanket slung over
his shoulder.

'Hau, Jackabo!' he grinned, the whites of his eyes startling against his
dusty face. 'What are you doing on the war trail of the Zulus?'

Sigonyola!

Jackabo grinned back at him. His friend seemed to have sprouted an
inch or so since he'd last seen him. They'd met at a village kraal one
afternoon. Undaunted by the lack of cohesive language, they had quickly
become friends. Sigonyola was a year older, his brother, Mangila, two years
younger.

Mangila dodged between the bellowing cattle and launched himself
bodily at him. The three of them boxed and tussled, while the elder of his
charges sat watching. The toddler had fallen asleep and was curled up like
a puppy in the dust with his thumb jammed into his mouth.

Sigonyola hoisted the sleeping child onto his back. The little one's arms
and legs moved instinctively, moulding his small frame to the boy's body.

Mangila picked up one of the packs, put it on his head and they set off
again. 'Do you know him?' Jackabo asked Sigonyola, indicating the small
boy on his back. The lolling head still had the thumb stuck in its mouth.
The gangling boy shook his head.

'But who does he belong to?' Jackabo persisted.

Sigonyola looked sideways at him, his brows drawn in a frown, puzzled
by the question. 'He is a Zulu,' he said, shrugging his shoulders. 'What else
must I know?'

They walked all that day through the dry, stony landscape, stopping now and
again for a rest. Sigonyola produced some dried strips of meat and they
chewed them to quell the rumbling in their bellies. Thirst haunted them,
and they took to sucking pebbles to keep their mouths from drying up.

By sunset, the air was cold, the shadows blue and sharply defined. As if
at some pre-arranged signal – the proximity to a source of water, judging
by the unmistakable smell of river water – the two armies, both military
and civilian, began the process of stopping to camp for the night.

Wearily, Jackabo sank to his knees, then rolled over and played dead,
his arms and legs thrown akimbo. After a bit he sat up, kicked off his
sandals and began to examine his feet. Bruised and battered from the long
day's march, his toes were bleeding from small cuts and bruises. Sigonyola
leaned over and looked at them with some curiosity.

'Eh, my friend, the feet of the *umlungu* are not strong enough.'

Thrusting out a foot, he compared it to Jackabo's. Like all Zulus, he
had developed a thick ridge of hard skin on the soles, as iron-hard as
horses' hooves.

'This is the foot of a Zulu,' he said, solemnly. 'It is a foot for walking,
marching, and running. A Zulu foot is the best foot, Jackabo.'

The others squatted round, their small round heads nodding earnestly
as they examined Jackabo's battered and less efficient appendages.

The next few hours were a haze of fetching and carrying, distributing
food and sleeping mats to the regiments. Jackabo ran with the others, his
battered feet forgotten. More than one warrior started in surprise, as his
bed mat, head-rest, pipe and tobacco pouch were delivered by a red-
haired, pale-skinned spectre that suddenly vanished as quickly as it had
come.

It was during one of these forays that he almost ran into Jakot. Too late,
he tried to dodge out of sight. Startled, Jakot made a grab at him. Ducking
quickly under the Xhosa's arm, Jackabo disappeared into the shadows.

On the sixth day out, a runner came looking for him. The message he
carried was from Shaka. Febana ka ma jo-ji was seriously injured, and
Jackabo was needed to look after him.

His heart sank. He didn't want to be with Farewell. He wanted to be
with his friends, moving up to the battle lines.

The small boys wanted to come with him, but Jackabo had no option
but to leave them behind with Sigonyolo. The *toto* stood rubbing his eyes,
the strips of red beads stretched over his little belly.

As Jackabo turned to wave goodbye, the *toto's* thumb crept back into his mouth. He and his brother stood watching him until the bend in the path hid him from sight.

The former naval officer was sitting in the shade propped up against the horse's saddle, his torn shirt draped loosely around his shoulders. His face was pale and pinched with pain, his legs held awkwardly in front of him.

Dried blood spattered his breeches from waist to knee, and fresh blood had already soaked through the bindings Fynn had used to dress the wound.

As soon as he appeared, Fynn rounded on him. 'Jack, what in the hell d'you think you're doing here, eh? This is no place for you, lad.'

Jackabo stood his ground. 'There's much younger fry than me out here, Fynn.' Fynn eyed him sceptically. '*Yebo*, boy, there are. But they're Zulus, you aren't. Born to it, see, comes with their mother's milk. Boys practice their trade early hereabouts.'

Biting down the need to rebel, knowing it would get him nowhere, Jackabo scuffed his toes in the dust and balled his fists in his pockets. After a bit, he forced himself to ask: 'What happened to Mr Farewell? Did he get wounded in the battle?'

Fynn shook his head. 'Not a bit of it, we've seen no action yet. Bloody ox gored him this morning.'

'Is it bad, then?'

'Only flesh wounds, but nasty,' said Fynn, wiping his hands on the seat of his trousers. 'The beast's horns got him in the ribs, gored him and scraped the length o' his hip bone. He's lost a lot of blood, but as far as I can tell, none o' his vitals seem to be harmed. He's very weak, though. Shock an' such.'

On Shaka's orders, Jackabo had been delegated to remain with Farewell, to look after him and administer any necessary medicines.

Fynn explained the necessity of keeping everything as clean as possible. 'It's the infection we have to watch for, Jack. Any sign of red around the wounds, this is what you have to do...'

At sunset, it grew bitterly cold and a thin wind blew up from the south. They sat huddled in blankets around the fire, the Lieutenant's head propped up against his horse's saddle, a blanket tucked around him. His blonde hair looked silver in the firelight, his face waxy, aged by the loss of blood.

'Where will you be heading tomorrow, Fynn?' Jackabo asked. Fynn pointed to a mountain ridge silhouetted against the fiery red sky.

'That's where they say Shaka will face down Sikhunyana. So, boy, that's where old Fynn will be going.' Hitching up his blanket, he turned round to toast his backside at the fire.

Jackabo stared at the brooding hills. 'My friends – what'll happen to them?'

Fynn shrugged his shoulders. 'What can I say, Jack? Many of the women and young children will have turned back by now. The feisty among 'em will stay on till the bitter end. The *udibi* boys too, Jack – they have to be on hand to look after the cattle and see to the warriors' comforts, such as they are.'

There was nothing left to say. Sadness crept back into him. He looked into the fire, and watched the embers glow then shrivel with each breath of wind.

'It's how it is, Jack,' Fynn said, softly, 'but I want you to remember one thing, and where you heard it first.' He shook his pipe into the fire, the old, mischievous smile back on his face.

'The Zulus are damn hard people to kill, Jack. Man or boy, they're uncommonly strong. Where others would falter, these bastards just keep on coming. They can stand up to punishment that'd kill lesser men. And I reckon that'll go for the *udubi* boys as well, so don't you be frettin' too much, see?'

His eyes changed and became icy chips in the firelight, the humour in them gone.

'I hope to Christ we never have to fight 'em, boy,' he swore softly 'because even with our guns and powder and an army of Redcoats, I ain't so sure we'd lick 'em. And so says Fynn, from his deepest heart. Amen.'

After Fynn and his men had gone, one day passed into the next. Days lengthened into a week, and then one week into another. The full moon came and went, and the skies were given back to the stars.

For Jackabo, the daily routine went on as usual; collecting firewood, seeing to their food, dressing the Lieutenant's wounds and watching for tell-tale streaks of infection. After a week or so, he could see the wounds were beginning to heal cleanly.

Just as he began to think they would be there forever, one day around mid-morning, a group of black men stepped out of the bush. Jackabo looked up from where he was changing Farewell's dressings. It was hard to tell who the strangers were. Ndwandwe or Zulu? Who could say.

'Fetch me the rifle, Jack,' Farewell muttered, hastily gathering the remnants of his shirt around him. 'I hope to God they're Zulus.'

Jackabo eyed the natives warily. Lean and hungry, they were men who had travelled far and fast, their caved-in bellies and faces sculpted by lack of food and sleep.

A click as Farewell cocked the musket. A tense few seconds followed.

A rustle of branches, then Fynn rode into the clearing. Apart from the drooping ostrich feathers in his hat, his sadly-depleted footwear and a hungry look about him, he seemed much the same as he had a month ago.

Farewell lowered the musket. 'Thank God it's you, Henry. What news from the front?'

'A complete rout,' Fynn answered. 'A fucking blood-bath, that's all you could say about it.'

'It was as cold as the grave up there,' Fynn said, holding his hands out to the blaze. 'Shaka's spies reported the kraals were deserted for miles around. The women and children had thrown in their lot with the army. All things considered, what else could they do? The Zulus would only have butchered them and run their cattle off.'

'Indeed,' said Farewell, tersely.

'Not a good place to be, in between two forces hell-bent on destruction,' Fynn added. A weary smile crossed his face. 'So I stayed out of harm's way, up on the mountain. That way, I didn't have to shoot anyone.'

'And from where, I presume, you had an excellent view of the proceedings?' Farewell commented, stretching out his hands to the fire. Fynn quickly looked away into the darkness. 'Aye, Farewell,' he said, at length, 'I saw it all.'

He studied the flames for a few moments. 'On the upper slopes of the mountain, there was a rocky ridge. It was here the Ndwandwe made their stand. Further up among the trees were the women, children and old folk, as well as the cattle, of course.'

Jackabo knew in his bones what was coming next. He stared unblinking at Fynn. Judging by the nervous tic jumping at his temple, the man known as Mbuyasi, the finch, had taken what he'd seen very hard.

He muttered, 'Poor bastards. What an almighty struggle it must have been to get all their people and cattle up there.'

Jackabo's stomach lurched. A sudden image of bewildered children dragging their feet in the dust, wailing in exhaustion, rose to haunt him.

'Even after Shaka's *impis* were facing them, no one moved, nary a one of them. It was only when Jakot fired off some shots that all hell broke loose.'

Then Fynn went on to describe the battle of Ndololwane.

Zhee, zhee, zhee… the drumming of spears on shields and the Zulu battle chants pouring contempt on the enemy as they advanced, the *impis* with their deadly, short blades, fanning out in long probing horns, their mission to encircle and destroy.

Up close now, coming under the long, unwieldy spears of the Ndwandwe, and oh, the wailing and crying among the women and children above. Terrified children and old people, cattle bawling and women clasping their babies to their breasts, the gut-wrenching horror of watching the Zulus swarm up the mountainside, the deep hissing and humming of animal and bird noises as they came.

'Thousands died that day,' Fynn said, 'and not just warriors either. As Shaka's warriors carried out his red war, *impi embovu*, a war to the finish, I had a bird's eye view of it all.'

Fynn's voice cracked. 'The Ndwandwe army broke and ran, thinking to escape into the forests. Mostly, though, they went back up the mountain, to stand or fall along with their people. For days afterwards, the skies were full of circling birds… '

Farewell stared down at his clenched fists, the knuckles white in the firelight. 'War's a bastard, Henry, whether it's on land or at sea – a bloody business, all in all.'

A lengthy silence followed, broken only by the crackle of flames and the whining of mosquitoes. Fynn cleared his throat, and spat into the fire.

'The Zulus also suffered casualties, of course. It was hardly a bloodless victory. Shaka paid a high price for it. Apart from the loss of hundreds of his warriors, he also lost Mgobozi, one of his best commanders, and a close friend of his, by all accounts.'

Jackabo's head came up. He knew Mgobozi, a tall, light-skinned man with any easy smile. Farewell got to his feet and rummaged in his baggage.

'What I have here, Henry, my boy, is a cure for most ills. And I think, as one English gentleman to another, this is a timely moment to partake of some of it.'

Uncorking the bottle of brandy, he offered it to Fynn. Turning to Jackabo, he said gruffly, 'War makes brutes out of most men, boy. I hate to say it, but Shaka's no different from any of us, in that respect.'

Fynn had the last word. 'Remember the last time we had this conversation, lad?'

Taking a long hard swallow of the fiery Cape brandy, he asked, 'What d'you think now of followin' your friends to war? Just be bloody glad you didn't see any of it. I reckon Shaka did you a favour, boy, by pinnin' you down here as part-time medical supervisor.'

Seventeen

After the army returned to kwaBulawayo and the obligatory period of mourning was observed, Shaka disappeared into the *isigodlo* and nothing more was heard of him.

An unnatural period of calm descended on the deserted royal quarters. The square in which he held court every day stood deserted with only the wind and the dried leaves and balls of dust to disturb the silence.

As for Jackabo, he was happy for the talk of wars, battles and the inevitable sorrow that followed, to be over and done with. Now he was free to spend time with his friends, his band of kindred spirits, for Sigonyolo, his brothers and the other *udibi* boys had returned none the worse after playing their part in Shaka's war.

In their spare time, they took to roaming the bush and vying with each other to see who could pee the furthest. They played games, had mock fights with sticks, racing each other until they fell down, exhausted. And finally, Jackabo learned to swim, egged on by his supporters.

He took to wearing only his under-drawers when out with his friends. As he said, 'It'll stop my breeks and shirts from wearing out and save on the washing of them, too.' His shock of red hair grew wild and tangled, much to the despair of Nontonella, Jakot's wife, who periodically captured him and subjected his unruly locks to a thorough washing, combing and plaiting.

The hills and valleys around kwaBulawayo became his playground, and it was a playground like no other. To him, Zululand was a paradise, teeming with infinite varieties of creatures, both large and small, four-footed, feathered, or with no legs at all, the dangerous, the deadly and the timid.

After he fell in with a group of hunters, he learned how to be alert to the dangers of the vast, unpredictable land as well as to its beauty. Over time, he was able to tell which species had come to drink at the waterholes the night before, and from the scuffed tracks and spattered drops of blood, which had lived and which had not.

His newfound freedom was a lightsome thing. It was the seashores and braes of Buchan all over again, but on a much grander scale. Unfettered by time of day and released from the shackles of school, parents, stern Kirk and sea-faring duties, his boyhood, quite simply, was given back to him.

And with it came a new awareness of time and space, the grandeur, and the wonder of all life, both animal and human, and the infinite variety of both that abounded in the kingdom of the People of the Heavens.

One day, the hunters found a bush baby clinging to its dead mother and brought it back for him. The bundle of bloodstained fur clung to his shirt with almost human fingers, its huge eyes filled with terror. At first he wasn't sure what he could do to help it, but somehow it survived.

Now, *itombi* – little lady – slept all day curled up in a basket lined with a pair of his old drawers. When she wasn't out on the hillsides at night, she would chatter and jink around his quarters, keeping him awake.

His fame soon spread. In no time at all, other small animals and creatures began to find their way to him. First to arrive was a pair of tiny orphan deer, followed by several birds, then some rabbit-like animals that had become trapped in a grain store. After that, there were several cats; the offspring of those brought to Shaka as gifts by James King or others who had travelled from the bay to visit kwaBulawayo. Half wild, and spitting like furies, at first if he tried to touch them, their fur would stand up along their backs. Gradually though, the juicy morsels of food he provided proved too tempting to remain stand-offish for long.

The Zulus were observant folk, quick to get to the heart of a person. They would say, 'Eh, see this Jackabo, the *umlungu* child who has come to live with us – surely he must be an *inyanga* of animals? To live with them as he does, it must be so.'

The odd, humorous glance would be directed his way. 'Aii, truly this child is a wise one, though strange in his ways.'

The cold season was a time of tawny grasslands and the high-vaulted blue of winter skies. It was bounded by the spicy smell of earth and wood smoke, of blazing fires burning clear and sharp in the night air, with people huddled round them for warmth.

One bright cold day, as they sat hunched over the fire, trying to keep warm, Farewell, not yet able to undertake the long return journey to the bay, produced some woollen blankets to wrap round themselves. One of them he laid aside. Officer or not, Jackabo found out that the usually taciturn former Lieutenant was a dab hand at sewing, because there and then, he made him a coat.

Cutting the blanket in two, he took one half, folded it in two and cut out an opening for his head. After sewing up part of the sides, he left the rest to drape down over his arms like sleeves. With naval precision, he finished off the raw edges in blanket stitch to stop it fraying.

That winter, Jackabo ran about Zululand like Joseph in his coat of many colours, the only difference being that his was made of best York-shire wool, grey with a fine, red and blue stripe through it, and neatly blanket-stitched in red.

On nights like these, the African skies surpassed themselves. To step out into the crisp, cold darkness was to step into another world, one where the canopy above your head seemed as deep as the deepest ocean and studded with glittering jewels.

It wasn't only Jackabo who was mesmerised by the stars. After all, as the people reminded themselves: 'Are we not the amaZulu, the People of the Heavens?'

He learned the names of some of the stars and the glittering, remote constellations spanning the heavens.

Komotsho, the evening star; Indusa, the star that pulls the night across the sky; Dithutlwa- the Giraffe; the Three Healers, The Virgin's Fire, the Stars of Planting and the River of Peace.

Jackabo, in turn, pointed out the Southern Cross, and tried to explain how the people of the sea to whom he belonged used the stars to help them find their way over the darkened ocean when no land or sun was in sight.

One day at sunset, a man came. The whisper went round that he was a famous storyteller, a mystic man of great age, who went from village to village, fire to fire, telling stories as he went. So wise was he, that none could challenge him on any point.

No one seemed to know his tribe, or where he had come from. He spoke many tongues and knew all there was to know about almost everything; from the most recent battle to those of many years ago, who had won and lost and how many had been left behind on the field of battle, their faces covered by their shield and their bellies slit open.

But it was not only war he spoke of. Many were his stories; from the animals and birds of the plains to the legends and myths of all the tribes, not only in Zululand, but also from those other far-off lands of Africa that lay beyond the sunset.

That night, he came to their fire. Jakot was there, wrapped in his deerskin karosse, for the night was cold. The interpreter wasn't pleased that Farewell was still in residence, and showing no signs of leaving, for he had wives and cattle waiting for him beyond the confines of kwaBulawayo, and wanted to go and see to them. While Febana ka ma jo-ji was still there, requiring his services, Shaka had refused to let him leave.

Jackabo was glad when he saw the storyteller moving over to their fire, hoping it might take Jakot's mind off his troubles. When the old man caught sight of him, he stopped short and stared hard at him, before easing himself down into a cross-legged position on the opposite side of the fire.

His whiskers shone silver in the firelight, the same luminous colour threaded through his grizzled peppercorn hair. He wore the *isi coco* – the woven head-ring used by all older married men. Age had begun to wither the muscles on his haunches and upper arms for the flesh had sunk back to expose the clean lines of sinew and muscle, the puckered wounds on his body at thigh and shoulder, the unmistakable marks of the warrior he had once been. Draped around his shoulders was a tattered cape of leopard skin, and round his neck he wore a necklace of its teeth and claws threaded on a length of dried animal gut.

He's either a chief or a great warrior, Jackabo thought. Only those of royal blood or warriors of proven bravery had the right to wear the skins, teeth and claws of the leopard, lion or cheetah, the great cats, the *isilozemosi,* the Beasts belonging to the King of the Zulus.

The old man took some snuff, sneezed a few times then blew his nose into the fire in a splatter of mucus.

'I am Lumukanda,' he said, looking round the circle of faces. He peered at Jackabo across the firelight, his eyes bright and curious as black polished buttons among the spider webs of wrinkles. He motioned for him to stand up and turn around slowly a few times so he could see him better.

In the silence, the fire crackled and spat out small blue flames. Jackabo was careful to sit down again only when Lumukanda bade him. As they waited for the wise man to speak, an air of great expectancy hung in the air, for others had crept over to join them.

At length, Lumukanda gestured to where the Southern Cross hung glittering in the night sky. 'Far away to the south and west where the desert winds blow,' he said, 'there is a cave. It lies in the land of the people who are called the Batwa. On the wall of this hole in the rock, there is the drawing of a man. It is very old, from a long time ago.'

The knotted fingers picked a stick out of the fire then rubbed the glowing point against a stone to sharpen it. A few sweeps of his hand cleared the earth by the fire. Then he began to draw on it.

A buzz of whispering rose as people craned their necks trying to see what he was doing. When he'd finished, he beckoned to Jackabo to come and look.

Jackabo peered down at what Lumukanda had drawn in the sand. Jakot pushed the karosse aside, and leaned over his shoulder to see.

A tall, stylised figure emerged out of the dust. Striding out purposefully, it held a hunting bow in one hand and two short daggers in the other.

As he looked closer, he saw that the man was wearing what looked like a helmet, not unlike those worn by the Roman centurions in his history books. Below the helmet, long, flowing hair reached down to the small of his back.

Without warning, the outlines of the drawing seemed to shift and change. Jackabo blinked, thinking his eyes were playing tricks on him. As he watched, the long hair below the helmet seemed to turn red as did the figure's short beard, while the skin grew paler and a white light began to radiate out of the eyes...

Startled, he pulled back on his heels. His reactions had not been lost on Lumukanda. When Jackabo glanced over at him, shocked and confused, the old man's eyes were intense and full of humour as they looked back at him.

'This is the son of Karesu, the Fire-Beard,' he said. 'A long time ago, he and others like him came to the land of the Batwa.'

Around them, the whispers rose and fell, while the hairs stood up along the back of Jackabo's neck and down his arms.

Karesu, the Fire Beard, the old man had said. Had what he'd just seen been as clear to others as well, or had he been the only one to see the red hair and beard in the drawing in the sand?

Jakot drew the karosse around his shoulders and eased himself back into his place. Although he said nothing, Jackabo could feel his eyes boring into him.

Lumukanda muttered to himself in another tongue. Soon afterwards, he appeared to be asleep, except for the moving of his lips in incantation or prayer. Jackabo dared another quick look at the drawing. This time, all he saw in the firelight was a crude sketch drawn in the sand.

The vivid image of Karesu, the Fire Beard, still burned behind his eyes. There had been no mistaking the red glint of the man's long hair, his pale skin, or the white light shooting out of his eyes.

But who was he? Where had he come from, to appear in the desert lands of the Batwa, so long ago? And what had prompted someone to draw him on the wall of a desert cave?

Lumukanda's monologue came to an end. His eyes flicked open. With a quick wipe of his hand, the drawing was no more, the sand smooth once again in the firelight.

All that remained was the spark of knowing, and the kindliness in the bright black eyes that met Jackabo's across the smoke curling skyward.

One morning not long afterwards, Jackabo was heading for the main gates, whistling as he went. Today was a special day, for at long last he and Sigonyolo were going on a foray into the bush in search of honey.

First, they would have to find a honeybird, for without one they would have little chance of locating the exact spot where the wild bees had built their hives. They would have to listen for the bird's call, a loud, rattling noise that sounded much like a handful of pebbles being shaken up and down in an empty gourd.

The small brown and yellow bird would eventually lead them to the wild bees, fluttering from bush to bush ahead of them, for it was as keen as they were to reach the honey and taste the sweet nectar. Once they'd found the hives, a small fire would have to be lit and fed with green wood chips to smoke the bees out. Only then would the dripping honey be theirs. Sigonyolo warned him that the little bird would have to get its share, too, including the fat, juicy larvae stored in the waxy cells, otherwise next time they came looking for honey, it would lead them away from the bees and into danger, possibly to where lions or other predators lay in wait.

Jackabo's mouth was already watering with the thought of the warm, sticky honey. The last time he'd had anything quite so sweet was when Biddle had emptied his pockets and discovered a twist of brown paper and what was left of three striped humbugs stuck together by salt water and time.

His mind being occupied with thoughts of such delights, he failed to hear his name being called. When a hand fell on his shoulder, he whirled round, startled.

The face that met his gaze was round, a rather naïve moon below a greying cap of peppercorn curls. Normally, a man of his mature years should be wearing the *isi coco*, the woven head-ring denoting his status as a married man. But there was no such *isi coco* for Malusi.

He was one of those called *Qwayi Nyanga*, the Moon Gazers; men who were scarred, crippled at birth or generally disinterested in women. They were usually employed as guards, and eunuch servants in the *isigodlo*, the place where Shaka's women lived. There was nothing remotely sinister about Malusi. He was clad in a short kilt of leather and a faded length of blue cotton draped round his ample shoulders. It clung damply to the folds of his body emphasising the pads of fat around his nipples. Sweat dripped fom him, his robe dark in patches where sweat had soaked through.

Jackabo greeted him with some surprise. 'Hau, Malusi! What brings you here today?'

Struggling to get his breath back, Malusi blurted out his message. Shaka has sent me to look for you. Must go at once, urgent, Nkosi say

Jackabo's heart sank. *Urgent.* The word had a nasty ring to it. What could Shaka possibly want him for? He had retired to the women's quarters long ago and had not been seen since. Groaning, he glanced down at his none-too-clean drawers, his sole item of clothing. He was hardly attired to meet royalty. And there was Sigonyolo who would be waiting for him...not to mention the bees...*and the honey!*

Bulongwe! He said a few more swear words below his breath, then gave in with ill grace. They would have to wait until another day.

Malusi stopped in front of the small gate set in the high fences, the one through which no male was allowed to pass on pain of death – apart from Shaka himself, or one of the Qwayi Nyanga, of course.

Jackabo stared at the barred gate. Beyond it lay the secret world of the *isigodlo*. According to Jakot, hundreds if not thousands of young women and girls lived there, with many more scattered throughout the kingdom, under the eagle eyes of the formidable female military commanders Shaka had chosen for the task.

Malusi scratched softly on the gate. A woman's voice, sharp and imperious, called out, 'Who is calling at this gate? The Lord of the World does not wish to be disturbed.'

As he muttered a response, a trickle of sweat ran down Malusi's face and into the folds of his neck. There was a soft click of wood on wood. The gate creaked then swung open a crack. Malusi ushered him forward, clucking like a broody hen.

A hand reached out, clutched Jackabo's arm and pulled him through. A shove in the back told him to keep facing the other way. A rustle of clothing followed then a clunk as the wooden batten dropped down, sealing them inside.

Isabella Bleszynski

The keeper of the gate moved in behind him and nudged him forward. Jackabo badly wanted to turn round to see who was doing the poking, but a sharp hiss warned him to keep his eyes to the front. Then his silent guide proceeded to herd him along the dusty paths with an occasional hiss and a prod to stop him turning round.

As they moved deeper into the maze of twisting alleys, he caught sight of an occasional flash of teeth and gleam of inquisitive eyes from inside the shadowy interior of the beehive huts, accompanied by a scamper of bare feet and giggling, a slap followed by a scream as girls vied with each other to snatch a glimpse of him passing by.

The *isigodlo* seemed vast; no hint of where it ended or began, only the blue sky above and the huge sprawl of huts and narrow passageways on either side.

Eventually, they came out into a large, open square. In the middle of it stood three or four superbly constructed dwellings, their high, arched doorways and smoothly thatched domes indicative of royalty.

The centre of the spider's web, Jackabo thought. Why am I being brought to this place? But there was no more time to think. Whoever was behind him gave a sharp tug to his hair then blew into his ear, small quick puffs of warm breath that sent shivers down his back. Jackabo spun round.

A pair of dark, mischievous eyes flashed at him. Both hands were clapped over the girl's mouth in attempt to muffle her laughter.

Marie One! There was no mistaking her small breasts; just as pert and bobbing as the last time he'd seen them. 'Sibongile! What are you doing here?' he croaked.

'Eh, Jackabo,' she murmured, pinching him on the cheek, her breath warm and sweet in his ear. 'We are lonely for you, grow quickly into a man, we beg you.'

Giving him another radiant smile, she nudged him towards the doorway of the largest of the dwellings. Another friendly nip for old times' sake, then she sped back the way she'd come, giggling as she ran.

Jackabo moved to the threshold and stood at the arched doorway waiting to be called. After a few moments, receiving no response, he dared a quick look inside. Shaka was slumped in a carved chair, seemingly lost in thought, watching the smoke from the fire drift up towards the gap in the thatch.

Sensing his presence, the Zulu king turned his head. When he saw Jackabo standing on the threshold, the look of weariness on him lifted. Rising from the chair, he motioned for him to enter, the beginnings of a smile on his face.

What he saw in the face of the King of the Zulus at that moment shocked him. The whites of his eyes were strained and bloodshot, as if he hadn't slept for days, his normally smooth skin sagging with weariness and lines of pain.

With a sudden flash of insight, it became clear to him. *It's Mgobozi...* he thought, *he's grieving for his friend.* One of his oldest friends and a fellow cadet from the early days in Dingiswayo's army, Mbobozi had been killed during the recent battles with the Ndwandwe.

The revelation that a man like Shaka of the Zulus could suffer grief and the pain at the loss of a friend confused him. In spite of himself, Jackabo felt a lump rise in his throat, as he looked at the raw suffering in the eyes of the man who was feared by so many.

So that was why he's hidden himself away, he thought. So nobody except the women and girls of the *isigodlo* could see that the warrior king was mortal, vulnerable in the face of the death of a friend.

With a sudden jolt, he realised Shaka was speaking to him. 'You did well in tending to Febana ka ma-jo-ji. It was fortunate you were on hand to tend to his wounds after he was injured.' Jackabo nodded, and looked down at his dusty feet.

Silence followed. Then Shaka spoke again.

'You followed my people to where you had no need to go,' he said, 'you helped the *totos* and ran with the *udibi* boys to bring food and drink to my warriors. You have a good heart, and you are also very brave. This is what I want to say.'

A flash of weariness crossed his face. 'Even the young find death waiting for them in unexpected places. It is not my wish that it will seek you out while you are in the house of Shaka, or anywhere else within my kingdom.'

Jackabo's thoughts were in turmoil. Could he have been wrong about the Zulu king's motives in keeping him in kwaBulawayo? What if he'd only thought to protect him, realising that he was safer here than anywhere else –

including eThekwini? Perhaps his comments the first time he'd set eyes on him about being 'too young to fight' and ' not strong enough to build ships' had been behind his decision all along?

Hastily, he thrust such thoughts away. Though the matter of his following the army had obviously been on Shaka's mind, Jackabo knew there must be another reason for sending Malusi to find him. He was right. Shaka came to it without further ado.

'A woman, here in the *isigodlo,* is very sick,' he said, 'the *muthi* given her by the *inyanga* has not helped.' He shook his head. 'I must see what the white man's medicines will do. Since Mbuyasi is away, you must take care of her.'

Jackabo shot him an agonised glance. *Surely to God he doesn't think I'm able to work a miracle like Fynn did?*

'I have much faith in your people's medicines,' Shaka went on. Jackabo looked at the ground, and said nothing. Inside, he was in a blind panic.

His experience of medicines was scanty, to say the least. Being fed castor oil for a sore belly or dosed with toddy and gruel when he had the 'flu was no great qualification for what might be expected of him now. He broke into a cold sweat. *Och, why didn't I just run before Malusi caught up with me?*

Marie One appeared at the doorway, carrying a box. Fynn's medicines, he supposed. As Jackabo stumbled back into the sunlight after her, he contemplated the consequences of administering the wrong kind of medicine to one of Shaka's women.

Chattering away, oblivious to his worried silence, Marie One led him back through the maze of huts to where a neat residence was set well back from the others. Ducking down, she lifted the goatskin flap and scrambled through the low doorway. Jackabo bent down and followed her wriggling buttocks inside.

The smoke from a small fire burning in the centre was overpowering. Only by crouching down near the floor was it possible to breathe easily. The smell of vomit, sweat and body odours added to the thick atmosphere. Eyes smarting, he peered around the smoky interior. The huddled body of a woman lay on a sleeping mat, her head moving from side to side as she moaned and plucked at her clothing.

A dig in the ribs from Marie One reminded him of why he was there. Struggling for breath, he moved closer. Two objects had been placed near the woman's head; a sinister-looking, misshapen mass in a skin pouch and a bundle of what looked like herbs. He eyed both uneasily.

I'd better keep my *umlungu* nose out of this, he thought, remembering Jakot's advice. Whatever *muthi* or magic charm the *inyanga* had put in place would stay where it was.

Bouts of deep coughing racked the huddled form and the skin was slick with greasy sweat. Marie One squatted beside him, her eyes as red and watering as his own. She shook her head. 'In here,' she said, patting her own breast.

Jackabo was completely out of his depth. Desperately, he tried to think what a real doctor might do. After a bit, he motioned to Marie One to turn the sick girl on to her back.

The face was young, smooth and oval, the colour of milky coffee, with a small flat nose and full mouth, her hair plaited in tiny braids that stuck out around her head. When he touched her forehead, her eyes fluttered open. A flicker of alarm rose in them when she saw him bending over her. Weakly, she turned her head away, tears trickling from the corner of her eyes.

As she moved, Jackabo caught the flash of gold in her ear lobes. Cautiously, he lowered his head to her chest, and listened. Her breathing was laboured, and to his inexperienced ear, the rattle and gurgling in her lungs sounded alarming.

Oh, God, she's really sick, he thought. *If she dies, Shaka will blame me.*

Without warning, the hum of voices dribbled away into silence, as a tall figure entered from outside, blocking the doorway. Jackabo turned his head and peered through the smoke to see who it was.

As always, Nandi, the Nkosikazi of all Zululand, dominated her surroundings. A strong hand gripped his arm, and hoisted him to his feet. He found himself clasped against the familiar voluptuous bosom, while her voice, still as soft as melted butter, crooned in his ear, 'Eh, Jackabo, how you have grown. Almost a man now.'

After a few more affectionate squeezes, Nandi eased herself down on to her knees beside the sick girl and called softly, 'Mbuzikazi...Mbuzikazi.'

The girl drew her knees up to her chest, her body racked by another fit of coughing. When Nandi looked up at Marie One, lines of concern were grooved around her mouth. They exchanged a meaningful glance.

Jackabo's eyes swivelled from one to the other. He knew a secretive look when he saw one. *Something's going on here, something I'm no' supposed to know about....*

Nandi was a shrewd woman. Aware of his curiosity, she flicked a quick glance in his direction, a warning frown crossing her face. But the knowing nod of Marie One's head in response failed to escape his notice either.

For the second time in as many minutes, he told himself, Something's going on here. Whatever it is, these two are in it together. So much for thinking it was Shaka who sent Malusi for me. It's pretty clear whose idea it really was...

Nandi eyed the contents of the medicine box. 'Jackabo,' she pleaded, holding out a hand to him. 'What can you do for this girl, this Mbuzikazi? She is very sick.'

His mind was racing. *This is your fault, Fynn. You started this.'*

Within days of coming face to face with Shaka's army when he'd first landed on the shores of Zululand, Henry Fynn had saved the life of an old woman the *izinyanga* had given up for dead.

Naturally, such news had flown like wildfire straight to the ears of Shaka himself. The legend that the twenty-year-old Fynn had brought someone 'back from the dead' had helped in no uncertain way to pave the way for Shaka's acceptance of the white men into the Zulu heartland.

And if that hadn't been enough, a few weeks later, Fynn had just happened to be on hand to save Shaka's life after an assassin stabbed him while dancing among his people. From then on, the *umlungu's* medicines and potions were considered all-powerful, though Fynn, canny as always, had been shrewd enough to keep the medicine men on his side, sharing his knowledge with them and discussing their own methods of treatment.

Now, through no fault of his own, the eleven-year-old known as Jackabo had inherited Fynn's mantle, as well as the possibility of reaping the whirlwind if anything went wrong. Wiping his sweaty hands on the seat of his drawers, he sat back on his heels and took a deep breath.

'The fire must be put out,' he said, 'it is very bad for her. Then bring water, hot water, also many covers to put over her.'

While Nandi relayed his orders to the women hovering by the doorway, Jackabo set about investigating the contents of the medicine box.

Printed in Fynn's slanting hand, three glass jars bore the legends, '*Oil of Peppermint*' '*Stomach Powder*' and '*Rock Salt.*' Next came a small blue bottle. When he unscrewed the silver top and took a sniff of the contents, he was almost knocked sideways.

Eyes watering, he managed to decipher the cramped writing on the label. *Sal ammonia* – smelling salts! After the smelling salts came witch hazel for bathing swollen eyes, followed by iodine, for treating cuts and stings. He breathed a sigh of relief. So far, so good... A dark green bottle was next. Drawn on the label was a skull and cross-bones, on it the legend: '*SLEEPING DRAUGHT. 1-2 drops only. WITH CARE.*'

Tins of salve and wintergreen for chilblains – he took those out and placed them to one side, along with the sleeping draught. Nestling at the bottom of the chest, wrapped in an old woollen sock, he found something else.

The label on the dark brown bottle told its own story. A bearded Jack Tar gazed out over a stormy sea, one hand shielding his eyes. Written in large gilt lettering on the blue label, he read '*THE SAILOR'S FRIEND*' and below it: '*BEST JAMAICA RUM, WARMS THE COCKLES OF THE HEART.*' He placed it to one side, along with the other items.

By the time the women returned with what he'd asked for, his drawers were plastered to his body in a stew of fear and sweat and his red hair was curling in the heat. Seeing no way out of his predicament, he got to work.

Now that the smoke's cleared, fresh air will no harm her, he thought. I'll get the women to wash her down, to cool her and ease the fever. Next, should be the wintergreen. It'll need to be rubbed into her back and chest.

The smell of the wintergreen was sharp, familiar and comforting. How often had his mother vigorously rubbed it in, then wrapped him in flannel and covered him with feather quilts to sweat out whatever was ailing him. What else could he do but try it out on Mbuzikazi?

He contemplated the bottle of rum. A dram or two of whisky, laced with heather honey and boiling hot water had always proved a sure remedy for colds and feverish chills. Had he not been given it himself more than once during the bitter Scottish winters?

Gathering up the bottle of rum, the wintergreen and the sleeping draught, he turned to where his patient, Nandi and a delegation of women from the royal *isigodlo* were waiting for him to perform another of the white man's miracles.

At last it was finished. The place reeked with the pungent smell of rum and wintergreen. Below the mound of covers, Mbuzikazi had lapsed into a deep sleep, her breath rattling and gurgling in her chest. He'd done all he could. As far as he was concerned, the Navy rum, the two to three drops of sleeping draught, and whatever other dark spirits were at work in the secret places of King Shaka's *isigodlo* could fight it out among themselves.

After a few days of high anxiety while tending the sick girl, a great improvement in her condition was noted. It was with great relief that Jackabo finally managed to escape from the *isigodlo*. Not only had he done his duty, but had also maintained the reputation of the white man's medicines.

But that was not to be the end of it. Shaka, being so impressed with the skills and understanding Jackabo had shown when called on to deal with the illness of the young woman, Mbusikazi, had created a new post for him, that of ' medical doctor to the women of the *isigodlo*.'

Henry Fynn laughed uproariously when he heard about the new appointment, teasing Jackabo about all the young girls who'd soon coming looking for him – but, after sobering down, promised to advise him and keep him right concerning the potions and herbal treatments to be used on his new patients.

Eighteen

Farewell carefully eased one arm into his jacket and slid the other into the remaining sleeve. He had just returned from a hunting trip with Shaka and ached in every muscle.

After several weeks' absence, Shaka had emerged from the *isigodlo* looking refreshed and rested. Almost the first thing he did was to organise a hunting trip to which he'd invited Farewell, also his half-brother, Dingane and his commanders, Mdlaka and Nqoboka.

Secretly, he'd been encouraged by Shaka's invitation to join in the hunt. The longer I can stay around, he thought, the more likely it is that Shaka will grant me a concession to hunt elephant. Must play my cards right, though.

During the expedition, several leopards and lions had been killed, solely for the use of the Royal house, of course. Hundreds of birds and scores of monkeys had been trapped, their feathers and fur required for the trimming of head-dresses and war costumes. And then there were the elephant –

Farewell drew in breath sharply. In India, he had been used to seeing the smaller, brown variety of Asian elephant, domesticated and patiently biddable under the control of their mahouts. Nothing, but *nothing*, had prepared him for the sheer size of the African elephants, those massive grey pachyderms, as they came stampeding out of the bush, ripping off branches and knocking aside trees, the sound of their trumpeting enough to shrivel the balls of any man.

By the time the hunt was over, a dozen or so tusks had been loaded up ready to be transported back to kwaBulawayo by the bearers. Naturally, they were Shaka's property... no doubt to be set aside for trading with the Portuguese, Farewell thought tartly, remembering his first sight of the magnificent tusks he'd glimpsed at Delagoa a few years back.

He smoothed down his moustache, lost in thought.

Seeing Shaka in action at close quarters had been quite an experience. The man had been tireless, his ability to co-ordinate and organise the hunt clearly demonstrating the military skills at which he excelled. Grudgingly, he had to admit that the sense of order and discipline of the Zulus was impressive, from the king down to the lowliest tracker.

Stepping outside his quarters, he looked up at the sky, and was immediately dazzled by the brilliant display of stars. Must keep all this in perspective, old boy, he reminded himself. All too easy to get seduced by this damn country, and forget why you came here in the first place.

As Farewell's footsteps crunched past him, Langani pressed back into the shadows and waited until he was out of sight.

The hour was late. By observing the daily routine of the man Shaka called Febana ka ma jo-ji, the diviner had noted that it followed much the same pattern. Every night, he would come out of his hut, look up at the heavens as if seeking some message in the stars before moving on to the King's residence where he would stay for some time.

Aii, but he still reminds me of the wolf, the diviner thought; the long snout, the cunning in the eyes. Why is he he staying so long in kwaBulawayo? The wounds inflicted on him by the ox have long since healed.

Langani did not trust Farewell. But then, he saw little reason to fully trust any of the pale-skinned strangers who had recently entered the kingdom – not yet, at any rate.

He was not alone in this, he knew. He had seen suspicion leap into the eyes of more than one Zulu, some of them high-placed, as they watched the *abelungu* hold the ear of Shaka, their king, and receive gifts of cattle and land.

The young boy, the one the Zulus called Jackabo, was a different matter altogether. Because of his youth and friendly ways, there was no bad feeling towards him, rather the opposite, for he was welcomed everywhere. Shaka had been right in what he'd said during their last meeting. The boy with the hair like fire had indeed found safety within the royal house.

Langani rubbed his eyes. Even in the soothing darkness, they were troubling him. It was what came of spending too much time watching the images he'd recently begun to see in the coiling smoke and flames.

The throwing of the bones had hinted at something lurking in the place where the physical and the spirit worlds overlapped. Of late, he had also been receiving half-formed fragments of strange images and weird sounds that welled up then died away. Something was afoot in the spirit world, although its true shape or intent had not yet been revealed to him.

Moving out of the shadows, he stepped on to the path that led to the massive, domed structure where Shaka was entertaining his guests. The muffled sound of a woman's laughter floated in on the night air from the direction of the women's quarters. It served to remind Langani of something else, a matter of some seriousness, which he believed might possibly be linked to the old she-cat herself, Nandi, the King's mother.

The deepest and most secret of the whispers he'd intercepted had hinted of a woman, possibly a wife, for Shaka. Were they the first stirrings of something new, a beginning, perhaps – or even a birth?

Langani shivered. What he'd learned of the time when *itshaka* himself had been conceived had alarmed him. The *amadhlozi*, the ancestors, would indeed be vengeful if history were to repeat itself.

It was not quite clear what the rumours meant, but one thing Langani did know. If they were true, then they were unlikely to bring anything good in their wake, either for the amaZulu, the People of the Heavens, or for Shaka himself.

He needed to keep a close eye on what was happening nearer the heart of things. As an idea came to him, Langani's eyes gleamed in the darkness.

He would place a spy in an unlikely place, one that nobody would ever suspect. And they would report anything of interest back to him.

Nineteen

The cold, dry days of the winter season had almost passed and now the cattle stood knee-high among the lush grass of the Nkwalini valley. Leaves were beginning to unfold on trees and bushes and the hillsides were studded with bursts of yellow mimosa and sprinklings of spring flowers.

Each day, the sun rose earlier and climbed a little higher. Ragged cracks began to appear in the ground of the cattle enclosures, and the nights were filled with the high singing of cicadas and the distant roaring of mating animals out on the plains.

One afternoon, Jackabo was visiting old man Mtimkhulu, the father of his friend Viyasi, the young warrior who had carried him over the burning sands while on his way to kwaBulawayo, over a year ago.

After he'd made his farewells and was about to leave, he noticed a bundle of dusty feathers beneath the *msasa* tree in the corner of the kraal. Seeing a faint movement, he squatted down beside it. The wounded bird tried to flutter away, one wing drooping awkwardly.

Jackabo knelt in the dust beside it. Making small comforting noises, he gently smoothed its rumpled feathers. A bright yellow eye opened, and the bird looked fearlessly back at him, its beak half-open, as if it was trying to say something.

Running an eye over the shiny black feathers, Jackabo put his head to one side, and said, 'You're either a crow or a raven. And quite young, I'll be thinking.' Then he picked it up gently and carried it home inside his shirt, being careful not to jostle the broken wing.

After a few days, he gave it a name. Because it was a brave wee bird, though not so wee as all that, he called it Hector, after a famous Maclean who had more than held his own in a battle against his enemies.

Slowly, the wing began to mend, although he suspected it might never allow the bird to do more than flutter from the cross-struts of the hut down to the perch he'd made for it in the shade by the doorway.

Jackabo also kept a dozen or so stick insects in a wicker cage. Now and again, he would catch Hector watching them intently. The bird never sought to do more than look at them, in much the same way that the half-wild tabbies who also lived there, tended to acknowledge Hector's presence without trying to catch him or do him a mischief.

A few days later, a messenger came running to tell Jackabo that two *umlungu* had arrived. Pulling a pair of trews on over his ragged drawers, he rushed out, excited to see who had travelled from the bay. Apart from Fynn and the Lieutenant, he had seen no one else for almost a year.

The stir of porters outside Farewell's living quarters told him where they were. Just visible inside the dark interior, he spotted the unmistakable bulk of John Cane, also the drooping ostrich feathers on Fynn's hat. Standing with their backs to the doorway, facing Farewell, they were completely unaware that Jackabo was only a few yards away.

The Lieutenant's face was as pale as death. Words tumbled out from between his bloodless lips. 'Elizabeth, my wife Elizabeth, you say? How in God's name did she get here?' Jackabo turned away quickly, but not before he heard an explosion of rage burst from him.

'*James King!*' he shouted. 'I should have known that bastard would've had a hand in it. Thought I'd got rid of him for good – and good riddance, too!'

With a jolt, Jackabo realised that he hadn't known that James King had left the bay. But then, anything could have happened during the last twelve months.

With an effort, Farewell quickly regained his equilibrium. 'Good God, I would have thought he'd have stopped short at encouraging my wife to follow him here! But then, what else can one expect from a liar and a fraud?'

Jackabo squatted down in the shade of a nearby hut to wait until the quarrelling was over. After a time, the shouting stopped and things grew quieter. John Cane ducked his head to clear the doorway and emerged with Fynn close behind. Seeing Jackabo squatting in the shade, Fynn shot him a rakish grin, and strolled over to talk to him.

The first thing he noticed were the rings Fynn was sporting on each of his big toes. They'd been fashioned from pieces of polished wire and rows of small blue and red beads. Seeing where his interest lay, Fynn laughed.

'A present from a lady, d'you fancy a pair, boy?'

'I couldn't help overhearing what was said,' Jackabo said, getting to the nub of things. 'Is there going to be trouble?'

'You could say that,' Cane replied, jutting out his bearded chin. 'It's been on the cards since the *Anne* arrived a fortnight ago. Off the ship steps James King, alongside him Mrs Farewell herself, come a-lookin' for her long-lost spouse.'

He laughed his big man's laugh. 'I says to meself – John Cane, now there's a gel with steel in her stays if ever there was one! As pretty as a picture, enterin' Shaka's kingdom, cool as you like!'

Fynn winked. 'Well, Cane, you're the man with the expertise on corsets in this neck o' the woods. Myself, I prefer my women without 'em – and you can take that anyway you like!'

It was too hot, even for joking, so they moved into the shade. 'Where is she now?' Jackabo asked, 'Mrs Farewell, I mean…'

John Cane roared with laughter. 'Well, she ain't here, that's for sure! If we'd brought her with us, the Lieutenant would likely have spit us through with that fancy naval sword of his.'

Scratching his bearded chin, he looked at Jackabo thoughtfully. 'To have his Majesty take a notion to keep the Lieutenant's wife here as well as yourself – now, that *would* set the cat among the pigeons, an' no mistake!'

Later that day, the men gathered to discuss the situation. Farewell was surly and uncommunicative, obviously extremely unwilling to say why he had chosen to stay on in kwaBulawayo for so long after his recuperation.

Fynn looked into his pot of beer. Why didn't the man want to leave? When Shaka, understandably, had insisted that he must now leave kwaBulawayo and join his wife as soon as possible, his face had taken on a closed-off, stubborn look.

Good God, Fynn thought, if I had a wife who'd left the comforts of Cape Town to come lookin' for me, the very least I'd do would be to go and welcome her!

In spite of not setting eyes on the young woman he was married to, for over two years, Farewell seemed strangely reluctant to go and welcome her. In fact, hadn't he steadfastly refused to even go aboard the Royal Navy frigate she had pleaded with the Cape Governor to dispatch into unknown territorial waters in the hope of finding him and bringing him home?

Now, wouldn't that just aggravate the hell out of any woman! Fynn let out a sigh of exasperation. And there was another thing… what, if anything had James King to do with Elizabeth Farewell suddenly turning up in Zululand?

To have a woman, and a white woman at that, arrive unexpectedly in a place like eThekwini, had been something of a shock to the beleaguered crew. But the fact that the woman in question was the wife of their self-styled leader and had sailed in accompanied by the former partner her husband was in strife with – well, it boded no good at all. A woman with a grievance could turn out to be something far worse than a mere inconvenience.

Fynn took a long, slow swallow of beer. eThekwini was a place dominated by men, most of them unorthodox characters. Cut adrift from civilisation, living on the edge of barbarity and facing an uncertain future – well, anything could happen. As regards Elizabeth Farewell, being the only white woman within hundreds of miles could spark off any number of reactions.

He wiped froth from his moustache. Well, there was jealousy, for a start, rivalry, hidden resentment – or just plain lust.

And then there was Shaka; a wholly unpredictable factor in the mix. It was clear he'd no liking for Farewell, the man who was her husband. Who knew what he might make of her arrival, especially if word of the conflict between Farewell and King were to reach his ears?

And, sweet Jesus! Any suggestion of impropriety between King and

Elizabeth Farewell would not sit well with the strict moral and sexual code Shaka had imposed on the Zulu kingdom... better to throw gunpowder into the fire than that!

Drat the woman! Fynn thought. Why couldn't she stay at home and busy herself with tea parties and suchlike, instead of pitching up in a tinderbox of male strife like eThekwini?

That night, after the arrival of earthenware platters laden with the steaming fried beef Fynn had shown the Zulu cooks how to prepare, the atmosphere became unusually cordial.

For the first time, a few of the girls from the *isigodlo* were present. This, in itself, spoke volumes about the regard in which Shaka held Henry Fynn. Normally, it was forbidden for a man other than the King to look on the faces of the women of the royal *seraglio*.

Jackabo could see that Fynn was very taken with them, although he had the good sense not to stare too much. Dressed in short, tailed skirts of leather, they wore plumes of feathers in their hair and strings of beads coiled around their necks and wrists.

Some held flickering tapers and bowls of sputtering wax while others presided over gourds of beer and platters of food. As they moved quietly about in the background, the gleam of their brass rings and necklets was reflected in the polished floors.

Among them was a familiar face. Jackabo had no difficulty in recognising its delicate oval shape, or the flash of gold in her long ear lobes. When her eyes met his over the smoking tapers, he saw the flash of recognition in them before she bent her head and turned away, smiling.

No doubt about it, he thought. She was the girl called Mbuzikazi, the recipient of the wintergreen rub and the hot toddy containing 1-2 drops of sleeping draught and several generous tots of *'Sailor's Friend.'*

Intrigued, Jackabo found himself shooting a cautious glance at her from time to time. After a bit, he began to notice things – a soft look here, a brief, but intense glance from below her long lashes – and all of them directed at Shaka himself.

Oh ho, he thought. As Ned would say, 'as sure as eggs is eggs, Heelander, something's going on here.'

Usually, if he'd been invited to attend and it grew late, he would curl up on one of the karosses and go to sleep. More than once, he had wakened at first light to find himself alone, with Shaka's great domed palace empty and smelling faintly of beer, dried grass and smoking beeswax.

That night was no exception. Except that Jackabo stirred from his sleep long before cockcrow. Yawning, he reached down to scratch an insect bite on his ankle. Beyond the arched doorway the sky was still dark, the smoking wisps from the tapers still casting flickering shadows over the plaited walls and bead-covered columns of the huge, domed structure.

Thrown into relief were two elongated shadows, one of a man while the other was the slight figure of a woman. Still half-asleep, Jackabo raised himself on one elbow and peered around.

As he did so, he saw the shadows merge. A sharp intake of breath, muttered words and a woman's low moan prompted him to sink back down again, draw the soft fur of the karosse around him and close his eyes.

After a time, if he had been awake, he would have noticed the shadows become two again and would have seen the man and the woman pass through the arched doorway and into the early dawn light.

A month or so later, Fynn and Jackabo were sitting in the shade cleaning his hunting guns. One of Shaka's servants appeared with the news that a group of natives, two white men, and several unidentifiable animals had been spotted a day or two away.

'My bet is that it's Lieutenant King,' Fynn said, 'the other will be that lanky streak of piss, Nat Isaacs.'

'Why not Tom Halstead or Ogle?' Jackabo enquired, 'or Ned even. I haven't seen him for such a long time.'

Fynn shot him a crafty look. 'Because, lad, they're Farewell's men – at least, Tom Halstead is. Ohlo? Well, I'm not so sure about him. He's his own man. Neither of them would have any interest in coming here.'

'Why couldn't it be Mr Hatton?'

'Because he wouldn't leave the bay unless it was an emergency,' Fynn responded, 'he's too busy with the new boat to go travelling. It'll be Isaacs, you mark my words.'

And he was right. Around noon on the following day, James King, Nat Isaacs and their entourage arrived. The 'unidentifiable' animals turned out to be a discontented piglet, four dogs, a pair of yellow canaries in a gilt cage, and two white goats wearing blue leather collars. The minute he set eyes on the menagerie, Jackabo suspected that, with the possible exception of the pig, they would all end up in his care.

King looked well and fit. He was dressed in new clothes and his beard and moustaches were neatly trimmed. He greeted Jackabo with affection, relieved to see him again. Immediately, he explained his decision to go aboard the frigate sent by the Governor to deliver Farewell back to his wife.

'I could scarcely believe my eyes when I saw it lying at anchor,' he said soberly, 'I had to make a quick decision whether to go or stay. If I got to the Cape, I could try to raise some money to finish the ship and put things right.'

Reaching into his breast pocket, King extracted several crumpled envelopes and held them out. Jackabo's heart leapt when he recognised the slanted handwriting.

Postmarked Aberdeen, Scotland, they were from his father, Francis Maclean. Judging by their condition, they had passed through quite a few hands before reaching the Cape.

Tears stung his eyes, and he bent his head to hide them. Two years without sight or sound of his family was a very long time, especially for a lad who had left home at the tender age of nine and a half.

'I wrote to your father, Charlie,' King said, darting a quick glance at him. 'I wanted to set his mind at rest, and your mother's as well, of course, to say you were safe – although, God's life, boy, I wasn't even sure of *that,* not knowing how you were faring.'

'So what did ye say, sir, about… about where I was?' Jackabo asked, the words sticking in his throat. 'Did ye mention –'

James King looked at his naval apprentice, hiding nothing. Not only had the boy been shipwrecked while in his charge, he had also been detained hundreds of miles from the nearest point of civilisation by a man whose reputation for mercy was negligible.

'I tossed and turned a few nights over it, I can tell you,' he admitted. 'In the end, I decided to trust to Providence. God help me, boy, but I intimated that you were safe and well. I had no reason to think otherwise.'

'Aye, captain,' Jackabo said, with a quick nod, 'that was the right thing to do. I *was* safe and well, here with the Zulus, so you told my folks no lie.'

'Thank God you were,' King said, gripping his shoulder, 'because what I'd have done if you weren't, Lord only knows.'

As soon as he could, Jackabo retreated to his quarters with his father's letters clutched tightly in his hand. I'll just read them one at a time, he promised himself. I'll begin with the most recent then make my way back to the start. That way I'll no' miss anything.

But once he was alone, his resolve crumbled. He read and read until the light gave way, then fell asleep with the pages of his father's letters spread out around him

Next day he received the 'few things' the Captain had brought him. New clothes and boots, bars of soap, scissors and penknives; pens with all sizes of nibs; bottles of different coloured inks; chalks, pencils and paints.

And books! A virtual treasure trove that included books for reading and writing in; books for drawing, with soft tissue paper between each page.

Like a squirrel with a store of nuts, Jackabo bore them off to his quarters. There he examined each precious thing over and again- smelling chalks and paints, unscrewing the tops from the bottles of inks, testing out the nibs and sniffing the intoxicating scent of printer's ink on books fresh from the printing machines of the Cape.

An hour or so later, King re-appeared. Jackabo looked up from where he was chopping up some worms for Hector. 'Great news, Jack,' he said, triumph glittering in his eyes. 'Shaka's granted us permission to look for a new site along the northern coast. In short, lad, we're going to create a rival to eThekwini.'

Flushed with success, he added, 'and here's more good news, boy. The King's also given Fynn a concession to hunt a few elephant along the Black Umfolozi. Excellent news, don't you think?'

From its perch, the bird eyed the mess of worms expectantly. Cocking its head to one side, it opened its beak as if to say something. King, oblivious to the raven's watchful yellow eyes, paced up and down.

'Fynn's done it, Jack,' he crowed. 'Shaka allowing an outsider to hunt in the royal grounds – it's unprecedented. I expect he'll be strictly limited in what he can hunt, but it's a start.'

So, Fynn, Mbuyasi, the finch, was on the brink of achieving what had drawn him to Zululand in the first place. The ivory tusks from Shaka's own hunting grounds were almost within his grasp.

Some time later that day, Shaka sent for him. Without warning, he sprang a surprising piece of news on him.

There was a new lean look to the Zulu ruler's powerful physique. His eyes were clear, the whites almost blue against his dark skin. They were also full of humour as he looked at the eleven-year old boy. 'I must have a special ambassador,' he said, 'someone who will carry my most important messages, someone I can trust with secrets.'

Twirling his forefinger, he announced, 'Since you can speak my language, and already are physician to the *isigodlo*, I have decided that you will be this person, Jackabo.'

He was stunned. Taking his silence as tacit agreement, Shaka beamed at him. 'The day after tomorrow you will leave for eThekwini. I have something very important to tell Febana ka ma Jo-ji and the white chiefs of eThekwini.'

His black eyes gleamed. 'But, I will not tell you what it is until you are ready to leave. It is still unknown, even among most of my own people.'

Two days later, Jackabo set out at dawn on the hundred and fifty mile journey to eThekwini. With him were a group of young warriors, an *induna* called Busa and three of the dogs James King had brought as a gift for Shaka.

Just before they reached the outer gates, something struck Jackabo as being very odd. When one of the dogs stuck its black and white snout back inside again to see what was keeping them, he was puzzled. How had the dogs got out?

It meant that the huge gates must have been open. Usually, they were kept closed until the sun was well up, because of the risk of scavengers or predators finding their way inside. Nobody would have dared leave the gates of Shaka's citadel unbarred all night – so who had left kwaBulawayo so early?

As they began to make their way down the slope to the river below, one of the hunters pointed to a trail of crushed grass leading in the same direction. Scouting around, his keen eyes missed nothing. He held up a hand. Five people passed this way, three women and two men.

Jackabo hesitated. It was probably nothing. Someone could have set out early to visit a relative or someone sick. On the other hand, though-

His curiosity won by a short head. He nodded to the *induna*. *Alone, go alone.* This way, only Busa and he would know who had left Shaka's citadel in the dawn light.

Ten minutes later, the *induna* returned, his legs glistening with dew and spattered with grass seeds. '*Ndlovukazi,* the Great She Elephant,' he said cryptically, close to Jackabo's ear. 'Also two women from the *isigodlo.*'

Jackabo was surprised. Nandi! He had no idea she had even been in kwaBulawayo. A sudden thought struck him. Could it be that, for some reason, she had stayed on after the day Shaka had summoned him to the *isigodlo* to tend to Mbusikazi? If so, wasn't it odd that he hadn't set eyes on her since, or even heard a whisper about her still being in residence?

And another thing – there would most certainly be male guards or servants accompanying the King's mother, because she would never undertake a journey, unprotected, especially travelling with young women from the *isigodlo*. 'And the men, who are the men travelling with them?' he asked.

Busa's lip curled. 'Two of those called the *Qwayi Nyanga.*' 'Did they see you?' The *induna's* look of disdain was proof enough that they hadn't.

Jackabo felt somewhat deflated. So, the mysterious women and their escorts were no longer a mystery. Only Nandi and her people then, setting out early for emKindini, most likely to escape the heat of the day.

It was Marie One who turned round and spotted Jackabo, the dogs and the group of hunters coming up behind them. Quickly, she darted forward and tugged at Nandi's cloak to get her attention, before whispering urgently. Other faces began to turn in their direction, and Jackabo recognised one of them as belonging to the moon-faced Malusi.

The Nkosikazi of all Zululand stood regally in the middle of the path, dew soaking the hem of her cloak; the stubborn lift of her chin a forceful reminder of her status. The morning sunlight fell on the sweet, oval face of someone standing just behind her. With a start, Jackabo realised that it was Mbuzikazi, holding a blanket around her shoulders to ward off the morning chill.

The tableau of mistress and servants remained strangely immobile. A breeze stirred the grass and plucked gently at the folds of the women's clothing.

As Jackabo came up to them, the girl, Mbuzikazi, put her head on Nandi's shoulder much like a child would do. This'll be the third time we've met in what might be called unusual circumstances, lady, Jackabo thought to himself.

He motioned for Busa and the others to go on ahead. He would catch up with them later. The men made a wide detour around the group, keeping their eyes carefully averted. Offending the King's mother, or casting a sideways glance at any of his women tended to carry severe penalties.

Marie One offered him a tremulous smile. Nandi stood with her feet planted firmly apart in an oddly defensive gesture. Although her smile was as generous as ever, her eyes were wary, as if scenting trouble.

'*Sawubona,* Jackabo! What good fortune to see you. Did Shaka send you? To bring a message perhaps, or wish us a good journey?'

Jackabo shook his head. '*Cha!* I have not seen him today. I am on my way to eThekwini to deliver a message. That's all.'

'So, he does not send you to look for me? You are sure of this?' There was a curious relief in her voice. He shook his head in response. In an instant, her ready smile flashed out at him, her dark eyes restored to their usual good humour.

As Mbuzikazi moved closer to Nandi, clearly anxious about his presence, the blanket around her shoulders slipped. Before she could cover herself, Jackabo caught a glimpse of an unexpected swelling in the smooth, brown belly that was revealed.

At the age of eleven, he knew precious little about the mysteries of women and birth. Where he came from, it was not a domain into which a male of the species, of any age, willingly sought entry. In fact, it would be safe to say that all men – including fathers, but excluding doctors – were firmly kept out of the way until well after the event.

If only Marie One hadn't tried to stifle a scream, and if Mbuzikazi hadn't panicked and frantically tried to cover herself up, then Jackabo probably wouldn't have noticed much out of the ordinary – except maybe to assume that she'd put on a little weight since the last time he'd seen her.

But Mbuzikazi slumped to the ground, visibly upset. Burying her head in her hands, she started to whimper like a lost child. Marie One fluttered around her, near to tears, while Malusi and the other member of the Qayi Nyanga cringed and moaned and covered their heads.

A hand shot out and caught Jackabo in a vice-like grip. Making shushing noises in Mbuzikazi's direction, Nandi dug her fingers into his shoulder.

'*Shaka must not hear of this! Do not tell him! No, no, no, he will kill us all, even myself!*'

The words spilling out of her were barely coherent. Gripping him tightly, she willed him to understand the magnitude of the situation. Patting and stroking his head in a fever of desperation, she tried to reassure him that all would be well if only he kept silent, and told no one. Jackabo found it hard to speak, even harder to look at the girl.

Breathlessly, Shaka's mother told him how Shaka had refused to provide her with grandchildren. Aided by Mbuzikazi, she had taken matters into her own hands. Once she had the girl safely within emKindini, no one would ever find out about the coming child.

Nodding his head frantically, Jackabo tried to reassure her that he wouldn't breathe a word to anyone. It was all he could do. With his heart pumping furiously against his ribs, he somehow managed to extricate himself from her pincer-like grip, swearing that his lips would remain firmly and permanently sealed.

As he ran hell for leather to catch up with the others, he kept thinking: If only we'd been earlier or later, or chosen another day altogether, our paths would never have crossed, then Nandi andMbuzikazi would have slipped off to emKindini, carrying their secret with them, instead of which–

The secret he now shared with them was as dangerous as a keg of gunpowder left too close to a blazing fire. Nandi's reactions had been totally unrehearsed – and very telling.

If Shaka ever found out the extent of her involvement in the begetting of Mbuzikazi's unborn child, she *knew*, yes, she knew in her heart what the outcome would be. Mother or not, Shaka would never forgive her for such betrayal and manipulation. *But would he really be driven to kill her?*

Jackabo's heart lurched. If even his own mother was terrified of Shaka discovering her duplicity, and finding out that a child of his existed, what chance did anyone else have of surviving his vengeance?

There was nothing else for it. From now on, all he could do was to keep his mouth shut and try to keep Nandi's explosive secret, just that. A great and terrible secret...

Twenty

J ackabo stopped dead in his tracks. Lifting his head, he sniffed the air. This time there was no mistaking it. The whiff of salt, brine and seaweed, the smell of the ocean, the sea, was unmistakable.

A few yards further on and he caught a glimpse of it; deep blue, green and turquoise, with a strip of brilliant white sands shimmering through a fringe of wind-bent trees. Racing off down the track, he headed for the dull thunder of the surf splintering and crashing on to the sands, yelling and whooping as he went.

Someone shouted after him, but he ignored them. Bare feet thudding on the ground, he ran with beating heart towards the one great continuum that had been part and parcel of his life since the day he'd first drawn breath.

Dazed by the smell and the sound and the sight of it, struck dumb by its sheer roaring presence, Jackabo flew over the dunes, the hot sand burning the soles of his feet and leaped straight into the surf, yelling like a dervish. The strong undertow knocked him off his feet and sent him flying headfirst into a soup of warm brine and grainy seaweeds.

For the next half-hour or so, among a melee of laughing, shouting Zulus and barking dogs, he capered and cavorted until he was exhausted.

Eventually, he dragged himself out of the water, stripped off his sodden clothes then collapsed on to the hot sand.

By noon the next day, they had entered the final phase of their long journey. The last breath of wind had died away and the skies had changed to a leaden grey. Leaves hung motionless and shrivelled in the heat and the shirring of cicadas and crickets rose up in deafening waves from the tall grass on either side of the track.

By the time they struggled up the old elephant trail and reached the top of the ridge overlooking the bay, it was late afternoon. Below them lay eThekwini, the greens and blues of the lagoon reduced to a uniform blue-grey, the islands and their bird colonies veiled by heat haze.

As they followed the winding elephant trail down the hill, even the chattering of the impish monkey colonies was stilled as man and beast waited for the on-shore evening breeze to bring some relief from the heat.

The woman appeared as if by magic out of the red glow of the setting sun. One moment there was only the darkening bush and the glinting lagoon, the next she was there, bathed in the strange bronze light.

Like some surreal ghost, she glided out of the dusk, and moved towards them in a fluttering mass of ruffles and wind-tossed ribbons, a little brown and white fox terrier bounding ahead of her.

Jackabo stopped dead in his tracks. A long hiss of surprise as the Zulus caught sight of her. The dogs took their cue from the sudden tension in the air. The collie cocked an eye in her direction, a growl starting in his throat, while the other dogs prowled around, stiff-legged, hair standing up along their backs.

It was the terrier's shrill yap of alarm that alerted her. Shading her eyes, she stared at them, long tendrils of hair whipping loose to stream Medusa-like around her head and shoulders, golden snakes in the dying light. The fox terrier backed up against her skirts and bared its teeth.

Busa hissed in Jackabo's ear. 'What is it? Give me the word, and I will take my spear to it!'

The unexpected sight of a white woman appearing out of the sunset was so mesmerising that when she spoke, Jackabo almost jumped out of his skin.

'Where in the world have you sprung from, young man?' she asked, as her cool blue eyes moved over him. 'Are you real, or will you vanish if I close my eyes?' Jackabo thought he could well have asked her the same question.

Suddenly, he was painfully aware of how he and the Zulus must appear to her: an unkempt boy in tattered clothes, and a handful of black men with spears betraying varying stages of suspicion, a pack of dogs snarling at their heels.

'No, ma'am.' he said. Remembering his manners, he hastily pulled off his hat. 'I'm no ghost. I'm called Jackabo.'

'Then good evening, Jackabo,' she said, her furled parasol aiming a deflective poke at the collie's inquisitive nose. 'I'm Elizabeth – Elizabeth Farewell.'

Jackabo nodded. 'Aye, we heard you had arrived on the *Anne.*'

As she swept the loose strands of blonde hair back from her face, the light caught the glitter of gold rings and ruffles of fine lace at her wrists. Close to, he saw she had a fine, strong jaw and a determined mouth. What was it John Cane had said about her? *"A lady with steel in her stays."*

Indicating his travelling companions, she asked, 'And who might these fine fellows be?' 'They're Zulus,' he replied, 'King Shaka's people.'

She made another feint at the dog's nose with the tip of her parasol. 'Ah, yes,' she replied, coolly, 'the native king who so angered my step-father.' Jackabo looked at her blankly. 'Johann Petersen,' she explained, 'perhaps you've heard of him? He came up with Francis on the first expedition, a year or two ago.'

A few more tendrils of blonde hair came loose and whipped around her head. 'Pompous man.' she said, smiling. 'Got everything he deserved. Came scuttling back to the Cape as fast as his legs could carry him.'

Now Jackabo remembered. *That* Mr Petersen. Fynn had a few tales to tell of the antics of the temperamental sixty-year-old hotel-keeper who had the dubious honour of being Farewell's father-in-law.

Jackabo couldn't take his eyes off her, as he tried to remember when he had last seen a white woman. Tiny pearl studs adorned her ears, and a delicate cameo brooch, the profile of a man wearing a top hat and high collar nestled in the ruffles of lace at her throat.

'So, tell me, Jack,' she said, fixing her cool eyes on him. 'Where do you live? It can't be here, at the bay, otherwise I would have met you by now.'

He nodded towards Busa and the others. 'I live with the Zulus, ma'am. I'm only here to deliver a message from the king.'

As she digested this latest piece of information, her grey eyes looked him over without blinking. Then her delicate brows drew together in a frown.

'You mean to say you actually *live* with the natives? Who else lives there, pray?'

Now it was his turn to stare. 'Zulus, Ma'am, it's where the Zulus live.'

There was a hint of impatience in her voice as she asked him, 'No, Jack. I meant one of your own kind, white people. Who else is with you there?'

He shook his head. 'No one... but Mr Farewell, Fynn and the others come quite often to *indaba* with Shaka.'

The cameo at her throat winked in the bronze light. 'Jack, aren't you afraid to be there alone?'

Alone? How could anyone be alone in kwaBulawayo? he thought, in amazement The Zulus were his friends. Hadn't he lived among them for more than a year now, and no harm had come to him, no hand or voice raised against him in anger, not even that of Shaka. He shook his head, his unruly red hair whipping about in the hot wind.

Elizabeth Farewell brought her hands together in applause. 'Splendid, Jack! A lone white boy, living happily among the savages,' she cried. 'I'll be able to dine out for a twelve-month on this tale alone! I shall prevail on Francis to bring this native king along to see me.'

Jackabo opened his mouth to say something then closed it quickly. Elizabeth, the lady with 'steel in her stays' obviously had little concept of the realities of life in the kingdom of the Zulus.

At that point, they parted company. She turned in through the open gates of Fort Farewell, where the rusting ship's cannon still lay in the long grass, while Jackabo, mindful of his manners, waited until she and the small terrier were safely inside.

Busa cleared his throat, hawked and spat into the dust before coming to the point with little delicacy. 'This woman *umlungu*, aiii, but she is a strange one.'

Jackabo turned to him, surprised. 'What do you mean? What's strange about her?' The young *induna* scratched his head in confusion. 'I saw no feet. I saw no legs. How does she move?'

Mimicking the dipping and swaying of the hooped hem of her dress and the smoothness of her walk, Busa asked in all innocence. 'If this woman *umlungu* has neither feet nor legs, what lies below the covering? Perhaps she is made with only a belly, like the snake?'

A low rumble of laughter came from the other Zulus. Jackabo joined in with them. As to how Mistress Farewell would react to being compared to a snake's belly, he could only guess!

Jackabo woke as the last twinkling stars were paling in the sky. Instead of continuing on the track around the bay as darkness was falling, they had elected to camp for the night before proceeding on to the main camp at the boatyard.

The whole feathered population of eThekwini seemed to be up and about, serenading the day. Yawning and scratching, he wondered if anyone was awake yet at Townsend.

Dawn was never the high point of Aloysius Biddle's day, especially after a night on the grog. He could almost hear the bosun's dulcet tones echoing across the bay. 'Avast with yer bleedin' racket, ye feathered bastids! Yer chirpin' an' cheepin's enough to waken the bleedin' dead.'

As soon as it was light, they would set off for the other side of the bay and the boatyard. Excitement gripped him. Very soon now, after a whole long year, he would see his old friends again. Ned, Aldred Williams, Biddle and Cookie…

Parting the thick bush surrounding the clearing, Jackabo peered out through the foliage. Behind him the Zulus waited in the shadows, holding back the dogs.

The half-built ship dominated the boatyard, rising like a Phoenix out of the solid log base on which the keel had been laid. The last time he'd seen it, almost a year ago now, the keel had only just been put down. Now, cradled in webs of scaffolding, the sleek lines of a sea-going schooner were beginning to emerge.

Perched up on one of the trestle walkways was his friend, Ned Camer-on. With a red bandana around his brow and stripped to the waist, he was busy hammering in nails. Aloysius Biddle, clad in a gaudy striped weskit, his swollen feet thrust into a pair of shabby ruby-red carpet slippers, was in the process of inching his way up a ladder. In one hand was a paint pot and brush, while the other was awkwardly holding on to the next rung while he decided whether or not he was going to manage to get his leg up.

Jackabo could tell from the back of his neck that the bo'sun wasn't in the best of humours. From past experience, he knew that particular shade of red meant that either his bunions were bothering him or he'd drunk too much rum the night before.

At the edge of the clearing, he spotted Hatton leaning over a table, intent on his plans and charts, his sandy hair ruffling in the breeze. The black and white collie at Jackabo's feet whined softly in his throat, impatient at the delay.

Hatton glanced up. Frowning a little, he looked around the clearing, as if wondering where it came from. On catching sight of the red-haired boy, he stared at him in disbelief, his eyes flicking rapidly to the spears of the Zulus standing behind him.

Jackabo put his finger to his lips, pointed at Ned, then at the bo'sun. Hatton's sunburned face broke into a grin. Cupping his hands round his mouth, Jackabo waited. Then just as the bo'sun's slippered foot reached for the next rung, he broke cover and raced out of the bushes, yelling, 'Yoo, hoo, Mr Biddle! It's Ja-ack! I'm ba-ack.'

It had the desired effect. Biddle swung round, eyes like poached eggs in his sun-reddened face. His right foot, having not quite reached the safety of the next rung, slipped and he lurched off balance. Hastily, he turned to face the ladder to save it from toppling, the fate of the paint pot hanging in the balance.

'Holy Mother o' God!' he swore as the ladder teetered. 'Bleedin' boy – you'll be the death o' me, you mark my words.'

Ned had spotted him. Clearing the scaffolding easily, he swung down the last few feet, whooping as he came. Grabbing Jackabo, he whirled him round and round so his feet were off the ground. He roared in his ear, 'How's the world with you then, Heelander?'

Jackabo held on to him for dear life. 'All the better for seeing you, Jamaica – but mind you don't let go of me!'

It was only when his feet were back on the ground that he noticed the vicious bruise on Ned's cheekbone. His eye was half-closed and swollen, the bruising around it fading into shades of yellow and brown.

'You should have seen it a few days ago,' Ned boasted.' A real shiner it was – purple, blue an' puffed out like a scallop.' Holding out his battered knuckles, he closed them into awkward swollen fists and jabbed the air in mock combat.

Ned's cocky grin didn't fool Jackabo for a minute. Beneath the bravado, his friend from Jamaica was angry, very angry, hoppin' mad, in fact

Busa and the Zulus came over to look at Ned's injuries. This was just what men did; fight with each other over an insult, cattle, a woman, or some other thing. The real source of their interest, however, was Ned's gold ear-ring and his shock of sun-bleached hair.

Jackabo sighed. Now, there would be even more questions about the strange ways of the *umlungu* issuing from the perennially inquisitive Zulus. Though he knew Ned was no below-decks scrapper, he was sure he could give a good account of himself, if the need arose. Ned didn't wait for him to ask who'd been on the other end of his fists.

'That damn Thompson,' he snorted, 'the man's got a gob on him that needed sortin'. Spiteful bastard's aye lookin' for someone to put his needle into – as if we didn't have enough trouble here already.'

Before Jackabo could question him about the last part, Hatton intervened.

'Right then, Biddle, tell Thompson we're off, and you make sure he leaves the yard shipshape.'

His grey eyes sought Jackabo's, and he smiled. 'It's good to see you, lad. From the looks of you, you're in fine fettle, which I'm pretty relieved to see.'

He touched him on the shoulder. 'There'll be plenty time for us to catch up. But before that, I reckon you and your mates must be hungry. No breakfast yet, I bet?'

'Talking of having plenty news,' said Ned with a grin. 'I'm sure Jack'll be real interested in hearin' yours.' A flush crept into the first officer's face.

'I'll tell ye later, Heelander,' Ned replied, his good eye sparkling with devilment. 'In the meantime, just you keep your eyes peeled for a certain shadow. You can't miss her, 'cos she'll be wearin' a man's shirt.'

Hatton said nothing, just hurried off up the path leading to the camp.

Although intrigued by Ned's jibing at the first officer, Jackabo's interest lay in another direction. 'What sparked off the scrap between you and Thompson, then?'

'Thought you'd never ask,' Ned drawled, 'and there's no need to enquire as to Thompson's condition. Let's just say the man in question will no' be climbing any ladders for a wee while.'

At that point, he seemed oddly reticent about what had actually started the set-to, but Jackabo knew that sooner or later he would find out.

As they wound their way up to the campsite, the mouth-watering aroma of roasting beef came drifting along on the breeze.

'Oh, man,' Jackabo moaned. 'I'd forgotten about Cookie's roast dinners. Lead me to it, Ned.'

Later that night, after polishing off yet more of Cookie's roast beef, they settled down round the fire, John Hatton bringing out a tot of brandy to toast his safe return.

The cook spoke up. 'Thee do look uncommonly well, boy, considerin' you're fresh from that hornet's nest,' he said, poking the fire with a stick. 'When we heard the news you'd been scuttled by that chief, I thought to meself "Well, so long, Jack, me old shipmate…"'

'Did ye think they'd kill me, then?' he asked.

Avoiding the boy's eyes, the cook shrugged his shoulders and sniffed.

'Dunno, lad. Who can say what'd be in the mind o' a savage like yon? Young lad like you, hair red as fire, no knowin' what he might get into 'is mind.'

Jackabo sensed an undercurrent among his shipmates, one he didn't particularly care for. Ned cut in, his eyes giving off blue sparks in the firelight.

'Any fool can see Jack's in the pink, fit as a fiddler's dog, an' in better shape than most of us here, hey, Heelander?'

Laughter flowed around the fire as the awkward moment passed. 'Aye, so,' agreed Biddle. 'The lad's back safe and sound. No harm done. You can put it behind you now, boy.'

Before Jackabo could stop himself, the words spilled out. 'But I'm no' here to stay. I have to go back. There's business to attend to...' His words tailed off.

'And just what business might this be, lad?' Hatton asked. Suddenly, Jackabo could see how it might look to the crew if he told them the truth.

A mere lad of eleven elected to a position of trust in the court of King Shaka, not only as Shaka's ambassador, but also as a trusted physician to the King's women? Who would believe it?

By a stroke of luck, it was then he caught sight of the 'shadow' Ned had been teasing Hatton about. What he'd said was true. The 'shadow' *was* wearing a man's shirt.

Jackabo's mouth dropped open. This was the second time in the last day or so that he'd been caught unawares by women appearing like ghosts out of the twilight. First, Elizabeth Farewell, and now, a mysterious African girl . . .

The shirt fell to just below her knee. It glowed white against her brown skin so that she resembled a pale butterfly fluttering in the dusk. Just then, a log shifted and tumbled in a shower of sparks. She froze like a young deer caught in the light of a hunter's lantern. A quick flash as her eyes met his before she melted away into the darkness.

Caught between Hatton's intriguing 'shadow' and the reality of his own situation, Jackabo realised he had some fast thinking to do.

Things at the bay had changed. It wasn't the same as before...but then neither was he. Experiences of the past year flitted through his mind; the fever, Ned's ghostly flute, wandering into the terrible boneyard; being spirited away to emKindini by Shaka's mother, struggling with a new language; following Shaka's army to war, the friends he'd made among the Zulus...

And that wasn't all, not by a long shot. A jolting reminder of the dangerous secret he now carried returned with all the force of a thunderclap. And there was also the message Shaka had sent him to deliver to the 'white chiefs' of eThekwini –

They'd never believe me if I told them, he thought. And who could blame them?

Jackabo had been back for a few days before he saw her again. There was little of the unwilling ghost about the girl this time. She appeared from behind the huts, tall and graceful, one hand steadying the earthenware pot on her head. Catching sight of him, she smiled. She was young, with a round soft face, her hair plaited close to her head in the intricate patterns favoured by Zulu women.

Although the blue, faded shirt she was wearing fell demurely to her knees, it only served to accentuate the grace and shapeliness of the body beneath it.

Water from the bucket had dribbled on to her shoulder and the wet cotton clung to one breast, exposing the outline of a nipple. Hastily, Jackabo tore his eyes away.

Later on, as they were stacking wood ready for the evening fires, Jackabo quizzed Ned about seeing her that day in full sunlight. 'Is that the shadow you were telling me about the other day, the one that got you the black eye?'

Cookie and Biddle had hinted broadly that the fracas between Thompson and Ned had flared up over the girl. It had, but not in the way they'd imagined.

'The very same,' Ned answered.

'How did she come to be living in the camp, then?'

'One day Hatton was out looking for new timber, up beyond the ridge an' over a ways. All of a sudden, he hears someone screamin' an' hollerin' fit to bust. Anyway, he goes to see what's amiss. The girl was in a sorry state, a deep wound on her head, soaked in blood she was, a man layin' in to her with a stick.'

'Mr Hatton wouldn't like that.' Jackabo said.

'Damn right there,' retorted Ned, 'so he steps up, grabs the stick and tosses it aside. A wrong is a wrong, in any colour or creed.'

'Was that the end of it?' he asked.

'Not a bit of it,' said Ned, stacking some more branches. 'By this time, a crowd had gathered. This wasn't the first time the old man – the girl's own father as it turned out – had beaten the lights out of her.'

Jackabo stared at him. 'You mean he was in the habit of doing it?'

'Too true, Heelander – accordin' to the friends, who by this time have appeared out of the bushes and are gathered around her. Hatton picks up his axe an' gives it a shake. No need for fancy interpreters. He meant business, an' no mistake. Then the father, a brave kind o' bastard, runs off – not wantin' to square up to him. Hatton, bein' the gentleman he is, tears a strip off his shirt an' binds up the girl's head to stop her bleedin' to death.'

Ned wiped his face with his bandana. 'Next thing, she wouldn't let go of him, holds on to him when he tries to leave, her eyes wellin' up with tears. Then a parcel of her friends starts pleadin' with Hatton to take her with him. By all accounts, the old boy had killed her mother, beaten the woman to death.'

'What else could he do?' Jackabo said, dumping an armful of branches on to the pile. Ned laughed. 'It's obvious the wiles o' women haven't come your way, yet!'

Jackabo said nothing, remembering how he had to contend with the Three Maries and their attempts to strip off his clothes to satisfy their curiosity.

'But how did the crew take it, when he brought her back here with him?'

Ned roared with laughter. 'I'll not go into what exactly was said, but it fair turned the place on its head, I can tell you. I mean, the first officer arrives back at camp with a young, near-naked gel in tow. It'd be a hard heart would look at her, all battered an' bloody, and say he was wrong. The sail maker had to stitch up her head to stop the bleeding. But Jack tars bein' what they are, Heelander, plenty was said in jest, I can tell you! '

'What about the father – did he make any trouble?'

Ned gave a snort. 'Hatton went back to the village and sorted things out. For the girl's sake, y'see Heelander, for her standin' in the eyes of her people. The old bastard got a mess o' beads and a couple of cows for the loss o' his daughter's services, pleased as anything with the trade-off.'

From the corner of his eye, Jackabo caught sight of a pale splash of colour moving between the huts. Ned grinned. 'Like a puppy dog, she was, followin' Hatton everywhere, even down to the yard.'

'The boatyard?' Jackabo blinked in surprise.

'Aye,' said Ned, 'the poor lass set about tryin' to lift the timbers and look to see how she could help him.'

'Don't tell me she works at the yard!'

'No, Heelander, I've a feelin' she might have been too much of a distraction. In any case, it's not women's work. John put her to work with the washing tub. Anything that pleases Hatton makes Dommana happy. And that's no lie.'

'What did you say her name was?' Jackabo asked, as he listened to the sound of singing and the slap, slap of water from behind the huts.

'Dommana,' Ned replied, 'her name's Dommana.'

After supper that night, Ned struck his forehead with the heel of his hand and said, 'Bye the bye, Heelander, I meant to tell you – but what with one thing and another, it clean slipped my mind.'

Jackabo cast a suspicious eye at him. 'Is it a good surprise or the other sort?'

'Now why do ye always think the worst of me?' Ned replied, as he headed for one of the storage huts. Burrowing beneath a pile of tarpaulins, he emerged, dragging a battered tin trunk after him.

'Ta-ra! Your sea-box!' he said, wiping a mess of spiders' webs away. 'We found it a few months ago, high and dry in the sand, tangled up in some weeds an' mangrove roots.'

Jackabo could hardly believe his eyes. His sea chest! It was a bit the worse for wear, a few dents and the odd spot of rust here and there on the blue paint, the white lettering a bit chipped to be sure, but still readable.

C R MACLEAN
FRASERBURGH
SCOTLAND

He stared at it, a lump rising in his throat, as he remembered the day his father had printed his name and details on it with a small, finely-tipped brush.

After some gentle persuasion with a crowbar and some lamp oil, they managed to prise open the lid. 'Is that no remarkable, it finding its way back to me after all this time?' Jackabo said, pulling out things he had long since forgotten about; cream pantaloons and buckled shoes, trousers, knitted sweaters and a pile of vests, underdrawers, shirts and stockings for all seasons.

Ned held up a pair of red flannel body-warmers. 'What in hell's teeth are these for?' 'You mind your own business!' Jackabo cried, wrestling the offending garments from his clutches. 'My mother made these for me to wear in cold weather.'

Ned hooted in laughter, 'Cold weather, eh? Did you no tell her ye were sailing for Africa, then?'

Ignoring him, Jackabo delved to the bottom of the trunk. Apart from a thin dribble of seawater, the kist had lived up to the reputation guaranteed by the ships' chandlers in Aberdeen.

Eventually, he found what he'd been looking for. A handful of sea shells from Sandend, and the drawings and little letters given to him by his brother and sisters.

A lump rose in his throat as he gathered them together. Wisely, for once his friend from Jamaica said nothing, just put a hand on his shoulder.

Next day, a message came from Farewell. An urgent meeting had been called *"to discuss the matter of general discipline at Port Natal."*

With a stab of guilt, Jackabo thought of the message he had been sent by Shaka to deliver. What with the excitement of seeing everyone again, Ned's fight with Thompson, meeting Farewell's wife and hearing Dommana's story – half of the time he'd either forgotten about it or wondering how, where and when he could bring up something everyone at Townsend might prefer not to hear about.

But it was time. Shaka's message could wait no longer.

The atmosphere in the meeting hut could best be described as venomous. The camp had obviously split into two factions. Lieutenant Farewell and his supporters were seated on one side of the table, while arranged on the other were the representatives of the shipwrecked mariners.

Gone was the Lieutenant's previously shabby look. His wife had seen to it that her husband had been restored to his true estate, that of an English gentleman. From his tailored jacket down to the fine leather boots, every stitch he was wearing looked new. The aroma of bay rum wafting its way round the table was an evocative reminder of a lost world where a man with a few coins could go into a barber's shop and obtain, not only a close shave, but also have his beard, moustaches and finger nails trimmed, as well.

Cane had taken up a position on Farewell's right, his arms folded over his massive chest. On his left were Halstead and Ogle, eyeing the proceedings from below the brims of their sweat-stained hats. Facing them across the table were Hatton, Biddle, Thompson and Ned. Of Fynn, there was no sign.

Looking around the grim faces, Jackabo's spirits drooped. The stifling heat, the hard, grinding labour and constrictions of life at the bay were taking their toll on everyone, and the hut was rife with underlying tensions.

Even to his young eyes, it was clear that the resentment was mainly focused on one man. Looking at the hard, unforgiving eyes and clenched fists of some of the sailors, there was the strong possibility that sections of the elements present might lose control of their tempers.

Henry Fynn chose that moment to breeze in, as large as life.

'Mornin' all,' he said, sweeping off his battered straw hat. His gaze swept around the room. With studied indifference, he sauntered across to join Hatton and the sailors.

The irony of his action was lost on no one. Fynn was, or should have been, Farewell's man. He'd been the first to sign up with him, first to step on to the shores of Zululand and the first to meet the Zulus and make contact with Shaka.

Suddenly, before the meeting even had a chance to begin, the square outside erupted into a melee of angry shouting and scuffling. Farewell turned round, frowning, then got up and strode out to investigate. No one else moved.

Long minutes dragged by. Farewell swept back in again. It was not for nothing that Lieutenant Francis George Farewell had been mentioned in dispatches and awarded naval honours during Bonaparte's long-runnng war. Ignoring the sweat trickling down his brow, he took up his place at the head of the table.

Straightening his shoulders, he put his hands behind his back, and announced, 'Gentlemen, I'm afraid I have some rather serious news to impart.'

The silence was laden with tension. *What now?*

Farewell cleared his throat. 'It seems our native interpreters have been guilty of a flagrant breach of discipline. Not too put too fine a point on it, they've assaulted a Zulu woman – and not just any woman, either. Not only was she the wife of one of Shaka's chiefs, she was also a princess in her own right. Apparently all hell has broken loose.'

Someone swore, the obscenity rattling round the room like a loose cannonball. Farewell removed the gold-rimmed eyeglass. Looking down the length of the table, he announced, 'they're calling for all white men to be killed, along with the perpetrators. I'm afraid we now have what could be termed 'a situation.'

A stunned silence followed. He added softly. 'I should remind you, gentlemen, that rape is a crime that demands instant death here. Shaka's beside himself with rage, which is quite understandable.'

Chairs scraped back as men got to their feet in protest. Jackabo kept his head down and busied himself picking at a scab on his knee.

Someone demanded. 'Weren't the bastards with King and Isaacs at the time? Surely they'd have put a stop to it?''

Farewell shook his head. 'Well, no. The bold boys had gone off on some ploy of their own, came across the woman, started pestering her. When she started to raise a fuss – well, they'd been drinking, and things got out of hand. They held a knife to her throat then held her down. Jakot sent a messenger to let King and Isaacs know about it. They were some miles away, hunting, at the time.'

'So, what's the situation?' Fynn asked. 'Does Shaka have the bastards under lock an' key?'

Farewell stared into the hot sunlight beyond the doorway. 'As to that, I couldn't say. After that, unfortunately, things took a turn for the worse.'

'Christ!' someone swore. 'How much worse can they get?'

'As soon as King heard the news, he sent a message to the pair ordering them to high tail it back here to the bay. Under no circumstances were they to return to kwaBulawayo.'

'King and Isaacs, where are they now?'

Farewell swayed gently on the balls of his feet. 'Naturally, they returned to kwaBulawayo to plead the case with Shaka. Any other course of action would be construed by him as either cowardice, or compliance with the swine.'

Fynn spoke up. 'Why do I have the feeling there's more?'

Farewell shot him an acid look. 'Unknown to King, the bloody interpreters ignored his orders, still drunk, I suppose.'

He let out an exasperated sigh. 'In short, the stupid bastards headed straight back to kwaBulawayo. Where they are now, or whether they're still alive, is a matter of conjecture.' Muttered oaths greeted the news.

'How did we get to hear about it?' asked Fynn.

'Jakot sent runners to warn us,' Farewell replied. Everyone in the room was busy with their thoughts, trying to work out how long it had taken the runners to make the hundred and fifty mile journey to the bay. By now, anything could have happened back there.

'Which means,' Fynn added slowly, 'that James King and Isaacs walked into an even bigger hornet's nest than expected.'

He whistled loud and long, the expression on his face saying it all.

This was as good a time, or as bad a time as any, Jackabo thought, to pass on Shaka's message. At least the major players were all in one place.

Ignoring the hubbub of angry voices around him, he got up onto his chair, and stood there with his arms folded. Gradually, the talk dribbled away into silence. Curious heads turned in his direction.

'What is it, Jack, lad?' Hatton asked, 'it must be mighty important to forget your manners.'

'Aye, it's important enough,' Jackabo replied, standing his ground 'It's what I was sent here to tell you, but then with one thing and another, the time was never right.'

'And you think *this* is the right time?' snapped Farewell, his eyes angry blue sparks. Fynn cut him short. 'Let the lad speak, Farewell.'

Everything went quiet. No one, with the exception of James King, had ever openly challenged the Lieutenant's authority.

'Given who the lad lives with, and in the light of recent events, don't you think we should hear what he has to say?' Fynn added, coolly.

With a curt nod, Farewell motioned for Jackabo to continue. He stepped down off the chair and took a deep breath before beginning what he wanted to tell them.

'Shaka's planning to move the Zulu court from kwaBulawayo across the

Tugela – to this side of the river.' He waited a moment to allow the message to sink in. 'He sent me here specially to tell you what his plans were before you heard it from anyone else.'

'*This* side of the river?' Fynn echoed. 'And just how close to eThekwini is he going to build this new place, may I ask?'

Jackabo considered the question for a moment. 'It's to be on the banks of the Mvoti River. A day or two from here, I think – about twenty-five or thirty miles away.'

A babble of voices broke out. 'What's it about? Why's he doin' it?'

'So he can spy on us, no doubt –'

'Aye, well, there's no need to move hisself and his whole bleedin' court to do that. We're well reported on and have been from the start.'

Farewell stared at him through the monocle. 'And when will this event take place, Jack? Did His Majesty see fit to let you know?'

Jackabo delivered the final piece of news. 'Shaka's already ordered his people to start work. By the time the rains set in properly, most of the Zulu court will have moved across the river.'

Someone muttered, 'Jesus, Mary an' Joseph! Even if we escape getting' slaughtered for a rape we ain't done, we'll still have 'is Majesty breathing down our necks!'

During the ensuing fracas, Jackabo slipped quietly away, his duty done. Busa and the others would be waiting for him along the old elephant road heading out from the bay. It was time to go home.

By the time the meeting broke up, the first sliver of a new moon had risen. There was no wind, and the leaves of the bamboos hung unmoving in the humid air.

Fynn stepped into the bushes to relieve himself. As the stream of urine hit the ground, he let out a long sigh of relief. Hitching up his baggy trousers, he pulled his belt a notch or two tighter.

This last trip had left him feeling low. His insides had been playing up. Added to that, his men had been a pain in the arse. A few fights had broken out, so he'd had to give one or two of them a good hiding.

His mind drifted back to the meeting and how it had ended. Farewell had called the boy back and given him an urgent, hand-written message to

238 *Isabella Bleszynski*

take to Shaka without delay. In it, he had taken full responsibility for the actions of the interpreters. Whether it would save their bacon or not, only time would tell.

Fynn cleared his throat and spat into the dust. And then there was the question of Shaka's move south.

No one could keep a large, well-trained army endlessly occupied with routine training. The army feared him, to be sure, but even the effects of the most gruelling night marches didn't last forever.

Ten years ago, Shaka had taken the rag-tag, ill-disciplined young men of the tiny Zulu nation and, with all the passion and fire in his soul, had drilled and schooled them into the most feared warriors in all of Africa.

And for this, they revered him, idolised him.

Yebo, Nkosi, Fynn thought, I know what you have created, but I fear it might well turn out to be your downfall.

Shaka had taken a mixture of tribes and peoples and welded them into one great nation, a people with one heart, one allegiance – and one Nkosi.

The Zulu kingdom was a decent one, with an inherent morality running through every aspect of life. *Ubuntu* they called it – the great capacity for generosity towards humanity espoused by Shaka's people.

Industrious and intelligent, bounded and shaped by the laws of their ancestors and Shaka's swift justice, many of the Zulus looked on him almost as a god. A terrible, punishing god, it had to be said, but also one who ultimately had their best interests at heart.

Shaka was the heart and soul of their nation. And, because of all these things, they looked to him, often in fear, but mostly with trust, for the next step forward.

Fynn drew in a deep breath of air, savouring its salty taste. He knew of only one thing beyond the Tugela River of any possible interest to the Zulu king. *The open road south…*

It led to Chief Faku and the amaPondo, one of the few large unconquered tribes still beyond the influence of the Zulus. Their traditional lands were vast, and stretched almost to the northern borders of the British-held Cape Colony.

Moving the Zulu court south, across the Tugela, would leave Shaka free to move at any time of the year. Unhindered by the annual summer floods, which kept them confined beyond the River Tugela, nothing would then stand between him and Faku.

Fynn sighed, deep in his throat. Once the amaPondo were conquered, Shaka's influence would stretch from beyond Delagoa Bay in Mozambique all the way to the borders of the Colony. *And then what?*

The first stars had come out above the lagoon. Fynn was within a hundred yards of his compound, and he could already see the flicker of cooking fires through the trees. The air was spiced with the enticing aroma of roasting beef.

He quickened his step. A dog barked and a woman's voice shushed it quiet. Life's good here, he thought, I don't want it to change.

Twenty-One

Shaka sat motionless in the carved chair, his anger ruthlessly held in check, the lines of his body stiff with hostility. He had kept King and Nat Isaacs waiting for more than an hour in the heat and under the watchful eyes of his elite bodyguard, the Fasimba.

With his lips set in a tight line of disapproval, Mbopha, his major domo, stood looking down his long nose at them. James King deliberately kept his eyes focused on Jakot. Although the message being channelled through the Xhosa interpreter was chilling in the extreme, the man still managed to keep his tone neutral while conveying an accurate account of what Shaka was saying.

As the full implication of Shaka's diatribe began to sink in, King became aware of the tremors running through Isaacs' body next to him.

'I should have you all killed…' Jakot translated, his eyes fixed on the ground. 'Masters must control their servants, or suffer the same fate. These yellow dogs of yours are not fit to live. If you have no stomach to do it yourself, I will gladly kill them for you.'

James King winced. *Execution! How in hell am I going to handle this?*

Jakot's left eyelid fluttered slightly as he looked directly at him. Whether it was plain fear, or something else, King had no way of telling. The interpreter carried on, his face expressionless.

King motioned for Jakot to let Shaka know he wanted to speak. The monarch's forefinger snaked upwards in agreement. King cleared his throat.

'In umGeorge's land, we have the same law as you do for this crime. And yes, they are sometimes executed for it. But all I ask is that you let us deal with these men, for they are the subjects of umGeorge, as we are. They will pay a heavy penalty for their crimes and I can promise you they will never be allowed to set foot outside eThekwini ever again.'

A long silence, then Shaka's voice cut through it, an edge of impatience in the tone. 'So you will not have them put to death?'

King hesitated for a fraction too long. A fist thumped the arm of the carved chair. 'Hah! It is as I thought!' Shaka spat out. 'The white man is too merciful. This is why his servants behave as they do, believing nothing will happen to them.'

A dutiful chorus of 'Yebo, Nkosi' arose. A casual flick of his fingers and the Fasimba guards stepped forward to surround Isaacs and King.

Shaka got to his feet, towering over them. 'Go now. I shall send for you when I have decided on this matter.'

King glanced sideways at Isaacs, and saw that his face had turned several shades whiter. Seeing him begin to sag at the knees, King took hold of his arm.

'Get a grip on yourself, for God's sake, Nat!' he muttered. 'Every move is being watched. Keep walking, lad. All's not lost. Didn't ye see the glimmer in his eye when I mentioned King George? Magic words, Nat, my boy, magic words.'

Jackabo arrived back in kwaBulawayo in time to see King and Isaacs being led away by the Fasimba guards. A moment later, Jakot brushed past him with barely a word, muttering in Xhosa as he went.

He gazed after them in bewilderment. Where were the Fasimba taking them? And Jakot – where was he going at such a lick?

Sensing trouble, he began to run, heading for his own quarters, Farewell's urgent letter to Shaka more important than ever. Aye, the Lieutenant's pretty shrewd, Jackabo thought. Writing Shaka a letter on such braw paper will flatter him no end – and what he says in it even more, maybe.

Farewell had told Jackabo how impressed Shaka had been with the thick vellum of the formal land grant he'd presented to him for his approval, also the rituals that went with its signing; the thumb-print signatures, the witnesses and the solemnity that had defined its value.

'You know what to do, Jack,' the Lieutenant had said, his pale eyes drilling into him. 'Offer it to him as a valuable document – which, under the circumstances, it *damn well is!* Maybe it's the only chance we've got to save our necks – so do it right, boy, exactly the way I've told you.'

Jackabo found Shaka alone, pacing up and down like a caged lion, his formal leopard skin cape and elaborate head-dress tossed aside.

At the sound of footsteps, Shaka wheeled round, scowling. On seeing who was hovering in the doorway, the scowl changed to a smile. He beckoned to him to come in, as if glad of the distraction.

After questioning him on how his message had been received at iThekwini, his face changed from approval to a scowl of displeasure

'Eh, Jackabo, have you heard of the bad thing that has happened with the yellow dogs belonging to Kingi and Febana ka ma Jo-Ji?' Jackabo nodded and sat down cross-legged on the floor.

'It is very difficult for me,' the king of the Zulus said, resuming his agitated pacing. 'The chiefs look for justice. They demand that I should kill all the white people because they were the ones who brought these *nyale* to our shores.'

He snapped his fingers. Then, echoing his mother Nandi's past sentiments, he said, 'The Zulus are a bad people, Jackabo. That is why I have to kill some of them from time to time. If I did not, they would cease to fear me. Then they would turn against me and say I am not worthy to rule them.'

Shaka sat down heavily in the carved chair. His eyes were red and strained as if he'd been sleeping badly or looking into too many smoky fires.

'I do not wish to kill the white people – not *any* of them,' he announced, as casually as if he were discussing the latest hunt. Shooting a brief glance in his direction, the slight flicker in the black eyes made Jackabo's stomach lurch in fear.

Oh, God! It had never occurred to him that he might be included among those the chiefs wanted to see dead. He dug his nails into the palms of his hands, acutely aware of his heart thumping against his ribs. A long silence followed.

'How happy umGeorge must be to be King of the white people,' Shaka said, with a sigh. 'I feel you are a good people, a strange and wonderful people. If I understood writing, I would send a message to umGeorge and tell him all I feel, and what I think.'

Jackabo stared at the man who, a few moments earlier, had calmly admitted that he frequently disposed of some of his subjects to keep their respect. Realising that his mouth was hanging open, he closed it quickly. Shaka pointed at the sketchbook Jackabo had brought with him. Jackabo's heart began its crazy thumping again.

Farewell's letter! He had almost forgotten about it!

All he could do now was to trust the instincts of the tall, cynical Lieutenant who had entrusted him with delivering it. Opening the book, he took out the long parchment envelope he'd placed inside to protect it from the heat and dust on the long, hot journey. Handling it carefully, he held it out to Shaka.

'For you, Nkosi, from Febana ka ma jo-ji,' he said.

Shaka's eyes roved over the elegant, scrolled writing and the creamy vellum. Taking it from him, he raised the envelope to his nose and breathed in its scent. After closely examining Farewell's elegant handwriting for a few moments, he traced the letters of his name with his forefinger. Then he motioned for Jackabo to open it and read what Febana ka ma jo-ji had to say.

Jackabo's imperfect Zulu was strained to the limit as he tried to convey exactly what Farewell wanted the Zulu king to know. By the time he'd finished, he was in a lather of sweat and anxiety, his hair plastered to his forehead.

Shaka nodded, seemingly satisfied. Putting a hand on Jackabo's head, he patted it a few times then wiped the beads of sweat from his forehead with a broad thumb.

'*Ngiyabonga,* Jackabo, you have done well. I understand what Far-well wanted me to know.' Resuming his pacing, he said, 'Go now. I have much to think about.'

Keen to escape, Jackabo slipped the letter on to Shaka's chair and made for the door. Before slipping out, he shot a glance over his shoulder.

Shaka's broad, muscled back was towards him. Something in his stance reminded Jackabo forcibly of his mother, Nandi. Her face, as he had last seen it, floated in front of his eyes, and he saw again the long forefinger pressed to her trembling lips and the fear and desperate pleading in her eyes.

His stomach gave a jolt. *Och, God…and there was that too, the terrible secret they both shared.*

The call for him came early next morning. By the time he reached the royal residence, King and Isaacs were already there, the Fasimba standing over them. Jakot was in his usual place, betwixt and between the two factions.

Shaka swept in, courtesy itself, smiling and hoping they had slept well. He obviously had, for his skin gleamed with health and his eyes were clear. He came straight to the point, with no preamble.

'My people call for justice. For the violation of a woman, our laws are clear. Death is the punishment. Taking account of all things, I have made my judgment.'

The black eyes were hooded and watchful as they scanned the faces of the white men in front of him. A master of manipulation, he waited for several long moments before speaking.

'Since the foul dogs who committed this offence are under the command of the *abelungu*, some of my people are calling for you, their masters, to pay for it with your lives. However, I have denied them this.'

Someone nearby gasped, the sound almost strangled in their throat.

Jackabo silently prayed that Jakot had translated the last part correctly. Shaka's voice was as smooth as silk as he went on.

'How could I answer umGeorge if it came to his ears that I had killed his people because of the acts of a few yellow dogs? He would not look on me kindly and would demand to know how his people could be held responsible for the acts of such vermin. He would surely send his soldiers here. So, for these reasons, I have told my chiefs I will not have you put to death.'

Shaka rose effortlessly from the impressive carved chair, a supreme actor on stage before a captive audience.

'However, some amends must be made to my people for this grievous crime. So this is what I have decided. My *indunas*, councillors and others have been persuaded to accept my judgment.'

"Persuaded" wasn't a word that came to mind when considering Shaka's usual methods of getting his own way, Jackabo thought. The warrior king's voice was hard and imperious as he continued.

'Beje of the Kumalo must be found and dealt with. For too long, this running hyena has been a thorn in the flesh of my people, hiding in the forests and refusing to come out and fight like a man.'

A crackle of anger coloured his next words. 'The *umlungu* and their weapons must flush him out.' A broad forefinger stabbed in Nat Isaacs' direction. 'I have decided you will be the one to do it. Order your men to proceed to Ngome. Seek Beje out and deal with him.'

Every eye in the place turned to Isaacs. The colour drained from the eighteen-year old's face, and, for a minute or two it looked as if he might have stopped breathing altogether. His lanky body sagged like a doll with the stuffing trickling from it.

King swiftly stepped into the breach and offered to go instead, but Shaka would have none of it.

'*Cha!* ' he snapped. 'You will too busy with the building of the *umkombe*, and Mbuyazi must hunt for more elephant before the rains come.'

Stepping forward, he clapped Nat on the shoulder with a hand that could splinter bones. 'Find the Kumalo troublemakers, then it will be finished. All will be forgiven. Justice will be done.'

Jakot's face remained blank and expressionless as he translated. King stepped in front of Isaacs to shield his obvious distress from Shaka's eyes and give him time to compose himself.

'We must be clear what it is you are asking us to do,' King said, the colour high in his face. 'If Mr Isaacs succeeds in finding Beje, what must be done with him?'

The eyes of warrior King glittered, hard black pools of mocking humour in a stern face. 'Kingi, you know the ways of war. Beje must be killed, his people destroyed and their villages burned. Then Kumalo will be no more. *Impi embovu... a red war, a war to the finish* – the Zulu way, my way.'

There was no mercy in the eyes observing Nat Isaacs and James King, no glimmer of compromise, just the implacable will of a man holding all the aces.

Shaka had been clever, devilishly so, Jackabo thought, as they made their back through the gates. He could have solved the matter with a flick of his hand and had them killed. Instead, he had seen an opportunity to rid himself of several problems at the same time, all in one brilliant move.

How to free the *umlungu* from the expected sentence of death, and still placate his people over the rape of the wife of a Zulu chief? Shaka had mollified those that needed to be mollified, by offering them a different kind of justice – not by killing a handful of white men, which he'd persuaded them would solve nothing – but by using their skills and their guns, he would put an end to the long-running war with the Kumalo and bring years of fruitless bloodshed to an end.

And, along the way, also create another supreme victory for Shaka, the warrior king, he added, trying hard not to feel a huge sense of relief.

What was not discovered until some time later was why he had seen Jakot racing off at such a lick the moment he'd entered kwaBulawayo, at the same time as James King and Nat Isaacs were being escorted, under guard, back to their quarters after their bruising meeting with Shaka.

What no one knew was that the ever-resourceful and quick-witted Xhosa, realising the implications that the rape of the Zulu princess would unleash on the unsuspecting white men, had quickly seized the two drunken miscreants the minute they'd stupidly staggered back in through the gates of kwaBulawayo instead of making their way back to the bay as they'd been ordered to by King and Isaacs.

Unknown to anyone, including Shaka, he had secreted them, bound and gagged, in an out of the way hut where someone had recently died. Because of the fearful stigma, and its location close to the outer fence, his decision had been a wise one, for he knew full well the hut would be given a wide berth by the superstitious Zulus.

Added to which, once the duo had slept off their drunken spree, they had utterly accepted that, if they didn't co-operate and keep quiet, Jakot would either slit their throats himself or hand them over to Shaka.

Once the hue and cry had died down, he had arranged to leave open the gates of kwaBulawayo just long enough to allow them to make their escape in the dead of night and head off as best they could towards the bay.

'Long time I owe Kingi for my life,' he said later when the story came out.

'This time my turn to repay.'

Twenty-Two

Langani's eyes began to close. Gradually, his head sank on to his chest. The smoke from the fire writhed upwards; thin spirals of vapour seeking to escape into the night sky. Some time before taking *lesedi,* the potion that would help to induce a trance state and aid his powers of meditation, he had thrown the bones.

They lay scattered before him in seemingly random patterns. Langani knew each of them intimately – who they belonged to, how old they were and how they had come into his possession. Here, for swiftness and cunning, were the knuckles of monkeys and baboons; for strength, the spinal bones of leopard, cheetah and lion, the small skulls of snakes and birds for lightness and secrecy.

Lying slightly apart from the others were a few rounded knobs of bone, brown with age, smooth and glossy with use. These had come from old enemies, long battled with and finally overcome, their skills and knowledge now part of Langani's own.

The tips of his fingers rested on a small, but select group. Aah…here were the most powerful of them all; human bones; parts once clothed with flesh and linked by nerves, sinews and muscles, the steady flow of a heart's blood pumping through them.

The bones lay where they had fallen, waiting patiently until their mysteries were unravelled. Long moments passed by. Gradually, the pattern of Langani's breathing altered as his pulse and heart rate began to slow down.

Deep within the place where he now found himself, the spirit that belonged to Langani recoiled in fear and astonishment. The things he saw around him were both frightening and hard to understand. This was nothing new, for there were always dangers in the place where time and the worlds of the spirit and the physical merged and became one, even if only for a brief time.

The fluttering of white wings came closer and beat around him until he could feel the fierce, hot breath of their passing. There appeared to be neither sea nor water around them, so he did not think they represented the great sails belonging to the vessels of the white men, those he had seen many times before in his dreaming.

Perhaps they were some other kind of ship, though what they carried and or what drove them, he did not know. Then the scene changed.

Bearing down on him out of the mists were creatures he found it hard to believe could ever exist outside of a nightmare. Hot winds and plumes of smoke came snorting down their long noses and their glossy coats were foam-flecked and heavy with sweat. Sounds, frightening sounds accompanied them; the sharp crack and rattle of thunder, puffs of smoke and tongues of fire; the screams of men wounded and dying…black men, white men, their blood stinking in the heat as it spilled from their broken bodies.

The smoke from the fire coiled around him once, twice and then three times then writhed silently upwards, carrying its secrets and the frightening visions with it.

While Langani rocked to and fro, sweat dripped down his face. His instincts told him there was some link between the frightening images and the strangers who had recently come to the land of the amaZulu. This had long been at the root of his long-standing distrust of what they respresented.

Seeking to understand, he began to repeat the ancient incantations that were a part of his *isangoma* heritage. Frantically, he searched for the key, the key that would show him more –

An unexpected movement close by caused his eyes to snap open. The smoke from the small fire in his hut billowed inwards and was sucked up towards the space in the thatch. A disembodied figure seemed to materialise in the doorway. When he saw that it was that of the *umlungu* child, he of the hair like fire, he was overcome with curiosity.

His sudden appearance was very strange indeed, and especially here, in the secret dwelling of an *isangoma*, high up on a mountainside.

A boy like this, with his child's body and soft heart, surely could pose no threat either to the mighty king Shaka, or to Zululand itself. Langani had known this for a long time. So, could it be that he was a messenger, an omen of what was to come…or something more?

When Langani's eyes flicked back to the doorway, he saw that it was empty. The boy known as Jackabo was no longer there. Only the lighter patches of starlight beyond and the ticking of cooling embers in the fire remained.

Fully awake and clear-headed, his trance state at an end, the diviner stretched out a trembling hand and swept up the sacred bones from where they lay scattered on the ground. Then he returned them safely to the bag made from the skin of the lion that had killed his brother many years ago.

Smoothing out the patch of earth in front of him with the flat of his hand, he wiped away any trace of the patterns that had been made by the throwing of the bones.

Miles away from kwaBulawayo and the mountainside where the diviner Langani lived, a group of hunters rose at first light, as was their custom. After taking a pinch or two of snuff, one of them came over to where the boy lay wrapped in his blanket, still fast asleep.

'Time to wake, *mdodo*,' the man said, as he yawned and stretched. Smiling at the muffled response, he strolled over to where one of his fellow hunters was stirring the embers of last night's fire.

The rains were late. Every day became more oppressive and sultry than the last. By mid-morning, every patch of blue in the sky would have retreated behind a soup of grey clouds, the sun a pitiless yellow eye sucking life and colour from the world. Best then, to be on their way while it was still cool.

By the time Jackabo and the hunters reached the banks of the Mvoti River, the sun was nearing its highest point in the sky. Waves of heat shimmered on the horizon, distorting the line of scorched hills in the background, while mirages of rippling water danced and wavered across the sun-baked land.

Suddenly, there it was, directly ahead of them. The new capital of the Zulu kingdom – or what it would become one day, very soon now. A surge of speculation and excitement ran through the hunters.

At first glance it looked even larger than kwaBulawayo. Perched on the low lying curve of hills above the river, the half-built skeleton of Shaka's new capital reared out of the raw, red earth, its massive oval shape dominating the landscape. Miles of fencing had been erected around its perimeter and pair of huge gates stood wide open at the lower end.

Inside, it was a hive of activity. The virtual army of people that had been despatched south some time earlier, now sweated and laboured to finish their work before the rains set in properly.

The heart of the Zulu kingdom had begun its shift south.

'Jackabo! Hau, Jackabo, come and lend us a hand!'

Moments after passing through the gates, Jackabo heard his name being called, as people who recognised him greeted him on every side, the rhythmic chant of work songs ringing out as men sweated and strained in the heat, carrying out the multitude of tasks needing to be done.

Wood carvers were working patiently in the shade of awnings set up to shield them from the fierce sun. Under their skilful hands, hardwoods such as ebony and mahogany were turned into stools, chairs, bowls and all manner of decorative items.

Jackabo stopped to watch weavers binding mountains of tall elephant grass and reeds into bundles. The beautiful thatches of the beehive shaped huts were created with skill and flair, each one uniquely different from the other. The more skilful of the weavers would also put the finishing touches to the interiors of the more important structures, such as those belonging to Shaka.

As he moved on, he passed men perched on top of half-completed huts, manhandling the curved framework of the roof into place, while others hurried by, balancing long bamboo poles and bundles of grass netting on their heads.

A familiar face caught Jackabo's eye. Sigonyolo's mother waved to him from where she was sitting in the shade with a group of women, their nimble fingers creating the intricate, patterned strips of beads that would decorate the massive central posts of Shaka's residences.

While the hunters went in search of friends or family, Jackabo padded up through the empty heart of the new citadel, whistling as he went.

Shaka's magnificent, high domed dwellings stood in splendid isolation. As yet there was no sprawl of servants' quarters or *isigodlo,* although areas had been clearly been marked out for their construction. Even half-finished, the Great Hut drew the eye, its imposing size and beautiful cascades of thatch superb examples of Zulu skill and innovation.

At the top of the slope, an expanse of mature woodland had been left untouched, for Shaka's habit was to take a stroll at sunset every day. he liked nothing more, especially at the end of a long day full of the tiresome, but necessary regular meetings with his chiefs and councillors, than to walk in the cool shade among growing things.

Jackabo picked his way over a patch of rough ground towards what would soon become Shaka's seat of power. Hovering on the threshold, being careful not to step over it, he took a look inside. The intricate, high-arched doorway permitted only a brief patch of sunlight to enter what would soon become the holy of holies, one of the places where the mighty Shaka would live.

The smell of new grass, reeds and fresh earth wafted out of it. As yet, there was no hint of the sweet honey smell of beeswax and smoky tapers, but that would come later. Shrouded in shadows, the vast interior exuded an air of mystery and silent majesty.

Suddenly, a blur of white came swooping out from somewhere high up among the huge crossbeams supporting the thatch. It flew over his head in a flutter of wings, forcing him to duck. Heart thundering, Jackabo stepped away quickly from the threshold. Though reason told him it was probably only a hunting owl, another deeper instinct reminded him of the Zulu belief that the spirits of their ancestors took up residence on the threshold of a new residence, close to their living descendants.

Maybe the Nkosi's *amadhlozi* are already here, he thought. If they're anything like him, I'd better not get on their wrong side…

The heat was oppressive. Sullen waves of shimmering air rose up from the hard-baked earth. As he turned away, a sudden wave of tiredness swept over him. It had been a long time since sun-up, and even longer since he'd had much to eat. He looked around for somewhere to sit down.

About a hundred yards away he spied a *mkhula* tree, its wide, spreading branches forming a tempting pool of shade. Jackabo padded over to it.

Letting his pack slide off his shoulders, he took off his hat and tossed it aside. Spreading out his blanket, he sat down on it and propped himself up against the base of the tree, his legs stretched out before him. Tiny chinks of sunlight strayed through the dense foliage and dappled the ground around him

This is the place the Nkosi will likely choose to *indaba* with his people and his elders and councillors. He'll hold court here, and sing too, if the mood's on him. A small inner voice responded: *Yebo*, and very likely he'll clap his hands for the slayers to dispatch some poor devil careless enough to drop a soap dish!

Yawning, he pushed the thought away. For the moment, the *mkhula* tree was just an ordinary tree, standing on the edge of things. Sliding down into a more comfortable position, he pillowed his head on his pack and tipped his hat over his face.

Even the bees seemed to have stopped buzzing. The smell of resin and the sap of growing things rose from the warm earth. Drowsy now, he brushed an ant from his bare arm, closed his eyes and allowed his thoughts to drift.

How long had the tree had stood there, he wondered. How many seasons of rain and storms had it seen, how many nights with the full moon shining down on it?

It was still a young tree; somehow he knew it was. He imagined its roots burrowing below the earth, rustling deeper, seeking moisture, space and room to grow. He yawned again and eased his head into a more comfortable position. Images began to flow slowly and peacefully through his mind; trickling water; the smell of earth and rising sap; small creatures burrowing through leaf mould; layers of rocks and stones, down to places where there was no light and the earth was older than time.

When the first jagged flashes of lightning came, he could see them clearly from behind his closed eyelids. Maybe going to sleep below a tree with lightning about wasn't the safest thing to do…

Och, well, he thought, a person has to trust in something. His lips curved in a grin. It would be a pretty brave bolt of lightning that would dare to strike a tree destined to shelter Shaka of the Zulus.

When Jackabo next opened his eyes, he found himself looking into the face of a man sitting cross-legged a few feet away from him. His hair was long and braided into plaits which lay on his shoulders like coiled snakes. The dark eyes observing him were young, surprisingly so, the lids smooth and showing no trace of age. Blinking, he struggled to sit upright. Cautiously, he glanced over at the man.

When Jackabo's eyes met his, those of the stranger betrayed no flicker of surprise. Even half-awake, this struck him as odd.

Usually, when people met him for the first time, the colour of his eyes and hair surprised and intrigued them. This man, however, showed no such reaction. This, to Jackabo's way of thinking, meant that he must have seen him before somewhere – and up close at that, so the colour of his eyes or hair was no longer a surprise, something to '*tch*' or peer at.

Two things suddenly leapt into his mind, one following close on the heels of the other. They *had* met before! Now he remembered – it had been on the sands of eThekwini, on the day he'd been washed ashore after the storm and wrecking of the brig. *And there was something else…*

Although there was nothing in his appearance or dress to alert him as to the nature of the man's calling, Jackabo knew, without a shadow of a doubt, the identity of man sitting opposite him.

He was the mysterious diviner known as Langani. He'd heard his name whispered around the campfires, although very few had claimed to have actually seen him in the flesh. Why he was so sure of this, he had no idea, but every instinct in his body told him he was right.

Twenty-Three

Townsend Boatyard, eThekwini

S ome thirty miles away, the mood among the heat-stricken exhausted crew members was sullen and tense. A short time later, when the shaft of a broken chisel slipped, almost severing two of McCoy's fingers, it was the signal for the trouble that had been brewing to finally erupt.

Amid the shouting and swearing that broke out, somebody had the good sense to run and find Henry Fynn so McCoy could be attended to. Luckily, he was still in his compound and hadn't set off on his planned hunting trip down the Wild Coast.

First, the bleeding had to be staunched and the wounds cleaned, then a length of sail twine boiled and sterilised. Finally, a draught or two of neat rum was poured down McCoy's throat so the sailmaker could sew the lips of the jagged wounds together.

After McCoy's oaths had died down to a drunken mumbling, the rest of the crew downed their tools and refused to go back to work.

An ugly mood emanated from the group of men surrounding Hatton, the first officer. Violence thrummed in the air, a hairsbreadth away from spilling over.

As usual, Thompson was the ringleader. Openly contemptuous of Hatton's attempts to keep things on an even keel, his stocky frame was rigid with hostility. Jerking a thumb over his shoulder at the half-built vessel, he snarled, ' See that! It's a bleedin' disaster, that's what it is. It's jinxed, I tell you! What that heap o' shit has cost us in blood, sweat an' aggravation ain't worth mentionin'. '

A flood of catcalls and oaths broke out in response, not all of them in agreement with the man's comments.

Seventeen-year-old Ned Cameron elbowed his way to Hatton's side, a heavy hammer clutched in his fist. Shooting a warning glare at the older, more seasoned Thompson, he tried to reinforce Hatton's authority by appealing directly to the men.

'Don't let this tub o' lard rile you, lads. God knows thing are bad enough already. No offence to McCoy, poor bastard, but to put Mr Hatton here on the block for an accident, which it was – well, it just ain't the act o' rational men, and ye all know it.'

Thompson jostled up against him, his face inches away from Ned's.

'Aye, and who else is responsible, I ask ye? Officers – that's who, bleedin' liability, every last one of 'em!'

Ned's eyes struck blue sparks. Jabbing stiff fingers into Thompson's ragged shirtfront, he said, 'Talking o' liabilities, Thompson. You're a fine one to talk. Don't recollect *you* comin' up with any ideas as to how to improve matters.'

Wafting a hand below his nose, he added, 'An while ye're at it, take your pig's breath away from me, before I spew.'

'An' if I don't?' sneered Thompson, trying to regain the upper hand.

Ned's drawl was slow and deliberate. 'Well now, you sow's arse, I think ye should cast your mind back to what happened the last time your gob got carried away with itself.'

Guffaws ran through the crowd. Thompson flushed, his face reddening. He hadn't forgotten the humiliation he'd received at the end of young Cameron's fists, either. Muttering below his breath, he turned on his heel and angrily shoved his way through the group of men.

One of the seamen spoke up. 'At this rate, we'll be here till Doomsday. Nigh on two years now, we've patched an' made do. Mr Hatton, them tools is buggered, and that's the truth of it. Same as Thompson, I sez…what's to be done?'

Before Hatton had a chance to reply, another gruff voice butted in. 'It ain't only the bleedin' tools, though is it? Have a keek at me legs, here.'

Biddle, the bo'sun, stepped forward and rolled up his shirt sleeves then his ragged trousers. Angry red boils and open, suppurating ulcers peppered his forearms, calves and ankles.

'Bleedin' insects, the bites won't heal,' Biddle said, mournfully. 'Man-eaters, they are, me flesh bein' so tender. All of us is feelin' poorly, and that's no lie.'

Hatton accepted what the bo'sun had just said. In fact, he'd been feeling below par himself; one bout of fever after another, and now a constant ache in his lower back. Looking at the faces around him, none were free of the signs of strain or illness.

Something had to be done, and soon. Another incident like today – and there was no knowing what could happen. All it took was for a chisel to slip, a man to gash his hand – petty grievances get added to the mix, then before you know it, it escalates into real violence. It could have easily ended up with someone getting a knife in the ribs –most likely myself, he thought.

The first officer had seen more than one mutiny in his time. He knew only too well what could happen when men were pushed to the limit. He had no great inclination to look on the results of another – especially not here, on this remote coast of Africa, with no way out, and a half-built vessel their only option for survival.

The only thing was – what could be done about it? It was time he had a serious talk with James King, before anything else happened.

Two days later, in the early morning, the scaffolding below Ned's feet gave way and he dropped like a stone through the broken planking and fell some twenty feet on to the ground below.

Seeing him lying there with an arm and a leg twisted awkwardly below him and blood trickling out of his mouth, there was a moment's frozen silence. Then Townsend boatyard erupted into bedlam.

In the end, Hatton had no choice but to draw his naval revolver and threaten to shoot the next man who lifted a hand in violence against anyone else.

By the time Jackabo and the hunters arrived at the bay later that morning, heard the news and made their way to Fynn's place, Ned had regained consciousness.

Once again Fynn had been sent for. After dozing Ned with a few drops of laudanum, he organised a stretcher and had him carried to his own compound, rather than up the steep hill to the camp site. Afterwards, he'd straightened out the broken arm and leg and bound them up with splints and bandages, so Ned had no option but to stay where he was, flat on his back.

Luckily, he seemed to have suffered no serious injuries, apart from the broken arm and leg. His ribs were badly bruised, but not fractured. The blood trickling from his mouth had been the result of biting his tongue, or so Fynn hoped.

'There's still a chance you might have ruptured something in your innards,' Fynn warned him, 'so you'll have to stay here with me, just in case you start bleedin' from the mouth again.'

After going cross-eyed trying to measure the state of his tongue, Ned stuck it out for Jackabo to assess the damage.

'I have to admit it's no' a bonny sight,' Jackabo replied, screwing up his face. 'It's dark red and purple where your teeth bit into it an' twice its size. I don't know how you're going to manage to chew your grub, though.'

'With any luck, it'll shut his gob for a while,' Fynn said. 'As for victuals, he'll have to dine on gruel till his damn tongue heals.'

Ned's tongue might have been out of order, as well as an arm and leg, but his right foot wasn't. When Fynn bent down to exit the hut through the low doorway, his bare foot caught him on the backside, knocking him flying.

'You won't be laughing, my lad, when you get the bill for medical services rendered,' scoffed Fynn, wiping the dust and chaff off his person. 'Booting the doctor in the arse isn't included in the fee. That's going to cost you extra!'

That night, Jackabo found it hard to sleep. The ground was hard and lumpy, and something, probably a rat, kept rustling about in the thatch above his head. Every so often, one of the dogs would scratch or bite at fleas.

Every time he closed his eyes, he saw Biddle's suppurating ankles. Very few of the men were in good shape. McCoy, out of action with his damaged hand, Hatton poorly withn a pain in his back – even the invincible Fynn was suffering from what he descriptively called 'the skitters.'

'It's this bloody rain,' he'd said, gripping his belly, 'or maybe it's the pellets of rat shit everywhere.'

And now there was Ned, lucky to be alive. By all accounts it had been no accident. Thompson was the likely suspect, everybody knew it, although there was no proof, and nobody had seen him lurking. Unfortunately, his influence had spread to a few other malcontents among the crew, so it could have been any of them.

Jackabo lay there, fretting. Things must be really bad, he thought, if Hatton had to threaten to shoot one of the crew. Two men were already injured over the heads of it, while Ned's falling from a broken walkway had clearly been a planned act of revenge for his backing of the first officer and his put-down of Thompson.

As if sensing his unease, the black and white collie called Fergus whined in its throat, and beat its tail gently against the ground, the whites of its eyes luminous in the darkness.

The sound of the surf filtering through the tangled screen of windswept scrub provided a soothing background to what was developing into a tense situation.

Shaka was sitting on a flat boulder watching James King, his keen eyes taking stock of the slumped shoulders and the weariness stamped on the man's face. He said, not unkindly, 'I have given you my best answer, Kingi. The road you think to travel with your people is hard, very hard. You would end up food for the hyenas, your bones picked clean by ants.'

Without preamble, he came straight to the point. 'Some of your men of the sea are old, and know nothing of this country and the strange nations who live here. Is it not so?'

Reluctantly, King had to agree. When it came to handling anything on the high seas, experienced old seadogs like Biddle were worth their weight in gold. On dry land, and especially out there in the wilderness of

African bush, it would be a different matter altogether. The Zulu king's hard assessment of what he'd discussed earlier with him could not be denied.

Shaka rose off the mossy boulder, the wind fluttering the plumes of his head dress and pointed north to the long, curved beaches dwindling away into the haze.

'If you follow the sea this way, you will come to bad country; swamps, disease and the risk of predators, even in the waters. My own people prefer not to risk its dangers. Although the other way is longer, it will take you to where you want to go just the same.'

Panther-like, he paced to and fro. 'Some of my Zulu people have already travelled to the lands of the bearded ones you call Portuguese. You may know this already, Kingi.'

King nodded. He hadn't forgotten Shaka's connections with Portuguese traders. Bluntly, he again stated the current problems bedevilling his crew at eThekwini regarding the interruptions affecting the boat building.

'If we do not get the tools and supplies we need and sufficient medicines, we will not be able to finish the *umkumbe*. Soon, some of my crew will either be dead, or too weak to work.'

Subtly, he had tried to emphasise the importance of being able to complete the ship – not only for the ultimate survival of he and the crew, but also as regards what he suspected Shaka's own agenda and plans concerning the schooner might be.

Shaka waved an impatient hand. '*Yebo,* all this I know. But tell me, Kingi, will you be able to find all you need in the land of the Portuguese *umlungu?*'

King ran his tongue over his cracked lips. 'Yes, I believe so.'

Shaka clapped his hands. '*Hau!* Then it is settled. Someone must go to Delagoa. The *umkumbe* will be finished – and all else will proceed.'

'The Portuguese also build ships, so there will be tools and everything we need to finish the ship,' King explained. 'As for medicines and other supplies, I can bring back what we need.'

The Zulu king shook his head. '*Cha*, Kingi, you will not be the one to travel to Delagoa. You must stay here. If you go, your men may cause more mischief. Then I will have to deal with them.'

King stared at him. Oh, my God, he thought, his heart sinking, he already knows about the strife at the yard! I've long suspected he has spies at eThekwini, reporting back to him.

'But who – who will go to Delagoa?' he stammered, tripping over his words. 'Isaacs is away fighting the Kumalo, Mr Hatton has been ill. Even Mbuyasi is not strong enough to make such a journey at this time.'

Feverishly, he ran over the names of the crew in his head. Ned had a broken leg and arm; McCoy's hand was shattered and infection had set in. None of the other crew was fit enough, or reliable enough, to undertake such a journey; that left only Biddle and Alex Thompson, the first mate. Biddle was out of the question. Not with his corns and bunions. That left only Thompson.

King stifled an oath. *Thompson!* The bastard was capable of anything, he'd probably abscond and swill the money down his gullet in some Portuguese grog shop. By chance, his eye fell on Jakot who had been standing quietly by while translating. He stared hard at him.

The interpreter spoke English and he'd already been to Delagoa Bay with the British fleet a few years ago, so the chances were he'd also picked up some Portuguese.

'*Cha!*'

The single word issuing from Shaka shrivelled King's brief hope that perhaps the Xhosa might make it to Delagoa and back in one piece. The man's uncanny, he thought, how in God's name did he know what was on my mind?

King saw by the narrowing of Shaka's eyes that it would be unwise to pursue the matter of Jakot. So he asked the only question left to ask.

'Then, Nkosi, who do you say must go to Delagoa?'

Two pairs of eyes were fixed on him. The more dominant of the pair held the amused smile of one regarding a somewhat backward child, while in the other, the gold segment in the left eye gleamed like that of a feral cat.

For James King, it was an odd moment. It seemed as if the three of them – the Zulu king, the Xhosa, and he, the man from North America, were poised on the brink of a moment of some significance.

Feeling as if he was standing on the edge of a steep cliff in a howling gale, he summoned up his courage and asked the warrior king one more time:

'So, Nkosi, who do you say must travel the long road to Delagoa?'

On the following day, Jackabo met up with Shaka's hunting party a few moments after they'd turned in through the top gates leading to the royal residences.

On catching sight of him, King's face turned a strange shade of grey. Suddenly, he looked old and crumpled, his eyes a washed-out blue. When he spoke, his words tumbled over one another, painful to hear.

'Jack – it's the only way, lad. Who else is there left who's fit to go to the Portuguese? But what if something else happens to you? Your father, what would I tell him?'

He swayed on his feet and was forced to lean heavily on his musket for support. Jakot's face was blank, unreadable as he reached out a hand to steady him. Shaka frowned, not understanding King's stumbling words. The interpreter muttered a hasty response.

Shaka nodded, then issued a curt command. 'Leave us now, Jackabo. First Kingi must rest. Hlambamanzi will come for you later.'

Jackabo had no idea how long he stood there after they moved away. Some part of him had already understood what lay behind James King's stumbling, agonized words.

A sense of disbelief washed over him. Mozambique? In his mind's eye, he could see the miles of dusty bush and winding tracks stretching ahead all the way to the unknown horizon.

After that came the fear, something that trickled and keened through him like grey smoke. It lingered for a while, then was gone.

By the time Jakot came to fetch him it was almost sunset. Jakot said little during the short walk to where Shaka and King were waiting for him, although the man's kindly hand resting on his shoulder spoke volumes.

When King began to call him Charlie, Jackabo knew things were serious.

'God knows, what with one thing and another, you've had enough to contend with in such a short time,' he said, soberly, a pulse beating erratically at his temple 'Your father would be mighty proud of you, Charlie…'

At the mention of Francis Maclean, King's words tapered away. His voice quavered then cracked. 'How can a lad like you be expected to undertake such a venture? Even with warriors looking out for you, as Shaka's promised, it's not right, it's just not right. I'm the one who should be going, but it's just not possible.'

He ran a hand distractedly through his hair. 'Better we give up the whole idea, let every man Jack of 'em take his chances. We either head north to Delagoa, or travel south as far as Algoa, sign on aboard a ship, and have an end to it – those that make it, that is.'

South, as far as Jackabo was concerned, didn't have a good ring to it. Travelling north was better. Shaka's influence spread far beyond the borders of Zululand. It meant they would be under his protection – for most of the way, anyway.

Some instinct made Jackabo's eyes shift to the silent presence in the carved chair. The black eyes held an unmistakable gleam in them, watchful, calculating even. While it was true they held a certain human compassion for the boy standing in front of him, there was also something else – the hint of challenge.

You are my ambassador, Jackabo. Who else must travel to the land of the Portuguese to save your people –and the umkumbe?

A jolt of almost savage excitement began in the pit of Jackabo's belly. In the eyes that met Shaka's, there was also a message. *Nkosi, I have not forgotten.* Shaka beckoned him to come closer. Jackabo padded forward.

Close to, Shaka's eyes were not as black as might be expected. They were deep brown with flecks of gold in the irises, the whites clear and strong. Lingering in their depths was an unspoken question along with a hint of calculation. *Will you be as strong as you need to be? And what of your spirit –is it big enough, strong enough?*

The thrawn heart of twelve-year-old Charles Rawden Maclean rose to meet Shaka's challenge. His silent response was much the same as it had been the last time he'd stood up to him, straight from his sickbed, feverish, but defiant.

If it's a fight you're after…I'll not let you see how feared I am, but I'll do it all the same. It was answered by an infinitesimal nod of the regal head and a slow but meaningful blink of the heavy-lidded eyes.

Turning back to James King, Jackabo said, 'I'll go to Delagoa. I'll come to no harm, cap'n – there's few would meddle with Shaka's warriors.'

An answering spark in Shaka's watchful eyes confirmed what Jackabo had long suspected – that the king of the Zulus understood the language of the white men better than anyone suspected.

And anyway, sometimes there was no need for words, for spoken language.

After leaving Shaka and King, he ran to his own quarters, desperate to be alone for a while. Once there, he went back over the events of the last few hours in some detail. Until he came to the final moment or two…

What really astonished him out of all that had transpired was the flash of emotion that had briefly crossed Shaka's face at the end. Undeniably, it had been a flicker of pride. And it had been for him – the twelve-year-old known as Jackabo, the stranger in the tribe.

A few days later, he travelled back to the bay with James King to be "kitted out." That meant a new bedroll, extra clothes; a woollen pullover, boots, and several pairs of socks, a warm jacket from the captain. Hatton added a small axe and a sharp knife in a leather scabbard. In case of emergencies, there was a stock of medicines from Fynn's depleted stores, as well as *muthi* for sunburn and insect bites.

Rolled up in the toe of a sock were the last of the Captain's gold sovereigns. It was placed in a leather pouch, which he would carry around his neck. With it was a list of what was needed as regards spare parts, ship's essentials, tools and medicines, detailing size, quantity and expected cost.

'Hey, boy!' Fynn said, coming upon him, as he was packing. 'It's about time you learned to use a firearm. As long as you remember which end's which, and can use it without blowing off your feet or hands, you'll be all right!'

And without ado, he took him into a clearing away from prying eyes and taught him the basics of ultimate survival – of how to defend himself.

As soon as everything was in hand, Jackabo slipped quietly away and set out back to kwaDukuza. Also included in his pack was James King's Navy revolver and supplies of powder and shot wrapped up in oilskin to keep them dry.

He said no goodbyes. The memory of another parting between himself and his shipmates still carried too much sadness. Better to slip away in the dawn light while everyone was still asleep.

As soon as they topped the ridge and left the bay behind, a queer kind of excitement began to run like a fever through him. Am I not off on one of the grandest adventures that ever was, he thought – and with an *impi* of Shaka's warriors to watch my back?

One goodbye, however, he couldn't refuse. The night before he was due to leave, Shaka sent for him. After he had inspected everything and examined the knife and the small axe and the revolver, he picked up the Bible that John Hatton had given him, and examined it curiously.

Indicating the darkening sky, he asked, 'This is the book of your Baba Phezulu, the one you say is up there?' Jackabo nodded.

Shaka frowned. 'What does it say in this book concerning long journeys in the lands of strange nations?'

The story of Moses and the children of Israel sprang instantly to Jackabo's mind. 'Tell me,' the King of the Zulus insisted.

When he began with the wars between the Egyptians and the Israelites, Shaka's face lit up with interest. However, Israelites being taken prisoner, and marched into slavery, produced a frown of disapproval. Knowing his views on the taking of prisoners, Jackabo hastily moved on to where the child Moses was rescued by Pharoah's daughter and raised as a prince in the house of his enemies.

God closing the waters of the Red Sea over the pursuing horsemen and the horses and chariots of the Pharoah met with his approval, and he nodded and clapped his hands in agreement.

And when the God of the Israelites spoke to Moses from the burning bush, Shaka accepted it without query. Being led across the great wilderness of sand by a pillar of fire by night and a cloud by day produced no trace of disbelief in him, either.

After he'd finished, Shaka asked, 'Was this story from your land, Jackabo?' Surprised, Jackabo answered, 'No. It happened here in Africa, far away in the north, in the place where the land ends and the sea begins. This is where it happened.'

Shaka stared at him, the light of discovery in his eyes. 'And if I travelled there, I might also find these great sands, where there is no water, only sand and where strange animals do live?'

'*Yebo.*' Jackabo said, 'but it lies many moons away, too far for anyone to walk to in one lifetime.'

Shaka pondered on this for a time. Then, changing the subject, he asked: 'Of how many seasons are you, Jackabo?' When he held up the fingers of both of his hands, then added two more, humour crinkled the corner of Shaka's eyes.

'When I was like you,' he said, 'I dreamed of being a warrior, a soldier – not a herder of cattle. Every passing moon made me more impatient. But I had lessons to learn. To be a warrior, other battles must first be fought, and those are not won with spear and assegai, but in the mind.'

The King of the Zulus leaned forward. 'Use first your head and only a little of your heart. This way you will always win.'

Servants came with lit tapers then retreated as quietly as they had come.

'The *induna* Langalibalele will go with you,' he said, after they'd gone. 'The warriors I have chosen will be as your own brothers. Runners have been sent ahead with orders to give you food, shelter and whatever you need. Nothing will be refused.'

He touched Jackabo on the shoulder as if to make sure his words had taken hold. 'Though your body is not yet grown, your spirit is great. This is what I believe.'

Picking up his pack, Jackabo turned to leave. Beyond the arched doorway, the eye of a moon that was almost full hung in the night sky.

As he was about to go, Shaka called out to him. Silhouetted against the glow of the tapers, the face of the warrior king was inscrutable in the half-light.

'Your Baba Phezulu,' he enquired, softly. 'Will he walk with you as he did with the others, those who travelled across the great sands?'

Jackabo smiled back with the undimmed confidence of all of his twelve years. '*Yebo*, Nkosi.' he replied, 'Baba Phezulu will walk with me.'

The *induna* Langalibalele was young, perhaps a few years older than Fynn. Wearing a knee-length *umutsha*, the fringes of soft cow tails wound round his upper arms signified his leadership.

Jackabo's eyes went to the leather thong around his neck, the one that bore the ritually blessed *isiqu* representing those he'd killed in battle and then to the puckered scars on his shoulder that told another story.

The *induna's* cool glance swept over the boy. Then he smiled. '*Sawubona*. Are you ready to walk, little brother? Only a short way, a stretch of the legs – is that not true, comrades?'

Good-natured bantering broke out as the men began to get ready. Langalibele indicated that Jackabo should take his place alongside him at the head of the group of twenty or so lean young warriors.

A stir of excitement swept through the people who had gathered to see them off. Jakot pushed his way through, an anxious look on his face.

'*Sala kahle, Jackabo,* stay well. I will look after everything until you return-even that black devil of a bird you keep in your house.'

A quick exchange of glances, a hand lifted in farewell, then he was gone, swallowed up by the crowds.

Once they were outside kwaDukusa, their followers began to fall away.

A gaggle of young boys ran alongside them for a while then they too turned back. Jackabo wondered briefly about his friend Sigonyolo in far-off Nkwalini and wished that he could have come with him.

The sun began to inch its way above the horizon. A long-horned gazelle leapt out of the bush closely followed by the buck, panic in their wide, flaring eyes as they swerved away.

Someone called out. 'You are safe enough, little brother, little sister. It is too early for hunting. Go back to bed.' High-spirited laughter rippled up the column.

Jackabo glanced sideways at the *induna*. Langalibalele had been very astute, he thought. By placing him in front, the *induna* had set the men's pace to the boy's stride, not the other way around. Portuguese territory was a long way off. If he tired too quickly, he would become seriously exhausted and then would hold them back.

After a mile or so, Jackabo looked back the way they'd come. The immense sprawl of kwaDukuza 'the place where people get lost' lay wreathed in the morning mists, its thatches mellow in the early light.

How long would it be before he saw it again? They might be away two or three moons, but it could be as long as four. A final glance, then he slipped back into place beside Langalibalele.

The leather pouch carrying the last of James King's gold sovereigns was a comfortable weight around his neck. Also inside was the all-important list of items needed to secure the survival of the crew of the *Mary*.

As he walked along, Ned's old song came to mind, the one he'd played on the flute while they'd been on that first trek to kwaBulawayo over two years ago. Jackabo began to whistle the melody of the bittersweet sailors' shanty. '*Oh Shanandoah, I long to see you…away you rolling river…*

Somewhere behind him, a fine, deep bass voice picked up the melody and carried it on. Then another joined in, and then another, until the trilling melody of Jackabo's whistling became a full-throated symphony.

Many miles stretched ahead, all the way to the land of the Portuguese and whatever awaited them there. The first rhythms of the journey had begun.

Twenty-Four

In the light of the full moon, the outlines of the flat-topped acacias stood out black against the star-dusted sky. Serene and hauntingly beautiful, it was a night to be remembered. The chill of the winter season was still to come, but tonight the air was warm and still.

Half a mile away, a lioness was teaching her half-grown cubs to hunt. Pausing in the moonlight, she flicked her tail from side to side then reared up to sharpen her claws on the trunk of a tree. The animal yawned widely, showing teeth that were white and very strong. Rolling over to scratch her back on the rough ground, she squirmed with pleasure, her belly pleasantly full after the recent kill.

A sharp sound, a wailing cry floated on the still night air. In one smooth movement, the lioness came off her back and into a low crouch, the end of her tail quivering. The cubs stopped halfway through their game of tag.

The cries came again, stronger now.

The lioness raised her head and sniffed the air. Her keen instincts told her the sound came from a newborn creature, but of what kind she was not sure.

After a while, the wailing ceased. Rumbling in her throat, the animal straightened up then called to her young. Padding silently across the moonlit clearing with her cubs gambolling at her heels, the lioness blended into the shadows and disappeared.

On the hillside overlooking the valley stood the place called emKindini, the home of Nandi, the Queen Mother of Zululand.

The furtive rustles and whispering that had been going on for some hours now within the confines of the private residence finally came to an end. The young woman Mbuzikazi had just given birth and was being tended by the midwives who had been secretly brought to emKindini by the Nkosikazi.

The woman with silver-streaks in her hair bent over the squirming bundle in her arms. Fierce pride and tenderness was etched on her strong features. Drawing back the swaddling cloth in which the newborn child was wrapped, she examined every inch of him, smiling when she saw how strong he was.

When the small face creased in a scowl, it took her breath away. Turning him over on to his belly, she saw how the hair curled into the folds of his plump little neck. Tears of joy spurted into her eyes. 'Aiii, it is himself all over again,' the child's grandmother crooned. *'iZulu nempela* – the Heaven and none other.'

The child's starfish fingers closed over hers and tried to guide her knuckles to his mouth. Holding him against her breast, she sang softly to him.

Soon she would hand him over to Nobagwegu, the woman chosen to be his wet nurse. To outsiders, the baby would be only the child of a maidservant. That way he would remain safe, his true identity concealed from those that might do him harm.

With Mbuzikazi his birth mother, and Nobagwegu, his surrogate mother to care for him, the child would live a safe and happy life, protected by their vow of silence and fearful obedience to his grandmother, Nandi, Nkosikazi of Zululand, the woman now holding him in her arms.

Many miles away, the diviner Langani woke with a jump in the smoky darkness, his heart pounding against his ribs. For a moment, he wondered if a bolt of lightning had come upon him in his sleep for the taste of blood was in his mouth, salty and metallic.

Had it been the cry of a wounded animal he'd heard, or perhaps the screaming of someone with bad dreams?

He lay for a moment looking into the darkness. From its perch on the crosstrees of the hut the rooster ducked its head and looked down at him, its round, golden eye fierce and unblinking.

Langani rose and pulled aside the goatskin flap covering the doorway. Outside, all was still and quiet. The full moon rode high, flooding the dried-up riverbed below with its silvery light.

His keen eyes searched for a telltale sign of movement. He listened, straining to pick up any unusual sounds, but there was nothing. It was quiet, unnaturally so, perhaps. The African night was very rarely silent, even in such a remote place like his sanctuary, halfway up a mountain.

His feeling of unease persisted. A frown marred his smooth forehead.

Lately, frightening images of things he had not been able to put a name to had been appearing with increasing regularity. Each time, they grew stronger and more detailed. This *umhlolo*, this bad thing, was unlike anything he had dealt with before. And as far as he could see, it had nothing at all to do with the white men now resident at eThekwini.

This was different; it was dark and brooding, with jagged teeth like those of the crocodile. And it was gathering strength. The *amadhlozi* were restless, beginning to express their feelings of disquiet about what was coming.

Somewhere out in the bush, a lioness roared and was answered by a male, some distance away, while closer an owl hooted mournfully as it glided down to take up its position on a tree split apart by lightning.

The young diviner shivered and made his way back to the warmth of his dwelling. Taking up a cross-legged position on his sleeping mat, he began to rock to and fro. Then he began to pray, to the old gods and to his ancestors, to help him clear the mists so he could see the nature of what was coming...*and whom it intended to destroy.*

Part Three

Twenty-Five

1827 Mozambique

Long shadows stretched across the beach, a welcome sign after the long day's trek in the heat. With sundown would come a lifting of the blanket of humidity shrouding the coast. Only then would they stop and set up camp for the night.

'Bad country,' the *induna* Langalibalele had said as he'd explained about the plan to avoid the wetlands along the northern coast of Zululand at the start of their journey: 'Too many rivers and dangerous waters, much sickness to be found there – also snakes and other dangers.'

The route they'd followed was safer and easier. It had also been the one Shaka had instructed them to take.

After leaving kwaDukuza, they had travelled northwest then crossed the Phongolo River into Swaziland. Keeping to the foothills of the Lebombo Mountains, they had then moved east into Mozambique, the cooler weather of the Swazi foothills eventually giving way to the sultry humidity of the sub tropical coastline.

When they rounded the next rocky point, a stunning vista of sea and sky opened up before them. It was still and calm and a placid sea mirrored the beauty of the early evening sky.

Suddenly, one of the Zulus called out and pointed seaward, a sharp note of warning in his voice. About a hundred and fifty yards off-shore, the silhouette of a ship stood out against the pale perfection of sea and sky, her tall masts and spider webs of rigging etched black against the sunset.

Jackabo immediately noticed the lack of mooring chains and the sails hanging limp and flat in the still air. No wonder she's not running out any cable, he thought, she's becalmed.

A buzz of interest rose at the sight of the vessel. Many of the Zulus had never seen a ship before. Their curiosity was destined to be short-lived, however. A foul smell began to drift across the water towards them; subtle and sweet at first, but also laced with rot, disease and the underlying stench of human waste. Even Shaka's hardened warriors turned their heads away in disgust.

Jackabo shot a glance at the *induna* Langalibalele. He was standing motionless with his eyes fixed on the vessel, the fringes of ox-hair around his upper arms stirring gently in the warm air.

Then from across the water, came sounds – shouts and terrible screams of terror which filtered towards the group of black men and the boy standing on the shore. Jackabo's heart constricted. A terrible sense of apprehension gripped him.

The decks of the ship were crowded with a struggling mass of near-naked bodies, men, women and children. Wielding whips, lengths of chain or knotted ropes, the lighter-skinned men, obviously members of the crew, began to herd the people towards the rails, much like they would animals in a slaughter house.

Other sounds, horribly amplified, began to drift across the water; the rattle of dragging chains; oaths and curses; the crack of whips and the thud of blows on flesh as people were beaten, kicked or dragged bodily across the decks. Women screaming in terror called out for their children, but were either thrown bodily over the side or forced to jump. Still chained to those coming behind, the weight of their bodies dragged others down with them into the water. Anyone trying to cling on to the ship or to fight their way back aboard was clubbed and kicked back into the sea.

As bodies began to hit the water, fear rolled towards the group of silent watchers in an awesome swell, as tangible as a fist in the belly.

Shouts of outrage exploded all around him as they saw what was happening. Jackabo was unable to drag his eyes away from the deadly triangular fins of the sharks scything their way through the mass of bobbing heads. Turning away, he dropped to his knees in the sand and covered his ears to block out the awful sounds.

God knows how many days the vessel had lain idle on the flat, gilded ocean with no wind to fill the sails, supplies of water and food running out and the cries and moans of the dying and thirst-crazed slaves dinning in the crew's ears.

He'd heard talk among the sailors about the Portuguese and Arab slavers who plied their trade along the coasts of Africa and how British naval vessels were busy scouring the seven seas in an effort to stop the vicious trade.

'About time, as well,' Hatton had said, acid in his voice. 'The British took their bloody time about stopping it in their own territories.'

Long moments passed. After a while, Jackabo lifted his head and looked out to sea. The black ship rode higher in the water, its holds lighter now. The lethal fins continued to cruise the waters around it, scouring for the last scraps of flesh. But it was quieter now, the battle over.

Jackabo wiped the sweat from his eyes. Were the Zulus aware of this terrible trade? Shaka undoubtedly was. The slavery business, something of this magnitude and seriousness so close to his own territory would not have escaped his attention. His network of spies and informers would have seen to that. Strange though, that he'd never heard a word of it around the camp fires, either in kwaBulawayo, kwaDukuza or anywhere else.

It was then he became aware of a new sound. A low, vibrant hissing from the men around him began to fan out like a wind tearing through long grass, rising and swelling into a growl of voices. This was the powerful war-chant of the Zulus invoking the spirits of their ancestors, a hymn of defiance and lament in the face of tribulation.

As the sound rolled out over the water towards the ship, the boy hoped that the crew would somehow be skewered to their masts with the anger and the passion contained in it.

At last the final notes of lament died away. The sombre lines of the slave ship rode the still waters, black against the last rays of the sun. Around it, the sea was calm, untroubled and clean, the recent blood and anguish stroked away by the dying light.

Jackabo took up his place again beside Langalibalele. Then the *induna*, the warriors and the boy travelling with them turned their backs on the black ship and the beautiful bay and kept on walking, determined to put as much distance between them as possible before darkness fell.

A few miles short of Delagoa Bay, Robert Duval's bearded face was a study of suspicion and avid interest as he came cantering up behind them.

Seeing a lone, red-haired boy tramping the dusty road with a group of hawk-eyed, muscular natives was not something he was used to seeing. Reining in his horse sharply, he issued a curt order to his men to go on and wait for him up ahead, before swinging down from the saddle.

Hailing Jackabo first in French and then in stilted English, he made no effort to mask his curiosity about where he had come from and where he was going. Jackabo looked the stranger over. About thirty years old, he reckoned, well dressed, raffishly handsome; decidedly Gallic in appearance and charm.

'Robert Duval,' the man announced in his strongly accented English. 'From Ile de France – I theenk you British call it Mauritius.'

With an expansive smile, he swept off his hat and slapped dust from his well-cut riding breeches. 'I, Duval, am here to conduct some business. And you, *petit monsieur* – what brings an English boy to these parts?'

Intercepting Langalibalele's warning look, Jackabo replied airily, 'Oh, just business, much like you, sir.'

'You are well protected, I think,' Robert Duval said, as he ran a shrewd eye over the Zulus. But Jackabo gave him nothing back, just a smile and a nod.

After the small talk dribbled away, Robert Duval had no option but to climb back on his horse and reluctantly canter off towards the town.

Some days later, Jackabo was sitting on the sea wall with Langani, looking out over the flat, oily glitter of Delagoa Bay. His feet hurt from tramping the streets and he was hot, thirsty and distinctly fed-up.

Shoals of small boats were busy plying their trade round the harbour, and more than a dozen large sailing ships lay at anchor, mostly foreign-owned, judging by their flags.

Twenty-five miles off the coast lay the island of Inhaca. He'd been told of its attractions by one of the few people he'd met who'd been able to summon up enough English to have a conversation with him. All he could see of Inhaca today, though, was a dusty smudge of brown on the horizon.

Turning his head, he gazed across the narrow strait towards the stone-built bulk of the *Fort de Nossa Senhora da Conceiao* – The Fort of Our Lady of Conception.

Built in 1787, almost forty years ago, the Mediterranean-style architecture with its turrets, crenellations, and rusty cannons dominated the skyline, a potent reminder of the Portuguese origins of the colonial rulers of the sprawling territory. The town had grown up and flourished around the harbour, and the garrisons based at the Fort.

It hadn't taken Jackabo long to discover that trying to trade with the Portuguese, the mixed-bag of foreign sailors, Arab traders and colourful itinerants of the markets and narrow alleys was not going to be easy. They'd been here for two or three weeks already, and so far, he'd made little progress. To make matters worse, few people spoke or understood English and he spoke neither Portuguese nor French, nor did any of the Zulus. Even those who'd been to Mozambique before knew little or nothing of the host language.

Early on, almost from their first hour there, they'd begun to attract attention of the wrong kind. Passing through the bustling market places and narrow, winding streets, suspicious stares would follow the red-haired boy and the group of Zulus, especially those of the ill-shaven Portuguese soldiers and local constabulary.

After that, he only took Langalibalele with him on his sorties into the city, while the others remained back in Chief Tembe's village, safely out of sight beyond the city boundaries.

Jackabo had already decided Delagoa wasn't a good place to be. At first, he'd been excited by the colour and vibrancy of the narrow streets and market places; intrigued by the smells of exotic spices, fresh from India,

Zanzibar and Goa; by the hawk-eyed Arabs in flowing robes and tasselled fez; the Dutch, German or Austrian sea-farers; the dubious traders and pirates, and by the merchandise, which ranged from gold, copper and beaten brass, to chunks of ambergris, exotic perfumes and colourful bolts of silks.

Perhaps it was the underlying unease, suspicion and the difficulty of being understood that had eventually dulled his excitement. On the other hand, it could also have been the stench emanating from the open sewers and gushing drains of the back streets.

After several fruitless sorties into the city, he was always glad to escape back into Chief Tembe's village, with its familiar odours of wood smoke and hubbub of African voices.

A few days later, when a voice hailed him from among the crowd, he was surprised to see Robert Duval pushing his way towards him. Greeting him as if he were a long-lost friend, the man insisted that he should accompany him on his search for whatever it was he was looking for.

'Better you come with Duval,' he said, with a sly wink. 'Otherwise the Portuguese will think you are an English spy come to steal their secrets.'

The man from Mauritius made it all look so easy. He helped Jackabo sell Shaka's ivory tusks for a good price and was able to charm his way around the boatyards of Delagoa, introducing Jackabo to those who could sell him what he needed, also showing him how to haggle like an Arab.

As the weeks passed, Hatton's list dwindled, until there was nothing else left to find. Back at Chief Tembe's village, Jackabo reached for the leather bag concealed below his shirt. Thanks to Duval, he still had three out of the original five gold sovereigns left.

'We've done it!' he crowed to Langalibalele, 'now the boat'll get finished and the captain's troubles will be over.'

A day or two later, while they were visiting a trading emporium near the Fort for some last minute purchases, a straggling line of dispirited black men, chained at wrist and ankle, appeared from the tunnels leading out from beneath the military compound. Langalibalele muttered something unintelligible in Zulu and spat into the gutter.

Blinking in the bright sunlight, and guarded by three or four men on horseback, the column passed slowly down the street, the clank, clink and drag of their chains and the soft shuffling of bare feet announcing their presence. Mangy, flea-bitten dogs darted out to sniff at their heels.

The crack of whips signalled the order for line of prisoners to turn into the maze of alleyways leading off the square. Jackabo and the *induna* waited for a few moments and then set off after them.

An open space overlooked by several ramshackle wooden buildings formed the slave market. On the raised platform that had been erected below some trees, a group of men, women and children were clustered together, their manacled hands clutching each other. Further back, pens similar to those used for herding cattle were packed full of those waiting to be put on the block.

The crowd, abuzz with chatter, was made up mostly of men, swarthy-skinned Portuguese and turbaned Arabs, with a scattering of Europeans, mostly Dutch, Austrian or German traders. Although it was still mid-morning, the fumes of brandy were raw in the air.

There were also women; dark-haired, olive-skinned women, in bustled dresses, their heads covered with shawls of fine wool or lace. Accompanied by an overseer, they were obviously there to purchase servants for their households or workers for their fields.

When a familiar full-bodied laugh rang out, the sound of a man enjoying a successful day out, Jackabo immediately swung round, startled. The voice was Duval's, unmistakably Duval's – he'd recognise that laugh anywhere. Inching his way through the crowd, he eventually spotted him.

Immaculate in a white shirt, fine polished boots and a hat set at a rakish angle, Robert Duval looked every inch the gentleman as he laughed and talked with a group of prosperous-looking men.

Puzzled, Jackabo kept out of sight. What was he doing here? Surely he wouldn't approve of what was going on?

Just then, Duval raised a hand to catch the auctioneer's eye. A quick assertive flick of the fingers, an answering nod then his hand came back to rest on the head of his ivory-headed cane.

Shame and a sense of indignation flooded through Jackabo. Business, indeed! It was obvious exactly what Duval's business was. He was nothing but a slaver, just like those aboard the black schooner.

A sour taste welled up in his throat. How stupid he must have appeared to the arrogant Duval, how he must have been secretly laughing at him, a twelve-year-old lad in a strange land, easy to fool.

Suddenly, he couldn't wait to be gone – out of Delagoa, and out of Mozambique. Thank God, Hatton's list was complete. There was nothing more to do. It was time to go home.

Blinking away tears of humiliation and dented pride, he tried to elbow his way through the crowd, but was hampered by the sheer press of people. A steely grip on his shoulder stopped him in his tracks.

'*Bon jour, petit monsieur! Ca va?*'

Robert Duval was looking down at him, his usual flashing smile in place. It faded somewhat when he registered the anger and confusion on Jackabo's face. In an instant, his Gallic charm disappeared.

'So now you know the nature of my business.' He shrugged his shoulders, sarcastically. 'There should be no secrets between friends.'

A quick glance around, then Duval grabbed him and attempted to shake him like a terrier would a rat. 'I can offer you a chance to make some money,' he snarled. 'What price will you take for those fine fellows of yours? *Mon Dieu*, think of the profit you could make!'

Just then, Langalibalele's voice rose over the noise of the crowd, calling for him. Duval's grip lessened a fraction. Jerking himself free, Jackabo ran, ducking and diving into the crowd, yelling out for the Zulu *induna* as he went.

'You owe me for services rendered,' Duval bellowed after him, 'no need to decide now, *petit monsieur*. I know where you are, and I will call on you soon, very soon. You can be sure of it!'

That night, in Chief Tembe's village, Jackabo lay awake, unable to sleep. In a fever to be gone, he was as restless as a cat on a day of high wind.

The poor devils on the slave block; the truth about Duval and his offer to make a deal with him to sell the Zulus refused to go away. How could he not have suspected why the man had come to Portuguese Delagoa in the first place? Mauritius, or *Ile de France* as it was better known, was famous for its sugar plantations. And plantations needed slaves to work in the fields, plenty of them, a ready supply of labour on hand.

And there was something else. Duval's hint about knowing where to find them might well have been a boastful trick, but then again, it might not.

After supper, he'd watched the Zulus honing their weapons. Did they suspect that trouble lay ahead? Were they getting ready for action?

He lay awake sweating in the insect-filled darkness, starting at every sound, imagining it to be the creak of leather saddles and the muffled hoofbeats of Duval's horsemen.

The chief had warned Langalibalele against leaving the village after dark, as Portuguese soldiers were constantly on the lookout for smugglers. If they were caught in the dead of night with boxes and packages, they would likely end up in the dungeons, their goods confiscated. And who knew what influence Duval might have in and around Delagoa?

'We leave at first light,' Langalibelele had said, 'the further away from that accursed place, the safer we will be.'

Leaning over, he'd spat into the fire. 'In any case, this *umlungu*, this piece of *utivi* does not know we are Zulus and that Shaka's warriors are not goats to run in circles making *meh meh* because of such a man.'

Jackabo fell into a doze in the early hours, exhausted by the day's events. Vivid dreams pursued him, but they were different dreams, not of Duval and the nightmare of slavery, but of other, deeper things.

As he slept fitfully beneath the thatch in Chief Tembe's village, deep in the province of Gaza, he saw them as clearly as if they were standing beside him in the flesh – those of his people from centuries past, come to stand by him in a time of great danger, his own *amadhlozi,* the long-dead Macleans of the Western Isles.

Some were fierce and some were tender, some were young and some were not. Some had fair, flaxen hair, others raven tresses, while many like himself were *gille beag ruadh,* the red-haired ones.

Not all of them were warriors, hardened in battle, but many were; fierce-eyed and unrepentant, the blood of battles past still spattered on their plaids, fallen for a cause, in defence of their own kind, or dead by some other misadventure.

One man in particular stood out above the others. Eachainn of Duart. With his long red hair and eyes as blue as cornflowers, his jaunty bonnet, adorned with the wings of pheasant and grouse cocked to one side, there he stood as large as life, with a nod and a smile, saying softly, '*Here we are, your kin folk, Tearlach ruadh…till the end of time.*'

And they had stayed with him until first light, until Langalibalele woke him, urging him to rise for it was time to go.

Dreams and the shades of things past fade with the rising of the sun, and those belonging to Jackabo were no exception. By the time it was light, all that remained with him was the haunting, but comforting memory of his *amadhlozi,* the Macleans of long ago.

The need to escape beyond the reach of Robert Duval took precedence over everything. They wouldn't be safe until they were free of Portuguese territory. So they slipped away from the village into the early dawn light, making no sound as they went.

Around noon, they were forced to slow down. Even the tireless Zulus carrying the bulky packages and boxes on their heads needed to take a break from the punishing pace they'd kept up since dawn. Finding a shady spot near a stream, the *induna* indicated that they could rest for a while and eat some food. Lookouts were posted on a wooded rise a hundred or so yards away.

Their respite was short lived. Half an hour later, one of the sentries came running 'The dust of many men, also *njomane* – horses.'

Jackabo's heart lurched. Duval, in his arrogance, wouldn't like to think he was being outwitted by a pack of natives and a twelve-year-old boy. Obviously, his intention to sell the Zulus had been real enough. In his blind arrogance, it would be reason enough for him to set out after them.

If Duval found them, they would have no chance of out-running men on horseback. If they took to the bush, they could scatter in different directions to avoid capture – but not if they were carrying the heavy boxes and packages. In that eventuality, the vital supplies might well prove to be their downfall.

For one wild moment, Jackabo considered abandoning it all – boxes, packages, everything – and just disappearing into the bush.

'No, dammit!' he swore, furious with himself for even thinking it. 'We'll no' run – we've come too far for that. The ship would be lost, the Captain lost, the whole game lost.'

The flare of the red fox began to rise in him. Seeing the glint of rage in the boy's eyes and the rising wash of hot blood to his face, Langalibalele smiled and slapped him on the back.

Running a thumb over the blade of his sharpened *assegai*, the *induna* smiled, 'Have no fear, Jackabo. We will finish what we came to do. The Zulus are ready.'

Rummaging in his pack, Jackabo brought out James King's Navy pistol. While he was priming and loading it, he prayed the riders would either pass by, or turn out to be anyone other than Duval.

The hoofbeats were louder now, coming their way. He signed to one of the men, a young tracker called Busa. *How many?*

Busa indicated ten, perhaps a dozen horsemen. By now, the supplies were safely hidden in thorn thickets some distance away. Obeying Langalibalele's signal, a handful of the Zulus melted back into the bush.

It was no surprise to see Duval at the head of the group of riders, a dozen or so armed, hard-faced men. Jackabo's heart sank when the sound of excited yelping and snuffling reached him.

Hounds! *Hunting dogs, the sort with keen noses…the kind used to track down runaway slaves.*

Langalibelele shot him a quick glance, something hard and indefinable in the dark eyes. A quick flick of his hand, and the rest of the Zulus silently fanned out and disappeared into the undergrowth.

With his mouth close to Jackabo's ear, he said, 'Stay here, *m'dodo*. Have no fear, Shaka's warriors will not be eaten by dogs, any kind of dogs.' A hand on his shoulder, then he was gone, the foliage closing behind him with scarcely a rustle.

The quick clip-clop of returning hoof-beats suggested the dogs must have lost their scent and were trying to pick it up again. Now there was urgency in the Portuguese voices and the excited whining of the dogs. Lust for blood was in the air, hot and heavy in the noonday heat.

A sense of bloody-mindedness ran through Jackabo like escaping steam. The desire to atone for his gullibility engulfed him. 'Stay here,' the induna had said. *No bloody fear!*

Searching around, he found a stick, much like a *knobkerrie*, with a gnarled knob of wood at the end. Tucking the pistol into the waistband of his ragged trews, he pulled the loose sailor's shirt down over it to hide the bulge. The shrill neighing of horses and men's voices expressing shock and anger suddenly split the air.

A quick glance through the screen of foliage told him that Langalibalele and a group of Zulus had spread out across the track and were facing the group of armed horsemen thirty yards away, effectively barring their way. Poised for action, the sun glinted off the razor-sharp tips of their *assegai*.

Jackabo stepped out of the bushes, intent on joining them. Duval caught sight of him and snorted in contempt as he roared out, 'So *petit m'sieur*, we meet again, just as I told you we would!'

Scenting the tension in the air, his horse snickered and reared up. Dogs milled around, hair bristling along their backs, snarling and growling. Duval quickly brought his horse under control.

'Being a gentleman, I would have preferred to conclude our business quickly, but if not, then I warn you – I will take not only your fine fellows, but you also, *petit rousse.*' His smile was wolfish in the hot glare.

'Your fair skin and blue eyes will fetch an excellent price, not on the common slave block, of course, so crude. But, in other quarters, a young boy like you would be much prized. For a while, that is…'

Jackabo yelled back at him. 'You'll no be taking anyone anywhere, *Monsieur* slave-trader.'

Indicating the Zulus, he shouted, 'Do you know who these are? They're no' just 'ordinary natives' as you'd have it. They're Shaka's Zulu warriors, the best in all of Africa. Unless you want to feel just how sharp their spears are, I suggest you turn round and skedaddle back the way you came.'

The answering guffaws and hoots of laughter were a mixture of contempt and menace at the twelve-year-old's affrontery. Jackabo heard the click of the Portuguese guns being cocked. Beside him, Langalibalele made the sharp, warning cry of a spotted plover.

Zulus suddenly spilled out of the bush behind and on either side of the horsemen, effectively cutting off their retreat and boxing them in. The dogs stalked stiff-legged round in circles, snarling and whining, unsure of what to do about the intruders.

The trap Langalibele had laid for Duval and his riders was the classic Zulu attack, scaled down to fit the present circumstances. The *induna* had placed himself and the first group as the head of the buffalo, facing the enemy, while the encircling 'horns' had slipped through the bush and come out behind and around them, making retreat difficult if not impossible, even on horseback.

As the reality of their situation and the nature of the men they faced became clear, the first crackles of apprehension among the riders became tangible.

No more time for words, or even thoughts. The *induna* and his men charged down the intervening thirty or so yards, while the encircling 'horns' closed in.*Zhee, zhee, zhee...* the low growling war cry and the fearsome ululating issuing from the throats of the Zulus stirred every hair on Jackabo's head. His belly cramped in raw excitement.

What happened next was brutal. Caught off-guard, Duval and his men struggled to control their horses, cursing and swearing as they fumbled with their guns. Langalibalele vaulted clean on to the saddle behind one of the riders. Jackabo saw his arm crook around the man's neck and the flash of the blade as he drew it across his throat. Blood pumped out, spattering the horse. Rolling its eyes wildly, terrified by the smell of blood, the animal reared up, throwing the dying rider on to the track.

Nearby, a burly, olive-skinned man was trying vainly to push his spilling entrails back into the gaping wound in his gut, his face twisted in shock and incredulity.

The dogs were ruthlessly dealt with, speared before they could do any damage. Next to come under attack were the horses. It was easier to fight a man on the ground than have him towering above you with a gun in his hand and mounted on a powerful animal with flailing hoofs.

The tips of the spears and assegais by now were red with blood, both human and animal. Men fell or were dragged down, their firearms clattering to the ground. The air was full of the yelping of dying dogs, the shrill neighing of horses and the acrid smell of gunpowder, while over and above it all were the cackling, shrilling animal and bird noises designed by the Zulus to put fear into the hearts of their enemies.

Jackabo stood there, frozen. For a moment he felt a stab of pity for the Portuguese. An unexpected trickle of fear escalated in him as he looked on the Zulus and their brutal handiwork.

Where were the amiable companions, singers, and storytellers with whom he'd travelled the long road into Portuguese territory – where had they gone? He realised that no quarter would be given, or expected, by these merciless strangers.

Cold reality flooded through him. This was how Shaka had trained his warriors – to be fast, disciplined, and deadly. Now the Zulus were fighting for their lives, and their freedom, just as they'd done many times before and would no doubt do again in the future.

Gunfire broke out, the smell of cordite hanging in the dusty air. Duval, still upright in the saddle, his shirt spattered with blood, was brandished a smoking weapon. Appalled, Jackabo saw Magema, one of the young warriors, disappear beneath the horse's hoofs.

Rolling away awkwardly, he came up in an unsteady crouch, blood streaming from a deep gash on his scalp, the short fighting blade still in his hand. Duval's boot shot out and caught him a glancing blow in the face. He went down like a stone, his bloody weapon falling into the dust.

Time slowed to a crawl. A triumphant smirk crossed Duval's bearded face. Deadly intent written clear across it, the gun began its slow trajectory towards the fallen Magema. Jackabo *felt,* rather than saw, the slaver's finger begin to tighten on the trigger.

Words of protest stuck in his throat. Then, with a jerk that almost drove the breath from him, he was off and running, his bare feet thudding down the dusty track towards the mass of dead and dying horses, men and dogs, screaming at the pitch of his voice, his boy's voice cracking with fear and rage.

'No-o-o-o! Duval . . .no!'

It was as if he were flying, not feeling the stones bruise his feet. The Maclean blood in him was up, the flare of the red fox lending him wings.

The gun barrel wavered. Duval's head swivelled round. 'Go away, *petit garcon,*' he yelled his voice hoarse with the swirling dust. 'This game is only for men. Stand and watch, learn something if you must – but get in my way, and I will kill you!'

Magema stirred, moaning, blood trickling from his mouth. Jackabo was only a few yards away now. No time to think. All he could see was Duval and the barrel of the gun. The cudgel with the knob on the end flew out of his hand, struck Duval a glancing blow on the shoulder and jarred his arm.

'Fuck you, boy!' Wheeling the horse round, he glared at him, murder in his eyes. 'A quick shot for the *kaffir*, then I'll deal with you.'

Jackabo's hand felt below his shirt for King's naval pistol. Fynn's voice echoed in his head. 'Remember what I showed you, boy, about handling a weapon. For God's sake don't blow your bloody foot off, or a hand!'

No fear, Fynn.

Using both hands, he brought the weapon up and held it steady. 'Duval!' His voice cracked and broke as he aimed it at the slaver. 'Shoot a man when he's down? I could ask what kind of a man you are – but then I already know the answer to that!'

The back of the slaver's neck turned brick red, and he swung round. His mouth sagged open in disbelief when he noticed the pistol in Jackabo's hand and the determined look on his face

Recovering his equilibrium, Duval moved fast and swung the hunting weapon away from Magema and aimed it in his direction.

The heavy pistol bucked between Jackabo's hands and spat fire, making his arm go numb down to his fingers. Duval swayed, twitching in shock. A hand reached up, trying to wipe away the blood streaming down his face. Jackabo felt as if he was standing on the edge of a precipice, waiting for the slaver to fall. But he didn't...

His aim had been too high! The ball had scored a deep groove along Duval's temple laying the scalp open. It was painful enough, bloody enough – but not disabling enough to stop him.

'*Cochon!*' he snarled. 'You think to kill Duval so easily? *Finis!* And so are you, *petit m'sieur!*'

A few yards away, Magema moaned, though barely conscious. Dry-mouthed, knowing he wouldn't be able to reload the pistol quickly enough, Jackabo flicked a quick glance in his direction. What he saw galvanised him into action. Diving down almost beneath the horse's hoofs, his fingers came in contact with the short, fighting assegai which Magema had dropped after Duval had kicked him in the face.

Rolling over, he was deafened by the roar of Duval's gun as it went off somewhere above his head. As he came to his feet, Magema's blade was in his hand, its grip as familiar as if it had always been there.

Shock registered in Duval's eyes. His glance flicked first to the blade, and then to the boy's face. Time slowed and seemed to stop. Jackabo was conscious of the heat and sweat rising from the horse's body and the smell of the tobacco on Duval's breath.

But as the slave trader raised the gun, his finger already tightening on the trigger, Jackabo brought Magema's bloody blade up, and drove it into Duval 's body with as much force as he could muster.

The man's mouth dropped open, blood spooling from it, the elegant silver-chased hunting gun falling away into the dust. The horse, maddened by the noise and the smell of blood reared up, dislodging him from the saddle.

Slowly, he began to topple sideways, his body sagging, both hands clutching the hilt of the blade embedded in his gut. As his booted feet came clear of the stirrups, Jackabo hastily stepped backwards, away from him – but not fast enough.

Duval continued to slip sideways, his flailing arms reaching out for him, as if for help. As Jackabo staggered, tripped and fell, the weight of Duval's body knocked the breath out of him and pinned him to the ground.

Crushed below the man's sprawling, inert body, he lay among the dust and hard-packed grit, stunned and stiff with horror, but unable to roll the dead weight off him or pull himself out from beneath it.

The slave trader's face was twisted sideways, mere inches from his own. A slowly glazing dark brown eye stared at him, the smell of warm blood thick and cloying in the heat. For what seemed like an eternity, Jackabo lay there listening to the terrible rattling in Duval's throat as his lifeblood slowly pumped away, while around him the fighting raged, punctuated by the terrible sounds of battle and the screams of dying men.

When it was over, and the man from Mauritius had taken his last breath, Jackabo opened his eyes and blinked away the tears.

And it was then that he saw Eachainn of the Macleans standing on the blood-spattered red earth of Mozambique a few yards away, as real as if he were made of flesh and blood, only the shimmering around the edges of him to say he was not.

The smile, though, was the same as the last time Jackabo had seen it, as were the cornflower-blue eyes, the long plaits of red hair falling down his back and the wings of pheasant and grouse set rakishly on his bonnet. But before he slowly faded away into the dusty sunlight, Jackabo saw his mouth form the words.

Tearlach ruadh…till the end of time…

And that was where the *induna* Langalibalele found them afterwards – Magema, Jackabo and Robert Duval – three inert, bloodied bodies lying among the others who had met their end on the road leading from Delagoa Bay.

Because the boy, Jackabo, was stricken dumb with shock and unable to put one foot in front of the other, Langalibelele carried him bodily down to the stream, and waded out with him into the clean, cold water until it was as high as his chest. And then he held him, and sang to him, while he washed Duval's blood from his body and his hair and from Magema's blade, until the water around them ran clear and clean.

An hour or two to rest and collect the goods from where they were secreted in a thorn thicket then, without the need for words, the *impi* and the red-haired youth turned their faces resolutely south and set out on the long road home.

Twenty-Six

September 1827

Henry Fynn tilted back his battered straw hat and squinted skywards. The noonday sky was deep blue and cloudless, from horizon to horizon. The breeze was warm, light and spiced with a tang of dry earth and rustling winter grasses. Swinging the rifle off his shoulder, he signalled to his men that it was time to take a break.

The group of hunters spread out among the aloes and scattered bush in search of a patch of shade, then squatting in a circle, they reached for the small boxes of snuff they usually kept round their necks or in slits in their ear lobes.

Stripping off his tattered shirt, Fynn sniffed it gingerly then spread it out on a bush to dry. Rinsing his mouth with a few sips of tepid water from his battered flask, he got down to the business of lighting his pipe.

There was real heat in the sun now. Flocks of swifts and swallows were winging their way south, wheeling, diving and catching insects in mid-flight.

He made a rapid calculation. August, it must be the end of August at least, or possibly the beginning of September. A smile flickered at the edges of his mouth. Old habits died hard. What did it matter what month it was? Time was measured in different ways here.

Stretching out in the shade, with the taste of the tobacco a welcome burr at the back of his throat, Fynn glanced over at the hunters.

They were taking their ease, squatting in the shade like skinny-legged storks. The husky voice regaling them with tales of his wives' antics elicited cackles of laughter from the listeners. The voice dropped to a whisper. 'Eh, in the end I had no choice but to threaten to beat the lot of them...especially my elder wife...eh, brothers, but that one makes my life verrry, verrry difficult...'

Fynn shook his head in amusement

Every mile he'd put between himself and the port was a good one, as far as he was concerned, and Shaka's invitation to come to kwaDukuza and join him on a hunting expedition couldn't have arrived at a better time.

These days, trouble was never far away in eThekwini. A witch's brew of resentment, petty jealousies, ill health and boredom bubbling below the surface meant that work on the partly built vessel was slow and laborious.

Because of the seamen's near-mutiny a few months ago, a boy barely twelve had been sent off on a six-hundred mile return journey through dangerous territory in an effort to save their sorry arses.

Fynn spat a stream of tobacco juice at a column of scurrying black ants. Undeterred, they regrouped and went on their way, abandoning their less fortunate brethren.

Bloody Africa, Fynn thought, philosophically. *As always, survival of the fittest.*

kwaDukuza, a few days later

Fynn tipped his hat over his eyes, yawned, and got ready for his mid-morning doze. It was cool in the shade, and his stomach was pleasantly full after the substantial morning meal he'd just eaten.

Ever since arriving in kwaDukuza, he'd spent his nights closeted with Shaka. After much talk and generous quantities of beer consumed between the hours of dusk and dawn, Fynn considered he'd earned a rest, even in mid-morning. Idly, he let his mind drift back over the past few days.

Although Shaka had made him more than welcome, he'd been conscious of a certain tension in the air, something underlying the bonhomie and talk. Nothing personal, he was sure; but the feeling had persisted.

What had really concerned him were the times when Shaka had stopped in mid-conversation, his words cut off as cleanly as if by a knife. Fynn would glance up to find him staring fixedly at something in the shadows, a strange look on his face. And that wasn't all. It appeared as if the King of the Zulus was almost afraid to be alone – especially during the hours of darkness. His almost feverish insistence that Fynn stay till daybreak was a new and quite disturbing turn of events.

Fynn felt his eyelids droop. He yawned again and stretched out his long legs. Shaka's problems, and everyone else's, would have to wait.

An hour or so later, he was wakened by the thud of running feet close by. Reluctantly, he removed the hat from his face and opened a bleary, bloodshot eye, just in time to catch the tail end of two runners disappearing up one of the narrow lanes nearby.

Someone shouted, asking what the hurry was. Fynn caught only a few words of the reply, but it was enough to jerk him fully awake.

By God, the boy's done it! He's made it back! He punched the air in triumph. *Well done, ye little cock sparrow, well done!*

Scooping up the earthenware pitcher from just inside the doorway of the hut, he tipped the contents over his head to waken himself up. Raking his fingers through his wet hair, he began to pace up and down. Little chance of having an audience with Shaka, he reckoned. At this time of day, he'll either be with his councillors, or asleep. The runners would have news, though.

Grabbing his hat, he set off for the top gates.

In his heart of hearts, Fynn had wondered, more than once, if they'd ever see the boy again. Not that he had any doubts as to either the capabilities, or the good intentions of the Zulus who'd been delegated to accompany him, because they would have done their best to see he came to no harm. The only trouble was that Africa, by its very nature, was both deadly and unpredictable. The survival of the fittest, both man and beast, lay at its very core.

He'd also entertained some doubts regarding the boy's stamina. Six hundred miles through dangerous terrain was a long, bloody way for a twelve-year-old boy.

Apart from Ogle, he was the only white man around who had any experience of what such an expedition entailed. Body and soul were pushed to the limit. To let weakness get the upper hand was to die, plain and simple.

When it came down to basic survival, in the end it was often the will alone that counted. That was the hard truth of it, and it was what he believed, from his own personal experiences. For a lad of Jackabo's age and slight physique – well, he'd kept his reservations to himself.

But, in spite of everything, the boy had made it back. He had survived.

Judging by the hum of voices, Shaka was still holding court in the shade below the mkhula tree. As Fynn drew nearer to the square, the voices grew louder, and were punctuated by endless murmurs of *'Yebo, baba.'*

Without warning, a tall figure insinuated itself smoothly in front of him, blocking his way. Below the plumed head dress, Mbopha's austere face was tightly guarded. His hooded eyes raked Fynn up and down. 'The Lord of the World is too busy to see you, *umlungu.'*

Fynn chose to ignore the hostility. He nodded mildly and replied in Zulu,

'I have no wish to disturb him. I only want to talk with those who brought news of the *induna* Langalibalele and the boy.'

Mbopha raised his voice as if to demonstrate his authority to everyone within earshot. 'You will wait in the outer area beyond the gate,' he ordered. 'After the messengers have reported their business to *Inkosi ye lizwe,* you can talk to them, but only if the Nkosi allows it –'

Just then, a voice boomed out, cutting him off in mid-sentence. 'Must the friends of the king be forced to wait like dogs in the hot sun?'

A flicker of scarlet in the dappled shade as Shaka rose to his feet, towering over the rows of bodies prostrated before him. 'You overstep yourself, Mbopha. Perhaps you grow tired of the high position I have given you, and would prefer to be relieved of it?'

Mbopha looked as if he had been physically struck across the face.

Shock chased humiliation and rage across his features. With a superhuman effort, he regained his composure. Only a flicker of naked hatred remained in his hard black eyes, something that was not lost on Henry Fynn.

The runners lay face down on the ground in a lather of sweat and dust, their exhausted breathing rasping in the silence. Jabbing a forefinger at their prostrated bodies, Shaka asked, 'You know the news they bring, Mbuyasi?'

Fynn cleared his throat. 'Only that the *impi* is on their way back.' After a few moments silence, he asked, tentatively. 'What news of the boy? How did he fare?'

Shaka looked across at Fynn, a flicker of humour in his eyes. 'He is well, very well, indeed.'

A long drawn-out sigh came from the people clustered around them. Shaka's voice rose as he turned to address them. 'You see what a wonderful people the nations of King Jo-ji are? Even their children are possessed of great courage, great heart.'

A rustle of obedient choruses: '*Yebo, baba*'

Shaka leaned down and spoke to Fynn quietly, 'Did you have doubts as to the boy's survival, Mbuyasi?'

Unsure as to where such a question might lead, Fynn decided to play safe. 'Not as regards the capability of your warriors, Nkosi, or their will to do their best for him. It was just…'

He struggled to find the appropriate Zulu words, the correct shade of meaning. 'It was the boy's own will to endure that I sometimes doubted.'

Shaka cut in. 'Man or boy, no one knows what he holds within him, the measure of his courage until the time comes to put it to the test.'

A ripple of agreement flowed out from the audience. The king's statement was something they could all agree with.

Shaka raised his voice a notch or two. 'In the case of Jackabo, I have been proved right. The boy surpassed all that was demanded of him. He has the heart of a warrior. That is beyond doubt.'

Rustling whispers greeted this public announcement of approval. Fynn digested this piece of information. Obviously, the Zulu ruler was in possession of more than just the bare details of what had happened on the journey.

KINGDOM OF A THOUSAND DAYS

'How soon do you expect them to return?'

Shaka's answer was swift. 'By the time the sun goes down.' Fynn stammered, 'Today? You mean they are almost here?'

A low chuckle came from the dais. Shaka's eyes were full of mischief as they met his. 'Mbuyasi, ever since the last full moon I have known when they would come. There was scarcely a day when I did not know exactly where they were. Why do you think I sent for you to come to kwaDukuza at this time?'

Fynn tried not to let his surprise show. How could he have forgotten the far-flung web of spies and informers Shaka had at his disposal?

'But why do you call only me here, Nkosi?' he asked, recovering quickly. 'Why not also ask Kingi? He is close to the boy.'

Shaka frowned, as if suddenly aware of the avid curiosity in the faces around them. Open talk had gone far enough. His look hardened, then turned into a glare. Heads dropped and bodies cringed to avoid drawing his eye.

'I will give you the answer to that later,' he replied, rising to his feet. 'At sunset, the gates of kwaDukuza will remain open. Fires will be lit to lead our people home.'

"*Our*" people, Fynn thought, sardonically. Well now, *Nkosi ye Lizwe*, the lad we always assumed was "ours" now seems to have crossed over to belong to you and the amaZulu.

In the morning, he would send a message for James King to come with all speed.

They came in the last of the dying light, just as Shaka had said they would.

Within the immense maze of beehive huts, evening fires had been lit and the air was full of the acrid smell of drifting woodsmoke. Drums were beating softly, their insistent rhythms adding a spice of excitement almost tangible in its intensity.

From where Fynn was sitting cleaning his weapon, he could hear people calling to one another from more than a mile away across on the other side of the settlement. With each passing hour, the fever of anticipation had grown.

Pushing aside the rifle, Fynn tilted his head back and looked up into the evening sky. The steady winking light of *Komotsho,* the evening star, was undiminished by the last flares of the dying sun. A solitary bird winged its way homeward against a darkening blue sky. Fynn watched the steady beat of its wings until it was lost in the dusk.

Suddenly, the shrill sound of women ululating rose up from the lower reaches of kwaDukuza. *My God...* Fynn thought, the hairs stirring on his arms. *They're here already!*

People ran down through the winding alleys, their torches bobbing and weaving as they went, while others ran to light the piles of firewood placed strategically down the length of kwaDukuza. Flames leapt skywards, sending showers of sparks into the darkening sky, while matchstick figures leapt and pranced round the burning pyres.

Stirred by the infectious mood, Fynn stowed his weapon safely away inside the hut. He wanted to be there when the boy came through the gates, because it was important that he knew that one of his own was there to welcome him back.

No sooner had he started off down the hill than the thud of feet coming up behind him made him turn round. A voice hailed him. 'Ho, Mbuyasi!'

It was Jakot, resplendent in a short kilt of animal tails and plumed head-dress of red and black feathers. '*Ninjani*, Mbuyasi! My heart is glad that our small *umlungu* has returned. Eh, but I have missed him.'

Fynn shot him a swift glance. There it was again, the collective, possessive word: '*our*'. Leaving aside the small touch of resentment this produced in him, he was touched by the man's genuine affection for the lad.

Drawn like moths to the heat and light, people danced and gyrated to the pulsating beat of the drums while waves of ululating and singing ebbed and flowed on the night air.

Suddenly, the noise died away. All was muted now; only the slow beat of the drums an insistent pulse in the background. Jakot gripped Fynn's arm and pointed towards the gates. 'See!'

Passing below the high arch was the *induna* Langalibalele, limping slightly, behind him a press of warriors, many bearing bundles and boxes on their heads. Fynn's eyes searched for the boy. And found him. *Was he imagining it... or did he look taller?*

With his hair hanging loose over his shoulders, a stream of red fire in the light of the torches, he had a long hunting rifle slung almost carelessly along his shoulders. Fynn frowned. There was something different about him.

Was it in the way he was holding himself, walking step for step with the *induna*, or the casual way the long hunting gun seemed part of him? Or was it something more?

He shook his head. Four, nearly five months was a long time. At that age, it could bring about a huge difference in a lad, especially after being on a mission with men twice his age.

The plumes of the Fasimba, Shaka's personal guards, dipped and swayed among the crowd as they forced people to stay back, to allow the returning warriors room to move forward.

Suddenly, Jakot put his head back and sent a long guttural cry of praise and greeting soaring out over the crowd. Fynn saw the boy's head turn, his eyes searching to see where it had come from.

Jakot raised his arm, the fist clenched in the age-old sign of victory and warrior comradeship. The wild ululating rose and spiralled into the night. When the chanting began, shivers ran up and down Fynn's back. Jakot turned round, triumph shining out of his eyes.

'Listen, Mbuyasi! Hear what they're saying!' The people of kwaDukuza were calling the boy's name, over and over.

Fynn saw the lad falter. The *induna* turned and said something to him, then put his head back and laughed. They came on together, Langalibalele's hand resting lightly on the boy's shoulder.

Fynn peered through the dusk, trying to get a closer look at him. The lad *was* taller, no doubt about it. There was a different set to the head and shoulders below the tattered shirt; the legs were longer, leaner and more muscular. His feet were thrust into dusty boots laced round his ankles, his trews slashed and ragged below the knee.

Fynn grinned when he noticed the birds' feathers woven into the boy's long red hair. Well, boy, now you're turning into a real vagabond, another Mbuyasi. His eyes narrowed. Sartorial elegance apart, though, there's something else about you, lad —

The last rays of the sun suddenly flared out, bathing the group in its crimson light. For a moment, it seemed as if the whole *impi*, including the boy, was drenched in blood. Beside him, Jakot's body stiffened. Fynn felt his mouth go dry.

The effect lasted only seconds. Now there was nothing to hold the darkness back. It filled the vast arena, throwing the blazing fires into sharp relief.

Fynn caught a stir of movement at the head of the slope. 'Shaka,' Jakot hissed. Then he indicated another group of figures streaking down the hill towards the arrivals. Fynn raised his eyebrows. *Izinyanga* – medicine men. Now, what were they after?

He saw the boy touch the *induna's* arm and nod towards the medicine men. A turn of the man's head then he rapped out a command. The line of warriors behind him lowered the boxes and packages to the ground, then waited. It was clear the *izinyanga* had work to do.

The tempo changed abruptly, and the ululating and chanting died away. In the silence, the crackling of the flames could be heard over the slow insistent rhythms of the drums. The boy came on alone, walking steadily towards them. Thirty yards away, now, twenty yards then ten...

Fynn was stunned by what he saw. Beneath the unruly bandeau of birds' feathers, the planes of the boy's face seemed to alter in the light of the flames. It was as if his childhood had been stripped away and another, more adult version, a vivid, but chilling glimpse of the man that he would one day become, had been stamped across the boyish features. And there was something else too, something about his eyes...

The smile on Fynn's lips faltered. The cool blue eyes looking straight at him were clear enough, but also in them was the look of one who had walked through the fires of hell and come out on the other side.

What in God's name had happened out there?

Tears suddenly pricking his eyes, Fynn reached out and gripped the boy's shoulder. Beneath the tattered blue shirt, the bones were slight but strong, with the unmistakable swell of hard muscle beneath the firm young flesh.

Blinking fiercely, he whispered, 'Are you all right, lad? You have the look about you of one who's had a pretty rough passage. What in the hell happened out there?'

Without warning, the *induna* Langalibalele was there, pushing his way between them. Good God, Fynn thought, I didn't even sense him coming up behind me...

'*Cha*, Mbuyasi!' the *induna* warned, keeping his powerful body between Fynn and the boy. 'Leave him alone, there are some things that do
not concern you.'

The boy flinched, as if he had just awakened from a bad dream. Fynn's
hand fell away from his shoulder. Trying not to betray the rampant
concern flooding through him, he said, 'Welcome back, Jackabo. Look,
Jakot's here to see you, too.'

The interpreter's plumes fluttered as he came forward, a flash of teeth as
he added his greetings. The boy stared at them both, the long, hard, blue
gaze back in his eyes. For a moment, Fynn wondered if he were suffering
from shock or injury. Then, remembering his own experiences, he grinned.

'Hard isn't it, Jackabo? Speaking the native lingo for months on end –
then before you know it, suddenly finding that you've forgotten your own
language!'

The boy stared beyond him, to where the medicine men were milling
about among the warriors. It was some moments before the words came
tumbling out. 'You know everything, don't you, Fynn?'

It came out jerkily, in a rush. Then his face crinkled up with laughter.

'I aim to please,' Fynn replied, with a wide grin, hitching up his baggy
trousers. A wave of relief passed through him.

The chanting of the *izinyanga* was louder now. Jakot stared warily at
the medicine men as they bobbed about among the squatting warriors,
dispensing their *muthi* and performing the ritual purification ceremonies
with a flick of animal hair whisks.

The boy's face went suddenly pale, exhaustion clear on it. He looked
past them up to the place where Shaka was waiting,

'The men won't be going near the Nkosi tonight,' he said softly, 'so
it's my place to go.' Holding out the hunting rifle to Fynn, he said,
'Keep it for me. It's not the thing to approach Shaka with a weapon in
your hand.'

Eyeing the smooth walnut and silver chasing of the long-barrelled gun,
Fynn raised his eyebrows. 'So they tell me, boy. Though I daresay he might
stretch a point in your case. No, I'd hold on to it, if I were you, finish your
journey the same way you began it. Take it from me, there's no way Shaka
will think you might do him an injury!'

A flicker of something deep stirred in the blue eyes then a faint smile crossed his face. Fynn pointed to the weapon. 'Where did you pick that up, if I may ask?'

Jackabo met his eyes square on. 'Spoils of war, Mbuyusi,' he said, with a spark of his usual boyish humour. 'You know how it is – spoils of war, and all that!'

Fynn stood with Jakot and watched the slight figure begin its lone walk up the hill to where the warrior king was waiting for him beyond the circle of firelight.

Twenty-Seven

Two weeks later

When King, Isaacs and Ned Cameron turned up at kwaDukuza a week or so later, they found Fynn dozing in the shade with his hat tipped over his eyes.

Slapping the dust from his clothes, King nudged him awake. 'Where is he, then? Where's the returning hero?' Fynn removed his hat and fanned away the flies buzzing round his head.

'Gentlemen,' he drawled, jerking a thumb towards the upper end of the settlement. 'Far be it from me to advise you as to the whereabouts of the one called Jackabo. Last I saw of him was yesterday, and he was heading that way.' Reaching inside the doorway, he brought out the pitcher of water and offered it to them. After taking a swallow or two and rinsing out his mouth, King passed the pitcher to Ned and slumped down beside Fynn. 'You say you haven't seen the lad since yesterday?'

'Nary a sign of him,' replied Fynn, shaking his head. 'But then kwaDukuza's a mighty big place, as you might have noticed. He could be anywhere, though I've a good idea where he's holed up.'

He cocked an ear. 'Hear that, gentlemen?' Isaacs paused with the pitcher halfway to his mouth and listened. Coming in on the still air, they all heard the distant sound of pounding drums and rhythmic chanting, punctuated from time to time by the full-throated roar of many voices.

'Sounds like there's no end of a good time going on,' Ned said. 'You reckon that's where wee Heelander is?'

Fynn nodded. 'They've been at it since yesterday. By the way, I'd lay off the "wee Heelander" if I were you, Ned. I think you'll find your chum's changed quite a bit.'

'What d' you mean by that, Fynn?' King asked, instantly alert. 'What kind of change? Did something happen to the lad? Spill it out, man.'

Curse my flapping tongue! Fynn thought. 'All I ask you,' he said quickly, 'is not to push the lad too hard about what happened on his travels. Give him time to tell you himself about it – or not, as the case may be.' The comment did nothing to remove the anxiety from James King's eyes.

'Savages!' It was the only word Isaacs had uttered since arriving.

Fynn shot the dark haired youth a quick glance. 'You might well call them that, Nat, but there's no denying they treat the boy right.'

Well, lad, he thought, eyeing the sullen-faced Isaacs, though you might not choose to believe it, wouldn't you say that it's been the same 'savages' who've given the boy friendship, protection and the comforts of life over the past two years?

Out of the whole stupefying situation the boy had found himself in, literally 'detained at His Majesty's pleasure' by the Zulu king, he had risen to the challenge with great courage. Added to which, he now also occupied a unique position close to Shaka, at the heart of the Zulu court…to the degree that he might even be heading into real danger.

This, in essence, was the crux of Fynn's present feeling of unease. The boy was at a vulnerable age; the stage where boyhood inevitably gave way to the stirrings of manhood, with all that it entailed.

Right now, Jackabo had chosen to stay beyond the closed gates with the Zulus, taking part in the ceremonies being conducted. For all Fynn knew, some kind of initiation rites might well be in progress. Mentally, he crossed himself that, on the latter, he would be proved wrong.

King broke in. 'What d'you think is going on up there, Henry?'

'Off-hand, I'd say it was one mighty big *indaba*, though I've no idea what they're up to.' Suspicion flared in King's eyes. 'You mean to tell me you weren't invited, Fynn? I'd have thought Shaka would have seen to it that you, of all people, were asked along.'

Fynn said nothing. The comment was a fair one. Why indeed had Shaka not invited him, especially after his earlier remarks that he'd specifically planned for him to be in kwaDukuza to wait for the boy's return?

What, if anything, was being hidden from him? Could there be a reason why the boy had been whisked off into thin air? The remote, chilling look he'd seen in the youngster's eyes still haunted him. All Fynn could say for certain was that whatever had happened out there had most certainly made an immense impact on him.

Finally, there was the matter of the *izinyanga* who had appeared almost immediately to conduct their purification ceremonies on the returning *impi*. That told Fynn something. Somewhere along the line, blood had been spilled and violence done. The Zulus delegated to accompany the boy were all battle experienced warriors, second instinct for them to take action if the need arose. It meant that some of the returning party, or all of them, had been involved in whatever had happened out there.

He narrowed his eyes. The image of the long-barrelled hunting gun, complete with walnut stock and silver chasings Jackabo had been carrying over his shoulder flashed into his mind. It was swiftly followed by the boy's response when he'd asked him about it. "Spoils of war, Fynn," he'd said, " spoils of war…"

Now what in the hell did you mean by that, boy? Fynn wondered.

At sunset, Jakot came to convey the king's greetings and to bid them attend a feast in honour of those who'd returned.

Years of living with various groups of African people had given Fynn insight into their ways, and he could usually tell when they were being less than liberal with the truth. It wasn't that they were deliberately lying, he conceded. It was just that they weren't telling him *everything*…

As he listened to what Jakot had to say, his unease intensified. His instincts very rarely led him astray. According to the interpreter, the Nkosi

had just honoured Jackabo and bestowed on him the praise name of
'*iQawu*' meaning '*the hero.*' Fynn was frankly stunned when he heard the
news.

The young *umlungu* fledgling who had come to roost in the court of
King Shaka had not only earned himself a place of pride among the people
of the amaZulu, but had also won high esteem in the eyes of Shaka, their
warrior king.

Fynn watched Jakot as he sauntered back in the direction of the celebrations. You know more than you're telling me, he thought. The piece of
news you've just delivered is astounding. For a supreme commander like
Shaka to deliver eulogies for bravery was not unknown. The human
attributes he respected above all else were courage and loyalty, and he was
reputed to be unstintingly generous towards those he publicly acknowledged.

But Jakot had given him only the bare details of what exactly was being
celebrated, here and now, in the great arena behind the guarded gates.
There was more to it than that, Fynn could feel it in his bones. The boy
himself had said nothing about the journey, nothing about Delagoa, not
one word – which, in itself, was telling. And pretty damning, he thought.

In his mind's eye, he saw again the boy's long, hard gaze, the fleeting
impression in the blue eyes of having been to hell and back.

So, what is it that you all know – and I don't?

Jackabo put the leather bag to one side, then spilled the remaining gold
sovereigns out of the rolled-up sock and on to the upended drum.

He stared hard at them. When he'd started out, five of them had nestled inside the leather bag around his neck. One had been handed over to
pay for goods bartered for in the markets and trading stores of Delagoa
Bay, the other given over to help pay for the ships' tools and boatyard
supplies.

The three remaining coins winked dully up at him, the date and the
King's head on them almost obliterated by years of use.

GEORGE REX 1: King George the First, the one the Scots had called
'the wee German lairdie.' He had been the first of the Georges, and now
they were on the Fourth. Sandy had told him about how the Hanoverian

princes had come to power, although he'd to make do with brown pennies instead of gold sovereigns to show him their heads.

The date on the next sovereign was 1783, the year the United States of America had fought a war to rid themselves of His Hanoverian Majesty's redcoats and their interfering taxes, especially those levied on the tea trade.

The third coin bore the heavy-jowled, bewigged head of George 1V, the present king. The date embossed on it was 1815, which made it the same age as he was.

James King looked over his shoulder to see what he was doing. 'By Harry, Jack!' he exclaimed. 'Three sovereigns left over, eh? How did you manage it?'

Jackabo looked away. He'd no wish to linger on thoughts of the slaver Duval or about Delagoa itself. By way of deflecting further questions, he commented, 'There was Shaka's ivory as well, remember? We got a very good price for it. I thought it best to keep hold of the gold.'

To his relief, his explanation was accepted. Slipping the coins back into the leather bag, James King joked, 'Next time I need someone to do a bit of horse trading, I'll know just who to send for. Well done, Charlie!'

At long last, he thought, the business end of the expedition is complete. Shaka had been given a fair share of the medicines and Langalibalele and the men had also been rewarded. Jackabo took a last look at the piles of boxes and packages waiting to be transported to the bay.

The sailors had what they needed to finish the ship. And now it was time for his own plans.

James King was in a good mood. The prospect of returning with the long-awaited tools, parts, ship's chandlery items and fresh stocks of medicines was a pleasing one.

'What say we take a turn by Jackabo's quarters?' he said to Isaacs and Fynn. 'Since we'll be setting off at first light, we should say our farewells now.'

There was no sign of life when they got there, only a small fire burning outside. If they were hoping to find Ned closeted with Jackabo, they were disappointed.

What they did find, though, was a large black bird flapping its wings and screeching in indignation from the crossbeams of the hut.

'*Mon Dieu!*' muttered Isaacs, unnerved by the yellow eyes glinting down at him. When several dark feline shapes also materialised out of the shadows, he flinched and backed away.

'At least Jack's safe from snakes,' laughed Fynn. 'It'd be a brave one who'd try anything with those cats around, not to mention yon black devil roosting up there.'

As he turned to leave, King caught sight of one of Jackabo's drawing pads lying open on the upturned drum that served as a table. Alongside it was a handful of pencils and chalks. 'Hold the light up a bit higher, Nat, so I can have a look.'

'Good God!' he exclaimed as he skipped over first one page, then another. They were crowded with drawings painstakingly executed in colour, and also in pencilled shades of black and grey. Fynn and Isaacs came to have a look.

Several pages were filled with sketches of ancient weapons; three or four-foot long double-edged swords with intricately-crafted basket hilts; huge two-handed swords; also the *Sgian Ochles,* the lethal small daggers of the Highland clans designed to be carried near the arm pit.

And, last but not least, there was the *skean dhu,* the small dagger, admirably suited to a surprise attack – designed for concealment in the waistband of homespun trews, in the folds of a plaid or in the top of a stocking – out and at the enemy's throat in a moment.

The centrepiece of the boy's collection, which filled a whole double page, was a huge battle-axe with a long shaft. Neatly printed below it was the title: *LOCHABER AXE.*

'Mphm, 'said King, marvelling at the boy's knowledge of weaponry. 'Most of this is from a century or more ago.'

'He must have a good memory to remember all this from his school books,' said Fynn, bemused. 'I don't recall ever seeing anything like this in mine.'

King laughed. 'Damn right, you wouldn't have seen them in your schoolbooks, Fynn! The only place you'd have run into these beauties would have been up some Highland glen – and you would've been at the wrong end of them, seeing as you're an Englishman!'

'Be careful who you're calling English!' Fynn protested, in mock offence. 'The Fynns are as solid Irish as the Blarney stone, I'll have you know!'

King looked thoughtful for a moment. 'The only thing is – all these sketches are pretty detailed. How would he have known all this? Weapons like these have been banned since the '45.'

Turnng over the next pages, he whistled softly. 'And where, Fynn, where in the hell did he get these ideas from?'

In the wavering light, a multitude of faces looked out at them from the page – young and old, male, female, some innocent babes, children with the bloom of childhood on them, others ancient and timeless. And all of them, without exception, bore the unmistakable stamp of being of another time, another place.

One in particular, struck King forcibly. Young and strong-featured, the man's eyes were direct and piercing, boldness in their depths. His hair was long and woven into plaits, with golden eagle feathers stuck into the jaunty tam o'shanter set at a rakish angle on his head.

'Look at this,' he said. Fynn shifted the torch into his other hand and peered closer. For a moment or two, he could have sworn the image seemed to waver then detach itself from the page. *A trick of the firelight?*

He blinked and looked again. There was something scrawled below it. A name. Fynn stared hard at it.

Eachainn Maclean...

'Hector,' said James King, 'now, I wonder just what his story was?'

'So do I,' Fynn echoed uneasily, as fingers of apprehension began to stroke down his spine.

King closed the drawing book with a snap. 'Boys of that age,' he remarked, a trifle awkwardly, 'you know what they're like, coming into manhood, feeling their oats. Think war and battles and soldiery no end of a fine thing. Follow the sound of the drum, fight for King and country, and all that.'

He threw a quick glance at Fynn. 'The only trouble is, Henry, by the time they find out that it's nothing of the sort it's often too late. They're either dead or maimed for life.'

King sighed. 'Better we don't mention this to the boy. Wouldn't like him to think we'd been prying into his affairs.' Straightening up, he said. 'I've a good idea where he and Cameron will be. Let's go and find him.'

They were easy to find. All they had to do was follow the sound of drumming. The crowd parted good-naturedly to let them through.

'There they are,' Nat said.

Clad in a pair of trews hacked off below the knee, Jackabo's red hair stood out like a flame in the firelight. Ned Cameron sat cross-legged with a drum wedged between his knees, conferring with one of the Zulu drummers. His hands beat out a brief tattoo on the drum, the Zulu drummer following it, beat for beat.

'If this is what I think it is,' King said, 'it would fit in with the drawings.' The other two looked puzzled. 'The Highlanders?' he reminded them, impatiently.

'How do you know so much about this, *capitaine*?' queried Isaacs. 'You are from North America, I believe?'

King's teeth flashed white below the dark moustache. 'I was born and bred in Nova Scotia,' he answered, 'but my mother and father weren't. They fled from Scotland during the Highland Clearances to start a new life in Canada. But they handed down the stories, the songs and the legends to my sister and myself to keep the traditions alive – so you could say I know a little about it. Nova Scotia wasn't called 'New Scotland' without good reason.'

'So what d' ye think is going to happen?' 'He's going to do the *Ghillie Callum*,' King replied. 'What in hell's teeth is that?' Fynn demanded

'A sword dance,' answered King, his eyes bright in the firelight. Warming to his subject, he said, 'Ghillie Callum was a Celtic prince, a hero of mortal combat. Lived around the turn of the 16th century, fought one of King MacBeth's chiefs at the battle of Dunsinane. After he'd killed him, so the story goes, he took the chief's sword out of the scabbard and laid it down on the ground. Then he crossed it with his own weapon and proceeded to perform a victory dance over the pair of them. An act of domination, pure and simple.'

Fynn bared his teeth in a grin. 'I can see the appeal such a symbolic gesture might have in certain quarters.'

In the area bounded by the circle of fires, the red-haired boy took up his position in the centre of it and began to speak slowly. In the silence that fell, only the crackling and spitting of the fires in the background could be heard.

Isaacs hissed something below his breath and nudged Fynn to look at the tall, cloaked figure moving out of the shadows and into the firelight. Shaka himself.

King lowered his voice to a whisper. 'What's he saying, Fynn?'

Fynn shrugged his shoulders. 'It's as you said. He's telling them the story of the battle and the crossed swords.'

After he'd finished, the boy nodded to Ned. Cameron's nimble fingers began to beat out a fast rhythm on the drum, the Zulu drummers joining in.

The boy began to dance. His bare feet leapt over the pair of *assegai* crossed over one another on the ground. Coming perilously close to the razor-sharp blades, beat for beat, he performed the intricate, complicated movements of the dance.

A great wave of excitement ran through the crowd. A sound tore out of Ned Cameron's throat, a wild yell that echoed out beyond the firelight.

'*Jesus!*' Fynn said. As the tempo of the drumming heightened, shouts of approval rose from the crowd. The boy's face was solemn as he concentrated on the dance steps, his feet flying between the dangerous quadrants as he re-enacted Ghillie Callum's sixteenth-century victory dance.

Ned and the drummer crouched over the drums, their hands a blur in the firelight as they pounded on the taut skins, holding the rhythm.

Just when the watchers thought they must surely falter, the boy leapt high over the crossed blades. Then, in one swift movement, he bent down, scooped them up and held them over his head.

The drums stopped. The roar of voices and the ululating that followed was overwhelming. Fynn's eyes were riveted on the boy as he stood there with the spears held in triumph above his head. Flushed with exertion and the heat from the fires, chest heaving, there was something different about him, different, yet familiar.

The face…the hair…what was it about his hair?

He peered at him across the fire-lit space. Jackabo's long red hair had been drawn into plaits on either side of his face – a face bearing the same look he'd observed on the night the *impi* had returned. The nerves at the base of Fynn's skull began to prickle.

Where had he seen that face before – the plaited hair, the eyes that seemed to follow you? He gave a start. *The drawing book, the man called Eachainn – Eachainn Maclean…Hector…*

As far as he could see all that was missing between the drawing and Jackabo himself was the bonnet, the flamboyant eagle feathers adorning it – and a few centuries in time.

Twenty-Eight

Fynn and James King had been summoned to an urgent meeting with Shaka. Both of them had intended to leave that day, but now they had little choice but to postpone their departure for another day or so.

King was the edgier of the two due to his anxiety to start out on the hundred and fifty-mile journey back to the bay so that the new tools and ship's supplies could be handed over to Hatton so the work on the vessel could resume in earnest.

Once they'd completed the initial formalities of the usual Zulu greetings and courtesies, the serious talking began. Shaka was in a serious mood, in spite of the fact that he'd sat up far into the night talking with Fynn.

As he sat listening to what was being discussed, it seemed to Fynn that King was having second thoughts concerning the site near the mouth of the umLalazi River that was earmarked for the future settlement he'd proposed earlier and to which Shaka had given his sound approval.

A gap in the conversation gave him an opportunity to speak his mind. 'I would've said it was just the place to build a harbour,' Fynn commented. 'Perfect, in fact. A large sheltered bay, ample fresh water, good supplies of timber – so what's changed your mind?'

'It's not that I've changed my mind,' King replied, 'but there's still a bit of groundwork to do.' He remained deep in thought for a moment, then added,

'For one thing, I need to do a proper marine survey, create a professional plan of action backed up with solid facts, technical details that will satisfy any reluctant money man as to the authenticity and viability of the project.'

He hesitated for a moment, unwilling to voice what was uppermost in his mind, the suspicion that Farewell- and Petersen, his father-in-law- had most certainly gone some way to damaging his reputation with the Cape authorities. Taking a deep breath, he pushed his fears aside and continued,

'If there's to be a new port in the north of Zululand with the potential to challenge the Portuguese for the market in ivory, hides and hardwoods, it has to be set out properly. Also, the advantages of using umLalazi as opposed to eThekwini have to to be made clear, very clear, for the whole operation will depend on it.'

He took a swallow of beer then wiped the froth from his moustache. 'But, first things first – it's imperative we get the supplies taken to the boatyard as soon as possible, so work can start in earnest on completing the vessel.'

Fynn became aware of a movement on Shaka's part and glanced over at him.For some time, he had suspected that the Zulu king understood more of the language spoken by the *abelungu* than he cared to demonstrate. So when Shaka nodded his head and added a few comments in Zulu, it was obvious that the gist of what James King said had not been lost on him. But what he had to say next, however, proved to be an even bigger shock.

Rising effortlessly from the carved chair, he folded his arms across his chest. His gazed rested on each of them, briefly. 'I would like to say something important to you both. It is why I have asked you to come here this morning.'

Fynn stared at him in amazement. The Zulu king was someone who rarely had to announce that he had something to say, because he was far too powerful for that. So whatever was on his mind would no doubt turn out to be pretty vital, earth shattering, even – and most likely cause a great shift in the balance of things.

His instincts were right. Shaka looked at each of them in turn, then said, 'I have been thinking for some time that I would like to meet umGeorge, the great king across the waters.'

Jackabo wondered whether he'd heard him right, but judging by Jakot's sudden in-drawn hiss of breath, he knew there had been no mistake.

'I have thought a long time on this matter,' Shaka went on. His face was serious as he announced, 'I want my people and those of umGeorge to be on good terms. We have much to learn from each other. But since no one knows of me in his country, I have decided it would be best to first send my highest chiefs to prepare the way for me.'

Staring straight at James King, he added, 'When the *umkumbe* is ready, you will accompany my Zulu chiefs and travel south on the waters to meet the Great Chief of umGeorge. You will bring greetings from me and let him know of my intentions to meet with King Jo-Ji one day – in his own country. And so it will begin – the friendship of the people of the amaZulu and those of umGeorge.'

Satisfied with the hush that greeted his announcement, Shaka sat down again. Jackabo avoided looking directly at any of the others – unsure or unwilling to see what might be revealed on their faces following the revealing of Shaka's plans.

'What d'you think of that, then?' Fynn asked James King as soon as they were safely out of earshot. 'Has he ever broached the subject before?'

King was silent for a bit. 'I can't really be sure. I speak no Zulu, remember, everything has to come through Jakot, but I do remember Shaka asking about how long it would take to sail to the Cape. And as for King George – well, you know yourself how interested he always is in all things royal – English royal, that is!'

He turned to look at Fynn. 'What about you? You're closer to him that anyone. Any hint of what was lurking in his mind?'

'Yes and no, to that one,' Fynn responded. 'I knew he had definite plans as regards what lies south of here – but I assumed it was to acquire control of more territory, amaPondo land, in particular. I know that's why he moved his court south across the Tugela, so he could march on 'em when he was ready and not be hindered by the high river levels and floods during the rains.'

'You surely don't think he's plotting to sneak into the Colony under the guise of friendship, one hand holding out peace and co-operation, the other with an assegai in it?'

Instantly, Fynn shook his head. 'One thing about Shaka of the Zulus – he's a master strategist, and no one's fool. He's heard enough about British firepower, ships, cannons and redcoats not to provoke them into any sort of military action without due cause. Hearing what we just have, I think we can dismiss any idea that he has his sights on any British-held territory, far less storing any hidden agenda like taking up arms against them.'

There was silence for a while, then Fynn remarked thoughtfully. 'I don't know if it's occurred to you yet, King, – but certain aspects concerning the events of the last few months are beginning to make sense.'

James King looked puzzled. 'What are you on about, Henry? Which events do you mean?

'The whole thing,' Fynn answered, as he began to pace up and down. 'I don't include the near mutiny you had on your hands, or the crew downing tools and refusing to work on the ship. Can't say I blame 'em, to be fair. No, I mean what happened after that.'

After a few moments, King said, 'You mean sending Jackabo and a parcel of Zulus off to the Portuguese to acquire the supplies necessary for our survival here, as well as finishing the ship?'

'The very same!' Fynn said, 'But think, man, which other plan will now be able to go ahead because of that?'

'The goddam ship, my friend!' he hooted, not waiting for a reply. 'Without that little escapade into Mozambique, the ship would have had to be abandoned, left to rot where it stood, given over to the ants and termites. Instead of which…think, man! Were you not given your orders, mere days after Jackabo here's safe return with the *impi*, plus of course, all the supplies needed for the vessel's completion – about your first port of call, who was going with you…and what your mission would be?'

At first, James King looked a little dazed. Then the reality of Fynn's words began to sink in.

'By God, Henry, I do believe you're right. The ship's been as much a part of Shaka's agenda as it has been mine. Not that I grudge the man anything. Without his assistance, yours truly, and the rest of my crew, would really have been sunk – and in more ways than one, I can tell you. From the start, he's been more than helpful...'

He let out a snort of laughter. 'Devilish cunning Shaka might well be – a master of subterfuge, a planner *par excellence* and a ruthless schemer as well, but without him, I reckon most of us would be in a pretty sorry state by now, what with one thing and another.'

Silence descended once more, while the two men each deliberated in their own way the implications of what had just unfolded.

After a while Fynn opened the subject again. 'Jesus, why didn't I realise before now what his grand plan must have been all along? All the talk of King George and matters pertaining to the Cape-he's been deadly serious, hence his avid interest concerning both of them. Now that the future of the ship's no longer in doubt, he's put his cards on the table.'

He whistled loudly. 'I reckon he's about to send a peace mission south to the Cape Colony. Hence his plan for you – a white man living in peace in his country, unharmed – to escort a delegation of his chiefs as an introduction to the Governor, 'King George's great *induna*'–showing him he has nothing to fear from the Zulus.'

Another brief silence, then Fynn said, grinning hugely, 'I'd love to be a fly on the wall on the day Shaka of the Zulus comes face to face with George the Fourth in London! Now wouldn't that be something!'

A few days later, Shaka, Fynn and his entourage set out on their hunting trip. Now that the expedition to the Cape had been agreed, a few tusks of quality ivory would be needed as gifts for the Cape Governor.

Jakot was overjoyed with the news that his duties as interpreter had been suspended for a while. Turning to where Jackabo was trying his hand at carving a small deer out of a piece of wood, he said, 'Good! Nix Nkosi, nix *umlungu*. You must come with me to my kraal at Nkwalini. I need your company on the long road.'

Jackabo stopped whittling his piece of wood and waggled his toes under Jakot's nose. 'Do you see this foot? It has not long returned from Mozambique and the land of the Swazis.'

The Xhosa regarded him lazily through a haze of pipe smoke. 'So, iQawu is tired and wants to sit by the fire like an old man. Come to my kraal and take your ease there, see my fine little herd of duikers. But if you are too tired…'

Jackabo grinned and flicked a few curls of wood shavings at him. 'All right, all right,' he agreed. 'But if this old man gets too tired, you will have to carry him. Promise?'

Jakot shook the wood shavings from his hair. 'Only if you will do the same for me, my friend,' he groaned. 'Now, let us prepare. We have a long way to go.'

After travelling north for many days, they made camp early that night. From the spot they had chosen, they could just make out the dark bulk of the hills that separated them from Shaka's old settlement of kwaBulawayo.

The air was cool and pleasant, a half-moon rising out of the bush, the mountains ahead dark and mysterious in the silvery light. The cough of a hunting leopard broke the silence. Jackabo guessed it might be anything up to a mile away, probably prowling on the mountain or on the lower foothills.

To reassure himself, he touched the stock of the elegant, silver-chased firearm cradled across his knees. Primed and loaded, it was ready to use.

Jakot was sitting by the fire with his eyes half-closed. Now and again, he would lay aside his pipe and break into a snatch or two of song. Emerging from his reverie, he said, 'When we get to my kraal, you must try my second wife's beer. It is very good.'

Jackabo noticed the gleam of mischief in his eyes as he spoke. His reluctance to drink beer had long since become a game between them.

Very soon, common courtesy would dictate that he take his place among the men and accept a swig or two when it was offered him. To refuse would be seen as a lack of civility, and worse still, a reluctance to embrace manhood.

Yawning, he placed the gun carefully to one side, reached for his blanket and settled down. As he lay staring up into the night sky, the twinkling of their fire seemed fragile against the immensity of the plains and the teeming African night. But of all the species out there, he knew they were the best equipped of all of them to survive its dangers.

Once they reached kwaBulawayo, Shaka's original centre of power, on the following day, Jackabo proceeded straight to his old quarters, while Jakot went looking for some old friends. Pushing aside the goatskin flap, he stepped inside the hut that had once been his home. Not only had it been his sleeping place, it had also served purpose as the sanctuary for the other species had he taken under his wing.

Except for a family of mice and a long-tailed blue lizard scuttling like lightning across the floor, everything seemed just as he'd left it. A moment or two later, his instincts told him that he was no longer alone. Hair stirred along his arms and the back of his neck. Swivelling round, he became aware of a bulky figure standing in the doorway, blocking the light.

Then he relaxed. There was no mistaking the plump body, the greying pep-percorn curls and the round moon face with its smooth, hairless skin. As usual, the length of brightly coloured cotton draped over his torso failed to conceal the plump belly bulging over the top of his knee-length *umutsha*.

'Malusi!' Jackabo's thoughts scurried like ants around his brain. *Why was he here? The child would have been born by now. Had something gone wrong?*

The last time he'd seen him had been on that fateful dawn morning over a year ago. It was when he'd inadvertently met Nandi's small entou-rage just after they'd stolen away from kwaBulawayo in the early morning to avoid being seen. The day when the pregnancy of Mbuzikasi, whom he'd treated for a feverish chill, and whom he'd later suspected of being enamoured of Shaka, had been discovered.

Malusi's anxious eyes met his. A clutch of dread rose in him. *Oh God, what if someone's found out about the child?* Forcing himself to swallow the sudden knot of anxiety in his throat, Jackabo smiled weakly at him.

'Hau, Malusi! *Sala gahle.*' The high voice with the slight lisp returned his greeting, before casting another frightened glance back over his shoulder.

Jackabo pushed past him to the doorway and took a quick look around outside. The coast was clear; no one was following or lurking about.

'What is it? Has something happened?'

A trickle of moisture ran from Malusi's scalp down to his chin. 'The Nkosikazi says you come to emKindini. The Great She Elephant says.'

'Did the Nkosikazi say why?' Jackabo asked.

Malusi stared back at him, incomprehension written large on his face. Jackabo could almost read his thoughts. Why would the Great She Elephant tell the most humble of her servants why she had ordered something?

So Jackabo just said, '*Yebo*, Malusi, *kusasa*-tomorrow-when the sunrise comes I will be ready. The same as last time, remember?'

The moon face broke into a furtive, childlike smile. Putting his finger to his lips, he made shushing noises as he backed out of the doorway.

After he'd gone, Jackabo lay down on his old sleeping mat, his thoughts chaotic. How did Nandi know I was here, in kwaBulawayo? he wondered. No one knew I was coming. The very minute I stepped inside the hut, Malusi was at my heels – almost as if he'd been waiting for me.

But Malusi was not the only one to come looking for him that night. Whether it was the rumbles of thunder that woke him, or the feeling that something, or someone else was there, he couldn't say. The next flash of lightning lit up a pair of huge, inquisitive eyes mere inches from his. A pair of small, knobby, almost human-looking hands clutched the edge of his blanket.

Yebo, news travels fast in Africa, he thought, smiling, as he reached out for his small nocturnal visitor. iTombi, the bush baby, had come to welcome him back.

The child surveyed Jackabo unblinkingly from a pair of huge, dark brown eyes. Apart from a string of beads around his belly and another around his chubby wrist, the child was naked. Jackabo eyed him warily, hoping they wouldn't expect him to hold the infant or make cooing noises, anything daft like that.

'This is Magaye, our little Nkosi,' Nandi announced, waggling a finger at her grandson. Dressed in a simple skirt, with her ample breasts modestly covered by a bandeau of vivid red and black patterned cotton, her only ornament was a heavy necklace of beads. When he looked closer, he saw that her hair was threaded with silver and there were telltale creases around the mouth and eyes.

She's changed, Jackabo thought, all this worry about Shaka finding out what she's been hiding has made her old.

The small Magaye beamed at Jackabo and flapped his hands. Straining to get a closer look at the intriguing stranger, a thin spool of dribble leaked from his toothless mouth. His grandmother laughed and wiped it away.

Nandi leaned towards Jackabo, anxiety in her voice. 'Tell me, does he look like his father? Would anyone recognise him?'

He hesitated for a few agonising moments. Should he tell her the truth, or not? Anyone with half an eye could see the family likeness. Magaye was clearly of the kaSenzangankhona bloodline and the spitting image of his father, the ruling King of Zululand.

In his heart, Jackabo knew trouble would come the minute someone suspected the truth. The child was also Nandi's flesh and blood and nothing could change that. The fierce pride on her face when she looked at him said it all. Would she be able to keep the look of joy off her face and hold every line of her body in check if need be? Knowing her as he did, he doubted it.

Fortunately, Mbuzikazi, the child's birth mother, chose that moment to appear. Smiling shyly, she knelt to lay out bowls of nuts, fruits and honey cakes. A howl went up as the child recognised her and demanded to be noticed. His baby face was drawn into a scowl, and his fat little hands were bunched into fists, waving in the air.

Startled, Jackabo glanced across at Nandi. No one who'd ever seen the Zulu king in a rage could fail to notice the family traits. Nandi caught Jackabo's eye, and burst out laughing.

'Eh, Jackabo,' she said, wiping the tears from her eyes. 'Magaye speaks for himself, a true Senzangakhona, bellowing when he doesn't get what he wants. Truly, he is his father's son.'

Mbuzikazi rose off her knees and took the child, rocking and crooning to him until he quietened down. Nandi sighed. '*Dadewetu!* What trickery we have to resort to. If he should ever find out who he really is...'

Reaching over, she offered Jackabo a bowl of honey cakes before sampling some herself. Sitting back on her heels, she glanced sideways at the red haired boy, then said, 'My son has honoured you, given you a high place. You are free to go anywhere you wish. Nowhere is denied you.'

Jackabo nodded. Magaye had stopped crying, his head lolling against his mother's breast. Nandi toyed with the beads around her neck. 'Because of this, you see and hear much, Jackabo.'

He could only nod his head. Now we're getting to the nub of why she's brought me to emKindini, he thought. Her face tightened. 'You know the hyena Mbopha, the only one trusted to carry a blade within sight of Shaka? *Aiee*! I have told my son often enough to be careful of this man, but he pays me no heed.'

Her hand shot out and gripped him by the wrist. 'Tell me what you know of this dog and the pack he runs with. And who among my son's enemies is the most dangerous?'

Her fingers were like steel. When Jackabo looked into her pain-filled eyes, his heart thudded with apprehension and fear. He had never voiced any of his suspicions before, not to a living soul. The treacherous whispers he'd overheard; catching sight of the unguarded hatred in certain eyes when they thought no one was watching.

Nandi already knew the answers to both questions; it was only confirmation she sought. She *was* Shaka's mother, after all, as fiercely protective of him as she was of Magaye.

Surrendering to the inevitable, he replied, 'The most dangerous of them all is Mkabayi, the sister of the Nkosi's father, the one called *impika*. Mbopha is part of the same.'

Her eyes closed briefly, and the grip on his wrist slackened. 'iQawu, you are very clever,' she said, 'you have good eyes and ears as well as a brave heart.'

On hearing his praise name, Jackabo's heart leapt. News travelled fast.

But then, she would have made a point of keeping a close eye on him. After all, they'd shared the same dangerous secret for the past year and more.

'Mkabayi is truly named *impika*,' she said, with contempt, ' she has hated me since the day I was brought to esiKlebeni, heavy with child. And once my son was born, she hated him also, because she had no child of her own. If she ever came to hear of our Magaye, she would destroy him – and all of us.'

Wearily, she wiped a hand across her face. 'There is another reason why she seeks Shaka's downfall.' The whites of the eyes boring into his were muddy and flecked with red. 'Do you know why, Jackabo?'

His response was swift. '*Yebo*, it is because she has other plans for who should be King of the Zulus.'

Nandi narrowed her eyes and looked at him for a moment. Then she smiled, her teeth white against her full lips, the Nkosikazi of old back again. She stroked the side of his face tenderly with a long forefinger.

'I see you understand everything, Jackabo. So, from your own lips, tell me the name of the one she favours.'

Jackabo hesitated. Oh, God, he thought, how much further into the secrets of the house of Zulu can I go? For a moment, he felt the scorching heat of danger and the blood smell of it pass close by. Then he said, 'The half-brother of Shaka, the one called Dingane.'

'*Yebo*, he is the one,' she agreed, her eyes full of anger. She sighed. 'Life has been hard, full of troubles. This little one, this Magaye, means much to me.' Another sigh, longer this time, trailing away into silence.

Eventually, Nandi said,' Do you see the white hairs on my head, Jackabo? I am growing old.' Her voice trembled, 'I am afraid someone will find out about the child. I fear for his life.'

What she then went on to suggest shocked him even more. 'The place called eThekwini is ruled by the white chiefs. All who live there are under their rule, and not that of Shaka. Is this not so?'

He stared at her in disbelief. A hot little wind had sprung up. It rustled along the smoothly swept ground, bringing the odour of baked earth and dust with it. Inside the Great Hut, someone sneezed, and then giggled.

Watching his face carefully, she spread out her hands in appeal. 'They could help Magaye and his mother. They could keep them safe.'

Jackabo blinked rapidly. Oh, God, did she seriously believe her grandson and his mother could find sanctuary anywhere within the kingdom, if Shaka – or worse still, if Mkabayi or Dingane discovered their existence?

Out of his depth, he struggled to find the right words. 'The white chiefs only rule in the place called eThekwini because Shaka allows it,' he said. 'They can hold courts and punish those who steal and suchlike, but in important matters, it is the king who has the real power. It is his land. This is the truth.'

She made a noise in her throat. 'My son put his mark in favour of the one called Febana ka ma Jo-Ji. It gave him land and power in the place called eThekwini. What do you know of this?'

Jackabo remembered what James King had told him of the land grant bearing Shaka's large sprawling X, along with those belonging to Chief Sotobe and Jakot Msimbithi, the piece of hand-made vellum which had made Farewell the master of eThekwini.

To gain time for him to think, he pretended to wipe a piece of grit from his eye. Meantime, his mind was racing. What do I know about land laws and who might own what?

He shrugged his shoulders. 'I do not think this means Febana ka ma jo-ji really *owns* the land,' he said, as truthfully as he could, while trying to ignore the look of desperation in Nandi's eyes.

'Shaka is Nkosi of all Zululand,' she insisted. 'If he gives someone a gift, then surely it must belong to the one he gave it to. Is this not so?'

Determined not to give her false hope, Jackabo added hastily. 'It is not because the white chiefs would not want to help Magaye and his mother, but eThekwini would be no safer than any other place in the kingdom.'

'*Or outside it…*' he could have added, but didn't.

The cry wrenched from her was heartbreaking. With a huge effort, she brought her emotions under control. Gripping his hand, she brought it to her breast and held it there.

'Then, Jackabo, I must tell you where the child will be taken if disaster befalls us… a place where he will be safe.'

He felt the anguish flood through her, as hot and virulent as a fever.

'You have kept our secrets well, Jackabo, but now I must trust you with another.' Through her tears, she whispered, 'It will be the last secret of Nandi, so listen well.'

Tears pricked at his eyes and he was forced to bend his head so she wouldn't see them. 'If the *amadhlozi* become angry or I smell treachery, I will send the child away,'she said. 'No enemy must find Magaye. I will give my heart's blood to prevent it.'

Shuddering, as if to rid herself of a shadow that was too close, she put her mouth close to his ear, and began to whisper.

Jackabo listened very carefully, as Nandi, Nkosikazi of all Zululand, told him her last secret; the place where Shaka's son would find sanctuary in the event of betrayal – or her death.

After leaving emKindini, he spent a week or two with Jakot at his farm, glad of no longer having to deal with Nandi's overwhelming sadness and her fears for the future.

One of the first things they did was to inspect the group of little duikers Jackabo had left with him before leaving for kwaDukuza. The miniature deer were sleek and fat, though not so small and defenceless now, and so tame that they'd taken to joining Jakot's cattle going out to graze in the mornings, returning at sunset each day.

On recognising his smell, they put their noses into his hand, their tails shaking in pleasure, their bright eyes innocent and childlike.

When Jakot offered him the beer pot after supper that night, Jackabo didn't hesitate. Reaching for it, he took several long, gurgling swallows of the potent, yeasty brew. Afterwards, he belched to show his appreciation, grinning as he wiped the froth from his mouth.

Jakot put back his head and laughed. 'Eh,' he said, his eyes wicked in the firelight. 'Soon I must find you a wife, one with plenty of meat on her bones!'

Every day, the weather grew more oppressive. By early afternoon, the underbellies of the clouds were black and full, darkening the world.

The ground was as hard as rock, and Jakot's wife had to toil hard, carrying water from the stream to water the gardens and keep the crops from dying.

All too soon, it was time to leave. Shaka would be returning from his hunting expedition soon and Kingi and Isaacs were also expected at kwaDukuza.

There was no need to visit kwaBulawayo again, Jakot said, for they would head directly south instead. Jackabo breathed a huge sigh of relief.

He had very good reason not to want to return to Shakaka's old citadel, because of what had happened there on his way back from visiting Nandi at emKindini.

The uncanny way Mkabayi seemed to materialise out of thin air on to the path in front of him had put the wind up him, and no mistake.

Although common sense told him witchcraft had nothing to do with her appearance, later on he couldn't help wondering if she'd been a phantom after all, conjured up by someone who'd recently overheard him discussing her with Nandi. What had leapt out at him, however, had been unmistakably flesh and blood, rank hostility glaring out of her coal-black eyes.

As he'd trailed wearily back into kwaBulawayo, all he could think of was how good a long cool drink of water was going to taste. As he padded along, his feet made no sound on the dusty paths. The former royal residences lay deserted in the glaring heat of afternoon, only the chirping of cicadas to disturb the stillness.

One moment, the path ahead of him lay empty, the next she was there, barring his way. *Mkabayi…*

There was no doubt in Jackabo's mind as to who she was – the sister of kaSenzangakhona, Shaka's father. For one thing, she bore the undeniable stamp of the Zulu royal house, even the barely-concealed rage lurking in her eyes looked familiar.

She was a rare example of a last-born twin who had cheated death. Instead of being sacrificed to release her sister from the curse of sharing the same womb, Mkabayi had been spared by a kindly father who had refused to have his infant daughter put to death.

Like most devils, the woman called *impika, the wild cat,* was good looking. Her hair was dressed in corncrake rows, woven flat to her head, her ear lobes elongated by a pair of heavy ear-rings while anklets and bracelets clinked with every move. Bold eyes raked over him, lingering a little too long on his mass of red hair before sliding to the firearm slung over his shoulder.

'From where are you come, white child?' she spat. 'You are far from home. What is so close to kwaBulawayo that you have no fear of travelling alone?'

Her smile was open, generous even. But her eyes said something else. Jackabo watched them closely.

'Ah!' She smiled, as if a sudden thought had just occurred to her. 'EmKindini, the great kraal of the Nkosikazi is not far from here. Perhaps you have been paying her a visit?'

The skin along his arms crawled as if soldier ants were parading over it. He said nothing, just kept his eyes steady on hers, hoping they wouldn't betray what he was thinking. Mkabayi regarded him much as a cat would a mouse. Her eyes glittered. 'I have heard of your courage, i*Qawu*. The Nkosi has also honoured you with cattle from his finest herds, I believe.'

She leaned forward, hissing, 'Take care, little *umlungu*. Do not be like the moth that flies too near the fire. You know what happens to these unfortunate creatures?'

The smell of her, feral and hot, was overwhelming. A trickle of sweat ran into the deep cleft between her breasts. Nostrils flaring, she reached out to touch his hair.

Instinctively, Jackabo pulled his head away. Anger flared in the handsome face. 'Then I shall tell you, boy! They shrivel and die, all the beautiful wings burned in the flames – such a pity.'

Fine spittle settled on his skin. Resisting the urge to wipe it away, Jackabo stood his ground and said nothing. She spat out a final warning. '*Stay where you belong, keep your nose out of matters that do not concern you!*'

Then in a whirl of fur-tailed skirts and clink of brass, she was gone. All that remained on the dusty path were her footprints and the lingering traces of her musky odour.

Twenty-Nine

Jackabo had always known that he would not have to go far to find Langani. It was what the diviner had told him before they parted below the *mkuhla* tree in the heart of Shaka's half-constructed new settlement.

'We shall meet again, iQawu,' he'd said with a smile. 'When the time is right, you will know how to find me.'

In spite of the strangeness of Langani's calling, Jackabo had liked the young diviner and they had spent a few hours together, talking and laughing in the dappled shade. The mysterious stranger with the long, braided hair was young and full of fun, not at all like the usual white-daubed *isangoma* who put the fear of God into folk.

'My name is Langani,' he'd said, then went on to tell him how he had come to be a diviner. 'As a young boy, I suffered the deep spiritual anguish known as *ukutwasa*. Driven frantic by dreams, voices and visions, fearing I was going mad, I had no choice but to accept the role the *amadhlozi*, the ancestors, had chosen for me.'

'Eh, it was hard, very hard,' he'd said, drawing in the sand with the point of a stick. 'I was young, no older than you are now, iQawu. I ran away many times, knowing I would have to give up everything to serve the ancestors and the people of my tribe. Eh, but it is hard to forget your mother and father, your brothers and sisters – especially young girls, *mdodo…*'

The corners of his mouth and eyes crinkled up, laughing when the colour rose in the boy's face. Then he'd shrugged his shoulders, his face solemn.

'There are some things you can never escape,' he said, 'no matter how far and fast you run.' Casting a long, sideways glance at Jackabo, he added softly, 'Like accepting *isipiwo* – one's destiny. What is to be, will be.'

During the three or four long years he had spent as a *twasa*, Langani had been apprenticed to a powerful *isangoma*, a woman known as Nthabiseng. Rising at dawn to start the day by ritual prayer and dance, he had worked tirelessly, cooking, cleaning, fetching and carrying for her.

This, as he'd explained, was to teach him humility and to prepare him to submit his will, first to her and then to the *amadhlozi*. Only after reaching an acceptable state of obedience and learning was he permitted to access the secrets of the ancient rituals.

The young diviner pointed to some *dassies,* little rock rabbits, that had hopped out from their burrows and were sitting cleaning their whiskers in the sunlight. With eyes that were suddenly mischievous, he said, 'The spirits of life are everywhere, iQawu – in the trees, the flowers, the roots below the ground – and especially in small creatures like these.'

Before they'd parted, he had whispered softly, 'When the spirits call, all must dance to their tune, black man, white man, it is all the same. It is how it is.'

When Jackabo returned to kwaDukusa, he waited until it was dark and then went to wait below the spreading branches of the *mkuhla* tree, the very spot where he had fallen asleep and wakened to find Langani watching him.

While he sat there, waiting, he thought about what the diviner had said as he had taken his leave of him. 'When the time is come, you and I shall meet again. Soon.'

Then he'd smiled and said, '*Yebo,* I have already seen it in the throwing of the bones. So it will be.'

On the way back to kwaDukuza, Jackabo had been preoccupied by his concern for Nandi and the stomach-churning confrontation with

Mkabayi. Now, listening to the rustling of the leaves above his head, he wondered whether Langani was aware of the dangers facing Nandi and the baby Magaye, or knew of Mkabayi's sinister appearance during his visit to kwaBulawayo. He really needed the diviner's help. Who else could understand these things?

The white blur of a hunting owl swooped down over the iron-hard ground of the empty square. A few moments later, a faint rustling sound close by told Jackabo that he was no longer alone.

'I have been expecting you, iQawu,' the diviner said. As he rose from the shadows, his body was as tall and straight as the *mkuhla* tree itself.

By noon on the following day, they were miles away from kwaDukuza. Although Jackabo had sensed the occasional village nearby, they had neither seen nor heard any one or anything, almost as if both human and animal life had stayed silent until they'd passed by.

Langani pointed to the dense thickets on either side of the track. 'Do not be tempted to come this way alone,' he said, with a disarming smile. 'There are many snakes here – and other things that would do you harm.'

Clad in a simple *umutsha,* with a goatskin bag slung over his shoulder, the young diviner wore nothing unusual to mark his calling or draw attention to himself. The long hair braided into plaits reminded Jackabo of the *iziYendane* tribesmen he had seen loping out of the bush in the dawn light during the time he'd spent with the Zulu army.

Now it looked as if they were just about to emerge from the miles of winding bush paths they had been following. Ahead appeared to be an old river-bed, long dried-up and overgrown with seedling trees, clumps of grass and wild flowers growing in profusion along its gravel-strewn course. Looming above it was a steep-sided ravine that might have once determined part of the river's meandering course.

Some small round pebbles embedded in the sand caught his eye. Jackabo bent down and picked them up. Washed down from the mountains called *uKhalamba, the barrier of spears,* they were as smooth as glass, and of interesting colours and textures. Some even had speckles of gold glittering in them. He thrust a few into his pocket. He would add them to his collection of sea-shells and other trophies.

Dead ahead, the side of a mountain rose sheer out of the river bed. A wall of dense bush covered its slopes, while higher up, outcrops of reddish sandstone and stunted trees were visible. Langani was waiting for Jackabo at the foot of it

Unlike the solemn *iziYendane* warriors, with their profusion of long plaits, Langani was smiling. 'I hear your doubts,' he said, indicating the mountain side. 'It is good you have trusted Langani enough not to speak them aloud.'

Jackabo crossed the last few yards of the dried up stream. 'Then you'll have all the answers ready for me,' he said, matching the smile.

The sound of Langani's laughter echoed along the ravine, bouncing off the rocky sandstone crags and sending a flock of brightly coloured birds squawking skywards. A troupe of baboons burst out of the scrub, the grizzled elder knuckling the ground and snarling his displeasure until his charges had disappeared safely into the bush.

Langani pointed up past the scree and dense shrubbery. 'Up there is where we will be sleeping tonight,' he said, mischief in his eyes.

Jackabo looked up the precipitous slope. 'You have a house up there?' he echoed. 'Are you sure it's not a *nest* you live in?'

'Well, iQawu,' Langani said, with a toss of his long plaits, 'you will just have to wait and see.' Still smiling, he ducked down, plunged into the jungle of stunted bushes and disappeared.

Jackabo lost no time in dodging in after him. Guided by the pale undersoles of Langani's feet, he followed him up through a twisting maze of paths and tunnels, slipping and slithering on fallen leaves. It was quiet in the dusky gloom, the air musky and smelling of dry earth.

Once or twice, something spun and slithered away from him into the dim silence. Judging by the tufts of wiry hair caught on barbed thorns and twigs, the burrows were well used. The thought of coming face to face with a porcupine or two or a family of warthogs was not something he exactly relished.

A slice of blue sky appeared up ahead. A brief flash of Langani's buttocks below the *umutsha* as he scrambled up the last few feet, then disappeared from sight. Jackabo crawled up the last few yards and came blinking out into the sunlight.

He found himself standing on a flat lip of ground that stretched back against the mountain for fifty yards or so. Tucked in close to the rocky hillside was a neat beehive hut, its thatches silvered by sun and rain and sheltered by a cluster of trees.

In the stillness, the sound of trickling water seemed unnaturally loud. Shading his eyes, Jackabo looked around for its source. He was surprised to see a small waterfall cascading down the rocks, splashing and leaping as it came.

An extensive garden lay close by. To his surprise, he saw rows of tall, yellowing corn, trailing pumpkin, succulent beans and a host of other vegetables creating a splash of green against the dun colours of rock and dusty foliage.

Langani flashed a roguish smile at him, his teeth white in the glare.

'Do you like my house, iQawu?' he asked, indicating the beehive hut. 'It is where I call home, although I have a few other places where I sleep from time to time. Sometimes even Langani does not know where he will lay his head at night, so it is best to be prepared.'

The view from up there was spectacular. Endless miles of bush stretched into the distance to end in a smudge of purple haze on the horizon, while far to the west he caught sight of a range of hills and the distant gleam of sun on water.

A *druidh,* a man of magic Langani might well be – a powerful one even – but Jackabo was glad the diviner had chosen a place of light and endless horizons to live, for it told him a lot about the kind of man he was.

Langani lives like a king with his kingdom spread out before him, he thought, master of all he can see. No one would ever suspect that the secret hideaway of a powerful *isangoma* was hidden three-quarters of the way up a mountain, a place you could only get to by scrambling up through a steep-sided jungle of twisted scrub and aloes.

Curious to see what the inside of an *isangoma's* house looked like, he turned round, expecting to see Langani, but there was no sign of him. What he did see, though, was a spotted cat-like creature moving towards him with an intense look of fierce concentration on its face.

Jackabo froze. The animal was smaller than a leopard; the body longer and more loose-limbed with distinctive black tear marks curving from eye to muzzle.

It took him a moment or two to remember where he'd seen it before – or one very like it. Of course! This was what had begun to materialise out of the heat haze on the sands of eThekwini on those very first hours ashore after the storm that wrecked their ship and cast them adrift. But this was no leopard. It was a cheetah, the animal that could outrun anything on four legs.

As it stretched out its small neat head towards him, Jackabo felt the brush of wiry whiskers and the delicate rasp of its black tongue against his skin, followed by a waft of fishy breath. A pair of exquisite golden eyes looked into his.

'I see you have met Celiwe,' Langani called out from the doorway of the hut. 'She is named after a warrior queen of the Nguni people. Don't worry, she will not harm you.'

Jackabo let out a ragged sigh of relief. Eyeing the cheetah, he could see a certain female delicacy in the beautifully marked face. When he went inside with Langani, the animal lay down across the doorway and watched them, the tip of its long, banded tail beating lazily.

When Langani announced, 'My house is yours, be comfortable,' Jackabo cast a curious glance around him. Apart from a few wooden stools and an upended drum which served as a table, there was only a homely clutter of earthenware pots, strings of dried herbs and gnarled roots strewn around, the air infused with the musky, exotic odours of herbs and spices.

The other end of the hut was in shadow, so he tried to hide his curiosity and not peer too closely into what the *isangoma* might have hidden away in the darker recesses of his home. What did catch his eye, though were a few soft deerskin bags laid out on top of another drum. Tied at the neck with animal gut, they had an air of mystery about them.

Seeing where his interest lay, Langani frowned and indicated the small skin purses with a long forefinger. 'These you must not touch. Never try to open them.'

A sharp clucking above his head made Jackabo look up. The sharp golden eyes of a rooster surveyed him from the crossbeams, its scarlet comb and jowls bridling.

Langani made a few soothing noises to it. 'This one is not as gentle as Celiwe,' he commented, his mouth twitching in a smile. 'Pay him no heed. He is just looking for attention.'

He put a hand on the boy's shoulder. 'Now it is time for us to eat – you must be hungry. Come, you can help me prepare the food. Afterwards, but only if you wish, you can tell me what is troubling you.'

To Jackabo's relief, the meal they sat down to share was entirely normal; good solid fare containing no apparent magical ingredients – or, at least, none that he could identify.

The Umfolozi hunting grounds.

The lifeless mass of a bull elephant lay on the ground, buzzing flies settling in clusters on the gaping wounds in the animal's leathery hide, the stench of blood thick and coppery in the heat.

Hunting spear in hand, spattered with blood and gore, Fynn stepped away from the bloody carcase and flicked a glance in Shaka's direction. A few moments ago, a messenger had arrived from emKindini with an urgent message. Shortly afterwards he had collapsed and now lay on the ground, gasping for breath.

Blank faced, Shaka eyed the man at his feet. The message he had brought had been simple. *The Nkozikazi is very sick...*

'What ails the Nkosikazi?' Fynn asked. He'd never known the matriarch to have a day's illness. Secretly he'd always doubted if anything would have the temerity to attack the indomitable woman who was Shaka's mother.

Shaka's only response was to brush away the flies buzzing round his head. 'I am told she has pains in the stomach.'

When Fynn offered his services, the suggestion was waved aside.

'I will send an *inyanga*,' Shaka said. 'He will give her *muthi*, also some of the medicines Kingi brought me.'

Nudging the messenger with his foot, he rattled out a series of instructions then strode off in the direction of the hunting kraal, while the exhausted man followed a respectful distance behind.

As days passed, each report from emKindini was more desperate than the one before. *The Nkosikazi is in great pain...the Great She Elephant cannot eat, or drink...*

In spite of it, Shaka insisted in rising at first light to continue the relentless hunt for elephant; each day yet another medicine man was dispatched to emKindini, while the heat and humidity grew ever more oppressive.

After darkness fell, though, the King of the Zulus hardly slept. Fynn watched him pace up and down in the firelight, while the thunder and lightning rumbled and flashed in the distance. The rains were very close, and it was stifling, even at midnight.

At last, Fynn could stand it no longer. He went to confront Shaka, steeling himself for refusal, argument, or even threats. 'At first light, I intend to leave for emKindini,' he stated bluntly, 'perhaps there is something I can do for the Nkozikazi; maybe something among my medicines will ease her pain.'

To his relief, Shaka agreed. 'You are right, Mbuyasi,' he said, staring up into the sullen, starless sky. 'The rains are almost here. The hunt must end. Tomorrow I will return to kwaBulawayo. But first, go to emKindini and see to my mother.'

Fynn made his excuses and left to prepare for the journey. Afterwards, he found it hard to sleep. Tonight, there were no glittering stars, only a low, brooding darkness pregnant with tension and an indefinable threat.

He lay awake for a long time, the nagging sense of unease in the pit of his stomach underscored by each flicker of lightning and rumble of distant thunder.

Some miles short of kwaBulawayo, Fynn parted company with Shaka, and headed for emKindini, pushing on through the sweltering heat. By the time he arrived at the Queen Mother's kraal, it was late afternoon. He lost no time in heading for her private quarters.

A group of *izinyanga zokwelapha*, medical practitioners, were squatting outside the royal hut, their faces closed and secretive. Also standing by were a few of Nandi's personal guards.

Fynn nodded to the doctors and exchanged the usual courtesies with them. Knowing from past experience what to expect, he took a few deep breaths before bending his head and entering Nansi's residence.

A fire had been lit in the middle of the floor. The pall of smoke was so intense that Fynn could hardly draw breath, let alone make out where the sick woman was. To make matters worse, the hut was also crowded with female servants and women from the *isigodlo*.

The air was heavy with the earthy smell of the *izinyanga's* herbs, roots and potions. Underlying it all, Fynn could detect the sickening odours of infection and stale urine. Hastily, he resisted the urge to cover his nose and mouth. While trying to find his way to the sick woman, his hands came in contact with more than one bare breast and pig-tailed head. Sweating profusely and muttering apologies, he finally gave up the struggle.

Raising his voice above the keening of the women, he announced loudly, 'The Nkosikazi must have air. Everyone must leave. Only the *izinyanga* may stay. If you are needed, I will send for you.' After that, he ordered the fire put out and the smoking debris disposed of.

Fynn knelt by the Queen Mother. Curled up in the foetal position, her knees drawn up to her chin, Nandi looked shrunken and old, drained of her usual vitality and strength.

Her skin was grey and clammy, though burning hot, her breathing heavy and laboured. Careful not to dislodge any of the artefacts placed around her by the *izinyanga zokubula*, Fynn set about examining her.

The watery fluid oozing from her bowels told him a lot. His diagnosis was the same as that of the *izinyanga*. Dysentery. Although her condition was far more acute than Fynn had expected, he could tell there was another infection, a different one, running below it. He could smell it.

When he sought to ease her gently on to her back, she jerked and moaned without regaining consciousness. Carefully, he eased the thin cotton away from the lower half of her body. The odour made him gag, and his eyes ran with salt tears and sweat.

Fynn recognised a spear wound when he saw one. The deep gash in the Queen Mother's thigh was unmistakably the result of a sharp weapon being used with force. The festering edges were dull red, oozing pus and deeply infected. The skin must have split open like a ripe melon when her attacker struck. He wiped away the pus and tried to clean the wound as best he could.

With a sinking feeling in his gut, he realised it was more than likely Shaka's mother was going to die. And there was little he could do about it. No *muthi* in his possession could stop either the infection or the inevitable end of her life.

In a woman of Nandi's age, one of the root causes of her illness would have been bad enough, but suffering from both an acute bowel disorder and a severe infection elsewhere in her body, there was little chance of her making a recovery.

All he could do was to see that she was made comfortable. Very carefully, Fynn covered the angry-looking gash in her thigh and then went to the door to call for the women to come back inside.

Once they'd gathered round, he drew aside the cloth, revealing the infected wound. As he did so, he watched every flicker of emotion crossing the faces of the women around him. 'What do you know of this?' he asked, indicating the suppurating wound. They moaned and shook their heads, the smell of fear rank in the air.

'Who has been here? Who has come to emKindini in the last days?'

The distraught women covered their heads, moaning and keening as they rocked to and fro beside the body of their dying mistress.

Although Fynn was convinced they were hiding something, he eyed the trembling women with some compassion. Whatever they knew, they couldn't, or wouldn't, dare to divulge it. Something bad had happened in emKindini. Fynn could feel it in his bones. But there was nothing he could do about it.

At the best of times, for a white stranger to interfere in Zulu matters would inevitably stir up a hornet's nest of suspicion and resentment. For him to become involved in the investigation of a suspicious injury to a Queen of the royal house of Zulu, Shaka's mother – he realised only too well that the repurcussions arising from such an action would be of unbelievable proportions.

Resigning himself to the inevitable, Fynn motioned for the *izinyanga* to assist him in making the last hours of Shaka's mother more comfortable.

The Place of Dreaming.

Langani's eyelids began to flutter. After the boy had gone to sleep, he had partaken of both the roots of the *lesedi* and the toxic bulb of *leshoma* to help him relax and attain the necessary level of meditation. Already he could feel their effects, although it would take some time before he slipped away.

The *lesedi* would help to clarify his mind and bring him deep calm. The *leshoma* now, was another thing altogether, a far more dangerous substance.

There was little chance iQawu would wake before first light. Just to make sure, he had mixed a little of the potato-like *labateka* root into the food they had shared. It would do him no harm and would help to repair any weakness in the core of his body.

The boy moved in his sleep, and muttered something. Langani's eyes scanned his boyish face for signs of unease or distress, but found none, although beads of sweat stood out on his upper lip and on the pale brow that lay below the tangle of red hair.

Langani had been aware for some time of the strong presences hovering around the boy. They were strange ones, these spirits from another time, another world. He had acknowledged them as such, recognising that they were to the boy what his own *amadhlozi* were to him. In turn, they had regarded him with great curiosity, but no hostility, before hooding their light-coloured eyes and drawing back to hover a watchful distance away.

Langani cast a thoughtful eye over the boy's face, relaxed in sleep. Some danger must have threatened you to draw your guardians from the spirit world to protect you, he thought, remembering the evil that had come upon him in the land of the bearded Portuguese.

The diviner thought back to the time he'd come across him sleeping beneath the spreading branches of the *mkhula* tree. His mouth lifted in a smile. You also have powers, although you do not know it yet. Even then, as I watched you, I knew you were dreaming, exploring, your awareness growing.

Boyhood is giving way to manhood, he thought, as he studied the planes and facial bone structure of the twelve-year old boy. For a moment, he saw clearly the face of the man he would one day become.

Yebo, Langani thought, you will be a good man, and a brave one. I know how you acquitted yourself in the land of the Portuguese. The great Shaka also knew how brave and true you were, otherwise he would not have given you the praise name of iQawu. To be known as 'Shaka's hero' is no small thing.

As the effects of the mystical roots began to take effect, the diviner's breathing deepened, then slowed down. That this child of the sea people had such a curious connection to the mighty King Shaka was indeed intriguing – but it was no surprise to him, as he'd already seen it in the

waters, and in the throwing of the bones, long before the boy had ever set
foot in Zululand.

The fact that he, Langani, the most elusive of all the *isangoma*, had brought
him here to the place to which no one, not even his own family members knew
about, was testimony enough to the strength of the connection between them,
for the boy had trusted him implicitly, with no trace of fear.

His face softened. Also, iQawu was in need of a friend...

The boy had not told him in so many words exactly what was troubling
him, but Langani knew that it lay very close to the *umhlolo*, the bad thing,
which in turn was linked to the present house of Zulu.

Suddenly, he remembered a night at the start of the cold, dry season, just
days after the boy had set out on the long journey to the land of the Portuguese.
The full moon was still high in the sky when the faint but insistent cries of a
newly born child had jolted him from sleep. Afterwards he'd wondered whether
it had been connected to the secretive whispers he'd intercepted concerning the
Nkosikazi and the hint of a wife for Shaka. Was it this, or something stemming
from it, which lay at the roots of iQawu's present anguish?

Langani had known they would meet again, but the timing and the
strength of the appeal sent out to him had greatly surprised him. Something must have happened to disturb the boy and make him fearful, either
for himself or for someone close to him...

The *leshoma* begin to take effect. Slowly, the colours and shapes and
textures around him began to shift and crystallise. Langani's sense of
hearing sharpened and became more acute.

Whatever the cost, he would seek out the meaning behind the inexplicable images that streamed and wound in and out of his dreams like
ribbons in the wind. Slowly, the diviner let himself slip away to the place
where the present, the past and the future were as one.

Next to him, the fingers on the sleeping twelve-year-old's hand curled
as if he was clasping the hand of a friend, and the ghost of a smile passed
over his face.

Some hours later, the rooster cocked an amber eye and bobbed its head
from side to side. From its perch on the crossbeams, it could look down
into the body of the hut and see everything.

Wisps of vapour from the smouldering incense known as *imphepho* were slowly writhing through every nook and cranny. It did not however seem to affect either the cockerel or the other fowl fluffed up on the rafters.

Its beady eye studied the figure sitting cross-legged below. It was rocking back and fore with its head bent, lips moving either in prayer or incantation. The man's hair was braided into long plaits and his face was daubed with white clay. Around his neck were strings of goats' bladders interwoven with the claws and teeth of lion and leopard, and on his head he wore the ceremonial head-dress made out of the skin of the goat sacrificed at his initiation ceremony.

A slight movement caught the rooster's attention. It cocked its head to see what it was, its scarlet comb quivering as it peered down. Another human, a smaller one, lay sleeping, curled on its side. The head was burrowed into the shoulder and the hands were clasped between the knees. Its hair was the colour of fire and the skin as pale as the ash dropping from the embers.

Seeing nothing more of interest, the black rooster preened its feathers and prepared to settle down again. However, another small but insistent movement caught its attention. Head bobbing, it stretched its neck forward, curious to see what it was.

An eye, a golden eye, stared imperiously back at it through the haze of incense. The feathers of the bird in the wicker cage were black and glossy, and the croak issuing from its open beak was neither a challenge nor a greeting.

It simply said: *Here am I, and there are you. Whatever the spirits decide, so it shall be.*

Thirty

emKindini- the place of sorrows

Fynn arrived back at kwaBulawayo on the following day, just as the
sun went down. He went straight to the King's quarters, just as he
stood, dusty and dishevelled from the journey.

Nandi, the Queen Mother of Zululand was dying. He dreaded having
to relay such a piece of news, but there was no other way. Her son had to
know before it was too late. Pausing on the threshold of the magnificent
domed construction, he bowed his head for a moment in an effort to
regain his composure and slow his ragged breathing.

A quick glance inside showed him that Shaka was alone. Seated in the carved
ebony chair, his body was rigid, his fingers beating a jerky tattoo on one of the
arms. As Fynn softly announced his presence from the doorway, Shaka's head
jerked up, and the incessant drumming of his fingers stopped abruptly.

He stared at Fynn for a long moment, his brows drawn in a frown.
Beckoning him to enter, he asked, 'What of my mother, Mbuyasi?'

'Nkosi, it is not good news I bring you,' he said as gently as he could.

Without going into great detail, Fynn explained that the Nkosikazi did
not have the strength to fight the severe illness in her bowels. The infected

wound on her thigh was not mentioned and he prayed fervently that the King of the Zulus would never find out about it.

Then he came to the crucial part. 'Nkosi, I fear your mother will not survive the night. It is why I came myself to bring you this sad news, rather than have you hear it from the lips of a servant.'

As he spoke, he kept his eyes pinned to the floor to avoid seeing whatever emotion might be visible on the face of the Zulu King. Every man had a right to privacy at such a moment.

The crash of the heavy chair falling over brought Fynn's head up sharply. Shaka looked as if he had been skewered to the heart, his expression bewildered, hurt. He took an uncertain step towards Fynn, his hands outstretched.

'You are certain of this, Mbuyasi? Can there be no mistake?'

Fynn shook his head. 'I wish I could say otherwise, Nkosi. No *muthi* can save her. If there was, I would have used it.'

But Shaka was no longer listening. He strode to the doorway calling for Mbopha. The night was suddenly riven with activity, servants running in all directions, their voices muted and terrified. 'We must leave for emKindini. Now! ' Shaka said, the lines of grief clear on his face.

Fynn looked around, dazed and disorientated. His eyes were bloodshot with exhaustion. Days of hard travelling and the bloody process of elephant hunting, combined with the lingering effects of his recent bouts of dysentery were beginning to take their toll on him.

Suddenly, he felt completely drained of energy. The world spun around him, and he made a grab at a corner post of the great arched doorway to stop from collapsing.

While he was struggling to control the dizziness, the shadow of a moth fluttering around one of the flickering tapers happened to fall on the finely plaited reed walls. In Fynn's current state of exhaustion, it seemed to assume the proportions of a huge black nemesis, struggling to free itself. He stared at it in horror, his imagination running wild.

Fortunately, his belly chose that moment to rumble in protest, reminding him that he hadn't eaten a bite since the day before. No wonder my imagination's playing tricks on me, he thought.

It would take some time for Shaka's men to get organised, the best part of an hour, he calculated. In the meantime, some food would do him the world of good, and keep his strength up for what lay ahead.

By the time they entered the gates of emKindini night was almost over.

Exhausted after hours of stumbling along in the pitch-black night, hedged in by the fast-moving Fasimba, Fynn was again close to total collapse.

One thought was uppermost in his mind. It was vital he check on the Nkosikazi before Shaka was allowed anywhere near her. As coolly as he dared, he advised him to wait while he examined his mother. Relief clutched at him as he hurried to her private quarters.

The keening of the women rose out of the pre-dawn darkness. The eyes of the group of *izinyanga*, luminous in the half-dark, turned in his direction as he approached the doorway of Nandi's residence. With only the briefest of nods, Fynn ducked his head and went inside. In the confined space, the smell of approaching death was thick and putrid.

A wild-eyed *isangoma* was crouched over the sick woman, flicking his gnu tail around her, muttering prayers and incantations. The eyes staring redly out of the bizarre, clay-daubed face held neither malice nor challenge in them; only mutual acceptance of the inevitable. With a final whisk of the gnu tail, the *isangoma* moved aside to let Fynn examine the dying woman.

Nandi was lying much as he had left her, her breathing and pulse erratic. Deeply unconscious, only the sound of her breathing and the rapid fluttering of her eyelids told him she was still alive. Her previously lustrous skin was the colour of dull clay, her full lips parted and slack.

Fynn drew his bandana from his pocket and dipped it into a nearby gourd of water. Carefully wiping the sweat from her face, he made sure the blanket remained firmly tucked round her lower body. Then he issued instructions to let Shaka know the Nkosikazi was ready to receive him. At the doorway, he turned back to look for the last time on Nandi's huddled body.

On a sudden impulse, borne out of the habits of his youth and the remnants of the faith still ingrained in his soul, Henry Francis Fynn turned back to kneel by the woman who was the mother of Shaka.

Swiftly, he traced the sign of the Cross on her forehead and whispered what he could remember of his long-ago prayers and the last rites of the Church. As he moved away, he fervently hoped that the mysterious bundles placed round her by the *isangoma* would not find themselves in conflict with the Christian ritual.

As he slipped out through the doorway and into the welcome darkness, waves of exhaustion rolled over him once more, leaving him drained of emotion and strength. Desperate to have a place to sit quietly and smoke his pipe, he eventually found a secluded spot close to the perimeter fence.

Slumping down, he fumbled for his pipe and tobacco pouch. As he stared into the soothing darkness, he was grateful for the deep silence that enshrouded emKindini.

Already he could sense an imperceptible change in the darkness around him, a breath of cool air and a brush of moisture on his skin. Dawn was not far off.

After what seemed only minutes, Fynn's head came up with a jerk, the taste of tobacco stale in his mouth. When he bent to pick up his pipe, the bowl was almost cold, so he reckoned he must have slept for an hour or more.

Looking around, he realised it was no longer still and quiet. As emKindini rapidly began to fill up with people, mostly villagers from the surrounding kraals flocking in to keep a vigil for Shaka's dying mother, pinpricks of light flickered in the darkness like fireflies. Finding the physical presence of so many people oddly disturbing, Fynn felt the first pangs of anxiety begin to gnaw at him.

He remembered all too well what had happened when Shaka's grandmother died. The scenes of frenzied grief and violence that had marked her passing had haunted Fynn for a long time afterwards. He was painfully aware that Nandi was a woman still in her prime, and also the mother of the present King.

His mouth dried in sudden apprehension. Suddenly, the man known as Mbuyasi the finch was afraid, very afraid.

The end of Nandi's life came during the time when the world seems to stand still and slip into a profound silence, a time when even the restless *crick-crick* of insects is silent.

And so it was that in this quiet period, in the place where it was neither night nor day, that the soul of Nandi, the Great She Elephant, Nkosikazi of all Zululand, and the mother of King Shaka, left her body.

Some of those who were there would later swear that they'd heard the soft, but distinct flutter of wings as her spirit rose to join her ancestors.

The Place of Dreaming

The sleek black rooster fluttered down from its perch and strutted across the floor towards the patch of light at the doorway.

Langani's eyes snapped open. The sudden rush of feathered wings had confused him. For a moment or two he was not sure of which world he was in – the waking world, or the one where dreams and visions held sway.

A quick glance showed him the boy was still asleep. The rapid movement behind the delicate blue-veined eyelids showed Langani that he was dreaming. He also noticed that the fierce, alien presences that had been hovering protectively around the boy were no longer there.

Langani did not know what to make of it. Had they withdrawn because they could no longer stay – or was it because they deemed the boy to be safe where he was, with him? He shook his head. Such alien beings were not his to either command, or understand.

With a conscious effort, he dismissed them from his mind, and looked down at the sleeping boy. Such a short time for him to be here with me, he thought, with a pang of regret. But it is how it must be.

Of course, iQawu does not know about the small dancing orb that used to jink playfully over the roof of the rock pool close by to where he now sleeps. How could I explain such a thing to him? And I can also never tell him about how I saw him being saved from the sea, not once but three times in his short life. First by the old story teller in his far-off homeland when he was still only a *toto*; then not so long ago, by the dog that saw him fall into the water from a great height, and the third time, in front of my own eyes and within sight of the headland of eThekwini.

Langani got to his feet reluctantly. Soon I must return him to kwaDukuza, but perhaps one or two more days here with me, for the comfort of his heart, and my own, would be a good thing.

Outside, the cockerel put its head back and crowed, once, twice, then three times in quick succession. Shortly afterwards, the bird with the black feathers stood up and beat its one good wing against the side of the wicker cage. Although its beak was open, no sound came from it.

Langani picked up the cage and crossed over to the doorway, treading carefully so as not to waken the boy.

Outside, the morning air was cool, raising gooseflesh on his body. The far-off hills lay dark on the horizon like the humped backs of slumbering giants. Away to the east, above the vast expanse of bush, a rose blush was beginning to colour the sky.

The bird in the wicker cage had stopped fluttering and beating its wings. Instead, a bright, intelligent eye was fixed steadily on the diviner as he placed the cage on the ground close to where the ground fell away.

Langani faced the dawn, his lips moving in silent incantation. The moments slid slowly past. Bending down, he swiftly undid the catch on the small door of the wicker cage. Then, lifting both cage and bird up in both hands, he held it up as high as he could.

With a flutter of wings, the bird launched itself out into the pale morning sky. It dipped earthwards, its one good wing beating frantically as it struggled to stay in the air.

The diviner's eyes followed the bird's progress. When he saw both wings begin to beat steadily in unison and the frail body swoop upwards, a smile lit up his face.

As the bird sped away towards the rising sun, he walked over to the edge of the steep incline, then threw the empty cage as far out over it as he could. It sailed out into space, tumbling over and over until it was lost the tangled scrub below.

The freeing of the soul changes everything...

Langani now knew more than he had done before. The identity of the one who had just passed out of life, and the one who had done her a great injustice, and so hastened the end of her life, were no longer a secret to him. He also understood what had been troubling the boy. So loyal and protective concerning those he had given his promise to, he thought.

The *umhlolo,* the evil thing, would not end with her passing. But when its evil would finally be spent, he did not know, because he was forced to acknowledge that it was gathering strength by the day.

Langani sighed. The long night was over, but the first of many sorrowful and dangerous days was about to begin.

EmKindini, the place of Sorrows

After the news came that his mother, Nandi, had passed away, Shaka got to his feet without a word. Stiffly, betraying no outward signs of emotion, he turned on his heel and disappeared into the finely constructed edifice that had once been the centre of his mother's power.

A low moaning swept through the crowd. His principal chiefs waited until he had gone, then they too left to prepare themselves for the mourning.

The spirit of the Nkosikazi has flown . . .

Fynn's plan had been to edge away discreetly, and find a quiet place for himself. Instead, he found himself wedged in, unable to move in any direction. More and more people were arriving, pressing in behind those already there, adding to the crush of humanity that smelled strongly of sweat and wood smoke.

Small children with huge eyes clung to their mothers' legs, heads drooping in fatigue, while the heads of babies lolled against their backs, oblivion in their pouted lips and seamless, closed eyelids. Grief and fear now began to pass from one trembling body to the next.

Fynn swore long and low below his breath. *It was beginning...*

When Shaka appeared some time later in full regalia, his stricken face was smeared with clay as a sign of mourning. Slowly, he made his way to the hut where his dead mother lay.

He stood before it with his head bowed. Tears streamed down his face carving runnels through the layer of clay. Occasionally, he lifted a hand to wipe his eyes.

One by one, his chiefs returned, dressed for mourning, to stand respectfully close by. Time passed. No one in crowd stirred and no child cried. The silence was uncanny. Fynn was sweating profusely. Caught like a fly in a web, he devoutly wished that he were elsewhere.

At last, the unearthly quiet came to an abrupt end. A long, drawn-out cry of agony burst its way out of the man bowed over his great shield. It was followed by a few deep, sighs and great, shuddering breaths.

'*Maye ngo Mama*! Alas, my mother!' Shaka of the Zulus could contain his grief no longer. Sobs of anguish rang out, sounds that were terrible to hear.

At first, the people of the amaZulu were stunned to see their warrior King exhibit such agony of mind. But then they remembered that he was also a human being just as they were, a man mourning his mother, the one who had given him life.

A cockerel began to crow somewhere inside emKindini – once, twice, then three times. Cockerels, as everyone knew, were often used as familiars by *izisangoma* and were commonly known to be harbingers of bad omens and death.

The waiting crowds took it as a sign. The King's wailing cry of lament was taken up by thousands of frenzied voices. '*Maye ngo Mama…Maye ngo Mama!*'

Fynn felt the hair rise on the back of his neck. Instinctively, he turned round, looking for a way to escape. Instead, he found himself hemmed in by a mass of sweating humanity. Around him, people tore at their clothes, necklets and ornaments and threw them to the ground.

Fynn watched in horror as an old woman tore clumps of her grey hair out by the roots, leaving patches of raw flesh. The eyes of a young woman near him rolled back in her head showing only the whites. Before he could catch her, she fell backwards and disappeared beneath the feet of those behind, along with the small baby on her back.

'Oh, my God! My God!' Fynn's hoarse shouts of protest were lost in the waves of rising hysteria. Using the butt of his firearm, he pushed himself clear of the frenzy and dived bodily in through the doorway of a nearby hut, the gun clattering and sliding over the glassy floor. He came to a halt against the far wall with his hands over his head, covered in dust, rat droppings and wood ash.

'*Jesus! Jesus, God and Mary!*' It was all he could say, over and over again. The frenzied screaming and shouting outside rose and fell in waves, battering at his senses. The sounds rising from emKindini were like nothing Fynn had ever heard before. They were chilling, terrifying…and completely out of control.

He scrambled upright, put his back against the wall and drew his knees up to his chest. Wiping away tears with the back of his hand, he retrieved his firearm. Checking it carefully, he primed it then placed it ready to hand, as he faced the open doorway.

A few miles from kwaDukuza, Langani stopped in the middle of the dusty track. His eyes were fixed on something on the horizon. Jackabo shaded his eyes and squinted into the distance to see what he was looking at. But there was nothing, only a band of grey haze and the mirages created by the shimmering waves of heat rising from the dun coloured landscape.

'Someone has died,' the diviner said, his face inscrutable in the white-hot glare. Dazed by long hours of walking in the heat, Jackabo looked up at him dumbly, not sure if he'd heard him correctly.

Jackabo moved into the shade of a gnarled old *msasa* tree and sat down. Taking off his hat, he dragged his sleeve across his face and wiped the sweat away. 'Who was it? Who died?' There was no spit in his mouth, and the words came out in a croak.

Langani squatted on his haunches, his long plaits of hair falling over his shoulders. Swiping his hand across a stretch of powdery dust that smelled of heat, old ant workings and animal dung, he dipped a long forefinger into it, then drew some marks on Jackabo's forehead, then on his cheeks and chin, 'Someone with whom you shared a secret is no longer with us,' he said at last, viewing his handiwork. Jackabo's heart gave a lurch. Which one did he mean? Painfully, he remembered he was the guardian of more than one secret.

Langani's eyes looked through him and beyond. 'This secret is known to only a few,' he answered. Jackabo waited, sweat trickling down his back.

The ochre daubings on his face began to sting as if he had been brand-ed with a red-hot iron. He gritted his teeth and resisted the urge to wipe them away.

'Now that her spirit has flown, you are the true keeper of this secret. But then you already know this.' Jackabo's heart thudded. The diviner had said '*her*' spirit, so the one who had died was a woman, a woman who shared a secret with him?

There was only one who fitted the description. Horrified, the words spilled out of him. 'The Nkosikazi…Nandi, was she the one?'

The diviner's handsome face was sombre in the harsh glare. He nodded. Jackabo was stunned. 'What happened?'

Langani rubbed his stomach and his back. 'In these parts is the pain. Also here.' His hand moved to his leg, kneading the flesh on the upper thigh. 'This is the worst wound of all.'

Jackabo stared at him, his mind in a whirl. What kind of illness could strike a person in the stomach and the upper leg at the same time? At last, he asked, 'Why was the pain in the leg the worst?'

The young diviner's face was closed and secretive when he answered. 'Because this pain was delivered by someone she did not expect to hurt her. Such wounds are always so.'

And he would say no more.

Langani parted company with him a mile or so from kwaDukuza. The sky was a soup of grey cloud, the menacing heat pressing down on the lifeless landscape.

The boy and the diviner stood together for a few moments in the small patch of shade below the thorny branches of a flat-topped acacia.

'Go well, iQawu,' Langani said, placing his hand lightly on Jackabo's shoulder. 'Remember what we now know of each other, and use it well. *Hamba gahle* – until we meet again.'

After a bit, Jackabo turned round to wave him goodbye. Langani's tall figure was hard to make out among the shimmering waves of heat. From the distance, it seemed the acacia tree and the diviner were almost indistinguishable from one another.

The next time he turned round, both the tree and the man had vanished, drawn into the pool of dancing, twisting shapes on the horizon, where mirage and reality merged to become one.

Jackabo decided to keep quiet about everything that had happened over the last few days. Not a word even to Jakot. If the Nkosikazi had really died, it would not be at all wise to announce he'd spent the last few days with an *isangoma* who had seen it in a vision.

The moment he reached his quarters, his eyes instinctively travelled to the bird perch by the door hoping to see Hector there, but there was no curious yellow eye staring down at him, no soft *crrrk*, no flap of wings or clack of beak.

Inside, he glanced up at the rafters, fully expecting to find the bird there, but all he could see were a few chalky droppings on the floor. It seemed he had lost another friend. Hector, the bird with the broken wing, had disappeared. Tired out after the journey and the day's sad events, Jackabo lay down and fell asleep almost immediately.

Some time later, he woke with a jump, with sweat running into his eyes. He sat bolt upright, wondering what had wakened him. All seemed normal, only the familiar buzz of voices rising up from the depths of kwaDukuza, '*the place so large people get lost.*'

It was then he heard the faint sound of drumming coming in on the sullen air. His scalp prickled. Padding over to the doorway, he drew aside the goatskin flap, stuck his head out and listened carefully.

In some distant village, men were bending over their drums in the dying light, pounding out their urgent message. Jackabo waited, his heart in his mouth.

When he heard the great surge of wailing begin, he let the goatskin flap fall back into place, then went to lie down on his sleeping mat again.

Langani had been right. Nandi was gone.

EmKindini

A crowd of people surged past the hut, their voices hoarse and strained after a long night's weeping and crying. Fynn waited a few moments until they'd passed by, then cautiously drew the flap covering the doorway aside and squinted out.

First to hit him was the harsh glare of sunlight bouncing off the ground. The next was the unmistakable coppery smell of blood and the sour reek of vomit. Lifeless bodies lay around in curiously huddled heaps, flies already beginning to settle on the smears of blood and trickles of urine. Fynn was appalled. Rubbing his strained, gritty eyes he peered around at the devastation.

A child – no, many children were curled up like small puppies asleep in the dust. Here and there an arm or a leg twitched. A head lifted then fell back again. Voices moaned, asking for water.

Covering his nose and mouth, Fynn stumbled towards the pitiful bodies. Not all of the people were dead. Exhaustion, lack of food and water, fear and excessive strain had forced many of them into an almost catatonic state. Even if he had boxes of medicines at hand, faced with such numbers, he knew there was nothing he could have done to save them.

Somewhere ahead he could hear the sounds of men's voices, their chanting and shouting underscored by the rattle and pound of spears on shields. Sensing the underlying hysteria and aggression running below it, his flesh crawled. The central parade ground was where the men would be gathered, Shaka at the heart of it, no doubt.

For a moment, Fynn was tempted to retreat into the relative coolness of the hut, pull the goatskin flap over the door and block it all out. Ignoring both his instincts and better judgment, he set off through the maze of huts, guided by the sound of the frenetic chanting.

It didn't take long for the blood letting to begin. Out on the edge of the milling sea of black, sweating bodies, a man fell to the ground and disappeared beneath the pounding of iron-hard feet. Fynn could only watch as others wavered, fell to their knees and tried to crawl clear.

The chanting stopped and the beating of shields ceased. A long moment of deathly silence followed. Out of it came a voice, a voice more like the bellowing of a goaded animal than that of a human being.

Shaka – demanding revenge for the death of his mother…

As a wave of white-hot emotion spun like a whirlwind round emKindini, scouring the very heart of it, Fynn's knees shook and he almost fell. Then the killing began.

Using spears, knobkerries, sticks or even their bare hands, each man tried to inflict as much injury as possible on those around him. Like an abscess bursting, bloodlust, old enmities and madness came to a head and overflowed. Fynn stood on the edge of it all, unable to move.

This was not the first time he'd witnessed explosions of grief and violence after the death of a chief or someone of importance. For one wild

moment, he contemplated firing a few shots into the air to try to stop the
blood letting, before coming to his senses. No, the mob would only turn
their anger on him, the white man; the intruder who had dared to come
among them with his gun during a time of great mourning.

Fynn swore long and loud, the obscenities issuing from his mouth
drowned by the howling of the mob.

Having fled the scene of men killing each other with anything at hand,
he wandered, dazed and emotionally drained, from one pitiful scene to
another; a ghost whom no one appeared to either see or acknowledge.

Down by the river, the dead and dying lay on top of one another.
Suffocated by the clinging mud, their faces had been pressed down into
it by those pushing in from behind, frantic to reach water to quench
their raging thirst or relieve their stressed vocal chords. Anyone who
could no longer force tears from their eyes was sought out and hacked
to death.

At one point, a crowd of wild-eyed young soldiers rushed at him,
threatening him with their bloodied knobkerries, demanding to know why
he wasn't weeping and tearing his clothes like everyone else.

He said nothing, merely stared through them, hoping like hell that
their awareness of his friendship with Shaka would save his life. Eventually, they turned away muttering, glaring at him and brandishing their
weapons.

Fynn's legs suddenly gave way, and he fell to his knees in the middle of
the muddy pathway and buried his head in his hands. For once, his skills
and optimism had deserted him. His hands and heart were both empty of
the will and the means to either heal or cure.

The resolute spirit of Mbuyasi, the finch, was stunned into a crippling
paralysis. The love of adventure, which had carried him into some deep
and dangerous highways since leaving the eastend of London, dwindled
and died in the face of such barbarity. At that moment, for him, the gulf
between white and black had never been so wide, or so deep.

It was worse than anything he could ever have imagined. And Nandi
had been dead for less than a day.

Her burial took place three days later, but only after Shaka was prevailed upon by his chiefs to stop the mass killings. No sooner had she been laid to rest than another cry sprang up.

The Nkosikazi was surely killed by witchcraft. Find the witches! Kill them!

Fynn's soul shrivelled in horror. This time the terrifying bloodletting would not be confined to one place, but would sweep through the entire kingdom.

Death was about to stalk Zululand. He could smell it in the air. Revenge and grief would turn in on itself to foment political and tribal expediency and launch an opportunity to settle old scores and annihilate enemies.

Could guilt perhaps be added to the list? The word 'guilt' lingered in the recesses of Fynn's mind. Whoever had thrust a blade into the thigh of Shaka's mother might well be suffering – if not from remorse – then from the abject fear of being found out. What better way to cover it up than to light a fire elsewhere?

He groaned. Oh, God, where will it all end? Then a sudden horrifying thought shot through him.

Jackabo! The boy would have no way of knowing what was coming his way. KwaDukuza would not escape the purges, he was sure of that.

Fynn's thoughts were erratic. Should I slip away and warn him, also those at eThekwini? But if Shaka asks for me and discovers I've gone, he'll accuse me of deserting him... and it'll only make things worse. In his present frame of mind, there's no saying what he might do.

He began to pace up and down in agitation. No, I must stay here-I can't risk the alternative. I'll send on some of my hunters, the best runners. They can move fast, and by night, if necessary, try to persuade the boy to get himself to eThekwini and relative safety.

The only thing was, though – would the lad have the sense to leave kwaDukuza once he realised what was happening?

He grunted in frustration. Knowing what young sprouts of his age were like, probably not. After all, he'd been living with the Zulus for so long now, there was a distinct possibility he would refuse to see that he might be in real danger.

Fynn cracked his knuckles anxiously. He *was*, after all, iQawu, Shaka's hero. But would the praise name be enough to stop the knobkerrie of some blood-crazed footsoldier out on a killing spree?

Not knowing what else to do, he began to pray. *Run, lad! For God's sake, take the road to the bay, and don't look back.*

Thirty-One

'Myself, I hate death,' Jakot said, scowling into the heart of the flames. 'Too much I saw of it when we fought the *amabhuna*, then the British.'

Jackabo reckoned it was the talk of Nandi's death that had loosened his tongue on that particular subject. Jakot rarely mentioned the frontier skirmishes he'd been involved in, let alone that he'd fought hand-to-hand not only with Boer farmers, but also with the scarlet-jacketed soldiers of the British Army.

'*Hau,* Jackabo,' the Xhosa had said sourly when he'd brought up the subject of setting out for emKindini. 'Why travel a long way to look at a hole in the ground? Let the Zulus look at it.'

Jackabo fixed him with a sober blue eye. 'We have to make the journey. To stay away will be seen by the Nkosi as an insult to Nandi's memory.'

His internal thoughts, however, were a different matter altogether. How can I tell you the real reasons I *have to* go back? Nandi trusted me with her secrets and I can never talk about them – not to anyone. If the truth ever got out, it'd damn an innocent bairn, his mother and everyone else who's had a hand in it. And that includes me...

A son fathered by Shaka, without his knowledge, would create ripples the size of tidal waves. If the Nkosi found out his mother had deliberately manipulated events in pursuit of her own desires, he would be driven to a peak of rage where he would be capable of anything.

In the last days of her life, Nandi had trusted him with her final secret, the place where Shaka's child would be safe. "If anything should happen to me... here is where you will find Magaye."

Jackabo realised that the time might now have arrived, with frightening speed.

He had known for a long time that Jakot hid painful secrets from his past. Although he was less than half the Xhosa's age, he already had ghosts of his own to contend with. And like Jakot, he daren't speak of them.

Take Mkabayi, for example. The woman lurked in the corner of his mind like a phantom, feeding his suspicions about Nandi's unexpected death and the wound in her thigh. Things had changed for the worse. Because Nandi was dead, he *had to* see if the child and his mother were safe, or if they were still in emKindini. The truth was, he needed Jakot to come with him – not only for company, but to allay any suspicions about why he had turned up there on his own.

He addressed the top of Jakot's head. 'So when Shaka asks why his interpreter did not come to honour his mother, you will just tell him you didn't want to walk all that way just to look at a hole in the ground? Is that what you will say to him?'

The Xhosa sighed and stopped attending to his feet. 'You *umlungu* will be the death of me,' he said, muttering below his breath. 'I have always known it.'

In Zulu, "Nandi" meant "*sweet thing.*" But "the sweet thing" was no more. After her death, Shaka ordered that the word pass from the language, to be heard no more on the tongue.

Mtoti would now be used in its place. As she was the Mother of all Beasts, this was a fitting name for her. Mtoti, the former Queen and Mother of every man, woman, child, animal, bird and beast in the land, now lay below the rich soil of Zululand. A pit had been dug for her in the very place she had taken her last breath. As was the custom, she had been placed on a mat in a seated position with her back against the side of the pit, and her body covered with another large mat.

Her Royal hut with its beautiful, intricate thatches and high, arched doorway had been brought down over the place where she lay and then covered with earth. Sprouting branches of the milk tree were placed in the ground over and around her grave. In time, they would take root and grow into a pleasant grove to shelter her last resting place from the sun.

Hundreds of warriors had been drafted in to form a regiment whose duty it would be to guard her grave for a period of twelve months. Huge herds of cattle were offered throughout the length and breadth of the country to appease the spirit of the departed Queen.

EmKindini looked as if a giant had taken it to pieces and thrown it together again. Jakot shot uneasy glances around him and drew his cape tightly around his shoulders, while Jackabo said nothing at all.

Sorrow hung over it like a cloud. The atmosphere was sodden with grief and tears, the air rank with the stench of old blood and strife. On the hillsides beyond the fences, the air was thick with predatory birds wheeling and screaming. A putrid, sickening smell drifted in on the air, causing people to turn away to retch and cover their mouths and noses.

Instinctively, Jackabo glanced up the slope towards Nandi's royal quarters. A sense of shock swept over him. Both the fences and the finely constructed beehive huts had been completely demolished, as had the *isigodlo,* the place where the women lived.

In its place, standing alone in solitary splendour on the brow of the hill was her shrouded burial place, the piled earth still raw; a gash in the red earth. A phalanx of Zulu warriors, drawn from her personal regiments stood guard over it. Dressed in full ceremonial attire, they stood sweltering in the fierce sun, sweat trickling down their bodies.

Jackabo's thoughts ran in circles around the impossible. *Oh God, where are Magaye and his mother... the three Maries... where are they now?*

'Aiee, I do not like this,' groaned Jakot, eyeing the gravesite with a conspicuous lack of enthusiasm.

Bare, circular patches were dotted around the brow of the hill, all that was left to tell where the royal huts had once stood. The much-prized glossy floors were almost indestructible and would remain long after emKindini crumbled away or was finally abandoned.

As he looked from one sad, dusty circle to another, Jackabo found it hard to identify the places that had once been so familiar to him. The fig tree that he used to climb still stood over by the outer fence, but it looked forlorn, the glossy leaves drooping in the heat. A lump formed in his throat.

Was it only a short time ago I sat there with Nandi, eating honey cakes and watching her play with her grandson, Magaye?

Jakot's voice cut into his thoughts. 'Eh, there is nothing more to see. All is finished.' Jackabo badly wanted to reply that it hadn't, and in some ways, it had only just begun.

But he didn't. Suddenly, he felt empty, not sure of where to go, or what to do.

Later on that day, as he wandered aimlessly about with a stony-faced Jakot in tow, out of the corner of his eye he caught sight of a familiar flutter of black and white ostrich plumes among the crowds. Below the feathers bobbed the brim of an old battered straw hat. Jackabo's heart leapt.

Henry *bloody* Fynn! As large as life and here in emKindini! *Of course, he'd been hunting with Shaka...did it mean the Nkosi was here too?*

Dodging through the crowd, he yelled out, 'Fynn! Wait up!'

To say Fynn was surprised to see him was an understatement. 'Good God!' he exclaimed, his face white with shock. 'EmKindini's the last place I expected to find you, boy. What in the hell possessed you to come here?'

Around the fire that night, Fynn told them of the terrible loss of life following the death of Nandi, also about the orders that had gone out to every corner of Zululand.

Jackabo hung his head, sickened. No wonder Jakot had pleaded his dislike of death not to come here, he thought, he'd known all along what would happen when a King's mother dies. A wave of shame washed over him. *Poor devil, to think I practically bullied him into coming with me...*

Without warning, Jakot sprang to his feet, lithe and tall in the firelight, the amber-gold sliver in his eye suddenly feral and dangerous. Jackabo stared at him as if he'd never seen him before.

Here was the Jakot of old, the one who had fought the Boers and then the British, the man who had braved the treacherous waters of St Lucia to save the lives of sailors and earn the name of Hlambamanzi, the swimmer, after desperately seeking a place of refuge in Shaka's kingdom.

'My wife, my child,' he said, heavily. 'I must go to my kraal.'

Fynn rose to his feet, his face cast in bitter lines. 'Surely the Zulus know that you're Shaka's interpreter and which kraals are yours? They won't harm your family –'

The look on Jakot's face told them he was taking no chances concerning either his family or his cattle. 'We'll come with you,' Fynn said, halfway to his feet. 'I'll speak to the Nkosi –'

Jakot shook his head. 'I have not forgotten how to travel by night.' Pausing for a moment on the outer rim of firelight, he muttered, 'Never did Hlambamanzi expect to be running in the night with the British offering to light his way!'

A faint chuckle followed. 'Strange times, indeed, my friends – but Jakot thanks you all the same.' And then he was gone, the darkness closing in behind him.

After Jakot had gone, silence descended, the firelight suddenly filled with unanswered questions.

'The Nkosi, Fynn…how is he taking it, his mother's death, I mean?' Jackabo had been almost afraid to ask. Fynn shook his head and crossed one tattered trouser leg over the other.

'The man's demented, Jack.' he said, bluntly. 'He's in a queer kind of rage, black like the pit. Seeing no one, not eating, sleeping, pacing the floor, shouting and talking to himself, even poor old Napisongo's terrified to go near him. As for myself, I've stayed away. Apart from anything else, he needs time to grieve.'

Cautiously, Jackabo probed further. 'D'you think it's because of Nandi dying – or might there be something else troubling him?'

Fynn snatched the pipe from his mouth, a thin strand of saliva trailing from it. 'What are ye getting at, lad? Have ye heard something?'

Caution warred with a terrible need to know more. Jackabo looked straight at Fynn, his eyes a startling blue in the firelight. 'Did something else happen to Nandi – more than you said, I mean?'

Fynn stared at him, wild calculation in his eyes. His instincts told him that the boy knew, or suspected something. Suddenly, he had a dire need to share what he knew. Drawing a deep breath, he told the boy about the wound on Nandi's leg and his suspicions that someone had deliberately attacked her. Jackabo's throat was suddenly so dry he could hardly swallow.

This was far worse than he'd expected. His thoughts ran in every direction as he remembered Langani telling him how a wound in her thigh had been the worst of all for Nandi to bear... *'because it had been inflicted by someone she didn't expect to harm her.'*

He stammered, 'Was that what killed her?'

Fynn shrugged his shoulders. 'Who knows? But the bloody infection it caused did her no favours at all, probably hastened her end.'

'Did you tell Shaka about it, Fynn?'

They were on very dangerous ground here and it was getting more so by the moment. Fynn shot him a scathing glance.

'What d' ye take me for, lad? I hold no truck with death wishes. I've every intention o' dying in bed at a great age, not in the arse end of Africa with my guts hanging out like tripe.'

Apart from the person who had attacked Nandi, or some of her women, they were probably the only people who knew about it. That left only one question. Who had been angry enough, or insane enough to stab the mother of Shaka? And even if they knew, or discovered the identity of the attacker, what could either of them do about it?

Secrets, Jackabo thought, as a shaft of anguish pierced him. Will they ever stop coming?

One thing, however, became clear. He and Fynn were trapped in emKindini, a place of blood, hatred and the taint of madness – though whose madness Jackabo wasn't quite sure.

Next day, something, or in this case, *someone* else, caught his eye. This time it was a face, a familiar one, moon-shaped and anxious – Malusi, but a much-changed Malusi, who looked as if he had been severely beaten.

The man's eyes were bruised and swollen, while his body was covered with cuts and livid bruises.

He was no longer the plump, portly fellow Jackabo remembered. The fat seemed to have been stripped from his body, and even his pendulous jowls had shrunk, though the slightly vacant look in his eyes remained the same.

Jackabo jinked through the crowd to catch up with him. When he touched him on the shoulder, Malusi clapped his hands over his head, whimpering and cringing like a whipped dog.

'Malusi,' he said, gently, 'it's me, it's Jackabo.' Recognising his voice, the man slowly removed his hands and peered nervously at him. Taking his arm, Jackabo steered him away from the curious glances of passers by.

'What happened, *mdodo*?' he asked, once they'd got clear of the mourners. 'Who hurt you?'

Agitated, Malusi flapped his hands and put his finger over his lips, his eyes darting from side to side. The sinking feeling was back in Jackabo's belly. 'Malusi, old friend, it will be our secret. Secret, remember? Like the one with the Nkosikazi.'

At the mention of her name, a stifled wail burst from him. Jackabo managed to quieten him down before pressing him for answers. He just *had* to know about the child called Magaye, his mother, and the four Maries.

Gently, Jackabo repeated their Zulu names – Sibongile, Nhlala, Blekissa and Nokukhanya. Malusi shook his head, moaned deep in his throat, and began to rock from side to side.

'Malusi, you must tell me. Are they still in emKindini?'

Reluctantly, the bullet-shaped head jerked up and down. Jackabo sighed in relief. 'Where can I find them? Take me to them.'

When the eyes in the moon face stared back at him, Jackabo saw that he had lost most of his eyelashes and eyebrows. Malusi spun round and began to lurch back the way they'd come.

Puzzled, Jackabo fell in behind him. Where was he going? They were heading back up the slope to where the royal quarters used to be. Surely, the beating he had taken must be confusing him…

Closer now and he could see the warriors guarding the burial site. Malusi plucked nervously at his sleeve, his eyes rolling in his head. Sweat stood out on his smooth brow and upper lip. Agitated, he looked to the place where Nandi was buried. A great quivering sigh ran through his body.

'Malusi!' Jackabo hissed. 'Are you telling me they're dead?'

The great head nodded.

'Were they sick?'

Cha. The man shook his head, his lips closed tightly.

When he pressed him further, Malusi's head shook violently from side to side. Up to then, not a single word had come out of his mouth. But now it did.

A tiny child's voice issued from the slack mouth in a sing-song imitation of someone else's words, grotesque in a man of his size and age.

'*The Nkosikazi must not be left alone...someone stay with the Great She Elephant during the long night.*'

The truth began to sink in. So that was what Malusi meant when he told him the four Maries were still in emKindini.

They were. *But they were no longer alive. They were in the burial pit along with their mistress!*

He could read the horror of it in Malusi's eyes. The best and brightest of the girls and young women of the *isigodlo* had been committed to the darkness of the pit along with the dead Queen. *And among them had been the four laughing, mischievous Maries.*

The innocent moon-gazer Malusi, although stricken almost dumb with shock, was able to tell him what had happened.

When they buried her, Nandi, "the sweet thing" had been dead for three or four days. The dozen or so young women, including his friends, the four Maries had not been so fortunate. . . .

Jackabo sat down, put his hands over his face and sobbed his heart out.

Afterwards, they went back down the hill, found a quiet place and sat down together. Jackabo held Malusi's hand and they both shed tears of regret; first of all for the loss of the laughing girls who had been his friends and then for Nandi, the formidable mother of Shaka, and all the sadness and sorrows of emKindini. After they had dried their tears, he had one last thing to ask Malusi.

'You remember the *toto?*' he said, gently, 'the one called Magaye?'

It had been a terrible, terrible day. Jackabo held his breath, fearing the worst. Malusi nodded. His face cracked into a smile, and he put his stubby forefinger to his lips.

Jackabo nodded, his hopes rising. *Malusi was smiling. Please God, let it mean something good.* Carefully and slowly, he put it to him. 'Where is the *toto,* old man? Is he also here?'

The eyes went blank. Jackabo put an arm round Malusi's hunched shoulders and put the question another way.

'The *toto?* Is he also with the Nkosikazi?'

The face cracked into a smile. The huge head swung from side to side in negative response. Then the little singsong voice said, '*Gone far . . .*'

Relief ran through Jackabo like a hot tide. At least Magaye, the small, innocent son of Shaka, was still alive.

'*Yebo,* old man,' he said, 'that is a good place for the *toto* to be.'

Not everyone mourned the passing of Nandi, the Queen Mother. To some, she was a ruthless she-devil, as destructive a force as her son had been.

Her ambition, his ambition, all along, they said, had been to mould the Zulu people, and the others they had conquered, into a nation to serve their monstrous egos.

Thousands had gone to their deaths cursing them. The bloodline of those who had suffered at the hands of either mother or son had neither forgiven nor forgotten, but had learned to swallow their hatred and stay silent.

Now, under the weight of enforced grief and the rule of terror about to be unleashed on a suffering land, old enmities began to stir.

When Ngomane, Shaka's adoptive father, got up to propose yet another decree, the news was received in silent horror, then passed from one corner of the land to the other.

The rains came. Violent thunderstorms split both the earth and the heavens and rain poured out on the parched ground with a vengeance. While thousands starved, corn, fruits and vegetables flourished then went to waste in village gardens across the land.

Bands of soldiers scoured the country seeking out wrong doers. With the defeat of the Kumalo and the Ndwandwe, the last great enemy, the external threat to the People of the Heavens had diminished – but now the internal threat to the stability of the kingdom grew with each passing day.

Mkayabi, the sister of the dead Senzangakhona, Shaka's father, continued to whisper behind the King's back and spread her poison. The whispering was faint, it was true, but as rumour piled on rumour, it grew louder.

'See, the Lord of the World does not sleep,' the insidious voices said, 'but walks under the stars like a man possessed. Who does he talk to? He allows no one near him, not even his trusted servants.

Can it be that the mother and the son were really devils, pretending to be of humankind? And having rid the nation of the she-devil herself – are the *amadhlozi* slowly destroying her son by driving him mad?'

Night after night it rained. The storm-tossed skies were torn apart with jagged displays of lightning, and the earth trembled with cracks of thunder that rolled and reverberated round the skies, alarming the cattle and frightening the children.

Rain came down in slanting needles followed by pieces of ice as large as fowls' eggs. Calves were found drowned in the kraals, and the rivers burst their banks, uprooting trees and carrying away people, animals and even whole villages sometimes.

Jackabo began to wake in the night, the smell of dank, raw earth threatening to choke him, the weight of it pressing down on him. He would thrash about, yelling, until Fynn shook him awake.

In the end, he was too afraid to sleep, and would lie awake, wide-eyed and staring into the darkness. There were too many dead people in emKindini …and they were too close. Nandi, lying up there in her tomb with her favourites buried alive around her; the bodies of the men, women and children who had died in her name rotting on the hillsides, their bones picked clean by predators and crows.

And there was the King himself, the Nkosi, half-mad, some said, oblivious to the suffering of his people… and alone, so terribly alone.

Fynn decided the best thing to do was to stay away from him. 'He knows we're here,' he said, 'when he wants to, he'll send for us.'

Jackabo quietly mulled over what he daren't say aloud. Fynn, you and I both know the truth of it. You're feared the king's out of his mind and will do us an injury if we get too close or draw attention to ourselves. But, being of the nature he was, and not sleeping besides, there came a time when he could stand it no longer.

Pushing back his blanket, he crept silently past the sleeping Fynn and out into the stormy night. And as he made his way through the slanting rain to the place where Shaka paced the night alone, lightning continued to flicker menacingly above the blood-soaked earth of emKindini.

Thirty-Two

Townsend boatyard was a hubbub of activity. Today, the new schooner would be launched. Threads of excitement ran like wildfire round the braes while drums pounded softly in the background.

The amaTuli jostled in and out among the crowds, their feathered head-dresses, monkey skins and necklaces of quills and bones adding an exotic flavour to the proceedings. A group of indunas and local chiefs, attired in full ceremonial garb, were clearly mesmerised by the size of the vessel dominating the clearing.

A makeshift platform had been erected. James King was already there, wearing the elaborate, black-feathered head-dress presented to him by Shaka on being made a chief of kwaDukuza. The pale flash of a lace parasol and the high, flirtatious tinkle of a woman's laughter announced the presence of Elizabeth Farewell. A flutter of black and white ostrich plumes intimated that Henry Fynn had arrived.

A surge of pride went through Jackabo as he looked at the vessel. Could it really be true she was ready, at long last?

It had taken three long years to build her – years of striving, struggling and cursing. Almost impossible to believe she had flowered out of the awkward hulk that had so bedevilled them. With the salvaged flags from the *Mary* fluttering from her topmasts, the schooner looked sleek and powerful, ready for her christening, her bows pointing down the double track of logs laid to aid her passage into the sea.

Excitement gripped him. Soon they would be bound for the Cape, carrying Shaka's offer of a peaceful alliance to Sir Richard Bourke, King George IV's Governor.

All of a sudden, he couldn't wait to feel a deck heave below his feet and hear the billow and crack of sails above his head.

A sudden volley of shots brought everybody's attention back to the matter in hand. Fynn was on the platform, his smoking gun pointing skywards. Sweeping off his plumed hat, he bowed low, setting off roars of excitement among the crowd. He held up his hands for quiet.

'The *umkombe* is about to begin her great journey. To pacify the spirits of the sea and ensure her safe passage, we must perform a small ceremony.'

Ripples of approval ran through the throng. This was something they understood. Fynn pawed the air for silence. 'The ceremony must be performed by the hand of a beautiful woman so it will have the best chance of success.' Up on the hillsides, the rhythm of the drums increased in tempo.

James King stood up. Dressed in a dark blue jacket and trousers, the gold-braided epaulettes on his shoulders glittered in the sun. His shirt front was dazzling white, the sweep of the glossy black feathers of the head dress Shaka had presented to him looking not a whit out of place.

His address was short, but moving, his Nova Scotia twang more pronounced, as if the imminent launch of the Susan and Elizabeth had somehow brought him nearer to the North Atlantic waters of his homeland.

His voice was gruff as he thanked the seamen for their forbearance, their guts at seeing it through. Turning to the first officer, he seized his arm and held it aloft.

'I give you First Officer John Hatton,' he said, 'a true blue if ever there was one – a man not afraid to take his jacket off and work alongside his men. Without his great skills in boat building and draughtsmanship, we wouldn't be standing here today.'

Loud cheers and whistles broke out, followed by the shrilling ululating of the women on the hillsides. James King's eyes raked the crowd. 'Jack! Where's our Jack?'

A forest of hands reached out for him. 'Woza, Jackabo! Come out, come out!' Leaning down, King pulled him up on to the platform. 'Without this lad, the youngest of the crew, we'd not be standing here now, I can tell you.'

Jackabo, suddenly uncomfortable, tried not to look down at the sea of smiling faces. King's hand pressed his shoulder. 'And by God, he's earned the title Shaka has given him. The journey this lad undertook into Portuguese territory was no mean feat, even for a grown man. His father will be very proud of him. We all are.'

A trickle of sweat ran down from below the feathered head-dress. Clearing his throat, King held out his hand to Elizabeth Farewell. Placing her parasol to one side, she stood up and placed a gloved hand in his.

'This delightful lady has agreed to crack a bottle over her stern – of the vessel, that is,' he added with a wicked grin. With a small bow, he offered the beribboned bottle of brandy to Elizabeth Farewell. Her smile was gracious as she took it in her gloved hands. 'She's a cool one, an' no mistake,' Ned whispered.

Without preamble, and in a clear voice that carried out over the boatyard, she said, 'I name this vessel the *Susan and Elizabeth*. May God save all who sail in her.' Drawing back the bottle, she dashed it with surprising force against the ship's bows. It exploded into splinters of glass and a froth of liquid.

There were more than a few indrawn breaths of stunned disbelief from the crew. The double-edged meaning was lost on no one. "May God save all who sail in her" sounded like more of a curse than a blessing – at best, it seemed a petty echo of her husband's grudging nature.

Ned growled below his breath, 'An' a pox on you, too, lady.'

As the sailors began to remove the rest of the scaffolding, Thompson and James McCoy tried to clear excited people back from the area that had been roped off for safety. John Cane, the carpenter, stepped forward and spat into the palms of his hands. Taking up a wooden mallet, he aimed a few hefty whacks at the end roller.

Jackabo saw the hull move forward a few inches. The sailors and a few of the boatyard workers were at the bows, pulling on ropes. The schooner moved forward another few feet. A great shout went up from the amaTuli. Ned ran forward to take up one of the trailing ropes.

'Come on, Heelander,' he yelled. 'It's not every day ye get to launch a boat.'

Sailors moved up from the stern, rolling stout logs that were placed at the vessel's bows. The men on the ropes took the strain and pulled her forward a few feet, the rollers easing her way. Gradually, as logs were taken from the rear and brought to the front, the vessel began to roll down the homemade ramp. Suddenly, some of the amaTuli started running alongside the moving vessel grabbing at the ropes, one or two even trying to climb aboard.

Thompson's hoarse voice bellowed. 'If any of 'em gets himself crushed, we're scuppered! They'll put a curse on the bloody thing an' then we'll nivver get out o' here!'

Hatton made a quick decision. 'Let her go, loose the ropes!' he ordered. 'She'll make it on her own now.'

The *Susan and Elizabeth* slid the last few yards on her own, with ropes trailing behind her, sailors and natives alike jumping out of the way.

As she hit the water, two great fountains of spray spouted high into the air on either side of her plunging bows. Almost immediately she steadied, the lack of ballast allowing her to ride high in the water. Within minutes, sailors were swarming up the ropes, throwing buffers over her side and throwing out anchors to secure her.

Against a backdrop of shimmering lagoon, the schooner rose and fell gently at her moorings, while the tattered, faded flags salvaged from the *Mary* fluttered in the breeze.

A few days later, Shaka called them to kwaDukuza. A month earlier, he had signed a document empowering James King to take charge of his mission to the Cape Governor. In it, he was instructed to take care of his chiefs and deliver them safely back to Zululand.

In a second hand-written document, Shaka conveyed his wish for friendship to His Majesty King George IV. It authorised James King and a leading Chief of his choice to negotiate, on his behalf, "a treaty of friendly alliance between the two nations."

In return for these and other services, James King was to be given full possession of the lagoon at the mouth of the umLalazi River and the territory within a twenty-five mile radius. Also written into the document was his free and exclusive right to trade anywhere within Zululand.

The documents looked impressive. Written in James King's fine slanting hand the scroll had been witnessed by both Jakot and Henry Fynn.

There it was, Jackabo thought – Shaka's vision for the future of southern Africa, just as he'd proclaimed it three years ago on that very first day in kwaBulawayo during the festival of First Fruits.

"UmGeorge shall be King of the whites... and I shall rule the blacks."

If Farewell knew of the advances in James King's fortunes, he gave no indication of it. Standing head and shoulders above everyone was the impressive Chief Sothobe ka Mpangalala of the Sibuyu, while Mbopha ka Sithayi, Shaka's major domo, stood aloof, his smooth features impassive, disapproval in every line of his body. Clearly visible beneath his cloak was the short-bladed weapon he always carried.

The sight of Mbopha caused Jackabo's heart to lurch uneasily. A look of menace hung about the man, like mist rising from a swamp.

A rustle, then a sudden silence as Shaka swept in. Dressed in a simple kilt of monkey tails, with a length of bright green and gold cotton cloth draped around his torso, he was clearly in a good humour.

He came straight to the point. 'It is your business to sail the great waters on my behalf. This will include all the men of Kingi, whether they are present here or not –

Pausing deliberately to make sure they were hanging on his every word, he went on, ' – except for the one known as Dambusa. He must stay here with me until such time as Kingi brings my chiefs back. Only then will I release him.'

The abrupt statement of intent dropped into the silence like a well-placed rock into a pool. Fynn scratched his beard irritably. Damn it, he fumed, what devil's game is he playing now?

Wasting no time, Fynn stood up, stating his objections as bluntly as he dared. 'Nkosi, as you know, Dambusa is very sick. The wound he received at Ngome while fighting Beje of the Kumalo has not yet healed. If he stays here without me –'

Fynn shook his head, implying the worst. 'Let him go to the Cape with the others, he will find suitable medicines there. I will stay behind in his place.'

Shaka's eyes glittered in secret amusement. 'Ever a good friend, Mbuyasi – but I agree. You can stay here with me.' He smiled broadly. 'After all, Dambusa might die – and then there would be no one for me to kill if my chiefs fail to return.'

Ned bent down, pretending to tie his boot. He whispered below his breath, 'What did I tell ye? This cove's nobody's fool – he hedges his bets like a professional.'

Shaka's gaze swivelled to Farewell. By no stretch of the imagination could it have been construed as benevolent. 'Febana ka ma jo-ji, you have asked that your wife be allowed to accompany my envoys. Is this not so?'

A murmur of surprise sprang up. Farewell nodded, his eyes watchful.

Jabbing a forefinger at him, Shaka said in a voice as smooth as oil, 'I say that she may go – but only if Kingi is agreeable.'

A flush suffused Farewell's face. King stepped in. 'Mrs Farewell is welcome aboard. I shall see to it she reaches home safely.'

Shaka nodded, benevolence itself. Almost as an afterthought, he fixed Farewell with an icy stare. 'She is not to be the intermediary of Febana ka ma jo-ji. The *umkumbe* will carry no message from you to King George's Great Chief. If it does, I will not allow your wife to leave.'

A pulse throbbed on the Lieutenant's temple. Straightening his back, he said stiffly, 'My wife will carry no letter to the Governor. I am a man of my word.'

Seeing Ned gearing up to offer up a sarcastic reply, Jackabo kicked him surreptitiously on the shin to stop him adding insult to injury by saying something he might regret. Shaka swung round to impale Jakot with his commanding gaze.

'Hlambamanzi, your place will be with the chiefs so that at all times, they understand what is required of them. I will tell you your exact duties at a later time.'

Jackabo saw a look of deep anguish cross the Xhosa's face. A trip back to Cape Colony, the kingdom of the British, was the last thing Jakot Msimbithi wanted.

Fynn's face was inscrutable as he listened to what Shaka had to say.

Bloody amazing, he thought, watching him closely. A few months ago, I'd have said he was on the edge of madness. Now he's totally in control, down to the last detail.

The mere reminder of Nandi's death made his mouth go dry. For three, long, harrowing months after she died, the people of Zululand lived under conditions that could only be described as inhuman. Dangerously close to starvation, an entire nation was forbidden to harvest their crops; even the milk from thousands of cattle had to be poured away. During that time alone, thousands of people were reputed to have died.

Fynn rubbed the back of his neck, disturbed by the memories. It had taken the boy and himself weeks to extricate themselves from emKindini, and a damn sight longer to free themselves from the mental horrors of what they had witnessed. One thing, however, still eluded him.

Just who had persuaded the man to stop the killing and let his mother rest in peace? Could it have been the bribe of thousands of cattle his chiefs had offered him – or had it been down to someone else, someone uncommonly close to him?

Instinctively, his eyes travelled to the red haired boy who was sitting staring at Shaka, lost in thought.

After the meeting, Mbopha slipped silently away. His jaws ached from clenching his teeth and he was holding on to his temper with great difficulty.

'Out of my way!' he snarled, taking a vicious swipe at a passing servant. He swished past, muttering to himself. 'Aiii, by the day, by the hour, the *umlungu* chiefs gain more power. As if eThekwini was not enough, more land is given into their hands. Now, every treacherous dog in the land can slip in to receive their protection and hide from the King's law – not counting those from strange nations who follow on the heels of the fornicator, Mbuyasi.'

He suspected it would get worse. More goods would come from the lands of the white men. The people would clamour for them until Zululand was buried under trinkets. Then more white men would come to pick over the riches of the land. He had never trusted the pale-skinned whites. And that included umGeorge and his people in the south.

'Unless something is done,' he muttered, 'soon it will be beyond the power of the amaZulu to stop them. We must take action as long as we have the chance.'

There was no time to waste. He must deliver this latest piece of news to the appropriate quarters.

Thirty-Three

Tomorrow was the last day of April. It was also the time of the full moon, an auspicious time for new beginnings. Shaka's mission would set sail when the lunar influences were at their most powerful.

Aboard, everything had been stowed away. Food, drinking water, dishes, pots and pans, bedding – all was in order, the vessel made shipshape for her maiden voyage. Added to which, more than a dozen magnificent ivory tusks, a gift for the Cape Governor, had been wrapped in sailcloth then lashed together for safety.

'We sail on the morning tide,' Hatton announced, rubbing his hands together, briskly. 'So stir your backsides, and stow your personals.'

Shortly afterwards, Jackabo went aboard, carrying his pack. Clad in a new blue-checked shirt and decent trews and with his hair plaited and tied behind, he set off below, whistling, to sling his hammock and find Ned.

The following day, tribesmen arrived in droves to see them leave. A wailing dirge rose up from the women huddled on the jetty, convinced that the *umkumbe* would sink below the waves with everyone aboard.

Nat Isaacs came slowly up the gangway, looking pale and ill. Next to arrive were Elizabeth Farewell and her small terrier, a convoy of servants sweating under the weight of her boxes and trunks. Farewell, dressed in naval trim and looking suitably protective, followed her aboard.

'Ready for a soiree in Cape Town, is he?' Ned asked with heavy sarcasm.

Resplendent in their tribal finery were the two chiefs, Sothobe and Mbozamboza, accompanied by three of their wives. A scurry of half-naked servants brought up the rear, bearing their headrests, mats, blankets, cooking pots, clothing, fur capes and general finery.

Jakot and his wife Nontonella were last to come aboard, the man in question carrying a large bundle and looking slightly harassed. Jackabo fell into step beside him along the deck.

'What's the bother?' he asked.

Jakot rolled his eyes in the direction of the trio of well-built Zulu wives. Chattering, wobbling and giggling, they certainly drew the eye.

Clad in short leather skirts and capes of monkey tails, their hair was stiffened with layers of red clay and plaited in complex rows of plaits running from the crown to the nape of the neck. Adorned by rows of intricately woven necklaces, some of coloured beads and others of little brass balls, their anklets tinkled merrily as they padded along the deck.

Jakot eyed them with red-eyed intolerance. 'Eh, these womens,' he said, with feeling. 'All day, they are wailing, crying, afraid the spirits will not allow them to return. The chiefs make a sacrifice to the gods for their safe journey…but no difference.'

Shaking his head at such displays of female temperament, he said. 'Me, I would beat them with a stick and drop them in the sea for the fishes.'

His wife, Nontonella, who was not in the least put out by her husband's comments, beamed at Jackabo. Waiting until the chiefs' wives were safely out of earshot, Jakot sashayed along the deck, swinging his hips, imitating their voices in a high falsetto as he went.

'*Ay ay ay…* the other wives will take all my things, my children, my pots, my hut…*ay ay ay!*'

Jackabo put back his head and laughed. Jakot was back to his normal self.

At last it was time to go. Everyone and everything was aboard. The tide was right. The call went out. 'Cables up, cast off ropes!'

Anchors clattered and rumbled. A hiss as ropes were cast off; a scuffle of feet as the thick, hand-plaited sisal dripping with seaweed was hauled up and coiled on deck.

The schooner trembled and began to move. The deck thrummed and tilted beneath Jackabo's bare feet. Instinctively, he braced himself against the rising swell. Above his head were the familiar billow of canvas and the sway of tapering masts framed against a vivid blue sky, the ship's tattered flags fluttering in the wind.

Natives milled round on the jetty, wailing and crying, reluctant to see the sailors go, children spilling out from the boatyard and running along the shore. Fynn was there to see them off, waving his hat, the black and white ostrich plumes fluttering in the breeze.

Elizabeth Farewell stood by the rail, a broad-brimmed straw hat tied below her chin by a tulle scarf. As the figures on the pier began to dwindle into the distance, she took the dog's little paw and waved it to her husband, much as a mother would do with a small child.

The vessel gained speed, the whiff of fresh paint, varnish and tarry ropes adding to the indefinable smell of the sea. To starboard was the high, forested bluff and the rocky islands spattered with guano, with the usual regiments of long-legged storks, herons, pelicans, and ibis standing to attention, oblivious to the occasion, and the presence of the schooner slipping by.

Soon, both the islands and the colonies of birds fell away in the wake of the schooner and became part of the eternal, shimmering lagoon that was eThekwini.

Somewhere ahead, beyond the spit of sand known as Fynn's Point, lay the lurking, pitted sand-banks which had broken the back of the *Mary*, three years earlier. Jackabo glanced in the direction of the master cabin. King and John Hatton would be poring over the chart, double-checking the findings King had made some five years ago.

The ship had slowed to almost walking pace. Very soon now they would begin to edge their way into the narrow channel that would lead them out into the Indian Ocean, the bo'sun taking frequent soundings as they went.

The mood was tense. Memories of the shipwreck still ran deep among the seamen. Level with the long spit of sand now, easing past it, watching as it slid by on the port bow. A strident cry came from amidships. A sailor pointed to something.

A group of befeathered Zulus was silhouetted against a background of windswept sands. The wives raised a high chatter of Zulu, their fear of the ocean forgotten. Sothobe's voice was hoarse with excitement. 'See! The Nkosi has come to wish us good fortune.'

People clustered round the rail to catch a glimpse of Shaka. He stood motionless, the feathers of his head-dress and long fringes of cow tails at elbow and knee fluttering in the wind. No one moved, nor spoke. Even the wives were hushed into silence.

Jackabo saw the warriors' shields rise in salute as they drew level with them and he caught the faint snatch of voices drifting towards them on the wind.

Slowly but surely, the vessel slipped by; the figures of Shaka and the *impi* dwarfed by the immensity of sea, sky and wind-swept sands. Another moment or so and they were gone.

Jackabo's fingers clutched the rail. What was it the Nkosi had said to him as he was leaving?

"Today will soon become yesterday. There will be many such before you will say 'Tomorrow I will come again to the land of the amaZulu.' " There had been a strange sadness in his eyes, when he'd added, 'Remember me, Jackabo.'

The red-haired boy turned away, oddly moved by the vivid memory of the last words the warrior king had said to him.

Farewell stood alone on the stone jetty, his eyes fixed on the empty, shimmering lagoon. He had already dismissed both the ship and everyone aboard it from his mind. Instead, the focus of his attention was on the man he'd dispatched south a few months earlier. If anyone could find his way to the Cape overland, it would be John Cane.

His thoughts turned to the letter he'd entrusted to the carpenter. The last few sheets of decent writing paper he'd had left, carefully wrapped in oilskin to keep it dry and clean.

Farewell had taken great care over its wording. Elizabeth had set the tone. 'Just the right note, dear,' she'd said. 'A firm but polite reminder of past services you've rendered the Governor's office, a hint of your past Royal Navy record and decorations, nothing boastful, just a statement of fact.'

Elizabeth always had a nose for what was correct. But he also had his own instincts and agenda. He would couch certain aspects of the whole sorry business a shade more forcefully, and in terms that a man of the world like Sir Richard Bourke would understand.

Nobody would suspect a thing – until it was too late, of course.

Francis Farewell removed his eyeglass and placed it in his breast pocket. Clasping his hands behind his back, he set off on foot towards Fort Farewell, whistling a jaunty tune as he went.

His departure did not go unnoticed. Shrewd eyes had watched everything from high up on the Bluff. They had seen the vessel sail safely out beyond the point and head south and Shaka and his warriors turn back in the direction of kwaDukuza.

Now they were fixed solely on Farewell. Yebo, ever the sly fox, Langani thought, noting the swagger in the man's walk. Who can trust a word you say?

Ill at ease, and aware that trouble was mounting, the diviner watched him until he was out of sight.

Three days later, Shaka sent runners to eThekwini. A large herd of his prime white cattle had broken through their fences and were scattered over a wide area of bush. He appealed to the remaining *umlungu* to send people and horses to kwaDukuza to help round up the cattle before they became the prey of lions, leopards or the fly that carried the sleeping sickness. Farewell, Ogle and Halstead, needless to say, immediately complied with the request.

Henry Fynn, however, was nowhere to be found – not in any of his home-steads, nor anywhere else in the whole length and breadth of eThekwini.

Three weeks later. The Wild Coast, amaPondoland
Fynn strode naked from the River umZimkhulu, water trickling down his body. At this time of year the air was cool and pleasant, with a sharp, almost peppery taste.

He shook himself like a dog, spattering water in a wide arc around him. Combing his fingers through his sun-streaked hair, he tied it back with an old bootlace then rubbed himself down with his discarded shirt. Stretching out in the makeshift chair by the doorway of the hut, he relaxed and allowed the last of the sun to warm his body.

It had been good to wash away the dust and fatigue of the long trek. More than a hundred miles of hard terrain and tortuous bush trails took its toll on a man.

Fynn squinted up at the cloud-streaked skies. The setting sun hung in a shimmering ball of fire just above the trees, the cricking of cicadas and the nightly chorus of croaking bullfrogs forming a pleasant background to the early evening.

Drips of water from his hair trickled deliciously down his back. After the harrowing experiences of emKindini and the long months of retribution following Nandi's death, his soul had yearned for the peace and quiet of this small place beside the river.

The day after Shaka's delegation left for the Cape, he had slipped quietly away from the bay. Both of his wives were well provided for, and his homesteads were not dependent on his day-to-day presence.

As for his offer to stay behind as surety for the safe return of the chiefs, as far as he was concerned, that was just what he was doing. After all, Shaka hadn't said just where he expected him to wait!

A hundred miles away from eThekwini there were few complications; only his camp, his cattle, and his people to contend with. Fynn smiled. And there was his new wife, of course. She had her own code of behaviour – and it most definitely included a modicum of decorum. Reaching into the hut, he extricated a length of faded blue cotton and wrapped it around the lower half of his body.

The acrid smell of wood smoke drifted out of the gathering dusk. He wrinkled his nose appreciatively. Not long till supper.

His trackers came ambling over, displaying gap-toothed smiles. Squatting down companionably beside him, they reached for their snuff-boxes, winking and twinkling at him out of the corners of their eyes.

Fynn glanced at the trio with affection.

Jonas, Mbalijala and Ngoza were people the Zulus disdainfully called

Fingoes. They had been with him from the start and they had shared many a hard trail together. Hunger, danger and the thrill of the hunt wove powerful bonds between men.

The yeasty whiff of beer announced the arrival of Fynn's young wife. Bending down, she placed the gourd on the ground, her soft brown eyes seeking his approval. The men eyed the foaming beer appreciatively.

Fynn sighed. What more could a man want than to sit out under the stars, a gourd of beer at hand, a warm fire to light up the night – and a pretty young woman waiting at the end of it?

Soon the hunting season would begin. Once the summer grasses died away, the game would be more easily spotted.

Eh, but life was good.

Two days later Fynn was sitting by the doorway in the slanting rays of the morning sun, cleaning his guns. A shrill whistling made him glance up. The quick, flicking hand signals of the Fingoes alerted him. *Armed strangers approaching . . .*

Putting down the half-cleaned hunting rifle, he got to his feet and reached for the loaded firearm he kept inside the doorway. His eyes flicked between the armed Fingoes and the open gates. Minutes later, a tall grey-haired man followed by a score of young warriors pushed their way into the compound.

Zulus.

Fynn's hands froze on the gun. *What in God's name –*

He frowned. Surely to God Shaka wouldn't have sent people after me all the way down the Wild Coast – *or would he?*

With a sickening jolt, he realised he already knew the answer to that. Shaka, as he well knew, could be unpredictable. What he would, or wouldn't do if the mood took him, was anyone's guess.

And as for finding a white man in amaPondoland – well, that wouldn't be too difficult, considering he was probably the only one between here and Cape Colony.

Fynn narrowed his eyes. There was something very familiar about the *induna* leading the group of warriors; the lined face, the deep grooves around the mouth and eyes, the solid stance and the air of command.

Then he remembered. Chief Nkobe. He'd met him a few years ago. Hold on, though – Nkobe's territory lay in the hinterland of eThekwini, some fifty miles beyond the steep escarpment rising up from the humid coastline.

His inner voice started to play havoc with his peace of mind. *What in the devil brings you so far south, Nkobe? And why do I have the feeling that what you're going to tell me will come as no surprise?*

The old, familiar prickling at the nape of his neck told him he wouldn't have to wait long to find out. Putting his loaded firearm back inside the hut, he crossed the compound to greet the newcomers.

Zulu etiquette demanded that guests and passing strangers be refreshed in mind and body before any other subject was raised. Fynn had no choice but to bide his time, though he was inwardly seething with impatience.

Once tobacco was produced and the ritual of lighting pipes completed, Chief Nkobe brought his speculation to an end. Waving a hand northwards, he shook his silver-streaked head and announced, 'The Nkosi, he is only one or two days away.'

Fynn almost choked in mid-draw. *Why now, just after his mission has left for the Cape? What in God's name is he up to?*

Inwardly, he cursed the Zulu king to hell and back. He must have moved his regiments south with incredible speed. Fynn drew in a sharp breath. It had all the hallmarks of a planned operation.

Aware that the man across the fire was expecting a response, he addressed Chief Nkobe as calmly as he could. 'How many regiments are with the Nkosi?'

Nkobe sighed, his breathing laboured, a slight wheezing in his chest. Fynn noticed the signs of fatigue etched into the man's face. He was no longer young, and his body bore livid scars of the battles fought in Shaka's service.

'The army he brings is a mighty one, Mbuyazi. I do not know how many regiments, but he has made two camps, one for each force.'

'Two forces?' echoed Fynn, perplexed.

'Yebo. One will attack the amaPondo, south from here.' Fynn felt ice drip into his veins. Leaning forward, he asked softly, 'and the other one, *baba*?'

The eyes that looked back at Fynn were streaked with broken blood vessels, the faint blue rim of cataract around the pupils and the tiredness of age clearly visible.

'The Nkosikazi must be avenged.' he said, simply. His voice was steady, only the slight trembling of the hands on the stem of the pipe giving him away. 'Those who refuse to mourn her must be taught a lesson.'

Fynn swore, suddenly, violently and graphically.

The shock of his outburst caught Chief Nkobe unawares, and the pipe fell from his hands in a shower of burning tobacco. Although the blasphemies voiced in Mbuyasi's own tongue were indecipherable to the Zulu, the explosive force of the white man's anger was not.

A two-pronged attack such as the one Nkobe had just described wasn't something dreamed up in a moment. Neither was the assembling of the entire Zulu army in such a short time . . .

To send the fastest and the most ruthless part of the army to harry people on the Colony's frontiers, the *impis* fanning out deeper into country whose borders were, at best, imprecise, was risky, very risky indeed.

Shaka had known full well that the white chiefs of Natal would have bitterly opposed any move to involve either themselves or their men in such a dangerous move. And that was why he'd timed it when he did.

Fynn swore again. What a fool he'd been! He had walked straight into the trap Shaka had set for him.

His choice of Nat Isaacs as hostage had been no more than a ruse. You knew damn well I'd not let that happen, he thought, grinding his teeth. Yebo, Nkosi, you had plans for me, all right – but what in hell are they? His mind feverishly raced through all the possibilities.

Then it hit him. The fact that he'd come to the Wild Coast under his own steam meant nothing at all in the scheme of things. He was exactly where he was meant to be, or rather where Shaka had known he would be, all along.

With him – on whatever crazy mission he had in mind. All of a sudden Fynn was deeply afraid. Not only for himself, but for all the others caught in the web of Shaka's ambitions.

Discussing the possible opening up of a trade route to the south while sitting in the comparative safety of Natal was one thing – but to be halfway down the Wild Coast with an unpredictable force like Shaka, hell-bent on avenging his dead mother, as well as engaging with the amaPondo, was quite another.

Fynn groaned aloud. Oh God! And to compound matters, at this very minute Shaka's envoys were no doubt setting sail for Government House in Cape Town to meet with Sir Richard.

Their carefully laid plans were in danger of tumbling down like a pack of cards. All it would take was something they weren't prepared for – and coming from a quarter they weren't expecting it to. Shaka's arrival on the fragile borders of the British Colony, accompanied by a massive force of armed warriors, would fit the bill exactly.

Conscious of Chief Nkobe staring at him, he thrust his rising appre-hension aside. Offering him some more beer as an apology, Fynn put a final question to him.

'Tell me, *baba,*' he said, 'where exactly can I find the Nkosi? I have an urgent matter I must discuss with him.'

Part Four

Thirty-Four

From his place on the headland, Langani stood looking out over the lagoon. The cheetah was at his side, her amber eyes half-closed against the hot sunlight filtering through the pine trees. The animal purred softly in her throat and rubbed her finelymarked head against his thigh.

Shaka and the returning Zulu army were very close, although Langani had no way of telling exactly when the long head of the snaking columns would begin to appear. The diviner parted the leafy branches and peered down into the deserted clearing below.

Once it had housed the skeleton of a half-constructed ship, men busy around her, the air full of whistling, banging and the honey smell of freshly cut timber. Now both ship and men were gone and a green slick of new growth had begun to reclaim the clearing. A family of small deer stopped to nibble at the new shoots of grass, unaware of the human dramas that had once been played out there.

Four full moons had come and gone since the vessel carrying the white men and Shaka's chiefs had sailed away. Now the thin sliver of another new moon was in the night sky. Very soon, the vessel would return from its voyage.

A frown plucked at the corners of Langani's mouth. Distance meant nothing to the destructive power of the *umhlolo*. Unfortunately, its black heart had not remained in Zululand, as might have been expected, but had followed the vessel south. Clucking gently to the cheetah, he retreated into the thick undergrowth. While he did so, he wondered whether any of those aboard the vessel who were soon to die had any forewarning of it.

A few hours later, a low rumbling in the animal's throat made his eyes flick open. The cheetah was sniffing the air, her long, banded tail twitching in anticipation as her keen senses picked up some subtle change in atmosphere, or sounds outwith his normal range of hearing.

Langani pushed aside the cloak and rose to his feet. The lagoon had changed from blue to silver grey and the afternoon sun had shifted down behind the Bluff. He cocked his head to listen, but all he could hear was the faint sigh of the wind in the pine trees and the lapping of waves against the shore below.

The cheetah padded over to the opening in the screen of foliage. Langani followed her and glanced out over the bay. The lagoon lay empty, with only the sunlight dancing on the crests of the waves.

Nostrils flaring, Celiwe's head swung round, her eyes fixed on a point somewhere over his shoulder. Glancing up at him, she began to pant softly, a pink slip of tongue curling round her sharp incisors.

Some time later, Langeni felt vibrations coming through the sun-warmed earth below his feet. Men, many men and they were coming his way. Clucking gently to the cheetah, the *isangoma* melted back into the undergrowth to wait.

The head of the long snake of warriors moved up the wooded ridge, the faint, but unmistakable echo of their voices and the subdued clink of weapons filtering ahead of them. Feet slithering on the needle-strewn forest trails, the black tide of sweat-slicked bodies began to crest the rise.

Langani's eyes were riveted on the two men in the lead. Shaka, the warrior king and Fynn, also known as Mbuyasi, the finch; one with a flash of red *igwala gwala* feathers at his brow, the other with his weapon slung casually across his shoulder.

Behind them came a flood of men, travel-stained and weary. Bringing up the rear of the long columns, still some distance away, would be the *udibi* boys and the spoils of war, the huge sprawling herds of plundered amaPondo cattle. The diviner stirred restlessly. *So, mighty Shaka, another victory – but how many are left to you? Your people grow restless. They are tired of war and the spilling of blood.*

The beads entwined in his long plaits of hair clinked together softly as he shook his head. Seeing the hackles rise along the cheetah's spine, he put a hand out and stroked its head. *So you feel it too, my friend.*

Grey like the smoke of forest fire it comes...beware, time grows short, great warrior king...

Before the crew of the *Susan and Elizabeth* even had a chance to enter the bay and drop anchor, tragedy struck. When the sails of the schooner and the British warship escorting her were spotted, Henry Ogle and Tom Halstead just happened to be up on the headland having a scout around for game.

When the schooner turned the point and began to navigate the narrow channel leading into the lagoon, the crew noticed the two men dodging down through the trees, waving their hats and firing their muskets.

'That's Ogle an' Halstead, all right,' said Ned, peering at them through the ship's glass. 'But who's the bloody fool with them – an' what in the devil does he think he's doin'?'

All eyes were on someone racing down ahead of Ogle and Halstead. On reaching the rocks, the man waved excitedly then dived into the fast-flowing water and struck out towards the vessel, no doubt thinking to come aboard.

A ragged burst of cheering broke out. Sailors rushed to the rail, shouting encouragement. 'Come alongside, matey! We'll give you a leg up!'

Without warning, the swimmer threw up his arms and disappeared below the surface. Uneasily, they waited for his bobbing head to appear. Seconds dragged by. No sign of him – only the swift flowing water swirling over the pitted sand banks. A sense of urgency exploded along the decks.

Biddle yelled, 'Throw out a rope if ye catch sight o' him. Look lively, for pity's sake!'

The red-haired boy standing by the rail said nothing. A few moments later, he turned away and went below decks.

Later, they discovered the identity of the missing man. It was Michael, one of the interpreters who had been involved in the rape of the wife of Shaka's chief.

Considering he'd been partly responsible for having the sentence of death levied on them, most of the superstitious sailors were of the opinion that justice had finally been done. His body was never found.

When the crew brought James King ashore, he was so weak they had to lift him off the ship and on to the jetty on a hastily constructed stretcher.

Fynn was waiting for them on the quayside. When he saw how gravely ill King was, the look on his bearded face reflected his abject shock. The sallow-skinned, emaciated figure cocooned in ships' blankets reached out a trembling hand to him.

Recovering his composure, Fynn bent over the stretcher and took the pitiful hand in both of his. 'My God, James,' he said, joking to hide his concern. 'So this is what the fleshpots of the Colony have done to you. You'll have to lay off the grog for a bit.'

King smiled weakly. 'Aye, Henry, the pace o' life down south is what did it.' Fynn's eyes sought those of the thirteen-year-old standing by the makeshift stretcher. His silent plea demanded answers as to what in the hell had happened to reduce James King to such a pitiful condition.

The slight shake of the boy's head and the brief, haunted expression in his blue eyes made the shivers run down Fynn's back.

Some sixth sense made him glance over at the triple masts of the Royal Navy frigate anchored out beyond the rocky headland. Odd that it hadn't sailed into the lagoon along with the schooner, he thought. The sea's calm, tide's high, no risk of running aground. Stranger still, that none of the officers have made any attempt to communicate with them or come ashore to see how Lieutenant King had fared on the long journey.

The first inklings of unease began to spread through him. And as they did, the Gorgon-like spectre of the possible failure of Shaka's mission started to rear its ugly head.

Dear Christ, Fynn thought, dread washing over him in a wave of sweat. *If it's true, then there'll be no way out of this for any of us…*

A sense of urgency overcame further speculation. With Jackabo carrying King's personal effects, Hatton and Ned took turns with Jakot and Fynn in carrying the sick man up the steep, winding paths to the house he had built on the Bluff, while Pikwane, Shaka's servant, ran on ahead.

While the rest of the crew carried on to Townsend to put the camp to rights, others began to unload the supplies and take the dogs and other animals off the schooner. The chiefs and their wives would be spending the night at one of Fynn's homesteads.

Mount Pleasant, James King's house on the Bluff
After Fynn dosed the sick man with a few drops of laudanum and settled him down, he came back into the main room. The others were gathered round the table picking at the food Pikwane had prepared for them. The atmosphere was tense.

' I fear it's his liver,' he said, his face grey with concern. 'You only have to look at his colour to see that. The whole area is swollen and tender. My guess is that it's some fluke in the blood, though exactly what it is I can't say with any certainty. Further diagnosis is well out of my league, I fear.'

The finality of Fynn's words struck Jackabo like a knife. Pushing away his half-eaten supper, he stared blankly into space. A painful silence descended, each man taking refuge in his own thoughts and fears. It was followed by a dull awkwardness that restrained conversation and soured the atmosphere.

Isaacs broke the sombre mood. Fixing Fynn with his curious black gaze, his bony fingers idly toyed with his abandoned cutlery. 'Tell me, *mon ami, just* how have you spent the time since we saw you last? Here, playing the dutiful hostage – or were you somewhere else, acting out another kind of game?'

Fynn's reactions were quick and resentful. 'Are you accusing me of something, Isaacs? If so, hawk it out like a man, don't waste time talking in bloody riddles.'

Isaacs hissed. 'You have just returned from a sortie down the coast with your *bon ami,* King Shaka, have you not? What we want to know is this – did you know of his plans to attack the Colony before we set out on our mission? If you did, and said nothing, then you ought to be shot!'

Blood rushed to Fynn's face. Isaacs jumped to his feet, brushed aside Hatton's attempts to restrain him and thrust his face into Fynn's.

'Ah, so I was right! My little barb has hit the mark. What madness possessed you? Shaka planning to attack the borders of the Colony at the same time as sending a party on a mission of goodwill – *pouf,* it is the mark of a madman. And for you to aid him in this means you are a traitor of the worst kind!'

Bringing his fist down on the table with a crack, Fynn shot to his feet and made a lunge towards Isaacs. 'What in the hell are you talking about? Who's betrayed the mission? And who has accused Shaka of attacking the British? It's the first I've heard of it.'

Isaacs snapped, 'The British military has made the accusation! We were given the news courtesy of one Major Cloethe.'

Fynn stared at him, suddenly at a loss for words. The squat bulk of the naval warship anchored beyond the mouth of the bay began to take on even more sinister tones. 'How in God's name did the British military get involved in this?'

John Hatton scraped back his chair and stood up. 'Almost from the start, we were suspected of being spies and kept hanging about Algoa Bay. We weren't even allowed to sail to Cape Town. Eventually, we were informed that Zulus had attacked the border tribes and advanced into British territory. Added to which, a white man had been spotted with the raiding party, adding fuel to the general idea that we were part of Shaka's strategy to wage war on the British.'

He ran a hand through his sandy hair, his grey eyes pinned to Fynn's astonished face. 'I mean to say, Fynn – which other white man running with the Zulus could it have been except yourself! Tell me that?'

Fynn went on the attack. 'Goddamn these lying bastards! As God's my judge, I was nowhere near the frontier at any time, without or without the Zulus. I stayed holed up with Shaka, he being my guest at Mzimkhulu for the entire period. We never stirred from there, except to do a bit of hunting.'

A buzz of anger stirred the hot night air. Tension filled the room.

'Hold on, Fynn,' said Hatton, coolly, casting a warning frown round the table. 'You were supposed to stay here as Shaka's hostage, remember? So, climb down off your perch, nobody here is accusing you of anything, merely bringing to your notice what the British military told us.'

Isaacs was sceptical. 'So Shaka could not have given orders for his men to push deep into the territory, then attack?'

Fynn shook his head irritably. As he held a spill of wood over the funnel of the lamp to light his pipe, Jackabo noticed that his fingers were shaking.

'On the contrary, Isaacs, what I *can* tell you is that Shaka's commanders were ordered to make the warriors sit on their shields if they even clapped eyes on a white man. That was to prevent the Zulus being accused of aggression against the Colony.'

Squinting through a haze of tobacco smoke, Fynn fixed a pair of hard eyes first on Isaacs, then on Hatton. 'Mapitha, Shaka's own cousin, was the man given the responsibility of seeing it was carried out if the occasion arose. That way, the chiefs wouldn't suspect Shaka of favouring umGeorge's people, nor have the Zulus accused of being cowards for not attacking them. This I'll swear to, on a stack of Bibles.'

Isaacs cut in. 'So some of them might not be tempted to carry out a raid or two out of sight of the Nkosi?'

Jackabo's eyes travelled to where Isaacs was crouched at the end of the table like a thin, black haired spider. *Nat's nothing if not persistent,* he thought.

Fynn took the pipe out of his mouth. 'Now there's a bloody silly question, Nat! 'Temptation' ain't a word that springs readily to the Zulu mind – not if it means going against a direct order from Shaka.'

Jackabo spoke up from where he was fondling one of King's dogs.

'The way I see it, some other group must have been mistaken for the Zulus. Just think about it. I mean, the British army have never even *seen* a Zulu warrior, let alone fight one. How could they tell who the attackers were?'

A pregnant silence fell over the group of exhausted men. 'You're dead right, lad,' Hatton said. 'The border area's not exactly short of renegades.

It's a hotbed of unrest, and has been for some time. Most 'em fled before Shaka's rapid advance a few years back.'

'And just when was this "attack" supposed to have happened?' Fynn asked, laying his pipe aside. Hatton thought hard for a moment or two before replying. 'Late on in July, I'd say.'

Fynn considered his answer carefully. 'The Zulu army was back at Mzimkhulu with me by the middle of the month. I remember, because of how bitterly cold it was at the time. Poor bastards needed to be fed and rested before the long trek back to Zululand. I can vouch for that, because I had a devil of a job trying to find food for all of them!'

Both triumph and relief were in his voice when he spoke. 'That means they were well clear of the frontier by the time these attacks were supposed to have happened. The British are either lying or they've mistaken them for some other band of hostiles.'

'Or else they've been given wrong information by someone wanting to stir up trouble,' added Jackabo, quietly, without looking up. Fynn shot him a quick glance. 'What do you know, lad?'

This time, Ned cut in. 'Me an Heelander, we saw that wife o' Farewell's getting' aboard a vessel bound for Cape Town. Interestin' just who was seein' her aboard, you might say. A real military-lookin' gent, the same look about him as some of the other toffs from Algoa who were so keen on keepin' us from going about our business.'

A shamefaced Isaacs spoke up. '*Peut etre,* I think we should start at the beginning again, put the whole story together.'

'Before we go any further,' Fynn said, 'will someone kindly tell me what that bloody Royal Navy warship is doing moored out there with her guns broadside on to our only exit? Are they here to make sure we don't get out – or just breathe down our necks with menace aforethought?'

'Well, before we get to that,' Hatton said, 'maybe you should start at the beginning and tell us why you came to be half-way down the Wild Coast in the first place.'

'Aye, right,' Fynn responded. 'After you left, knowing bloody well Shaka wasn't likely to hold me to being a hostage for the duration, I decided to take a little trip down to Mzimkhulu, do a bit of hunting.'

Allowing himself a grin, he went on, 'At least, I hoped so. I'd only been there a few days, when an advance party of Zulus came a-calling, to slip me the wink that the Nkosi and the Zulu army were only a few hours away.'

'So you'd no idea what he'd been planning?' said Hatton.

'None,' answered Fynn, emphatically. 'Though I suspected sooner or later he intended to have another poke at Faku – never for one moment did I think he meant to do it at the same time as sending his mission south.'

Jackabo came to stand by him. 'Did you go and find the Nkosi, then?'

Fynn stared into his face. At close quarters, he could see the dark shadows below the lad's eyes, also a hint of the same uncanny stare he'd seen on his return from Delagoa.

Forcing a smile, he replied. 'Aye, that's what I did, lad. I went to see the Nkosi to talk things over with him.'

A sudden image of his two terrified Fingoe trackers, Jonas and Ngoza, came to mind. When they'd walked out of the darkness and seen the legendary King Shaka appear in the firelight, they'd been rigid with fear, unable to move a muscle.

Fynn blinked rapidly. 'And that was how it was,' he answered, truthfully, 'I was with him all the time, right up until we walked into eThekwini a few days ago.'

A lengthy silence followed. 'And did you broach the subject of exactly why he was there?' asked Hatton, quietly. 'Did you point out to him he might be endangering his mission by bringing his army so far south?'

Fynn stared hard at the boat builder. 'I should remind you nobody tells the King of the Zulus what to do – but yes, I did have one or two conversations with him on that score.'

'And?'

Fynn hesitated a moment. 'It was Faku he was after, mainly, a chance for his army to see some action an' acquire some more amaPondo cattle. Of course, there was also the matter of avenging his mother. That was really what he was after. A big mistake, as I tried to tell him.'

Unbidden, indelible glimpses of Shaka with his mighty army flooded into his mind.

A winter sky, deep blue and crystal clear, the air bitterly cold in spite of the sunshine, the vast sea of bodies swarming across the river: even without their regalia of feathered head-dresses, ox hair fringes and war paint, Shaka's warriors were superb looking and deadly.

On and on they came, regiment after regiment, the icy water surging up to their thighs, as whooping, yelling and singing they poured across the Mzimkhulu River.

Shaka's elite force, invincible and unstoppable, framed against a background of udibi boys urging bawling cattle into the water and across to the other side, the air full of their raucous cries and shrill whistling.

And there was the warrior king himself, striding down the river-bank towards him, the civet tails of his short kilt swirling round his muscular knees, the creamy long cow-tail fringes startling against his darkly oiled skin. As he surveyed his army, immense pride was etched on his face, the glint of unshed tears clear in his eyes.

'Mbuyazi,' he'd turned to him and said, 'Is this not the mightiest army you have ever seen?'

'Your pride and your passion, Nkosi,' Fynn had replied, unable at that moment to find it in his heart to grudge the man either his pleasure, or his pride, in what he had created.

Hatton broke in. 'You said 'mainly' Fynn, it was *mainly* Faku he was after. Did he have something else in mind as regards the British?'

Fynn hesitated, wondering how he could convey the Zulu king's point of view without prejudicing the fragile revival of goodwill in the room. At length he said, 'In many ways, Shaka's quite a simple man…'

A snort of disbelief came from Isaacs. Fynn ignored it. 'Situations that might seem 'delicate' or 'complex' to us, are comparatively straightforward to him.'

'Like ignoring the Colony's borders or wiping out whole tribes?' Hatton persisted.

'Yes, and no,' Fynn replied, 'Remember Shaka, or any leader around here, has no concept of "borders" as we know them. Take the River Thukela for instance. Before his move south, it only formed a natural border because of its tendency to flood, thus keeping his warriors penned up in the Kingdom.'

A grudging agreement passed around the group.

Fynn went on, 'Basically, he had no intention of attacking either the British or their territory. What he did bend his considerable talents towards, however, were two main things. First, his unshakeable belief that some former exiles, those who'd fled before his earlier advances, were guilty of either ignoring Nandi's death or not showing sufficient remorse. Secondly, he was quite aware of the general unrest in the region – also a source of great anxiety for those at the Cape, I can tell you.'

'I don't think we need the details of what his proposed solutions to the problems might have been,' said Hatton, with a rueful grin.

'Well, I'll repeat his exact words, just in case,' Fynn said, laughing. ' To quote the man himself, "*It is very clear to me. To open the road between Zululand and the lands of the white men, surely it is necessary to remove all the hyenas and wild dogs in between – do you not agree, Mbuyasi?*"

A ripple of subdued amusement went round the room. Fynn returned to the matter at hand.

'In the end, after conquering Faku, he decided to make peace with him. In return, that is, for the amaPondo agreeing to come under the Zulu sphere of influence – which is perhaps what the whole exercise was about in the first place, gents.'

The others exchanged thoughtful looks. Fynn continued.

'It was only then I began to see the logic of his argument. Zulu influence up to the Colony's border – then British control all the way to the Cape.'

Jackabo broke in. "And I shall be king of the blacks and umGeorge will rule the whites." It was what Shaka said the first time I ever set eyes on him.'

'Well, you've a better memory than anyone,' Hatton replied. 'I think it's maybe the nearest we'll get to what was really in that devious mind of his when he went south – a three-pronged attack, involving Faku, the avenging of his mother's honour and clearing the way for a treaty between the Zulus and the British.'

Fynn swept a determined gaze round the room. 'Now, gents, it's your turn. I want to know exactly what happened down there.'

'We never did get to Cape Town, Fynn,' Jackabo said. 'Algoa Bay was as far as we were allowed to go.'

Fynn stared at him in disbelief. 'But why in the hell not, what were you doing all those months?'

Hatton's reply was short and explosive. 'Wait – that's all we did! Wait, lying at anchor while Sir Richard Bourke deliberated as to whether he might allow us to present him with forty prime tusks of ivory and Shaka's hopes for peace with the British.'

His normally calm exterior splintered under the harsh memories of the cold futility of those winter months. His face white with suppressed rage, he snorted, 'There was Lieutenant King, trying to be patient and reasonable, playing the waiting game, hoping for the best. And, yes, damn it, *thinking* the best of the British authorities, convinced it was only a matter of time before they came round.'

Ned Cameron butted in. 'Poor old Sothobe and Mbozamboza ended up rat-arsed on cheap grog. They even ran off, trying to get back to Zululand. Then, after a month or two of freezing aboard ship... enter Major A.J.Cloethe of the Cape Rifles.'

Jackabo and Ned exchanged glances. They'd been on deck when the horse and carriage had drawn up on the quayside. The first they'd seen of the major was his pair of well-polished military boots stepping out of the carriage.

'Well, now, what have we here?' Ned had muttered, 'a dandy-lookin' kind of fish, an' no mistake.'

Almost as if he'd heard him, the tall man narrowed his eyes below the stiff, peaked cap. Mounting the gangplank with a firm tread, he stepped on to the deck beside them.

Even without the tailored uniform of fine khaki serge and the scarlet and gold insignia on the epaulettes of his greatcoat, there was no mistaking the ram-rod back and rigid bearing of the military. The cool, slate-grey eyes below the bushy brows were experienced, used to sifting out men's weaknesses.

Tapping his swagger stick against his boot, the Major addressed Nat Isaacs with the look of a man who would dearly love to send him on a long route march. Standing at a little over six feet tall, his complexion was ruddy, his silver hair and moustaches short-clipped, severe. On being informed that James King was away for a few days, he'd said,

"I can see no problem with interviewing the Zulus in your presence, since he has left you in charge." His English was delivered in the heavy accent of the anglicised Boer. "In the absence of the nominal spokesman of this 'expedition', you will have to do. What I must ascertain can be done as easily in your presence as Mr. King's."

The Major's blunt disregard for James King's status boded no good for the future. A surge of angry colour rose to Nat's cheeks. Cloethe clicked his swagger stick against his boot impatiently.

"You say the Zulus occupy rooms at the residence of the widow Robinson? Perhaps you would be good enough to send someone to bring them here. The Captain's cabin will suit my purpose."

'Aye,' Jackabo said, 'that was our first sight of the rogue. But no our last, more's the pity.

'Damn and blast the man,' Hatton spat out, 'he interrogated the chiefs as if they were criminals suspected of cattle stealing. The poor devils were totally at a loss, wondering what they were being accused of. And, to make matters worse, he came back a second time, insinuating that the Lieutenant was a charlatan and a liar who had tricked them. In the end, between the grog, the cold, and the Major, the poor bastards ran off, making for home.'

Fynn's brain reeled with the implications of what he was hearing. 'But it doesn't make sense. Why in hell should the Governor put up so many objections to receiving a peace mission from a distant war chief? I'd have thought the British would have welcomed such an overture, after all the years of trouble they've had with the Xhosa.'

Hatton shook his head in frustration. 'You may well ask! But why all the hostility and suspicion towards us? We were British subjects, shipwrecked mariners, James King a former serving naval officer who'd served his country in time of war? Why were we pinned down in Algoa Bay when we were fully entitled to sail on to Cape Town?'

A heavy silence fell. Beyond the shuttered windows the frenetic activity of insects seemed abnormally loud. Fynn resumed his pacing. A sudden thought struck him. He swivelled round, 'The personal attack on James King... exactly what was said?'

Hatton's eyes unconsciously flicked to the doorway leading to the room where the man lay, seriously ill.

'I overheard every word. I was meant to, of course, just to make sure there was a witness to his humiliation. By God, when the British decide to play dirty, there's none bloodier, I can tell you! They savaged the Captain like a wild dog, took him down lower than a bilge rat.'

'Tell me,' said Fynn, stony faced.

When he locked eyes with Major A.J. Cloethe across the table in the Port Authority office, James King could barely keep the hostility from his voice. 'I would like an explanation as to your conduct, Major – and forthwith.'

The steel grey eyebrows lifted in mock surprise. '*My* conduct, *meneer*? I'm afraid my conduct should be neither a source of concern to you, nor anyone else. I am, after all, here to carry out the task allocated me by the Governor.'

'And that is?' demanded King. His colour was high, a pulse beating erratically at his temple.

'You know *exactly* what it is, sir. To ascertain the full intent of this mission you have mounted within the Colony.'

'Did Sir Richard not receive the letter I sent to his office? The one where I set out the clear aims of this mission, namely to present the envoys of King Shaka of Zululand? I was under the impression he had, since I have in my possession a reply I received from him. In it, he requests us to stand by while transport was arranged for our travel to Cape Town.'

'And then what?' asked the Major, abruptly, flicking a piece of lint off his sleeve. 'What did you intend to do then, sir?'

King drew himself up to his full height. 'I had expected to be received, along with the Zulu king's envoys, with at least a modicum of the courtesy and civility one would expect from the office of King George's representative at the Cape. I also expected that the chiefs would have been welcome to present King Shaka's gifts and a letter in which he sets out his hopes of a friendly alliance between Zululand and the Colony.'

He glared at the Major, his blue eyes cold as ice. 'Instead I have been disregarded, my people kept isolated for months. Worst of all – you sir, have seen fit to interrogate the Zulu envoys without my permission, and in my absence. Not once, but twice. You have treated these decent men abominably, taking advantage of their ignorance of our ways and language to create confusion and despair in them. You have come within an ace of accusing them of being no better than spies or thieves.'

Anger ran high in James King, hot and sharp, a bitter release after months of anxiety.

'In short, Major Cloete, you are a disgrace, and I intend to make a complaint to Sir Richard concerning this whole situation. Your name, sir, will feature largely in my report.'

The Major's voice was as hard as the frost on the distant mountain peaks.

'I should advise you that you would be wasting your time, *Mr* King...or are you still calling yourself *Lieutenant?*'

His face twisted into the semblance of a smile. 'You seem to have a remarkable knack of collecting titles to which you aren't entitled. '*Lieutenant*' being one of them, '*Chief*' being another, I believe – how quaint!'

James King went red, and then white. With masterful recovery, he fixed his eyes on those of Cloethe.

'I served with distinction for ten years as a midshipman in His Majesty's Royal Navy,' he stated. 'If it weren't for the abrupt end to the war, my commission would have come through. I lost out by a matter of a week or two. I have more than fulfilled all the criteria for command. My record in these waters alone, including a survey I undertook on behalf of the Admiralty – is enough to justify it.'

'Ah, yes,' the Major taunted. '"*If only*" – the saddest words in the language.'

He leaned across the table, his cold grey eyes as flat as stones. 'I, on the other hand, *do* hold the King's commission. I am under orders to see to it that no more mistakes are made.'

'What d'you mean? Mistakes, what mistakes?' cried King, his temper flaring up. 'I am not aware of any mistakes we have made on this mission – other than being too patient.'

Cloethe picked up a letter-opener shaped like a dagger and pretended to examine it. Then he said, smoothly. 'Of late, your reputation in the Colony has worsened considerably. On a previous occasion, you invited several prominent citizens to invest in your intended trading project-on the premise that the British authorities would soon declare the province a colony.'

The look of alarm and despair in King's eyes was not lost on him

'I have to tell you now, that neither the Cape nor London has the slightest intention of extending their rule further north.'

He paused to let the full effects of his statement sink in. 'Therefore the Governor feels you have solicited funds from Cape citizens under false pretences. I can only suggest you reimburse them immediately.'

Cloethe drove home the next devastating piece of information as surely as if he had used the mock dagger in his hand to do it.

'Reports from the frontier suggest that the Zulus now poised to attack our borders are accompanied by either one, or more, white men. One can only suppose they are part of your settlement at Port Natal.'

King gasped as if struck in the stomach. Cloete ignored it and relentlessly bored on.'Consequently, in order to calm the frontier tribes who are milling about in terror, threatening the stability of an already highly unstable region, Major Dundas has set out north with an armed force. His orders are to repel any attackers. It goes without saying that you and your party will be confined to the town until further notice.'

After he had gone, James King sank his head into his hands in despair.

The stark account of the humiliation and breaking of James King filled the room. From the adjoining room came the rasping breath of the dying man.

In the silence, the night sounds beyond the shuttered windows seemed unnaturally loud. At last, Fynn spoke.

'Personal?' he said, without passion, 'that was just too bloody personal for hearsay, or mere rumour mongering. I'd say that someone pretty close to James King was behind it.'

'A rat,' Ned said, suddenly. 'I smell a dirty, big bastard rat –'

'Aye, one wearing a monocle,' Jackabo added.

'I'll lay a wager we'll find that Farewell didn't set foot outside eThekwini.' Isaacs said.

'No, but his wife did,' added Jackabo, softly, ' As I told you, we saw her going aboard a vessel bound for Cape Town while we were fishing off the quayside.'

Fynn stared at him. 'So you think it might have been the blonde bitch that tipped them off?' Jackabo shrugged his shoulders. 'Who else could it be? Who else was anywhere near the Cape at the time?'

A grin lit up his face. 'But the British didn't get it all their own way, though. No fear. The chiefs refused to desert the Cap'n. After the orders came for us to be escorted back to Zululand below *HMS* Helicon's guns and for him to be confined aboard the warship, they refused to go aboard the schooner unless he was with them. Jakot also refused.'

Suddenly, the room was warmed by the stoic loyalty of the black men who had gone through their own tribulations while with them.

'There's one other thing,' thirteen-year old Jackabo added. 'The Captain's no the only one to have been betrayed.' Tired eyes swivelled towards him.

'The Nkosi,' he said, 'all the goodwill, the preparation, the hand of friendship held out to umGeorge and his fine fellows at the Cape – not to mention a wee fortune in ivory given in trust and generosity. I'm wondering what price will have to be paid for all of that?'

Isaacs had been quiet for a while. Now, he blurted out, 'The *Helicon!* We must send a letter to the authorities, and set Major Cloete and Sir Richard Bourke right. Be busy, Mr Fynn. Write it all down. At first light I'll take it out to the frigate myself.'

But even though Fynn sat up half the night writing a full report of what had transpired at Umzimkhulu, it was to prove a futile gesture.

By the time Isaacs arrived at the jetty, it was too late. As the frigate began to move slowly on the tide, the rattle of anchor chains and shouted commands echoed over the still water. Although he shouted himself hoarse trying to attract someone's attention, her duty done, *HMS Helicon* slowly tacked about and headed south. Isaacs was left clutching the letter that would have exonerated Shaka and the Zulus.

As the sails of the British frigate disappeared beyond the headland, the fragile hope died a death among the keening of the sea birds, a sad requiem to the optimism with which Shaka's mission had left the shores of Zululand only a few months ago.

There was to be no respite from bad news. Barely an hour or so later, a Zulu messenger arrived in a flurry of dust, sweat and anxiety.

On the army's return to kwaDukuza, the Nkosi Shaka had refused his warriors to rest and had told them to prepare for a long siege. His orders were to make war on Shoshongane kaZikode, a chieftain whose territory lay in the far north of Mozambique.

Exhausted after being up all night, Fynn stared at the man in disbelief. 'But that's five hundred miles away at least,' he muttered. Staring glassily at the runner, he demanded, 'What in hell is he thinking about?'

'Eh, Mbuyasi,' the man sighed as he extricated thorns from the soles of his feet. 'The *impis* have been away too long, already much fighting and not enough food. They are tired and in need of rest. How will they fight a new enemy?'

Fynn was hit by a sense of foreboding. Normally, the Zulu King was extremely solicitous as to the care of his warriors after a campaign, giving them time to feast, drink beer, relive their triumphs and enjoy the spoils of victory.

Since when had the distant Shoshongane become so dangerous an enemy that he had to be challenged by the entire Zulu force – especially at this moment in time? The northern terrain would be largely unknown, with few friendly villages to rely on for food and shelter. If they were to survive in hostile territory, they would have to fall back on the twin evils of plunder and coercion.

Not for the first time, Fynn wondered whether the army itself was the source of Shaka's stress. Had the exaggerated claims that some distant tribes had been slow to mourn his mother been the motivation for the bullying of Faku and the amaPondo? Was it based simply on the need to provide his commanders and *indunas* with the spoils of war ... *or was there something else behind Shaka's erratic behaviour?*

His scalp tightened. Having dispatched his whole army into the back of beyond, Shaka had left Zululand unprotected. Unbelievable! Not only that, he had also left himself personally vulnerable, open to attack –

Wordlessly, he handed the runner a pitcher of water. After drinking deeply the man wiped his mouth with the back of his hand and hunkered down, stork-like. Then he went on with his story.

'After sending away his *impis*, what does he do next? Eh, I will tell you, Mbuyasi – he gives orders for all the *udibi* boys to report to him.'

Fynn was dumbfounded. *What next?*

'*Yebo*, Mbuyasi. Now the Nkosi needs the nation's children once again. Just as he trained the Fasimba many years ago, he hopes to do the same with these young ones. *Nyosi, the bees* – this is what he calls the regiment of children.'

Reaching for the pitcher, the messenger swirled water around his mouth, then spat it out onto the ground.

Thirty-Five

In due course, Hatton came across the box grudgingly sent by Sir Richard Bourke as a reciprocal gift for Shaka. It sat on the table in the Master's cabin, its squat presence a reminder of the ill-fated events of Algoa Bay.

Hatton eyed the squat box apprehensively. 'It might be wise to see what's inside first. You never know what those bastards might have put in it.'

'I agree,' echoed Nat Isaacs. '*Mon Dieu*, we are in enough trouble already. To show the contents unexamined would be stupid.'

Ever present was his dread of having to explain to Shaka why he had failed to bring back supplies of the much-desired hair lotion the Zulu King had set his heart on.

The lid of the plain wooden chest was fastened by a steel-grey metal hasp and padlock. Unfortunately, there was no sign of a key.

'Might be best to have some witnesses when we open it,' Hatton suggested. 'We don't want accusations flying around that we pilfered anything.'

While Jackabo went running to fetch Jakot and Sothobe, Ned was called on to exercise one of his many skills. By the time they arrived, he was flexing his fingers, cracking his knuckles and generally revelling in his moment of glory. A piece of wire inserted into the lock, an expert click or two, and the padlock hung open. The box was about to divulge its secrets. John Hatton raised the lid.

The gifts from His Majesty King George IV's Governor at the Cape consisted of two sheets of copper, neither of use or value to the Zulus; a few knives and trinkets and some cheap medicines. The only thing of any value was a length of scarlet broadcloth. The crew regarded the paltry items in silence. 'Weren't worth pickin' the lock for,' said Ned. 'Quite,' replied Hatton, his voice dry as tinder.

Sothobe rocked to and fro silently then sank his head into his hands. When he looked up, anger sparked in his eyes.

'The King will kill someone for this. Do the people of umGeorge think Shaka a fool as well as a liar, a man without honour?'

An uncomfortable silence descended. Jackabo had a fleeting, but powerful, sense of the danger that could rise from the shattering knowledge of betrayal about to fall on an unsuspecting Shaka. Hatton was pale. Even Ned looked serious, his lips pursed in a silent whistle. Jakot's face was like stone. The treacherous behaviour of the British had come as no surprise to him.

Jackabo's heart sank. We whiteys trusted our superiors at the Cape to act in a decent manner, he thought. In turn, the chiefs, even Jakot, trusted us and followed us to umGeorge's territory. And for that they might well have to pay the heaviest price of all.

He felt the chill of fear around him. They, most of all, had good reason to know just what Shaka might be capable of if he realised the full extent of his betrayal and what had happened during the ill-fated voyage.

Poor bastards…

In the end, they decided to add more medicines, beads, amusing little toys and a valuable looking-glass framed in heavy silver, embellished with carved cherubs and flowers bought by James King as a gift for his mother.

After they'd repacked the box and replaced the hasp and the lock, only one question remained. 'Now, then, mates,' asked Ned, his blue eyes bright with mischief. 'Which lucky son of a bitch is going to deliver Shaka's "treasure chest" to him?'

Lines of strain were carved into Hatton's face. 'I wish it was as simple as that, Ned.' He sighed deeply, a great shuddering breath.

'How are we going to explain the failure of King George's Colonial Office? How they accused a chief of Sothobe's stature of being a renegade thief, how a former serving officer was humiliated and stripped of respect? And worst of all, their blind, bloody stupidity in misinterpreting Shaka's offer of peace!'

A wave of regret for John Hatton swept over Jackabo. His fine ship, the one he and the men had laboured so long to build had not been blessed with much luck.

The first officer chose that moment to make a further announcement. 'Before you go,' he said, with deep bitterness in his voice,' there's something else you ought to know. I've just been brought another piece of news which has more than a passing bearing on recent events.'

Straightening his shoulders as if to brush off the exhaustion threatening to overwhelm him, he said, 'A certain gentleman has just returned to the bay after a mighty long walk. John Cane, it seems, has been to the Cape and back. I think you can all guess what his mission was.'

Ned struck Shaka's wooden box with his fist. 'If anybody could do it, an' live to tell the tale, Cane could. He's big enough, an' ugly enough.'

Nat Isaacs started to pace the floor. In the angry silence, the squeaking of his boots was irritating. Hatton spoke up. 'It's clear Farewell sent him to make trouble with the Governor and spoil any chance of James King carrying out the peace treaty on behalf of Shaka.'

He passed a hand over his face. 'As God's my judge, I'll not forgive him, or Farewell either, for what they've done – robbing a man of his health and good name and for the ruination of Shaka's hopes for a peaceful alliance with the British.'

He shot a glance over his shoulder. 'Lord knows how much of this might find its way to Shaka's ears. Can we depend on Sothobe or the Xhosa to keep mum, at least about what happened down south?'

A current of unease stirred among the men. Nat Isaacs' boots stopped squeaking. 'This brings us back to where we began, *mes amis*. Now, who is going to deliver the bad news – and the box – to Shaka?'

Next day, Mbozamboza offered to travel to kwaDakuza to let Shaka know they had returned and tell him of King's serious illness. A day or two later, he returned, harassed and sweating.

Shortly afterwards, hot on his heels, a messenger came from Shaka. With him were some brown and white cattle. The message was terse, ominous.

The bullocks were to be sacrificed to umKhulukhulu, the Great Spirit, for Kingi's speedy recovery. Chief Sothobe was to proceed to kwaDukuzu immediately. And, as he was particularly anxious to hear news of his mission, someone from Kingi's party had to to accompany him.

'*Oh, Mon Dieu*,' whispered Isaacs, slumping down on one of the half-barrel chairs. 'Now we find ourselves on the edge of the knife.'

'Better to be on the edge of it than have it drawn across your throat, matey,' said Ned, offering him some dubious comfort.

In the end, it was Isaacs who offered to go with Sothobe and face Shaka. As for Chief Mbozamboza, or "*My Bosom-Boozer*" as he was affectionately known, he categorically refused to return to kwaDukuzu at all.

Sticking out his stout belly, the chief said sourly: 'I have already been in the lion's mouth. A second time and he will chew my head off. No, I will stay with you here at eThekwini.'

The beginning of September brought back the summer heat. Up on the bluff, among the trees, though, it was still cool.

Jackabo stayed close to James King. Every night when darkness fell, he would sit by his bed while moths bumped against the funnel of the oil lamp, casting giant shadows on the walls. Then he would tell him stories of home, tales he'd learned at Sandy's or his mother's knee, until he fell asleep.

At sunrise, Napisongo would help Jackabo to take him out on to the brow of the hill overlooking the sea. There they would prop him up in his chair beneath the flame trees, the scarlet flowers a vivid canopy above his head.

'My favourite time of day,' King said, weakly. 'It comes from a sailor's life, Jack. My own grandfather, nearly ninety when he died. Up with the lark to check the skies and the wind as if his life depended on it – which it had for near on sixty years at sea. Happen you'll be the same, my boy.'

Then, with haze shimmering on the horizon and the hills across the lagoon etched against the morning sky, James King would fall asleep, the breath sighing and rattling in his throat.

One day went by and then another. The old elephant road across the lagoon remained empty. No messengers appeared over the brow of the hill. No Isaacs. No news of Shaka's distant army.

Jackabo was strangely restless. The air had a queer kind of feel to it, as if something was dragging at it, holding it back. And there was something else there, too – an odour, a smell, almost like that of burning feathers.

For days now, he had walked around with a choking sensation filling his nose and throat, a dry, singed taste that made him want to cough and gag. It made no sense at all, especially when he remembered where he had smelled it before.

Once, back in Fraserburgh, there had been a great to-do when the bachelor son of one of Sandy's neighbours had one dram of whisky too many – hardly a rare event, according to local gossip. Tired out after a long spell at sea, the man had fallen asleep with his pipe still in his mouth.

Not unexpectedly, it had set the bed on fire and he was lucky to have escaped with a few minor burns.

The smouldering feather mattress had to be dragged out on to the back green, and for days, the stink of burning feathers had permeated every nook and cranny of Broadsea. Now, that same smell was back in Jackabo's nose.

'Burning feathers!' he muttered, trying not to gag. *What in the world's it all about?*

It was King himself who suggested Jackabo should travel to kwaDukuza.

'Poor Nat, I fear Shaka will trounce him, like he did over the business with the interpreters. Look what it led to, Nat taking a spear in the back when he tried to handle the Kumalo more or less single handed.'

He tried to pull himself up against the pillows. 'It's *my* place to go,' he protested, 'my place to take whatever blame is going, not let others suffer.'

His struggles set off another bout of coughing. 'This blasted weakness…'

His servant Napisongo came bustling in, his face creased with worry. After King got his breath back, Jackabo tried to reassure him. 'But Nat wanted to go, Cap'n. He's got to be quite a *man* since Algoa.'

James King gripped his hand tightly. 'Aye, that's a fact, Jack. I see the difference in Nat, too. But it changes nothing. It's my place to face the consequences, not him. Now it seems another lad will have to run after the first, to do a man's job…'

His eyes were a piercing blue as they met Jackabo's and held them, unwavering. 'What am I saying, lad? You've been doing a man's work ever since we were tossed on to these shores like so much spindrift. And by God, you've proved it – and more than once, at that.'

While slow tears welled up in his eyes, the grip on Jackabo's hand tightened 'It's not for myself I'd have ye go, Jack, but if Nat should aggravate the King, there's no sayin'…I fear for him.'

Jackabo felt the erratic leap of the pulse in the frail wrist, the fever running through him like fire. 'No, Cap'n, it's not you that's to blame. '

For a moment, he was sorely tempted to blurt out the truth – that Farewell had conspired with Cane to make sure Shaka's mission would fail, and also set the scene for his own humiliation at Major Cloethe's hands.

With a monumental effort, he held his tongue. Instead, he said, 'Shaka has other things to bother him just now. And I doubt he'll lay the blame at your door, anyway.'

The deep blue eyes never left Jackabo's face. 'As usual, you know more than you let on, lad. Better you stay safe here at the Port.'

Jackabo shook his head. 'No. Shaka won't hurt me, Cap'n – though he might be a bit on the raging side by now, I expect.'

As King studied the thirteen-year-old with affection, a sudden flash of his old smile returned. Then a far-away look crossed his face. 'I can see your father plain as plain in you, Charlie. One of the best is Francis. One day, you'll be as good a man as he was. You are already – '

The slow tears welled up again, and Jackabo had to turn his head away so the dying man wouldn't see how much he was hurting.

He looked back only once, just before the path dipped below the brow of the hill. His eyes clung to every detail: James King raising himself off his pillows to wave goodbye, the silver streaks in his dark hair shining in the dappled sunshine filtering through the flame trees. The voice that carried to the brow of the hill, however, was firm and clear.

'God speed you, lad.'

Jackabo raised his hand, the words of farewell sticking in his throat. And then he ran, tears blinding him as he followed the path down the hillside and then on to the old elephant road that led around the bay and climbed up on to the ridge.

Jakot and his wife Nontonella were waiting for him near the turn off to Fort Farewell. The interpreter was in a morose mood, sunk deep in his own thoughts.

After being so close to his Xhosa homelands, experiencing the iron hand of the Colonial authorities and the power they wielded, Jackabo feared what happened at Algoa had only added to Jakot's general distrust of the white man's world.

'UmGeorge's people will take their time,' the Xhosa had retorted angrily, 'but in the end they will eat up the land of the Zulus as they have done mine, piece by piece, like the python swallowing a goat. First they come to hunt, and then they will want land, the next thing you are eaten up whole by them. It is how the British are.'

Thirty-Six

The huge settlement of kwaDukuza seemed strangely empty and silent. As they passed through the gates, the Xhosa hissed through his teeth. 'Eh, I do not like this,' he said, 'it is like a place of the dead.'

Nontonella pressed close to him, her dark eyes darting from hut to hut, searching for familiar faces. After refusing Jakot's offer to stay with them that night, Jackabo made his way through the gates separating the royal quarters from the vast concourse below. No Fasimba, only a few older men sitting in the shade.

His quarters were much the same as they had been four months ago. Dusty now, a few spiders' webs here and there, the tin box holding his father's letters, pens, colouring inks, sketch pads and books still lying on the drum top where he'd left it.

A fluttering in the shadows above his head startled him, and he spun round. The black bird with glossy feathers completed its flight round the hut then glided down to settle on his shoulder.

'Hector!'

Nearly a year ago, just before Nandi's death, the bird had mysteriously disappeared. Now, all these months later, it was back, just as if nothing had happened.

Something, though, clearly had. Its broken wing, the one Jackabo had thought beyond repair, had completely mended. Jackabo ran a finger over the bird's head, smoothing the sleek feathers. 'Hey, bird, are you going to tell me where you've been?'

It regarded him with a round golden eye, a look that was direct and unblinking, its beak half-open as if it were about to speak. Teasing out a strand of his hair, the bird tweaked it playfully, then a moment later flew up on to the shadowy cross-beams and began to preen its feathers.

Jackabo's eyed the floor immediately beneath it. Someone must have swept the floor recently, he thought. No bird droppings by the door, either. Now, he wondered, just who would take the trouble to keep an empty hut clean and tidy, just for a bird? Or did it mean that it had only recently returned, knowing that he was about to turn up in kwaDukuza?

He shook his head. Just one more mystery, in a place full of mysteries.

As darkness began to fall, Jackabo found the huge settlement eerie and echoing, full of shadows that seemed to shift uncannily.

It was humid and oppressive, far darker than usual, due to fewer fires being lit. In spite of the lack of people, however, there was a new restlessness about the place, a buzz of whispers and rumours that magnified and spread like mosquitoes over stagnant waters.

Some had it that King Shaka believed himself to be a wizard, empowered by the *amadhlozi,* so he had no need of an army to protect him, while others hinted that the army had been defeated by Faku and the remnants of it were fleeing north in disgrace, afraid to face Shaka's anger.

Worst of all were the stories of new cruelties being carried out by Shaka; slicing open the bellies of the pregnant wives of some of his chiefs to see what the unborn looked like; the murder of over five hundred of the wives of the older warriors who had been called away to fight.

Jackabo resolutely thrust them aside. Rumours were just rumours, like gnats snapping in the dark. Most worrying of all for him was the reappearance of the 'queer air' he had noticed a few days ago. If anything, it seemed to be stronger here in kwaDukuza.

Turning a corner among a maze of pathways, he would come upon it unexpectedly, and be forced to hold his breath against its invasive stench.

An hour or so later, and there it would be again, lingering around the night fires, near the cattle pens, even in his own quarters, grey and unpleasant, writhing and moving in sinuous coils around him.

The atmosphere around Jakot's fire that night was morose and no one spoke much. Gazing into the flames, Jackabo was brought face to face with hard reality.

Who was he to question Shaka's military decisions? How could a thirteen-year-old, iQawu or not, bring up the subject of why the mighty King of the Zulus had sent his army off on a wild goose chase hundreds of miles away, leaving himself open to attack? Surely he knew that already – otherwise why had he recalled the *udibi* boys?

But even if he did pluck up enough courage, where could he begin? How could he tell him about his meetings with the diviner, Langani, his visit to the secret place he called home, the 'dreaming' and what he had seen there?

And then there was the close relationship he'd shared with his mother, Nandi; the secrets he held in trust for her and the child Magaye, the son he knew nothing about – they would have to remain secret forever.

All he could try to do was to warn Shaka about what Nandi had long suspected; that Mbopha, his trusted major-domo, was in league with his father's sister, Mkabayi, his halfbrother, Dingane, and the others who were planning to destroy him.

He shivered, even though the night was warm. The subject of yet another betrayal by his blood relatives was not one that anyone in their right mind would want to bring to Shaka's attention.

Fynn's oft-repeated warning rang in his ears. *Stay well out of Zulu affairs, lad. They're nowt to do with you or me – and it's highly dangerous to poke your snout into things that don't concern you.*

Then there was that other betrayal – that of Shaka's friend, James King. Should he tell him about the struggle for land and trading rights that had soured the relationship between his former Captain and Francis Farewell – or did he already know?

Jackabo now found himself in very dangerous territory. He held his breath as the next question hung in the smoky air.

What if he were to tell Shaka how Farewell had sent John Cane a thousand miles to Cape Town to blacken King's name...and not giving a tinker's curse how it would affect his plans for a peaceful alliance with the British?

Or, worse still, that it had also been part of Farewell's plan to imply that Shaka was planning to invade the Colony? In which case, might not the British be forced to come to Zululand to "pacify" the troublesome Zulus, thus providing the Lieutenant what he had always wanted – a brand new British colony with himself at the helm?

As if sensing his troublesome thoughts, Jakot looked hard at him and raised his eyebrows, the brilliant segment in his eye glowing like that of a wild cat. Hurriedly, Jackabo shook his head. 'No, nothing's wrong, Jakot...I'm just thinking.'

The King of the Zulus was a highly intelligent man. No doubt he already suspected there was a rift among the white chiefs of Port Natal. And if he did probe further, or if he were to be nudged in that direction – Jackabo knew that Farewell and Cane would be finished. Nothing would save them from Shaka's rage.

A spurt of bitterness surged through him at the thought of James King's humiliation and betrayal and the way he had been treated at Algoa Bay

Should I leave it to chance? Or should I tell Shaka everything and see them both get what they deserve? The questions burned in him like smouldering embers plucked from the fire.

The silver looking-glass adorned with plump, naked cherubs, twined ivy and flowers, the one intended to grace a lady's dressing table in Nova Scotia, was being held up by a small page boy so that Shaka could view himself from various angles.

'Ha! Jackabo! There you are,' he cried, tilting the mirror this way and that. 'You see how clever a thing this is – I can see my own face and that of Jackabo at the same time!'

Laying it down, Shaka turned to greet him. When Jackabo presented him with the hunting knife and leather sheath he'd brought him as a gift, Shaka was touched by the gesture.

'*Ngiyabonga*,' he said, as he examined them carefully, testing the razor sharpness of the cutting edge of the blade. After admiring the boy's new blue and red plaid shirt, the dark blue weskit and trews also purchased at Algoa, he indicated that Jackabo should walk about so he could look at him.

He couldn't fail to notice the difference in Shaka. His body was leaner, more finely honed, the planes of his face sharper; the eye-sockets dark and sunk in his head. Jackabo felt a pang of compassion run through him.

Clearly, sorrow had laid its hand on the Zulu king. Something of his spirit seemed to have gone out of him, leaving a lingering weariness in its place.

Shaka's first questions were not about his ill-fated mission, but about James King. What was wrong with him? When did he become ill?

When Jackabo told him that the illness began in Algoa Bay, he gave a visible start. 'Poison,' he suggested, his eyes narrowing suspiciously, 'perhaps someone in umGeorge's land put a curse on him.' The sudden flare of loathing in his eyes shocked Jackabo.

Unwittingly or not, the King had put his finger on the truth. *All it would take would be a few words from him... no one need ever know who had told Shaka...*

The black eyes that met his were disconcertingly direct. But before Jackabo had time to consider this new complication, a shadow fell over the patch of sunlight by the doorway.

The scuff of bare feet on the polished floor, and the murmur of obeisance as the man knelt and bowed over to touch it with his forehead alerted Jackabo to his identity. Mbopha kaSithayi, Shaka's major domo... Was it only his imagination, or was there a faint smile of satisfaction on the man's face as he claimed to have urgent business for Shaka to attend to?

Jackabo took his leave of them, more unsettled than ever by the man's sudden appearance and the jolting reminder of his hidden agenda. Suddenly, he felt rootless, tired and overwhelmed by the complexity of events. Scuffing his feet in the dust, he wandered on through the square.

The space below the *mkhula* tree was empty, only the wind stirring dried leaves, rustling them along the ground. Jackabo suddenly thought of Langani. *I need you to help me ...*

An uncanny feeling came over him then, an instinctive awareness that perhaps he wouldn't find the diviner waiting for him that night, or any other night, no matter how long he waited.

Remember, iQawu, what we both now know of each other. Use it well.

Making his way through the gates now guarded by old men, he set off for Jakot's place. Suddenly, his need for companionship and the warmth of a fire was overwhelming.

Just as dusk was falling over the great empty heart of kwaDukuza, Jackabo came face to face with a new force in the land. The regiment called *Nyosi, the bees.*

The oldest was no more than sixteen. Some were about his age, many younger. Flushed and cocky with their newfound status, they were like bantam cockerels, tossing the shiny feathers of their new head-dresses and brandishing weapons too heavy and unwieldy for them.

When they spotted Jackabo, they stopped dead in their tracks. Fanning out round him whooping like banshees, they made a great play of lunging and jabbing the air with their weapons. Throwing up his hands in mock surrender, he entered into the spirit of things, laughing as they whirled round him.

Wait, though! A few of the faces grinning out at him through the ferocious streaks and daubs of war paint looked familiar – He peered at them more closely. The tallest of the scarecrow figures hailed him, his teeth gleaming in the fading light.

'*Hau*, Jackabo! *Ninjani*, how are you?'

The voice was unmistakable. *Sigonyolo!*

A second figure stepped forward, a bunch of spotted plover feathers bobbing on his brow, the mouth stretched in a wide grin. *Mangila!*

They had met as *udibi* boys while following in the van of Shaka's army, sharing a blanket on cold nights below the glittering stars and suffering hunger and thirst together. They had remained friends, companions in many a foray into the hills; fellow conspirators raiding wild bees' hives for honey.

The boys all seemed taller now; their limbs loose and lanky, new muscle in the calves, thighs and shoulders. But the smiles were the same, open and mischievous, flashing at him through the warlike white and ochre daubings, their calloused hands reaching out to grip his. On hearing their gruff, newly-broken voices, Sigonyolo and he grinned awkwardly at each other, sheepish in sudden embarrassment.

A short, compact body pushed itself to the fore. He was someone vaguely familiar, but for a moment or two, Jackabo couldn't quite place him – until the small face split into a grin. No mistaking the gap in his front teeth.

'*Umahlebe!*' Surely this miniature warrior in tattered and overlong ox-hair fringes couldn't be the little brother they'd had to carry on their backs on the long road north with the army?

The other boy soldiers clustered around them, laughing on hearing him speak Zulu. There was so much he wanted to ask them, so much to say.

Did they know why the Nkosi had sent his army north to fight Shoshangane? How long would they stay with their new regiment?

The youthful *indunas* up ahead called out to them impatiently. Time was fleeting. The N*yosi* had duties to perform, a King to guard.

Jackabo looked at them, helplessly. They looked back at him, knowing time was against them. *Shaka's soldiers...* Sigonyolo, at fourteen, only a year older than he was, Mangila at twelve, a year younger... and Umahlebe, nine, if he was a day. A great sadness rose in him. *Nkosi, what have you done?*

Their brief meeting was over too fast – only time for a few more words, a joke or two, before their reluctant hands fell away, unwilling to part.

Nothing had really been said; the memories of sunny days, the freedoms of the hills and valleys, and the much altered, dangerous present and uncertainty of the future coming between them.

Sigonyolo and Jackabo looked at each other for a long moment, boys no longer. Since they had last met, he had tasted the danger of the long road that led to Delagoa and the killing of a man; he had sailed south to another land to experience a different kind of treachery, while Sigonyolo and his brothers had been separated from their family and thrust into a rag-tag army and a possible arena of war.

What lay ahead for his old friends in the dangerous game of being boy soldiers in Shaka's new army, was something Jackabo found it hard to think about.

'Sigonyolo, Mangila, *sala kahle*, stay well. *Sala kahle*, Umahlebe.'

The words of farewell stuck in his throat. It was all he could bring himself to say. A flash of white teeth, a toss of bright feathers, an awkward last touch of hands and then they were gone.

'*Hamba kahle,* Jackabo, go well, iQawu.'

The words of farewell floated back to him out of the dusk, echoes of their boyhood days falling softly between them like blossoms dropping in the heat. Within moments, the fast approaching night and the deserted parade ground of kwaDukuza had swallowed them up.

Jackabo waited until the last sounds of the *Nyosi* had faded way, then turned and scuffled his way to Jakot's place, his head down, thoroughly unsettled by meeting his old friends in such circumstances.

So they'd heard about iQawu, he thought, sadly. The happy days at kwaBulawayo seemed so far away now; the freedom of the hills, and the stalking of animals and birds; the stick fighting at which they'd always beaten him; the laughter as they tried to see who could pee the furthest –

Nyosi, the bees – strange that Shaka would have called them that after the many hours they'd spent in the bush, following the honey birds.

For better or for worse, they were Shaka's soldiers now. Torn from their duties herding the family cattle, the boys with daubed faces and weapons that were too big for them was all that stood between Shaka of the Zulus and his enemies.

Thirty-Seven

September the fifth. Mount Pleasant.

Fynn's face was a study in abject misery. Closing the door gently behind him, he slumped against the wall of the house.

Isaacs called out to him from where he was sitting on the wide verandah in a half-barrel seat. A bulky, leather-bound tome with *Buchan's Medical Journal* inscribed on the spine, was spread open on his knee. 'What is it, Fynn? Has he taken a turn for the worse?'

Fynn's eyes glittered with unshed tears. 'You won't believe this, Nat. Do you know what the man is asking for?' Isaacs shook his head.

'He wants to see Farewell. Can you believe it? Says he needs to shake his hand, make his peace with him.' His voice trembled on the last words.

Isaacs looked down at the yellowing pages of the medical journal and touched them lightly with his forefinger. 'So there's no need to search for an answer to his troubles, our good captain has found his own way.'

Fynn began to pace in agitation up and down the boardwalk, his ox-hide sandals flapping with every step. 'God, Nat, I've tried all I know. There's nothing more to be done.'

'Our friend is aware of this,' said Isaacs, softly, 'he knows you've done everything in your power for him. And he knows also, that his end is near. This is why he needs to see Farewell, *mon ami*. He wishes to leave the world with no bitterness, shake the hand of the man who betrayed him.'

In a sudden flare of temper, Fynn kicked the door viciously, and then struck it a blow with his fist for good measure.

'Damn it! Damn it all to hell and back. The poor bastard doesn't realise just how great a betrayal it's been.' He groaned. 'Forgiveness? Farewell should be made to come up here on his bended knees to make amends for the harm he's done to that good, decent man.'

'*Peut etre,* maybe he will,' said Isaacs softly, looking round for his hat.

When Isaacs straggled back over the brow of the hill as dusk was falling, Fynn knew by the slump of his bony shoulders that his mission had been unsuccessful. Bitter disappointment flooded his soul.

'Oh, no,' he groaned, 'now we'll have to lie our arses off to save him more grief.' 'Farewell was adamant he wouldn't see the captain,' Isaacs said, bluntly, slumping down into the chair. 'Nothing would shift him, no matter how I tried.'

'How was he when you put King's request to him?'

Isaacs laid his clenched fist across his heart. 'Like a stone,' he said, heavily, 'like a stone, Fynn.' Henry Fynn swore loud and long into the fragrant dusk, blind rage starting to rise in him again.

And so they lied to James Saunders King. They told him Farewell was on a hunting trip but that they had sent someone to find him. The yellow, wasted face that had once been handsome turned to them, a fierce appeal burning in the sunken blue eyes.

'And Jack, my boy Jack – will ye send for him? Tell him his cap'n wants to see him one last time.'

Out of earshot, Fynn said, softly, 'Now, that we *can* do for you, my friend. Pick the fastest runners, Nat. Darkness or not, they'll have to set off for kwaDukuza right away.'

They came with the first flush of sunrise, the scattered tribal people of eThekwini, climbing the winding paths leading up through the forested slopes from the lakeshore.

Silently, they took up their places around the house called Mount Pleasant. James King's own people had been there all night, their eyes on the shuttered window of the room where he lay dying. Now, the citizens of eThekwini were coming to pay their respects and keep him company.

When Fynn and Isaacs rose from their chairs by his bedside and staggered outside to stretch their cramped limbs, they found themselves looking out on a sea of black faces. A vast hum rose from the crowds, a wave of sympathy and sorrow that was wordless.

'How did they know?' Fynn said, close to tears. 'How do they always know when something's in the air? Is it some kind of sense we don't have – or have lost?'

It was all he could offer by way of explanation. Often there were no words to describe Africa's mysterious ways of communication.

When he woke later that morning, James King asked again for Farewell, and also for John Hatton to come. He began to show signs of great distress, his thin fingers plucking at the coverlet.

Isaacs set off once again for Fort Farewell to prevent an incensed Fynn from going himself. Through clenched teeth, he'd spat out, 'May God forgive me, but if I have to track down that apology for a man, I couldn't swear that I wouldn't blow his brains out.'

An hour passed, then another and still no sign of Isaacs or Farewell. King was sinking fast, and there was nothing Fynn could do about it, except deliver a drop or two of laudanum for the pain, or wipe the sweat from his face.

Eventually, sighs and rustles of expectation from the mourners outside alerted Fynn. Someone had turned up at last. He rushed to the door.

Hatton and Isaacs arrived together, accompanied by the crew of the *Mary,* every man dressed decently out of respect for the man who was their Captain. The mariners silently filed into the main room of Mount Pleasant, removing their caps as they came.

Fynn's red-rimmed, exhausted eyes searched in vain for Farewell. Isaacs took him aside. Drawing a sealed letter out of his breast pocket, his fingers were trembling as he placed it on the dusty tabletop. He smoothed it out then stepped away from it.

'Is this all ye have?' Fynn growled, casting a warning look at the half-open bedroom door.

'It is,' answered Isaacs heavily, sweat glimmering on his sallow face. 'And the devil of a job I had to pull even that out of him.'

Fynn eyed the sealed letter with as much relish as he would a black mamba. 'There's no knowing what that son of a bitch wrote in it.'

Isaacs sighed. 'Perhaps he might say in a letter what he couldn't do openly. But, for the captain's sake, Fynn, we need to read it first.'

Reluctantly, Fynn nodded. Isaacs tore open the sealed envelope. Inside there was a single sheet of paper. He unfolded it.

Fynn and Hatton were watching Isaacs' face like hawks. As his eyes scanned what was written there, they saw it change, and the lines of exhaustion deepen. His hand was trembling as he lowered the sheet of paper

'*Mon Dieu,* it's not even for the captain. It's addressed to me. You were right, Fynn, it's unnatural and completely unfeeling – and this from a man who claims to be a gentleman, a leader of men. May God forgive him, for I never will.'

When they went into the bedroom, James King's eyes fluttered open. They were clear and calm.

'No more lies now, Henry,' he whispered, his breathing ragged. 'I wanted to part friends with him before departing this life. For old times' sake, you know, just to give him my hand for any misunderstandings between us.'

He reached out for Farewell's letter, the pale fingers trembling. 'Nat, let me read what he said. I can't hurt any more than I do.'

Wordlessly, Isaacs lifted him up against the pillows and placed the single sheet of paper in his hand. After a few excruciating moments of silence, Farewell's letter fluttered from his hand and fell to the floor. His head slumped back on the pillows and tears oozed out from between his eyelids.

'Oh, I wish I hadn't seen it,' he sighed, 'to think Cane went all that way to injure me. What will my friends think of me, now?'

Fynn's fists clenched. 'My way would have been best.' he muttered to Isaacs. 'A musket ball straight through that bastard's black heart.'

James King never mentioned Farewell again. Instead, he talked affectionately of his mother and his sister. He sighed. 'I would only wish to live for their sake. What will they do now, without a man in the house?'

Turning to Hatton, he clutched his hand and whispered, 'Burn my family letters, John, but anything of importance send to my family. Clothes and suchlike, see to it the men take what they want.'

Outside, a breeze wafted up from the lagoon and rustled through the pine trees. Fruit bats swooped through the air, their curved shapes black against the evening sky.

King woke later complaining that his feet were cold. Fynn bathed them in warm water, rubbing them briskly to get the feeling back before wrapping them up in a clean pair of woollen stockings.

A great change seemed to come over him at that point. He looked as if he were carved from alabaster, his live flesh as chill to the touch as stone.

'Hatton, give me your hand.' Grasping the first officer's hand, he pressed it weakly then did the same with everyone there, including his servant, Napisongo.

'For the last time, boys...' His voice tailed away, rallied again. 'I know I have your good wishes...we'll meet again in the realms of bliss, never fear. I wish you all the happiness Heaven can bestow.'

A sigh was followed by a ragged catch in his breath, the rise and fall of his chest slower now. Then his last words, 'Remember me to my boy, Jack.' A small breath, then his spirit left his body.

In the garden beyond the shuttered window of the room, African voices swelled in a great wailing cry. *The soul of Kingi has flown...*

The great white chief of eThekwini, who was also a chief of kwaDukuza and a friend of their Nkosi, was dead.

Before Jackabo and Jakot were even halfway there, the drums brought them the news. The first faint rhythms came in on the breeze from a small kraal tucked up on the hillside a few miles away. Then others took up the call, an urgency in them that stopped Jakot dead in his tracks. He cocked his head to the side, listening.

Then he turned and looked at the red-haired boy at his side. Jackabo could tell by the slump of his shoulders what the message was. The Xhosa bent his head, his eyes scrunched tightly in sorrow.

'*Eh, Kingi...*'

Jackabo stood, dumb and bereft, with his heart fit to burst.

By the time they reached eThekwini, the funeral service was already underway. It took place a mile or so from Mount Pleasant, the house James King had built on the Bluff. The vast crowd of mourners parted silently to let them through, their eyes full of dumb sorrow.

The crew were gathered around the gash of red earth in the ground, their heads bowed. Hatton, as first officer, was at their head. Isaacs stood next to Fynn, his hands clasped, swaying in prayer. Around his shoulders was a prayer shawl, and on his head, the *yamulka,* the skullcap of his Hebrew faith.

Ogle and Halstead were also there, Halstead, for once, was without his cat-skin cap, his mousy hair plastered down with water. Of John Cane, there was no sign.

Standing conspicuously on his own, in full naval attire, with his gold braided hat tucked below his arm, was Lieutenant Francis Farewell. No waves of hostility flowed from the men gathered to bury their dead Captain, only blank indifference, as cold as charity.

Jackabo's eyes flicked from one stony face to the other. It was only their innate sense of decency for the occasion that stopped some of them from launching themselves at the elegant figure with boot and fist.

King's body had been sewn into a length of canvas by the sailmaker. As the crew lowered the shrouded body into the grave, Jackabo stood rooted to the spot, bedraggled and footsore after the long trek from kwaDukusa.

Clustered on the hillside were the African people who had come to honour the man known as Kingi. The people from his kraals were pressed closest to the grave; beyond that there were many hundreds more.

The air was full of keening and wailing, the genuine distress of people mourning a man who had given them sanctuary.

Jackabo stared at the gash in the red earth. It was impossible to believe that this was where James King would lie for eternity, on the headland overlooking the sandbanks where the pitiful timbers of his ship, the *Mary*, could still be seen at low tide.

Now John Hatton was saying the final words.

'In sure and certain hope of the Life to come…we leave our dear friend, Lieutenant James Saunders King in the tender care of Our Lord Jesus Christ.

Rest in peace, my friend. Amen.'

Those who were of the Church of Rome crossed themselves, those who were not, bowed their heads and muttered 'Amen.'

While Nathaniel Isaacs' lips moved silently in his own words of fare-well, there was no outward sign of emotion on the face of Francis Farewell.

One by one, the men came forward. Picking up a handful of earth, they tossed it into the grave, muttering their own personal farewells as they did so.

Beside him, Jakot's fingers played over the scars on his wrists, his face twisted in sorrow. Whatever his suspicions concerning the white race in general, the Xhosa did not include Lieutenant James King among them. He had spoken often of the kindnesses he had shown him aboard the *Salisbury*, en route to a life sentence on Robben Island, and for later opening the prison doors on his behalf and setting him free.

Jackabo had a heart like lead. The Captain was gone. Who would they follow now, who would lead the crew the next step of the way?

He was so sunk in misery that he failed to hear his name being called. Jakot nudged him. Looking up, he found Hatton was speaking to him.

'Jack. Is there anything you'd like to say? His very last words were for you. "Remember me to my boy, Jack." He was mighty fond of you.'

Jackabo dragged the back of his hand across his eyes, fearing he would disgrace himself and burst into tears like a bairn. What can I say? he thought, numbly, they're all waiting-

Over the heads of the crowd, he caught a glimpse of the lagoon draped in early morning mist. *The sea…*

The brotherhood of the sea was what bound them to James King, and what bound them to each other. It was what had brought them to the place called eThekwini and it was what, in the end, would bear them away.

A vision of James King as he'd been on the day they'd first met leapt into his mind. The cold damp of February, the towering masts of ships lying at anchor at Southampton, and a man in a naval greatcoat with a colourful scarf wound round his neck, the distinctive streaks of silver in his hair shining in the gloom.

Jackabo's feet propelled him forward. Desperately, he tried not to look down into the gaping hole in the ground. Stumbling a little at first, he began to speak.

'He was my father's friend. And he was mine too. He was my first Captain – and I'll never forget him, not for as long as I live.'

After all the words were finished and done with, the haunting African voices sang their own farewell to Kingi. Slowly, the mourners began to drift away back down the hill, carrying the sounds of their singing with them until only the crew of the *Mary* were left.

As they began to fill in the grave, and carry out the last duties they would perform for their captain, Ned took out his flute. Even before he began to play, Jackabo knew what it would be.

The melody of the old sea shanty trembled out across the Bluff, a requiem for their lost mariner.

'Oh Shanandoah, I long to see you... A-a —way you rolling river...
Away I'm bound to go...'cross the wide Missouri...'

Thirty-Eight

12 September. KwaDukuza.

It was clear Shaka had been greatly affected by the death of James King. Black feathers had been woven into the leopard skin band circling his brow, while deep grooves of grief were carved into his face and his eyes were strained and shadowed.

Isaacs, especially, was uneasy. He was still in mortal dread of Shaka re-opening the subject he feared most, namely, the business of the missing macassar hair oil he believed would restore some of his grey hairs to their previous colour. If similar fears were on Farewell's mind, he said nothing, sitting apart from the others, his lips pressed into a thin line below the clipped moustache.

When Jackabo looked beyond the outward shell of the man, all he could see was a void with a coil of suppressed hatred at its core. Some instinct told Farewell he was being watched. The pale blue eyes raked the faces around him until he found whose eyes were on him.

A flush rose in his face and he hurriedly looked away, Jackabo's silent contempt pursuing him.

The atmosphere between the white men was tense in the extreme. No one had expected James King's former partner to attend the meeting with Shaka.

Fynn's Irish temper was on the rise and in imminent danger of boiling over. He badly wanted to smash the complacency out of the blank-faced man with the greying blonde hair walking stiffly a few paces ahead of him.

If it was to be done, it would have to be done out of sight and earshot of the Zulu king. No doubt Shaka would understand only too well how men fought one another for power, land, or both. That was not in debate. The betrayal of a friend was something else.

To remove a man's good name, to besmirch his honour with arrant lies was monstrous enough, but to deprive him of his last dying wish, to come to the end of his life in peace and in forgiveness of someone who had done him a great injustice – was something he knew even Shaka of the Zulus would neither allow nor forget.

Fynn was no fool. He realised that the reputation of the white men of eThekwini had been seriously damaged by the debacle over Shaka's mission, not only in the eyes of the ruler himself, but in those of the chiefs who'd travelled with them. If he were to learn the truth, even if he stopped short of killing Farewell, it would do none of them any good at all.

If Farewell were to be thrown out of Zululand, the lies emanating from him on his return to the Cape would be vicious and destructive in the extreme, and would only serve to further damage both the reputation of those still here – and especially that of the Zulus.

His head ached; his conscience warring with the desire for bloody revenge. *Could I live with myself if I handed him over to Shaka's tender mercies, knowing he'd end his life with a bamboo stake up his arse?*

Fynn grimaced. *Aye, there's a question, now...*

'Dambusa,' Shaka said, fixing a severe eye on Isaacs and gesturing for him to rise. Isaacs got to his feet, his heart knocking against his ribs. *Mon Dieu,* he thought, *that dratted business of the hair oil is going to see me dead-*

Shaka regarded him solemnly for a few moments. 'Dambusa, for the many services you have done me, for the wounds at the battle of Ngome – and for seeing to the affairs of Kingi, I make you a chief and grant you the land between the rivers umDlothi and umLazi. It includes a portion of seacoast and also country up to three days march inland. The bay and forests are yours, and I give you the right to trade within Zululand.'

Jakot held up the paper and the pen with a flourish, proof that the land grant was ready to be signed. In the silence, the release of Isaacs' pent-up breath seemed abnormally loud.

Fynn surveyed the fast-ticking pulse on Farewell's jaw with great satis-faction. Pleasure gave way to burning curiosity. His gaze switched back to the unsigned land grant in Jakot's hand.

Now just who's behind that little surprise? Who wrote it out, word, line and verse, ready for just such an occasion? His mind raced over the possibilities. Shaka had made no mention of it during their time together at Mzimkhulu. No one had been in kwaDukuza, close enough to Shaka to advise him of such a move and draft it out, except –

His head swivelled to where the thirteen-year old known as iQawu was sitting cross-legged watching Farewell. Well, lad, he thought, why am I not surprised you might have had a hand in it? If you stay here long enough, I reckon you might well end up as Shaka's prime minister...

When Shaka got to his feet, the head bearing the cluster of sweeping, black widow-bird feathers was drooping as if in fatigue, or prayer.

'Leave me, now,' he said, 'I have much to communicate with you, but at present I am very sad.'

There was a long silence before he spoke again. 'My heart will not let my tongue speak as I would wish. It is too soon after the death of one I held in great esteem.'

As they rose to take their leave, he bade them wait. Then he looked at each one of them in turn, as if to memorise their faces – Isaacs, now known as Dambusa, Mbuyasi and Febana ka ma jo-ji, the remaining white chiefs of eThekwini.

'I have one thing of which I am glad,' Shaka said, a hint of a smile playing round his lips. 'If all of you were to return to your own land tomorrow, I could say, with truth, that a white man who was also a chief lived a long time in my country, without molestation from myself or from my people, and that he died a natural death. *Yebo*, that will ever please me.'

Although a deep sadness remained etched onto the face that looked back at them, the head adorned with black feathers was raised a little higher.

And then he turned on his heel and left them.

Shortly afterwards, Fynn cornered Farewell as he was about to leave. Dismissing the servants, he held himself in check until they had scuttled out of sight.

Then, grabbing Farewell by the front of his shirt, he ripped the length of velvet ribbon from where it was pinned to his lapel and dangled the gold-rimmed eyeglass in front of him.

'That's the last time you'll look down the end o' your long neb at men whose arses you're not fit to wipe. Even those you call bilge rats are several steps above you.'

Momentarily taken off-guard, the former naval officer made a grab for the eyeglass, but found his movements restricted by the well-honed hunting knife his former employee was holding to his throat.

'Now, now,' Fynn hissed, pressing the edge of the blade into the soft flesh beneath Farewell's ear. 'Don't tempt me! I should have used this on you when we found out the extent of your cold-blooded treachery in sending Cane to the Cape. Don't think for a moment it had escaped our notice.'

A thin trickle of scarlet welled out from where Fynn's hunting knife had pierced his skin.

'The only reason I didn't tell Shaka about what your conniving treachery was that I didn't want to be responsible for seeing 'one of my own kind' given over to the tender mercies of his executioners.'

Farewell's blue eyes were like chips of ice as he stared at Fynn. In them the man called Mbuyasi saw his deep-seated contempt for such sentiments.

He pressed the point of the knife a shade deeper and was rewarded with a flash of fear in the cold eyes. 'But shall I tell you something, my man?' he hissed, knowing he was dangerously close to committing murder. 'If you send any more 'secret' instructions to the British, then I will have no scruples about telling Shaka *everything*. And which one of us do you think he'll believe?'

Each word was carefully delivered with a slight, but effective pressure of the blade. Fynn hissed, 'And, if it comes down to that, then, good Catholic that I am, I'll be begging forgiveness even as I'm watching you screaming your last!'

'Fynn!' A hand clutched his bulging forearm, the young fingers like steel.

'Don't do it,' Jackabo said, softly, 'his time will come – and sooner than he thinks. But somebody else will do it, not you.'

Fynn reluctantly removed the blade and casually wiped it clean on Farewell's sleeve. Then, before turning away, he deliberately let the gold-rimmed eyeglass fall to the ground then crushed it beneath his heel.

Mbopha, the King's *major domo,* stood in the shadows listening to what had j passed between the white men. Earlier on in the day, he had hidden at the rear of Shaka's residence. Once the *indaba* with the king was in progress, he was able to eavesdrop on what was being said.

He had listened in mounting frustration while land, much land, was granted to the one known as Dambusa. Something will have to be done, he fumed, and soon. More of them will arrive, and like the leopard preying on the soft-bellied impala, they will begin to eat up our land.

Just before sunset, he slipped out through the gates of kwaDukuza and hurried away into the night. First, he would send a message direct to Mkabayi, then another to Dingane and his brothers who were currently miles away, with their regiments. Mbopha quickened his step, anger giving him speed.

The arrogant tyrant, Shaka – all he has left now are a handful of *udibi* boys. Let us see how well they will guard him.

After the funeral, the men had piled stones over the gravesite to secure it and keep away the wild beasts that roamed the Bluff at night. Every day, Jackabo went back to the gravesite with Jakot and Ned to make King's resting place decent. They re-arranged the stones to better order, packed earth in between them and planted flowers. Jakot uprooted some small trees and placed them in a wide circle around the gravesite.

'To keep the sun off the head of my friend, so he can rest in the shade.' Jakot's words, Jakot's epitaph for the man who had saved his life by bringing him in chains up from the darkness of the hold of the *Salisbury* and into the sunlight.

Jackabo sat back on his heels, wiped the dirt from his hands, and cast an eye around the burial site. It was a lovely place, a green place with only the sky above it. Far below, the lagoon sparkled in the sunlight and a breeze drifted up from it to riffle through the long grass and stir the seedpods of the wild flowers. Mount Pleasant, the Captain had called it. And it was. Now James King would always be here, near the place he'd called home.

Just then, a small rabbit, a *dassie*, popped out of the long grass, sat up on its hind legs and began to clean its whiskers. Jackabo smiled. The first day he'd met Langani, the diviner had drawn his attention to one of the little creatures, intimating that they too had a spirit.

Shading his eyes, he looked out across the lagoon. There were reminders of James King everywhere. Somewhere below was the boatyard he had named after his sponsor, Sir James Townsend. Moored in the bay was the schooner that bore the name of his mother, Susan, the vessel that had cost him so dear; first his money, then his health, reputation, and finally, his life.

But the Captain had run the race, seen it to the end and to the best of his ability, as far as fate had allowed. Kneeling down, Jackabo looked at the rough lettering etched on the flat stone.

LIEUTENANT JAMES SAUNDERS KING R.N
JUNE 1794 – SEPTEMBER 1828

No matter how hard he stared at the words, Jackabo found it hard to believe that James King, the man who had been his captain, was really lying below it.

Soon, rumours began to trickle through concerning the fate of the Zulu army. It was not good. Whole regiments were in retreat, while others were refusing to fight in their weakened state. It was also whispered that warriors had deserted, and gone over the high mountain passes to join Mzilikazi, the young Kumalo chief who had defied Shaka a few years earlier.

Jackabo was sleeping badly, often wakening in the dark, fancying he heard a cry, or thunder, or both.

The three young brothers who were his friends and now part of the regiment of *Nyosi- the bees* were very much on his mind. No matter how bright and dazzling their head-dresses, or how ferocious their young faces beneath the warpaint, he knew they would never survive if they should come up against experienced warriors.

Torn between two courses of action, he fretted about abandoning King's lonely grave, while at the same time imagining Shaka alone in an eerie, echoing kwaDukuza. Time was trickling away like sand in an hour-glass. And worst of all, the queer kind of air, the smell of burning feathers had returned, stronger than ever.

Seeing his pale, worried face and the dark smudges beneath his eyes, Ned had tackled him about it. 'The captain's gone,' he said, 'there's no more to be done, Heelander. Nothing can bring him back.'

Reluctantly, Jackabo decided that Ned was right. He would set out with Jakot for kwaDukuza next morning.

At sunset, John Hatton was nowhere to be found. Not in the boat yard and not in the camp. When darkness fell, the crew began to search for him, calling and hallooing as they went.

Dommana fluttered here and there like a startled bird, a glimmering ghost in the twilight. Jackabo said, 'Maybe she thinks her father came back and did Mr Hatton an injury.'

'Away with ye,' Ned said, shaking his head, 'Her pappy was only too glad to hand her over for the bride-price Hatton gave him.' They tried to re-assure the girl as best they could, but she ran off into the darkness, sobbing.

The search for Hatton began in earnest. Ned sent McCoy for the amaTuli trackers, then, armed with guns, sticks and storm lanterns, they fanned out from the camp. With the dogs whining and straining on their leashes, they stayed no further than six feet apart, for it was dangerous to get separated in the dark.

Huge moths batted against the storm lanterns, drawn by the bobbing lights. Trees and bushes loomed out of the darkness in strangely distorted shapes. There were strange noises everywhere; branches creaking overhead, twigs snapping, furtive rustlings and the incessant chatter of tree frogs and insects.

'Gawd, what's that?' hissed Biddle, as glinting animal eyes appeared in the torchlight. Behind Jackabo someone swore as they tripped over a snarl of hidden roots.

Whatever had happened to Hatton, darkness would not be his friend. They were under no illusion about his chances of survival. If they didn't find him soon, if he was lying ill or injured somewhere, he would be at the mercy of the predators that stalked the night.

Somewhere ahead, dogs began to whine, and then bark furiously. A shrill whistling sounded then a couple of shots rang out. Startled birds flew up into the trees, followed by an angry screeching and crashing of branches as monkeys thrashed about, alarmed by the gunfire.

'We have him!' Fynn shouted from the darkness. 'He's alive!'

Jackabo glanced over to where Hatton was lying by the fire, wrapped in a blanket. 'What happened?' he whispered.

Fynn shook his head. 'Don't know, lad. He's exhausted and fevered. Damn hard to examine him properly in the dark. I'll let him sleep a while then maybe he can tell me more.'

In the firelight, the first officer looked ghastly. He was ashen, lines of pain grooved deep into his face, Dommana weeping as she wiped the sweat from his brow and stroked his head.

Fynn asked her if she'd noticed anything troubling Hatton, of late. She rubbed her middle and then her back, intimating that he'd been complaining of pain. 'How long?' She indicated five moons, perhaps six. Fynn cursed softly.

'He must have been feeling poorly when we were in Algoa,' Ned burst out. 'But why didn't he say anything? We could have got him a doctor.'

'The captain had enough worries without his only officer taken bad. That's how Hatton would have seen it,' said Fynn, glancing sideways at the still figure. 'He was a quiet man – he wouldn't want to bother anyone. And he knew just how much was riding on this mission. But at least now I've got something to go on.'

That much was true. But it was too late.

Next morning after completing his examination, Fynn said 'It's his spleen, his kidneys, or both. He's swollen, back and fore, painful to the touch, running a high fever. When I asked him how long he'd been feeling ill, he just smiled that long slow smile of his.'

Aiming a kick at a piece of wood in the grass, he muttered, 'Damn and blast – why couldn't he have said something sooner?'

That was at noon. A few hours later, Hatton began to vomit blood. At sundown, as the shadows lengthened, the dogs laid back their heads and began to howl like wolves.

About nine in the evening, John Hatton breathed his last. The anguished cry Dommana gave came from a soul that was sore wounded, and would have broken the heart of the hardest to hear it.

At noon the next day, they laid him to rest beneath a huge spreading tree on the lower slopes of the Bluff, chosen because it was the tallest they could find.

His grave faced the entrance to the lagoon, the place where they had come in on the longboat the day after the *Mary* had been lost three years earlier. It also overlooked the boatyard where he'd drawn up his plans, laid down the keel of the schooner and battled and fought to build it.

It was the most perfect of days, the sun slanting in over the lagoon, the *Susan and Elizabeth,* Hatton's ship, mirrored on its calm waters.

The news that a second white chief of eThekwini had died, spread like a bushfire fanned by a spirited wind. People had been arriving since sunrise to pay their respects. Once again the local chiefs made the sad journey to praise Hatton, for his saving of Dommana had not gone unnoticed.

Among the mourners was the girl's father, weeping and wailing as if he'd just lost a favourite son-in-law – which he had of course, in a manner of speaking, though the pair of them had never set eyes on each other since Hatton had handed over the *lobola,* the bride price, to save his daughter's reputation.

But of that daughter, Dommana, there was no sign. It was as if she had vanished from the face of the earth. Before the funeral, they had called and searched for her, but in vain. So they had to bury Hatton without her.

His body was sewn into ship's canvas and over him was laid a tattered, but clean, ensign flag. Then he was lifted up on to the shoulders of his crew, and carried through Townsend boatyard and up through the trees to the spot they had chosen for him, with the sea of mourners following behind.

After Fynn had taken the funeral service and the crew had done the honours, Jackabo stepped forward, Hatton's Bible open in his hand.

He held it up. 'Mr Hatton gave me this – just after I'd been invited to be a guest of His Majesty.' His remark induced a smile or two among the mourners.

'Seeing the captain and Mr Hatton died only a few days apart, I thought about two friends from the Old Testament who also died together.'

Jackabo read from the second Book of Samuel; all about King Saul, his son Jonathan, and a shepherd boy called David who slew a giant and became their friend before going on to become the mightiest of the Biblical kings. And then he read out what David had written, all those centuries ago.

> *"Saul and Jonathan were lovely and pleasant in their lives, and in their deaths they were not divided. They were swifter than eagles; they were stronger than lions.*
>
> *I am distressed for thee, my brother Jonathan; very pleasant hast thee been unto me. Thy love to me was wonderful, surpassing the love of women.*
>
> *How are the mighty fallen, and the weapons of war perished."*

After it was over, they built a cairn of stones over the grave and wedged his name stone firmly in place. Drifts of fallen pine needles lay around the gravesite, and the air was heavy with the smell of resin and the sound of the wind soughing through the pines.

As they turned to leave, out of the corner of his eye Jackabo caught a flutter of pale colour near some rocky crags jutting out of the wooded hillside.

He glanced up quickly, but there was nothing there; only the peaceful forest, the honey smell of resin, and the cairn of stones lying in the dappled sunlight.

Dommana was discovered next morning, curled up on Hatton's grave. The hunters who found her were reluctant to touch her or come too close, afraid that the spirit of the dead *umlungu* had put a spell on her. Not wanting her to haunt them for disturbing her body, they had come running in the grey light of dawn to raise the alarm.

Ned sent for Fynn then rallied men to go with him to carry her back. Jakot and Jackabo jumped into the jolly boat and set off to fetch Rachel, for a woman's touch would be needed. Although the former slave had lived with John Cane as his common-law wife, those who remained loyal to King's memory would not have held it against the woman for her choice of partner.

When they were halfway across the lagoon, Jakot stopped rowing. Leaning on the oars, his head dropped on to his chest. Jackabo eased off on the other oar and let the boat drift. After a few moments, the Xhosa lifted his head. 'I can tell you now that this woman will die, Jackabo.'

Jackabo rested his dripping oar on the rowlock, and stared at him. A flight of herons rose off one of the islands and passed over their heads on the way to the reed beds on the other side of the lagoon, the steady beat of their wings clearly audible in the stillness.

'No, Jakot,' he said, hauling furiously on the single oar in an effort to get going again. 'Dommana's not very happy, that's all. She's just lost Mr Hatton. People don't die because they're unhappy.'

'Hau,' Jakot said, glancing over his shoulder, 'we are not in white man's country now. Here is different. Here people die for many reasons.'

With that, he took up the oars again. Sick at heart, Jackabo bent his back to the rowing. Then, a liitle more than halfway across the bay, the acrid smell of burning feathers returned in full force to haunt him with renewed ferocity.

'Dommana came with us meek as a lamb. She was hard to rouse at first,' Fynn said, as he rinsed his hands in a bucket of water.

Glancing over at the *Buchan Medical Journal,* which was lying open on the table, he shook his head. 'I doubt I'll find anything in there to help. She's like an animal deep in its winter sleep – it's almost as if she doesn't want to wake up.'

Rachel put the bowl of untouched curds back on the table. 'So, *baas*…' she asked Fynn, wiping her hands on a piece of cloth. 'What do you say is wrong with her?'

'Shock,' answered Fynn. 'She's in a state of deep grief. She didn't expect Hatton to die, but then, none of us did. '

The gold rings in Rachel's long ear lobes glinted as she turned to look at him. 'Ever since the boat is finished, Dommana is worrying. When it goes away, she thinks maybe it not come back, Hat-ton not come back, leave Dommana alone.'

'But there was no chance we'd not come back,' Jackabo stammered. 'The captain promised Shaka to bring the chiefs back safely.'

' *Yebo,* or else Shaka would've chopped Mbuyasi's neck like a chicken! ' said Fynn, trying to lighten the situation. 'They had to come back, no matter what.'

She turned a fierce eye on him. 'No, Mbuyasi, never this King Shaka would put one finger on you, the white man. But Dommana is a poor girl, knows nothing. She was afraid to go back to the father that beat her. All she see is that Hat-ton, one time, two time, go south and then not come back.'

Protests sprang to Jackabo's lips, and then died as quickly. The reality of what Rachel had said hit him with the force of a musket ball.

He'd always known the crew of the *Mary* would eventually leave the bay. They were men of the sea after all, and most of them had family, wives and children, mothers and sisters at home.

The captain had seemed set to stay, establish his new place on the umLalazi and start trading with the Cape. Nat Isaacs and Fynn had backed him in this new project, and he had no doubt he would have made them both partners, if he'd lived.

But John Hatton was another thing, altogether – a quiet man, who never said much. He had been a seafarer since he was ten years old. During the last three years, all his energies had gone into the planning and building of the *Susan and Elizabeth.*

Come to think of it, he'd never heard Hatton's name mentioned in connection with anything except the ship, and had never heard him voice any desire to become a trader.

Poor Dommana, maybe she'd known more of John Hatton, the quiet man, than any of them ever had.

Fynn touched Rachel's hand. 'She's free to stay here with us as long as it suits her. Tell her, Rachel. It might make a difference.' He nodded towards the bowl of untouched curds. 'And try and get her to eat something.'

But that was something Dommana refused to do. Rachel tried to coax her into taking some food, but she turned her head away, her lips set in a stubborn line. Nor would she take the sip of water laced with brandy that Fynn thought might rally her. When he tried to ease the spoon between her dry lips, she closed her teeth tightly. Her eyes flickered open, once or twice, but they were blank, looking through them and beyond. When Jackabo looked in on her that night, she was curled up in the same position, with her face turned to the wall.

Another day passed, and there was no response, only a soft whimpering from time to time. Fynn sent for an *inyanga* and went into consultation with him. After the man had gone, he said, 'I doubt what ails her is more than any *muthi* in this world can cure. The medicine man agreed with me.'

A third day dawned bright and clear. The *inyanga* was in place outside the door, muttering incantations. A great change seemed to come over Dommana then. She looked somehow faded, diminished, like a leaf fallen from a tree, or a flower drooping on its stem. Her once gleaming skin was the colour of dull clay, her body curiously shrunken as if it had already returned to the earth.

As the day wore on, Jackabo began to wonder if Jakot hadn't been right all along about Dommana's dying. He found him by the fire, deep in conversation with Rachel.

On seeing him, their heads drew apart quickly. They made no mention of Dommana. And then it came to him fast, like the shot from a gun. They already knew. Her spirit's gone. Just the last of her breath, that's all that's left.

Rachel took his hand. 'Nothing to be done, Char-les, no one can help Dommana, never no more. She want only to go to where is Hat-ton.'

And it was true. Somewhere inside, the girl had decided that she no longer wanted to live. Jackabo knew then that nothing could save

Dommana; neither *muthi,* nor Fynn's care, diviner's magic or prayers. And that was what happened. Just before dawn on the fourth day, the gentle Dommana came to the end of her life.

Ned went through Hatton's belongings and found a brand new white shirt he had bought at Algoa. Rachel washed her, braided her hair then dressed her in it, ready for her last journey.

They did not disturb Hatton's grave, for it would have been neither Christian nor acceptable to African beliefs to do so. Instead, they laid her as close to him as they could. Side by side, they shared the same earth, and the same cairn of stones covered them both.

Dommana and Hatton had met in the forest. He had defended her against a tyrannical father with his fists and the axe, and somehow it was fitting that they should return to the greenwoods to lie beneath the trees that had brought them together.

When Jakot left for kwaDukuza, Jackabo didn't go with him. Unable to come to terms with the deaths of so many people he'd cared for – in the end, he let the interpreter go on without him. An hour later, he half-regretted it, but even then, he couldn't bear to leave the strangely silent bay and the lonely graves.

Townsend boatyard was deserted, grass and weeds growing over the place where the schooner's keel had been laid. It was eerie and still without the usual hammering, whistling and cursing, Ned's antics and the quiet presence of Hatton poring over his plans.

Jackabo watched a family of baboons scamper across the yard, the black, round-shouldered male baring his yellow fangs at a pair of warthogs. Ignoring his snarls, the warthogs trotted on, their tails stiffly alert. Soon the rains and the ants would reduce the old scaffolding to a pulp, the bush would reclaim the clearing, and one day no trace of the boatyard would remain.

At the back of it all, like a never-ending dark stream, ran Jackabo's dread of the unseen forces he knew lay out there. Langani had told him about the *umhlolo,* the dark and terrible power that threatened all in its path, something over which, it appeared, even Shaka had no control.

He was alone now – his trusted commanders and advisers out of reach, his army disillusioned and rebellious; his mother, Nandi, that ferocious defender of his birthright, lying on the hillside at emKindini, surrounded by the bodies of his Four Maries, the laughing girls who had been like sisters to him.

The faces of Sigonyolo, Mangila and their small brother Umhlebe, as he had last seen them in the twilight at kwaDukuza, swam in and out of his thoughts; poor young, barefoot boys not yet ready for fighting, let alone dying.

No matter how good their skills at stick fighting, no matter how fleet of foot, or brave they were, they would stand no chance against grown men seasoned in war with only one aim in mind – to reach Shaka of the Zulus.

Jackabo's heart ached with loss. First Nandi, then King, followed by Hatton and Dommana…

And still the stench of burning feathers pursued him wherever he went, a constant in his life now, rarely lessening, sometimes overpowering, threatening to cut his breath off completely.

After days of hard travel, Mkayabi's messenger reached the camp at Ceza Mountain near the headwaters of the Black Umfolozi River. On hearing what she had to say, Dingane and Mhlangana, Shaka's half-brothers, promptly abandoned their demoralised regiments. They also left behind their brothers Mpande and Nzibe; the former because he was too soft-hearted for what they had in mind, the latter because he was still only a child.

As they sped hotfoot towards kwaDukuza, Dingane was exultant. What he had long desired was almost within his reach. The long wait, which had begun for him on the day of Shaka's ascendancy to the throne of the Zulu kingdom, was almost here.

Thirty-Nine

22 September 1828

Shimmering waves of heat rose up from the baked earth and reduced the sky to a washed-out blue. The hot, dry season was beginning to mount its usual deadly assault on the land.

It was cool, however, in the place that Langani had chosen for his time of deep meditation. The rocky overhang protected him from the direct rays of the sun, while an occasional drift of fine spray from the nearby waterfall cooled his naked body. The white clay daubed on his face and body did not render him either grotesque or terrifying. His true nature was a benign one, and it showed even through the traditional mask of his calling.

On the patch of smoothed earth before him lay the sacred bones. To a casual onlooker, they would appear to be lying in scattered, random patterns, with neither rhyme nor reason as to the way they had fallen. To Langani, however, their arrangement meant a great deal. What he saw there did not fill him with either hope or peace – but then, this was nothing new.

The thing of violence, the *umhlolo*, was very close. Many times, he had forced himself to gaze into its black heart in an effort to understand the nature of it, for he believed that only then could he hope to summon up enough of his powers to lessen its impact, or even banish it altogether.

After careful consideration, Langani sought an answer to his question. *Are you now nearing the climax – and therefore your end?*

The answer was short and brutal. *No!*

Tremors ran through his body like a fever. Tendrils of smoke from the small fire of *lesedi* roots began to drift around him. Gradually, its soporific qualities took effect and he slipped away into the place of dreaming.

The nearer to the black heart of the *umhlolo* Langani approached, the more indecipherable it became. That it threatened the house of Zulu did not come as a surprise to him, but he now understood that would not stop there.

Other images began to appear, merging and drifting into one another, a kaleidoscope of shifting fragments that at first made no sense to him. Gradually, though, he began to see a pattern forming, one that both frightened and overawed him.

Before his astonished eyes, a great city of gold began to rise out of the plains of Africa. Men, black men, white men, seemed to be digging and tunnelling deep below the ground, gouging and tearing out yellow metal and other riches from the belly of the earth. As he watched, the trail of these riches spread out to encompass the land, bestowing power and wealth on some it touched, while bringing misery and death to others.

Other cities began to appear: high stone towers and clusters of buildings, stretching for as far as the eye could see, with gardens, fields, farms and twisting snakes of roads crossing and criss-crossing the land.

His sense of wonder turned to ashes as he began to witness the turmoil of many wars and battles. Some of the bloodshed and hatred was between white men, those of the *amabhuna,* the Boers, and the soldiers of a great white Queen who lived across the sea. Driven by the greed for power, land and the riches that lay beneath the earth, they fought and died in their hundreds and then their thousands, their blood seeping into the rich red loam of Africa.

And now, to Langani's shame, ebbing and flowing from the future came horrific scenes of black men fighting and killing other black men, putting women and children to the blade, reducing their homes to blazing torches. The stench of the cruelty and inhumanity caught at his throat and made him gag.

With a superhuman effort, the diviner tried to focus his considerable powers on what he saw unfolding before him. Sometimes the pictures were not clear, the images merely symbolic, open to his own interpretation.

Take the one before him now, for instance…

Trails of more than one animal were clearly visible in the dust. They formed part of a force, a single force with many heads that sought to encompass the world. It was then he saw clearly to whom the tentacles belonged. Not that this piece of knowledge surprised him greatly.

Using the power of wind and tide, the billowing sails of the white men's ships spanned the world, their vessels disgorging men possessing great knowledge, magical inventions and *muthi* so powerful it could cheat death, also weapons which could blow both people and stone buildings apart, so that they disappeared in showers of dust.

Mesmerised, he watched in disbelief as they travelled to strange nations and lands far beyond his knowledge, crossing the great waters and the high mountain ranges of the world in strange inventions that rumbled along the ground on shining tracks or flew through the air like great birds.

No place was left undiscovered, from the tops of the highest mountains to the ocean beds beneath the seas. Rendered dizzy by the rapidity of the flickering images passing before him, the diviner then found himself looking into the blackness of space.

His mouth fell open as he gazed deep into the heavens and stared at the galaxies of glittering stars and saw the sun and moon and other worlds spinning silently on their axes.

Langani uttered a primitive sound in his throat as he watched the terrible beauty of the shining vessels launching themselves into the heavens, free of the earth and trailing plumes of fire in their tails. Even the remote expanses of space would not remain secret from the invaders and explorers of the future.

Sweat rolled down his face as he struggled to stay abreast of the vivid images and the sights and sounds flooding in on him. One thing he did understand for certain, and the knowledge made him glad and relieved…what he was witnessing lay in a future time, though how far away, he had no way of knowing.

A terrifying thought came to him then. If what he was seeing came to pass, if the moon and the stars were not too far away for these men to reach …what of his land? What would become of the amaZulu, the People of the Heavens?

Desperately, Langani forced his diminishing strength to focus on what he had feared and dreaded most of all. And when he looked on the bloody war that would one day erupt between the scarlet-coated soldiers of the great white Queen and Shaka's Zulu warriors, his eyes brimmed over with scalding tears.

Exhausted, his eyelids began to flutter. His eyes rolled back in his head until only the whites were showing. He moaned and rocked, shuddering, as he watched his people and their great kingdom fall bloodied into the dust.

When Langani next opened his eyes, he saw that he was very close to Shaka, *very* close indeed. In fact, he was so near he could see the fine pores of his skin and watch the rise and fall of his chest as he breathed.

It appeared to be late afternoon, perhaps an hour or so before sunset. The monarch was seated on a rough-hewn chair outside the doorway of a small beehive hut. Clearly, he was waiting for someone. The place was unfamiliar; nowhere of consequence, only a small *umuzi* called Nyakamubi, a few miles from kwaDukuza, one of many out-of-the way places Shaka used when he wanted to meet with his spies and informers away from the prying eyes of the royal court.

Langani sensed the monarch's restlessness, his need to escape, to entertain himself with some little folly. Noticing the lines around his eyes, and the sprinkling of silver at his temples, he was filled with great sadness on seeing this on a man he had always considered so vital and unchanging, his great strength undimmed, for had he always known him this way, from the very first time they had met during that far-off day of the great storm when they were young.

The failure of his mission to the Cape authorities must be preying on his mind, the inherent sense of betrayal gnawing away at him like a rat.

The sudden, tragic death of his friend, Kingi, the man with the streaks of silver in his hair, had affected him greatly for he had valued his friendship.

His great sprawling capital of kwaDukuza had become increasingly fraught with tensions. Insidious rumours had filtered through of his prized regiments refusing to engage with Shoshangani's warriors in battle. Worst of all, it was being whispered that some of his ablest warriors were fleeing north to join Mzilikazi, the renegade Kumalo chief.

Below the white daubed clay, Langani's face betrayed his distress. There were other things, other deeply buried, fearful things affecting this powerful, flawed man –

A movement by the gates of the small *kraal* drew the diviner's attention.

Hastily, he scanned the faces of the men entering the gates. Simple hunters, judging by the assortment of colourful birds' feathers stuffed into the pouches slung over their shoulders.

Lulled by the effects of the *lesedi* and the harmless scene before him, Langani relaxed his vigil. King Shaka was safe with his hunters. A small dalliance choosing new feathers for his head-dresses and trimmings for his ceremonial costumes was a trivial matter. No harm there…

He allowed his head to droop down on to his chest. Shortly afterwards, he fell into a deep sleep, exhausted by everything he'd seen and experienced.

A change, some small shift in the atmosphere, brought Langani back to full awareness with a short, sharp snap. A flash of brilliant scarlet caught his eye, the colour deep and rich. Simultaneously, or so it seemed, the small kraal was bathed in the slanting rays of the dying sun.

Langani shivered. It could almost be mistaken for blood. The illusion was short-lived and soon began to fade. He leaned forward and peered into the rapidly dimming light. Surely, what he'd seen was merely the flash of the scarlet *igwala gwala* feathers, those much favoured by Shaka?

He swayed uneasily. There was a brooding quality to the evening air, a deathly stillness hanging over the small kraal. Dusk was beginning to fall and the servants were busy preparing torches so that the Nkosi would have enough light to finish his business.

Shaka was pleased with his consignment of feathers. His face was benign and relaxed, the underlying grief and volatile emotions much soothed by the quiet, ordinary dealings with simple men.

From the bush beyond the small *umuzi,* the long mournful hooting of a hunting owl came floating out of the dusk, a harbinger of the coming night. The hunters instinctively glanced towards the open gates, suddenly aware that darkness was closing in fast. They looked hesitantly towards the Nkosi, hoping he would allow them to leave before the dangers of the night came upon them.

To their great relief, he rose from the chair, thanked them for their services and dismissed them. Gratefully, they gathered up their displays of birds' plumage, packed them back into the pouches and prepared to leave.

Langani's attention however, was not on the hunters hurrying away into the dusk. He was far more interested in the ominous patch of shadow hovering beyond the gates. What lay there was more akin to the dead of night, the pernicious small hours when evil stalked the world, than to the hour of sunset.

He stiffened. Someone, or *something,* was moving, coming closer. Two figures stepped out of the patch of darkness. Langani sensed something of the hyena in the cringing glide that brought them to the open gates, and brushed away tendrils of smoke so that he could see them better.

The elder of the men saw this moment as the fulcrum upon which his dreams and ambitions turned, while the younger followed his brother blindly, his soul vacuous and empty, scenting only blood.

The diviner's gaze slid over them, and returned to the patch of darkness which lay out there waiting, like some terrible, faceless beast.

A third figure materialised. A man stepped forward to join the other two. Even though his identity was not unexpected, Langani's breath hissed sharply through his teeth when he saw who it was.

Wolf-like, the man's smooth features failed to hide his inner triumph. His sense of injustice had been carefully nurtured over many years. Whether or not his mother had perished through some action of the warrior king was not certain, but he had used it as the seedbed on which his deep hatred of him had been allowed to flourish.

Even on a sultry night, Mbopha, the King's major-domo, had chosen to wear a cloak. It enfolded his tall, spare figure and concealed what was hidden beneath it. As he strode forward, it swirled around his ankles raising puffs of sand.

As Langani watched, Shaka's half-brothers, Dingane and Mhlangana, fell into place behind him.

Twenty third September. eThekwini
For days now, Jackabo had been sleeping badly. Waking with his heart racing, not remembering what it was he'd been dreaming about, his eyes would search the thin drift of moonlight flooding through the doorway as if he were looking for something – or someone.

The dogs were restless too; scratching and nipping at themselves, whining mournfully before coming to nudge him with their hot, dry noses. The air was heavy, pressing in on him from all sides. Fergus, the collie, suddenly growled low in his throat, the hair standing up in a ridge along his back. He growled again, showing his teeth.

Jackabo sat up, crawled over to the door on his hands and knees and stuck his head out. The collie pressed up close behind him, its breath hot on the back of his neck. Tension ran through its body and a low snarl vibrated in its throat.

The compound was bathed in moonlight, the outlines of the beehive huts black against the pale night sky. Jackabo scanned the pools of shadow over by the high fence. The gates were closed, the stockade solid and intact, the sharpened bamboo stakes standing out clearly in the moonlight. The coughing snarl of a leopard up on the headland carried to him on the night air.

Sadness caught at him as he thought of the Captain lying up there in his lonely grave with only the prowling beasts for company, John Hatton and Dommana covered by drifts of pine needles down below in the forest.

He rubbed his face. A dull ache pounded behind his left eye and his head felt as it was going to burst. All he wanted was to lie down and go to sleep. The collie butted his head against him in sympathy, his tongue rough on the back of his hand. Taking hold of the ruff of hair at the dog's throat, he shook it gently. 'Daft dog,' he whispered. 'You're just dreaming. Away and lie down now, Fergus.' Reluctantly, the collie wagged its tail, ambled back inside and flopped down.

A few minutes later, Jackabo heard a long low rumble. Assuming it was the dog growling again, he looked round, fully expecting to see it on its feet, its lips drawn back in a snarl. To his surprise, the collie was busy licking his paws, seemingly unconcerned about the recent noise.

Puzzled, Jackabo got to his feet and went outside. The ground was dry and warm below his bare feet, the grass stubby and brittle after months without rain. He looked up into the night sky. A three-quarter moon, benign and peaceful, hung suspended in space. The sky was cloudless, with a multitude of stars twinkling across it.

Crossing over to the fence, he checked that the gates were still barred. It couldn't be that late, probably around midnight or so, for he could see the embers of the cooking fires still glowing dull red among the faded ash.

The cricking of insects seemed louder now, the air throbbing and pulsing with their chirping. Then he heard the noise again. This time, there was no mistaking the low, menacing rumbles of thunder.

A storm must be on its way, he thought. He stopped dead in his tracks. It was too early in the season for thunder. The sky was cloudless, calm...

Without warning, the ground seemed to tilt beneath his feet. Alarmed, his eyes cast wildly around, looking for an explanation. *What was happening?*

About fifty yards away stood the hut John Hatton had shared with Dommana. It lay silent and empty in a pool of shadow, its thatch pale silver in the moonlight. Jackabo stared at its shrouded bulk.

It was where both of them had died. No one would ever live in it again – at least none of the sailors would, for they were very superstitious. The same for the Zulus, he was sure. The hut would be left to moulder and decay until it was finally demolished, by the activities of ants and termites.

Jackabo rubbed his eyes. His head was throbbing, making him feel dizzy. All he wanted to do was to go back inside and lie down.

It was then he thought he saw something move among the trees, a flutter of pale colour. The hair stirred along the back of his neck. It was what he'd seen high up among the trees just after they'd buried John Hatton.

Blinking fiercely, he forced himself to look again. This time, he realised there really was *something* there. And it was coming his way. It reminded him of the first time he'd seen Dommana, a shy ghost in the dusk, flitting towards him like a pale butterfly.

Dommana! He couldn't bring himself to call out her name. But wait!

It couldn't be Dommana. He had been there when they'd closed the earth over her and covered her with a cairn of stones.

In any case, what was moving towards him was neither a ghost, nor a woman. As it stepped out of the shadows and into a patch of moonlight, he saw clearly what it was; an animal, a long-legged, lean animal.

Jackabo recognised the neat head sunk between the shoulders, the long swinging tail and the beautifully marked fur. The amber eyes with their striking tear-drop markings running down each side of the muzzle were fixed intently on him. It was so close he could hear the soft rasping of its pads on the ground.

Suddenly, Langani appeared close behind it, his tall, lean presence emerging from the dusky shadows. Both animal and man continued to glide soundlessly towards him.

Something was wrong with the air. His head was spinning, the odour of charred feathers overpowering. Irrationally, he wondered how the diviner had managed to get inside the camp. The stockade was high, and the spikes of bamboo along the top were razor sharp, designed to keep out trespassers, both animal and human. Added to which the gates were tightly barred.

With a painful thump of his heart, he remembered that when Dommana lay dying, he had sent out a call for the diviner to help her. Although it was too late now, maybe Langani had heard him and was coming to help.

He opened his mouth to call out that Dommana and the captain and John Hatton were gone – but no sound emerged.

Langani was very close now, so close Jackabo could see the long plaits of hair, the glint of the moonlight on his oiled body and the streaks of white chalk on his face. The diviner stretched out an urgent hand. In appeal, or warning, he was not sure. Then Jackabo saw his lips move.

'iQawu… beware!'

The flash of bright light came first. Jackabo was dazzled by it, its coppery tang acrid in his mouth. Next, a barrage of sound seemed to come up from below the earth, drowning out Langani's words.

He cried out and tried to move towards him through the heavy air, but no matter how hard he struggled, something seemed to be holding him back. Rough animal hair brushed his fingertips but whether it belonged to the cheetah or the dog he wasn't sure.

The brilliance of the moonlight faded, and it began to grow dark. A wind came, tearing out of nowhere, a stew of dried leaves, dust and twigs that threatened to snatch his breath away.

An enormous crack of thunder split the air, a great vibration of sound and fury. Trees bent and tossed in the howling wind, the sky above moving, racing, as dark cohorts of the storm rode the winds of heaven, their banners of black, scarlet, and gold streaming out behind them.

Jackabo was lost, confused. *Where was he?* Every jangling nerve in his body told him he was no longer in the camp at Townsend.

There were others out there in the dark with him now, black derisive shapes that swore and threatened. Jackabo felt their menace, sensed them gathering for the kill.

He was also very aware of a chilling spiral of fear. *Not his own... but someone else's.*

The heavens were ablaze, full of vengeful fury, the darkness split apart by a growling that seemed to shake the very ground. A jagged flash of lightning tore down the sky, making everything stand out in vivid detail.

It was then Jackabo saw him. A boy of about ten years old, pressed up against the *mopani* stakes of the cattle enclosure. He was shivering, naked, and clutching a pair of thorn sticks as if his life depended on it. He looked very alone, crushed in on himself, snail tracks of tears on his cheeks. A short distance away, a group of older boys, youths were jeering and throwing out insults.

A stone flew out of nowhere. The boy cried out, his hand flying up defensively to his face. Dark blood trickled out from between his fingers. They came away, red from the deep cut on his cheekbone.

The shock had made the boy bite his tongue. He leaned forward and spat a gobbet of blood into the dust. As the storm gathered overhead, he stared up into the night sky. Then his lips began to move soundlessly as if in prayer.

Jackabo wondered who or what he was praying to. As if in answer, an immense barrage of sound and fury erupted in the heavens. Flashes of eerie blue lightning lit up the compound. By its light he saw that the boy's face was still upturned, his eyes fixed rigidly on something above his head.

Jackabo stared at him. Something about him had altered. *The scowl on his young face…*

The youngster was no longer pinned against the stakes of the cattle pen. Instead, he seemed to be moving purposefully towards the leader of the youths, hefting the thorn stick from one hand to the other as he went.

Jackabo peered at him. Something about him was familiar…the angle of the head, the way he was striding forward. Then it hit him like a thunderbolt. His eyes flickered in disbelief. *It couldn't be…*

But the scowl on the boyish face was unmistakable – *as was the oozing crescent-shaped wound high up on his cheekbone.*

Terrified, Jackabo tried to convince himself that it was all an illusion; the storm, the boy, and those stalking him. But somewhere inside, he knew it was not. The electrifying power of the storm was real enough, as was the coppery taste in his mouth and the dust gritting between his teeth.

His eyes flew back to the boy. His lips were still moving, his eyes fixed on the lightning-streaked skies. Instinctively, Jackabo now knew who he was calling out to, and why. The boy called *itshaka, the beetle* was calling on the *amadhlozi,* his ancestors. Jackabo did not know what he was asking them; all he knew was that they were very, very close. And he was terrified all over again.

The youths were not so sure of themselves now. They were uneasy, avoiding each other's eyes. The vulnerable boy pressed up against the *mopani* stakes had gone, and in his place stood an opponent, a very determined one at that.

The wind shook the tops of the trees and whipped the dried grass, twigs and grit into a boiling stew that spiralled across the ground. The dark gods and their cohorts rode high and wild across the night sky. Clad in streaming clouds of black and grey, shot through with blood red and gold, they were full of sound and fury – and very close.

The blow to the leader's head came out of nowhere. An enormous flash of light engulfed him, his stocky body silhouetted for an instant against the bluish flame. Clutching his head, he fell to his knees. The next blow caught him in the same place, ripping the soft flesh.

The small mob jostled forward, intent on revenge. Fanning out, their ragged cries were swept away by the tearing wind.

The boy faced them, bloodied sticks in his hand. His enemies stopped circling and moved in for the kill, five against one. Suddenly, Jackabo was afraid for him. He called out a warning, but the young Shaka couldn't hear him. His enemies were almost upon him.

Jackabo yelled again. The acrid stench of burning feathers was over-powering, blurring his vision and making him gag. A second flash of blinding light came out of nowhere, followed by an enormous explosion of heat, sound and energy that seemed to suck all the air away.

The whole melee was caught up in a cacophony of sound that was beyond description. All Jackabo could do was to fall to his knees, clasp his hands over his head and wait until it was over.

When he next looked up, everything had changed. All was still. The storm had quietened, the terrifying sounds had gone, and a gentle rain was falling.

The young Shaka was standing with his head tilted back to let the rain wash the blood and dust from his body. And he was laughing into the face of the dying storm, loving its ferocity and rage.

Sheer, blind terror overwhelmed Jackabo. With it came the cloying odour of burning feathers, and the sudden awareness that there was someone else out there in the soft falling rain, someone intent on murder.

Someone the boy Shaka could neither see, nor hear.

He peered into the dusk, straining to see who it was. The sickening, charred odour rose with a vengeance, burning his throat and catching at his breath. In the flickering light, he caught the glint of sharp metal.

Nkosi! he screamed, trying to move towards him through air that was strangely heavy and cloying. *Nkosi, look out!*

In the small kraal, which was called Nyakamubi, Langani watched as the black patch of darkness beyond the gate began to drift towards the pool of flickering torchlight. Something terrible was about to happen. He could feel it gathering in strength.

Summoning up his considerable powers, he snarled defiance at the blackness to keep it at bay. Unwillingly, it shrank back. His attention swivelled to where another scene was being played out.

Quick…quick!

The assassins, fearful that their courage would dissipate in the face of the formidable warrior King, gripped their weapons in sweating hands and stepped forward to meet him, murmuring greetings.

Shaka seemed relaxed, suspecting nothing. If he thought it odd that his stepbrothers, accompanied by his major domo, thought to pay him a visit at this small, out of the way *kraal* just as night was falling, he gave no indication of it. With his customary open-handedness, he expressed regret that the small homestead was singularly lacking in hospitality.

Mbopha was silent, his impassive face revealing nothing. Leaving the brothers Dingane and Mhlangana to feign spurious interest in the King's new collection of ceremonial feathers, he moved surreptitiously to Shaka's side.

The short assegai concealed beneath his cloak slid into his hand with fearful certainty. His fingers, suddenly slippery with sweat, curled around it. The honed blade gleamed in the light of the sputtering torches before it descended.

Once…twice…three times, Mbopha grunted with effort at each blow, a thread of spittle spooling from his lips.

The first struck Shaka in the soft part between neck and shoulder, the second and third blows, though aimed at the heart, merely glanced off his ribs. A gout of dark blood erupted from his mouth. Shocked, Shaka slowly slumped forward on to his knees, clutching his throat as if to stem the flow of blood.

Speechless, he withdrew his hand and stared at it. Blood ran through his fingers. It began to pool around him soaking into the earth of the dusty compound. Langani groaned aloud, sweat running into his eyes. Here was the heart of the *umhlolo*, the darkness that had been directed at the centre of Zulu power.

Galvanised into action by the sight and smell of Shaka's blood, Mhlangana, the younger of the two, ran forward and made a wild slash at his half-brother. Dingane added his long-held venom to the savagery being unleashed.

A few yards away, a pair of terrified servants stood frozen in horror. The burning torches dropped from their nerveless fingers to sputter impotently on the hard packed ground.

Appalled by what was happening, they backed blindly away from the horrific scene. Unnoticed by the assassins, they slipped through the gates of Nyakamubi and fled into the darkness.

Langani saw the badly wounded Shaka made an attempt to get to his feet. His lips moved. The diviner strained to hear his stumbling words.

'What….what have I done to you, my brothers? Why are you killing me, kings of the earth? You will come to an end through killing one another.'

Even in the fading light, his pain and bewilderment was clear to see. He moaned as a surge of agony gripped him. But his legendary strength had not yet deserted him.

WIth an almost superhuman effort, he rolled over on to his knees and painfully levered himself to his feet. He took a tentative step towards them, one hand outstretched, the other trying to stem the flow of blood from his wounds.

Even badly injured and swaying with weakness, Shaka of the Zulus was a formidable opponent. His head came up, and to their horror they saw the old, deep rage begin to smoulder in his pain-filled eyes and his hands clench into fists.

Mhlangana, the younger brother, broke first. With a high pitched shriek, he let the bloodied weapon slip from his hand, then turned and fled towards the open gate. As the naked implications of the crime they had just committed began to flood in on them, Dingane was next to crumble. *What if Shaka survives? What if he lives?*

His own questions filled him with unspeakable dread. It was well known the Nkosi's stamina and fortitude was superior to that of other men.

What kind of vengeance might he launch on them if he survived?

The patch of blackness outside the gate swallowed both brothers up, and then lurked there, waiting. Mbopha stood rooted to the spot, unable to move. A strange lethargy seemed to have taken hold of him. His hooded eyes stared unblinking as the old nemesis, the cursed enemy, stumbled towards him.

His eyes were glazing over, looking through him to somewhere beyond. Mbopha could no longer bear to look on his handiwork. Moaning, he threw his cloak over his head and turned away, but not before he heard the whispered words issuing from the blood-filled mouth of Shaka of the Zulus.

'It is not you who will rule the land, my brothers. The swallows will come up from the sea and cover it. They are already here.'

In a flash of insight, Mbopha realised the truth of what had just been said. A stab of naked fear followed. What if he had misjudged the astute Zulu king?

What if the ill-fated mission to umGeorge's people at the Cape had been an attempt to delay their encroachment into Zululand? Suppose he had been trying to buy time for his People of the Heavens?

Then he, Mbopha ka Sithayi would have helped to slaughter the only man who could perhaps have altered the inevitable flow of history. Terror flooded his soul.

Langani felt no pity for the man hurrying away, for he could see the shades already gathering around him.

The betrayal of a man who had raised him in worldly status and levied such trust in him would be rightly considered a gross betrayal of the worst kind by the *amadhlozi*. The revenge that would eventually fall on the former servant of Shaka Zulu would be theirs and theirs alone.

The young diviner's compassion was reserved for the man lying before him in the dust of the small *umuzi*. Though deserted and in agony, the warrior king was still alive.

Summoning up his great reserves of strength, he began to inch his way towards the open gates, leaving a smeared trail of blood behind him. His breathing was ragged and laboured, terrible to hear.

In spirit, Langani knelt down beside the dying warrior king, his eyes full of tears, willing him to hear his words and know that he was there wth him.

'What of you now, my long-ago partner of the storm? Though I tried to warn you of the white men, in the end it was those of your own blood who brought you down. Even with all my powers, I failed to stop it.'

In his mind's eye, Langani caught a glimpse Shaka as he was the first time they had met, young, defiant, and on his way to great power and glory – but with heart enough to stop and dance with the rain-soaked three-year-old that had been himself, hoisting him onto his shoulders and dancing round and round, both of them laughing into the teeth of the storm...

One by one, the torches sputtered and went out, leaving the compound in darkness. Now there was only a suffering human being, a bloodstained assegai and some brilliant feathers trampled into the dust.

Rising out of the bush beyond the thorn fences, the only visible witness to his suffering was the honeycomb, yellow eye of a moon that was almost full.

When Jackabo next opened his eyes, his headache had gone, and so had the stench of charred feathers. The night was alive with the clicking of insects, and the air was light and cool, the heaviness drained out of it. The moon hung suspended in the peerless sky, its pale light flooding the camp and silvering the thatches of the beehive huts. Little time seemed to have passed.

He glanced towards the hut where Hatton and Dommana had died. He had been staring at it when the cheetah had appeared out of the silvery dusk.

It had been no dream, for he had heard the soft brush of the animal's pads on the ground and been close enough to see its beautiful markings. Added to which, the urgency in Langani's voice had been unmistakable.

The clearing was empty; the glade where Dommana used to lay out the washing lying silent under the moon, only the leaves stirring in the air filtering up from the bay.

Jackabo had already come to a decision. The Nkosi must be warned. No matter what he might think, or suspect, or how he might rage, he had to warn him of the danger he was in.

Forty

Twenty fourth of September, 1828

Jackabo waited impatiently for daylight to appear. The night predators would still be on the prowl, particularly close to streams and drinking holes, so he would have to wait.

Under normal circumstances it would take him a good day and a half to reach kwaDukuza – but then these were not ordinary times. He would try to get there by sundown. Jackabo whistled softly for the dog. The collie frisked around him, butting him with its nose, anxious to be off. He would be glad of its company and protection.

Silently, he raided Cookie's food store. Thrusting some bread and cheese into his pack, he rummaged about until he found some scraps of meat and a bone for the dog.

It was getting lighter with every moment. But there was something he had to do first. Retracing his steps, he came back to the hut where Dommana and Hatton had lived. Squatting down, he scanned the ground. It wasn't long before he found what he was looking for – proof that the animal which had padded towards him out of the moonlight had not been just a figment of his imagination.

He wasn't disappointed. The animal's prints were there clear to see – including the intractable claw marks of the species known as cheetah. Close by, there were also the footprints of a tall man used to walking barefoot.

Jackabo ran down the hill and on to the track that led round the lagoon. The winding path, which was marked '*to the Zoolah*' on the survey map James King had drawn up five years earlier, would lead him up and over the ridge.

Although it was well used, dangers large and small lurked in the dense thickets on either side. Only the week before, a leopard had broken into one of the nearby kraals, killing a tethered goat and the two women who had tried to chase it away. The week before that, three fishermen had been savaged by a hippo after it capsized their dugout canoe.

The collie stopped dead in the middle of the track, and turned to look at him, ears erect and tongue dripping with saliva.

'What is it, boy?'

Stiff-legged, the dog warily investigated huge balls of animal dung lying on the track. Elephant. The herds still passed through eThekwini at certain times of the year. Undeterred, boy and dog ran on.

At first light, the bay was a magical place. The lagoon lay silent under the dappled sky, its rocky islands wavering in the mists. Silhouetted against the dawn sky was the ill-fated schooner, *Susan and Elizabeth*.

Today, Jackabo refused to be beguiled by its beauty. Time's slipping away, he thought, in sudden desperation, I can feel it pulling at me. The ship's waiting on the tide, but I can't sail, not until I tell the Nkosi what's lying in wait for him. Even if it means he has to hear some of my secrets-bar the last of them, of course. For Magaye's sake, and because I promised Nandi, I have to keep his existence to myself, especially now.

Pushing such thoughts away, he tried to focus on the moment. *I need to hurry...*

A mongoose sprinted out of the thicket and disappeared into the long grass with scarcely a rustle. Too late, Fergus spotted it. The collie didn't try to give chase, just sidled along, throwing knowing glances at him from the corner of its fey, yellow eyes. *Clever dog... you know we've urgent business today.*

Smoke rose lazily from somewhere deep in the bush, probably from Fynn's compound. With a pang, he wondered what would happen to Mount Pleasant, the Captain's old house, now that John Hatton had no need of it.

The next fork in the track led to Fort Farewell. No doubt the tattered Union flag would still be hanging on the termite-riddled flagpole, the rusty ship's guns half-hidden in the grass.

They left the shore and started up the rise that led to the top of the ridge. Urgency clutched at him and he broke into a run. The collie barked and ran ahead, leading the way.

The wide path was ancient and worn, carved out of the living earth by the feet of thousands of elephants following the rhythms of the seasons and their own deep instincts. Jackabo had heard that somewhere in the vast trackless bush was a secret valley where elephants went to die. If only it could be found, the hunters said, then the *umlungu* could find all the ivory tusks they could carry and would not have to kill the great *ndlovu* to get it.

Glancing seaward, he saw that the sun had cleared the horizon and started its slow climb into the sky. By the time it stood overhead, he should be halfway to kwaDukuza. If darkness fell before he got there, he'd only have Fergus and a strong thorn stick to protect him.

A twinge of anxiety forced him to put a spurt on. Before long, he settled down into the steady lope that the Zulus had taught him.

In the cool of early morning, the air smelled of dry earth and the spicy aroma of new growth. Signs of spring were everywhere. Huge herds of zebra, impala and sable restlessly tossed their heads while bucks knocked horns with one another and bellowed out their challenges.

To while away the time as he jogged on, he began to scheme how he might warn the Nkosi of the imminent danger he was in. His mind steered away from the inexplicable events of the night before. To dwell on them would only sap his energy and interfere with his determination to do what he'd set out to do.

And so he kept running, his knapsack bouncing against his shoulder blades, the collie racing ahead, its slavering tongue lolling out of its mouth.

The fierce African sun was no friend to Jackabo, even at the best of times. His fair skin and colouring saw to that.

Now, hanging like a sword above him, in a sky that was white with heat, it was his most deadly of enemies. Lancing along his sweat-beaded cheekbones and the bridge of his nose, it struck the tender part of the exposed throat and breastbone, attacking the wrists protruding from the sleeves of the shirt he had outgrown and beating with monotonous regularity on the tender skin of his feet and ankles.

The animal, too, was suffering. Cobwebs and ticks from the long grass clung to its lifeless coat, and its flanks heaved like bellows. To get some respite, boy and dog lay down together in the dwindling streams or collapsed in the nearest pool of shade for a few precious moments.

After the first excruciating hours, they found their second wind. Jackabo's battered feet ceased to hurt and the ground literally fell away beneath his steady pace, his ragged breathing calmer now, steady and easy. Even the blistering heat seemed to have lost its power to slow him down,

The sun had shifted to Jackabo's left and begun its slide down behind the flat-topped acacias. Looking for familiar landmarks, he spotted the clump of trees where the weaver-birds had built their nests and knew he was on the right track.

Still five or six miles to go to kwaDukuza, he reckoned. The long miles and sustained pace of travelling were starting to take their toll on him. His legs were tiring. All the food was gone and the water bottle was empty.

Fergus had taken to flopping down for a rest every so often, his sides heaving. Poor brute, the boy thought, even his tail's too tired to wag.

A mile or two further on and Jackabo frowned as he squinted into the distance. The light had a sepia cast to it and the shadows had changed to amber, the sun a molten ball of red slipping down in the west.

Is it my imagination or is that smoke ahead? He stopped, shaded his eyes against the glare of the setting sun and sniffed the air. There was no mistaking the acrid tang of burning.

'It's smoke, all right,' he said aloud, his voice raw and unnatural in the stillness. The dog whined deep in its throat and listlessly waved the tattered plumes of its tail.

He could see it clearly now – a tall grey and white column of thick clouds, rising into the hazy distance. A bit too early for bush fires, he thought. Memories of the night before rushed back to him. *A cloudless moonlit sky. . . too early for thunder and storms, but yet...*

Jackabo's mouth went dry.

He couldn't take his eyes off the billowing smoke. Short and squat at the base, black around the edges, its long plumes curled lazily into the sky, fanning out and drifting upwards into the golden light of the setting sun.

Without warning, it returned to haunt him, the same sickening smell that had been in his nose for weeks. Only this time it was stronger than ever. Bending over, he retched again and again, saliva dripping from his mouth.

Those damn burning feathers! What he was seeing was no accident; no fluke of nature, no spark igniting tinder-dry grass and setting the bush alight.

KwaDukuza was on fire!

Clenching his fists on each side of his head in horror, his knapsack rolled away into the grass, unnoticed. Fergus whined and pushed his nose into his hand.

Jackabo was numb. For a moment or two, he teetered on the edge of panic. *Shall I stay, go on – or turn round and head back to the bay?*

His thrawn inner-self threw up an argument against retreat. But kwaDukuza's my home. All I have is there, apart from what's on my back. My friends, Hector and the cats, the white cattle Shaka gave me . . .

A familiar voice echoed in his head. '*You've come so far already, now you'll need to go the whole way, Charlie.*

A queer thing, he thought, with kwaDukuza burning before me, the voice I just heard belonged to my mother, Charlotte. Didn't I hear her speaking to me, clear as a bell, telling me what I had to do? But she's right. I have to finish what I started.

Scrabbling around for his pack, he whistled for Fergus and then set off at a run towards kwaDukuza and the black column of smoke spiralling into the sky.

Given the hypnotic glare of the flames, the maze of bush paths and the terrified women and children fleeing with bundles on their heads, it was lucky they met in the way they did, almost colliding with one another.

Lucky? Far too many queer things had been happening of late for Jackabo to think that luck had anything to do with it. It was only when the man uttered a few words that he realised who it was.

'Oh, God, Jakot – it's you! What's happening?'

The hands slowly relaxed their grip on him. Jakot looked as if he hadn't slept for days. His eyes were strained and bloodshot, lines of exhaustion carved into his face. No colourful strings of beads now to cover the marks of the rope on his wrists, no soft hide cape to hide the lash marks of the *sjambok*.

Near naked and with only his intriguing left eye and his quick wits to keep him alive, Jackabo thought that this was how Jakot must have been when he'd fled to Zululand looking for Shaka and a new life.

The Xhosa turned his back on the flames, sat down heavily on the ground and sank his head into his hands. Sensing his distress, the black and white dog whined and nuzzled his face. Jackabo squatted down beside him.

Somehow, he knew exactly what Jakot was going to say before he said it. A queer kind of pain struck him between the ribs.

Jakot lifted his bloodshot eyes to meet his. 'The Nkosi is dead,' he stated bluntly. 'Struck down like a dog by the snake Mbopha and his brothers, Dingane and Mhlangana. Yesterday, they came yesterday, at sunset. The Nkosi was with hunters who had brought him feathers.'

Jackabo squeezed his eyes shut. *The Nkosi, dead...*

A deep sense of futility ran through him. Now nothing could save the man he had been running to warn. The strange events of the night before flitted through his mind, adding to his sense of unreality.

Around them, the night echoed with the pitiful sounds of wailing and crying. Shadowy figures materialised out of the smoke-filled glare then disappeared into the darkness.

Both Jakot and he were sunk in their own thoughts, wordless and exhausted in the face of the latest tragedy. Without raising his head, he asked, 'What kind of feathers were they?'

The Xhosa looked up, puzzled by the seeming irrelevance of the question.

Jackabo repeated, 'What kind of feathers were the hunters bringing the Nkosi?'

'I do not know. I saw many kinds there – but I think mostly red, from the *igwala gwala* bird, the ones the Nkosi liked so much.'

A frown creased Jakot's glistening forehead. 'Why do you ask? What does it matter what kind of feathers they were?'

The boy turned and looked at the lurid glow in the distance and saw the showers of sparks flying up into the night. Now he knew what the cloying smell of burning feathers meant, and why it had dogged him so persistently over the last few weeks.

The blood-red feathers of the *igwala gwala* bird represented the funeral pyre of kwaDukuza, the seat of Shaka's power; all the King's fine feathers charring and burning as his great citadel blazed.

It had been part of a warning meant for Shaka, not himself – only he hadn't understood its significance at the time. How could he?

'*Yebo*, Jakot,' he said, dragging his filthy shirt-sleeve across his brow. 'You are right, what does it matter now?'

Jakot went on to tell him all he knew of Shaka's last day on earth. For himself, he had been a few miles away building a new kraal to house his cattle. Worn out by the day's labours, he'd decided to sleep there instead of trying to reach kwaDukuza before dark.

Rising at dawn, he had passed by the small *umuzi* of Nyakamubi. Fully intending to skirt around it, he suddenly remembered that it was one of the places Shaka used when he wanted privacy.

'Something was wrong,' he said, shaking his head and pressing a weary hand to his heart. 'The gates were wide open. Something – someone was on the ground. So I came closer to see who it was.'

The brutally savaged body of Shaka Zulu lay face down in the dust by the open gate. It looked as if he had been trying to crawl to safety – or for help. Trails of blood led back quite a distance, a tumble of scarlet feathers trapped in the gore.

Jackabo felt the hair stir on the back of his neck. There they were again, the scarlet feathers… They stared at each other, the feral golden chip in Jakot's eye glowing in the light of the smouldering flames.

'Did – did you find anyone else there?' Jackabo stammered, 'perhaps someone was hiding, had seen what happened?'

The Xhosa shook his head. A sudden thought struck the boy.

'Jakot – but how did you know who killed the Nkosi? Why are you sure it was Mbopha and Dingane?'

The Xhosa surveyed him soberly. Jackabo could see the dull red of the leaping flames reflected in his dark eyes.

'Because, iQawu, my friend,' replied the Xhosa, 'I met someone else there, not a servant. He was the one who told me.' A small smile lifted the corner of his mouth. 'He appeared on the path before me as I was hurrying to get away.'

Jackabo held his breath. Why did he have the feeling that he knew what was coming next? 'Who was it?' he asked.

Unsuspecting, Jakot replied, 'A young man, tall, with strangely plaited long hair. I had never seen him before. He was the one to tell me all the things I have told you.'

Fergus whined deep in his throat, the smell of the smoke distressing him. Jackabo bent to stroke the collie's head in an effort to hide his emotions.

Langani – who else could it have been? The skin began to crawl on his scalp. *But how could he have been in two places at the same time?*

I saw him clear as day last night in eThekwini, he thought, wildly. Now, Jakot's telling me he spoke to him near Nyakamubi at dawn early this morning, nearly fifty miles away –

After discovering Shaka's body, Jakot found himself in a difficult position. First of all, he had no idea what had really happened or whether what the man had told him was true, although he thought it very likely. The open gate, Shaka dying alone, the murderers gone, vanished into the night.

Jakot's sole thought had been for himself. There was nothing he could do for Shaka. 'If I was found kneeling by the dead Nkosi or anywhere near, I would be accused of having killed him,' he explained. 'There was no one to say that I did not. And no one had seen me in kwaDukuza the night before, so I could not say that was where I had slept.'

The Xhosa was shrewd enough to realise that once the death of the powerful Shaka became public knowledge, it would not be long before the killers came looking for those nearest to him. It was ever the tribal way.

'And so Jakot did not enter Nyakamubi,' he said, with a face like stone. 'I left quickly before the murderers returned – or someone passing by saw me there.'

Shaka had lain all night before the open gates of Nyakamubi, the hard-packed ground below him soaked with his blood.

The Lord of the World had fallen to earth from his high places, betrayed by his trusted major domo, two of his half-brothers and with the collusion of his father's sister, Mkabayi, a woman whom he'd honoured and promoted as commander of one of his garrisons.

Even in death, Shaka Zulu had defied his killers. Although the gates had remained wide open to the savage African night, even the wild animals of the veldt had left his dead body alone. Later, the tracks of predators, large and small, were found around the entrance to the place, though none had tried to enter or molest the body.

Long afterwards, around blazing fires below winter skies ablaze with stars, the storytellers would tell and re-tell the legends of the greatest Nkosi of them all, Shaka of the Zulus.

'See,' they would say to their captive audience. 'He truly was the Lord of the World, Lord over all of the Beasts. It is true. For none of them, not even the leopard, nor the lion, dared to dishonour his body, even after his spirit had flown.'

The mighty *Iziloze Nkosi,* Lord of the Beasts, still commanded their respect, even in death.'

Jakot, known as Hlambamanzi, the swimmer and Jackabo, the boy Shaka had named iQawu, the hero, stood together, dumb, bereft of words and watched while kwaDukuza burned.

The boy's quarters, the place where he'd lived close to the Nkosi Shaka had been part of the Royal palaces. Now they were gone. All he had left in the world was in the bundle Jakot had brought with him before fleeing to warn him not to try to enter kwaDukuza.

Jackabo thought sadly of his raven, Hector, and his other animals and wondered how they had fared. There was nothing left to say and yet too much. *What will happen? Where will we go now that the Nkosi has gone?*

Such questions would have to wait. For now, he and Jakot could only stand and watch. At last, the great straw wickerwork domes collapsed in on themselves in showers of sparks and flying ash. Blackened straw covered all that was once the magnificence of Shaka and his court.

Above their heads, the heavens were beautiful beyond belief. *Komotsho,* the evening star, hung suspended in the darkness of space, and shone with a steady, brilliant light. A moon that was almost full rose up from the vast bush, a great yellow eye into a cloudless sky.

There was no thunder tonight, only tranquillity, but from out of the nearby thickets, a ghostly white shape swooped out of a tall acacia tree and the sound of its mournful hooting made all who heard it shiver.

It was both a requiem for a dead king, and a warning of what was to come.

Epilogue

Langani had wakened just before first light. The diviner liked high places where no one except the birds of the air could see him. From his position on the headland, he had a perfect view of the ship lying at anchor in the bay. He noted the bustle of activity around it, two small boats ferrying to and fro, men hauling on ropes and calling out orders.

The lagoon of eThekwini is a magical place, he thought, as he watched the mists rising over the scattered islands. Then he shivered, remembering what he had seen of its future.

In time, tall towers of stone would cover the sweet meadows. The place where the hippos came to sport among the reed beds would dry up and the many small springs coming down from the hills would cease to flow.

The road leading round the lagoon and up the hill, the one that had been carved out the earth by the great padding feet of the *ndlovu* would be forgotten and another built over it. Strange vessels would glide on the waters of the bay and rush around at great speed both on land, and also in the air. His mouth dried with the thought of it.

No more would the grunting cough of hunting leopards or the howl of jackals and hyenas be heard in the night, for they too would disappear from eThekwini. The hills and the shore would swarm with people, many people of different kinds.

Too many people…too much noise. Like the loud, raucous humming of angry bees, never ceasing night and day, there would be many, many voices, shouting and cursing, bright lights, confusion…and great sorrow.

Sometimes Langani was afraid of what he saw; at other times he was curious, full of wonderment at the strange inventions of the future.

The Lord of the World had been right, he thought. With his dying breath, he had uttered a warning to the brothers who were murdering him:

'*Do not think you will rule this land,*' he had said. '*The 'swallows' will cover it from end to end. They are already here.*'

Langani could look into the future as clearly as he could see into the past. Shaka's words will come true, he thought. It is what I warned him about, though he would not listen – or so I thought.

A smile touched his face for a brief moment. But even when the white men eventually rule our land, it will not be the end of things.

'*Earthly power does not last forever…*' he reminded himself, '*and neither do the men, black or white, who imagine they hold it in their grasp.*'

This he had learned from the Creator of all things, N'khulunkhulu. And it gave him much comfort.

Today, the youth called iQawu would be on the ship preparing to leave on the tide. Langani was desolate to see him leave, but it was time for him to go, to return to whatever the future held for him. With the great King Shaka gone, also Kingi and Hatton, the boy had played his part. Things were about to change in Zululand, and much trouble lay ahead.

The young diviner had been close to the boy with the hair like fire and had shared many things with him. From him he had learned much about the better ways of the white men and some of the good things they would bring with them, but he also knew of their need to spread their power and lay claim to things that were not rightfully theirs.

Yebo, Langani thought, sadness catching at him. I will miss his brightness, his spirit…from the very beginning, even before he had set foot in Zululand, it was always a joy to think of him.

Strange to think there are those among the *umlungu* who also have powers, he mused. iQawu knows he has them, but fears them greatly and thinks they will pass.

Langani smiled to himself as he remembered his own struggles around the time of manhood, when he thought himself mad, possessed of devils.

The spirits had chosen him, although he might well have preferred it otherwise. iQawu also had strong presences around him. Langani thought of the fierce, alien forces he had observed after the boy had returned from the far-off land of the Portuguese.

He sighed. It will be the same for him, I fear, *umlungu* or not. Those who are chosen must accept what they are given.

The cheetah's ears pricked up, and she edged forward to stare out over the bay. Her nostrils twitched delicately as she scented the wind.

The waters of the bay were calm, with only a slight wind rippling the surface. The ship was moving slowly towards the narrow passage between the long spit of sand and the headland.

The diviner could see the youth standing at the rail, the sun glinting on his red hair. Tall and strong, growing into manhood, no longer the tender boy shipwrecked on the shores of Zululand, he held himself erect and proud, as was his right.

Langani was aware of everything that lay in his heart. At this moment, iQawu was looking back, his heart full of pain, thinking of those he was leaving behind, both the living and the dead. He could feel his sorrow like a sword in the flesh.

There was a strong link between the youth and the places and people of the Zulu, Langani thought, a curious connection for one so young, and from a different tribe and race. But then he had always known that, for had he not seen his coming, long before he had even set foot on the sands of eThekwini.

Even though the ship would bear him away, the diviner knew that part of iQawu would remain forever in the land of the amaZulu, along with the shades of those who had gone before.

The mighty Shaka had already acknowledged this by bestowing such a worthy praise name on him. To kill a man of his own race in defence of a fallen Zulu had touched the warrior king to the heart.

And for this, as well as for his courage, and his loyalty, Shaka had given him the title of *iQawu, the hero.* And it would stay with him until his last days on earth.

The ship eased safely out of the bay, keeping the tall, forested headland to starboard and the long spit of sand to port. The sea was benevolent today, creaming gently against the jagged rocks at the point. The vessel flew easily over the sandbars and merged with the ocean. Once it reached the open sea, its sails began to unfurl like the wings of a bird and it sped on.

Langani kept the ship in sight for as long as he could. The cheetah pressed herself against him, and he could feel the trembling running through her.

He looked down the long years into the future and smiled at what he saw there. Apart from his Zulu praise name, he had not allowed the youth to leave Zululand empty handed.

'I have not been wrong to place the carved box in your keeping,' he murmured. 'You are still young, and though you have suffered much and been greatly tested, your fear and uncertainty at what lies inside it is understandable. However, you will keep it close by you. Although you are mortally afraid of what the contents of the box represent, years hence, when you are grown into manhood, you will confront the past and remember that you are still iQawu, and what will be required of you.'

The *Susan and Elizabeth* swung out in a wide curve to clear the treacherous rocks of the wooded headland. As the wind filled the sails, the schooner began to speed away into the morning haze, heading south.

'*Nkosi umLilwane, Lord of the Red Fire.* One day, that is what men will call you, *iQawu.* You will be a good man – and your life will run for as long as Shaka's kingdom lives. *Hamba gahle,* my friend. Go well. Until we meet again.'

The diviner bent his head in farewell and let his words carry on the wind. By the time he looked up, the ill-fated vessel known as the *Susan and Elizabeth* had disappeared into the morning haze.

As it followed Langani back into the sheltering trees, the cheetah was purring softly in her throat. Clad in their new spring foliage, the branches closed softly behind them.

Nearby, the bird with glossy black feathers cocked a sharp, golden eye in their direction. Then, after preening its feathers for a moment or two, the raven, which had once been called Hector, rose into the air and began to fly home ahead of them.

About the Author

Isabella was born and educated in the north east of Scotland. After entering the teaching profession, she took up a contract with the Ministry of Overseas Development, London and left for Ndola, Zambia, with her sons then aged 6 and 4.

Next came Malawi and the Bishop MacKenzie International School in Lilongwe. Her final tour in Africa took her to Libya where she worked for Sirte Oil Company in Marsa el Brega. A year after the Americans bombed Tripoli she left Libya and returned to Scotland, after more than twenty years of *'interesting living'* as she puts it!

Isabella now writes full time, and spends part of each year in Australia. She has four grandchildren.

*

KINGDOM OF A THOUSAND DAYS the second book in **THE 'JOHN ROSS' TRILOGY** *was the winner of the Pitlochry Quaich Award for Historical Fiction at the 2016 Annual Conference of the Scottish Association of Writers. The adjudicator was Alanna Knight, MBE Honorary President.*

Acknowledgements

My first thank you must go to all the on-line and off-line folks, too numerous to mention by name, whose books, blogs, advice columns, comments, and courses I've responded to during the long gestation period of writing these novels.

Neil Paterson of Findhorn Boatyard, Moray offered practical information on the launching of a boat down a slip in the old way. A big thank you to Rachel Mackay of Strathnaver, Sutherland for the Gaelic version of the Lord's Prayer.

Also thanks to Dennis deAgostini of kwaZuluNatal for sending me the biography of John Dunn, whose father came from Inverness; a Scot who, after the time of John Ross, became a Chief among the Zulus and founded a proud lineage which still exists today; also, the wonderful book, *Bessie,* based on the true story of one of the English children shipwrecked on the dreaded Wild Coast of South Africa. It made the wanderings of Henry Francis Fynn come alive for me, and I hope this is reflected in my writing of his expeditions down the same coast 200 years ago.

To members of the New South Wales Writers' Centre, Sydney, for their invaluable help with the reading, critiquing and suggestions for the trilogy during one of my visits to Australia. A big thank you to James Vella Bardon, formerly of Malta, now an Aussie and current member of the Australasia Historical Writers Association of which I am also a member. Good on you, James! Also Kate Matthews, another generous Ozzie who helped me at that time. I still have the well-thought out critique and suggestions you sent me!

While we are on the subject of James Vella Bardon, I must congratulate him on the sparkling victory he's just achieved with regard to the long-awaited historical fiction debut of his five part epic 'SASSENA STONE.'

For my own part, I was honoured to have 'KINGDOM OF A THOUSAND DAYS' awarded the Pitlochry Quaich Award for Historical Fiction at the 2016 Annual Conference of the Scottish Association of Writers. My thanks and appreciation must go to Alanna Knight MBE, Honorary Chairman, for choosing my book. It meant a great deal to me.

And last, but certainly not least, to all those who've read A DANCE CALLED AFRICA, enjoyed it, and came forward to tell me so. A big thank you! You made my day. I hope you'll also enjoy KINGDOM OF A THOUSAND DAYS the second book in the trilogy and, in due course, Book 3 LORD OF THE RED FIRE.

Author Notes

Now that you've met 'John Ross' aka Jackabo aka Charles Rawden Maclean, I hope you've enjoyed reading about what happened during his 'thousand days' at the heart of the Zulu court. Perhaps you haven't yet read A DANCE CALLED AFRICA?

If not, you can find it here: www.Amazon.com/dp/B01082KLV2K

REVIEWS

If you've enjoyed reading KINGDOM OF A THOUSAND DAYS I would greatly appreciate it if you would take a few minutes to POST a review on Amazon using the link above.

Reviews really matter to authors. I can't stress enough how important they are. In this way we find out what readers think of us and they encourage others to read our books.

Thank you, in anticipation. Your support is genuinely appreciated.

If you have any queries or questions, please contact me directly at isabellableszynski@gmail.com. **I'll be pleased to hear from you.**

If you'd like to read about the fascinating background to The 'John Ross' Trilogy you can **FIND OUT MORE** by visiting my website at: http://www.stravaig-books.com.

WHAT'S COMING NEXT?

COMING SOON

Golden Eye

THE MAN WHO SWAM TO AFRICA

*The untold story of Jakot Msimbithi
Xhosa rebel, freedom fighter and spy…
Even the notorious penitentiary of Robben Island could not hold him*

This novella briefly covers the extraordinary life of a Xhosa rebel who accidentally strayed into the forefront of one of the most compelling and dramatic periods in the history of 19th century south-east Africa.

Jakot was 'the man with the golden eye' and the luck of the devil. Although he features prominently in the first two books of 'THE 'JOHN ROSS' TRILOGY a series classed as Historical Fiction, neither he nor any of the other characters- with the exception of only ONE – were figments of my imagination.

Consequently, like the others, he lived, breathed and died, upright and on his feet, true to himself to the end, and very much a man of his time.

My main focus in 2018 will be the publication of **LORD OF THE RED FIRE** the final part of the story of the lad known as **'JOHN ROSS.'**

Lord of the Red Fire
NKOSI UM LILWANE

CHARLES RAWDEN MACLEAN, once known as *'Jackabo'* is now 23 years old, a successful ship's Master, and a husband and father. Although he now lives on the Caribbean island of St Lucia, he soon discovers that the old mystic influences of Africa are still very close.

In September 1838, on the tenth anniversary of the murder of Shaka, the Zulu King, he re-lives a mind-shattering experience from his boyhood past, and is forcibly reminded that he is still *iQawu, Shaka's hero*. What does it mean—and what new challenges will he have to face, even though he's half a world away from Africa? Very quickly, he learns the fate of some of those he left behind in Zululand.

Known to the freed slaves aboard his ship as *Nkosi umLilwane, Lord of the Red Fire,* he remains fiercely loyal to the people of his past and to those enslaved on the plantations of the Caribbean and the southern states of America. A fiery opponent of injustice, his defiance frequently demands violent action. A series of inexplicable events arise and must be dealt with.

The Victorian Age brings great change. As the age of sail gives way to that of steam, Maclean's life is once again in danger from the sea. Disaster follows. It soon becomes clear that his own troubled future is beginning to mirror that of the African people in the far-off land of his youth. Are the *isangoma* Langani's dire warnings beginning to come true?

Events in South Africa move quickly to crisis point. With growing horror, he can only stand and watch as the tragedies of the Anglo-Zulu War begin to unfold. A familiar name from the past comes to his attention and he springs to his defence. The final battle of Ulundi in 1879 brings about the fall of the Zulu kingdom as prophesied by Langani, the diviner, more than 50 years earlier.

Once again, the pattern of Maclean's life seems, by some uncanny alchemy, to follow the rise and fall of the Zulu kingdom. Sadly, one more of the diviner's prophecy begins to come true. Maclean sets off on a desperate journey to England.

Read an excerpt...

Lord of the Red Fire

St Lucia. September 1838.

I n the dead, small hours of night, the lamp swinging from the cabin beams suddenly guttered and went out. In the suffocating blackness, trails of cold and nameless dread began to uncoil in Maclean's stomach. Sweat beaded his forehead and matted the shock of red hair braided into a pigtail at the nape of his neck. The summer lightning flickering on the horizon lit up the interior in eerie flashes of black and white revealing the map table strewn with charts and nautical instruments and the oak table at which he found himself sitting bolt upright.

Beyond the master's cabin, there was only the night sounds of the ship, the flap of sails, creak of ropes and the sigh of hissing waters at the bow as the brig sailed on. No crack of rolling thunder, howling winds or lashing rain…

The enormity of what he'd just experienced made his heart pound like a hammer. He groaned, and clutched his head between his hands. *Dear God… good Christ, save me…* It was all he could say, over and over again.

The remaining fragments of the old, half-remembered dream slowly wisped away from him and the images of the boy and the awesome power unleashed over half a century ago faded away into the ever-changing light and shadows of the present.

Gradually, his pulse slowed and his breathing returned to normal. Soon, all that was left to connect him to what had been so vivid and real a short time ago was the mute display of lightning beyond the cabin – that, and the lingering taste of the red dust of Africa in his mouth.

Still dazed, he darted a glance around the cabin. *Why did it happen now, at this point in time? Last time, I was half a world away, a lad of barely thirteen.*

It had been no dream. Not then, and certainly not now – God knows, the distinctive odour of rain falling on the parched earth and the peppery sting of it on his flesh had been real enough.

The killers he had seen lurking had not been shadows either, he thought, but men of solid flesh and blood; the sinister flash of the blades and the sour, savage stink of betrayal as potent as they had been all those years ago.

On that long ago night, he, Charles Maclean, also known as Jackabo, a lad on the cusp of manhood, had stepped out of the everyday and into the extraordinary, the truly terrifying extraordinary, to witness a series of events from the past. *Not his own...but someone else's.*

He had never been able to explain or quantify what he had experienced that night. In the time it took to blink, he had travelled from a calm moonlit night to a place where a storm was brewing and where a youngster, terrified for his life, was attempting to call down the wrath of his ancestors on the heads of his abusers.

Chills had run down his spine when he'd identified the boy, both by the familiar scowl and the crescent-shaped wound high on his cheekbone. Without doubt, the frightened, yet defiant youngster had been none other than Shaka of the Zulus himself, already carrying the distinctive scar he would bear for the rest of his life.

Too much for his thirteen-year old self to come to terms with, the implications were terrifying beyond belief. But that had not been all he'd seen that night. Time had shifted once again, back to his present, and he'd caught a glimpse of King Shaka's killers lurking in the shadows, their knives glinting in the smouldering flames of a lightning-struck tree.

Beyond the sturdy oak ribs of the *Susan King,* a gust of hot wind began to fill the sails with a snap and a surge of power.

Ten years ago in Africa, it had also been the start of the hot season. Late September, the heat rising in waves from dry, cracked earth, the high shrilling of cicadas in grass that stood brown and lifeless under the pitiless sun, hard beneath his feet as he'd set off running to warn Shaka that his half-brothers were planning to kill him.

Reckless as to his own safety, he had set out alone for kwaDukuza, Shaka's sprawling citadel some twenty-five miles away, with only Fergus, a black and white collie, to protect him from the dangers of the bush.

But, as he was to find out later, Shaka, the warrior king, was already dead, lying bloodied by the open gates of a small out-of-the-way homestead a few miles from kwaDukuza.

Another wave of tropical heat and humidity seeped into the Master's cabin, causing beads of sweat to trickle down Maclean's face. A half-buried memory jolted through him, and his scalp prickled with a sense of inevitability. Something crucial seemed to be lingering on the edge of his consciousness, tantalisingly close and very relevant to the momentous events of the night. *What was it?*

A few days ago, a troubled feeling of loss, or impending loss, had haunted him until almost daylight before vanishing into the dawn, leaving no trace behind. But this was not the same. This *'something'* was sharp, immediate, and demanding.

September... the hot season... September...Africa, half a world away from the Caribbean...

A lurch in the pit of his stomach confirmed what he'd already begun to suspect. Frantically, his brain scanned recent events; bills of lading, port dues, departure dates, arrivals. *For God's sake...think, man! What's the date?*

Realisation hit him like a sledgehammer. His breath came out in a long, slow hiss. *Oh, my God – today's the twenty-fourth...it can't be...*

Exactly ten years ago to the day, on the twenty-fourth of September, 1828, the man who had dominated a thousand days and nights of his young life had met a brutal end at the hands of his half-brothers and a trusted aide.

And, putting aside the nightmare impossibility of what had he'd just experienced he, Charles Maclean, also known as *iQawu,* had set off in a surge of blind loyalty to try to warn Shaka of the Zulus of the impending danger he'd seen.

Maclean's mouth went dry with fear. Dear God, to re-live such an experience for a second time, he thought, to see it all again as clearly as the first time. Either madness or sorcery is at work here. The only question being...is it due to my own mental aberration... *or someone else's sorcery?*

The lightning had died away and was confined to an occasional sullen flicker of temper on the horizon. Anxious to dispel the eerie half-light and restore some semblance of normality, Maclean got to his feet and lit a few candles.

The beeswax smoked, sputtered then settled down, the flames steady in the sultry night air. Suddenly drained of energy, he reached for the firkin of water and drank deeply, water trickling into his beard.

Gradually, the knot of dread in his guts began to unwind. Picking up one of the candlesticks, he made his way through to his sleeping quarters. Ruefully, he eyed the tangle of bedclothes.

Shortly after midnight, he had been jolted awake by a strange rumbling sound. Calling out to the men on watch to investigate, he was surprised when the report came back that they'd found nothing untoward. He'd lain awake, staring into the darkness, unable to drop off again. Finally, he'd given up thoughts of sleep and returned to the Master's cabin to work on the journal he'd begun to keep a few months earlier.

Without warning, the flame of the candle began to flicker, sending shadows leaping in the far corner of the cabin. At the same time, Maclean became aware of the sweet, aromatic smell of beeswax flooding the cabin.

He drew in a sharp breath. Achingly redolent of another time, another place, triggering further bitter sweet memories of his past. The Natal days were a long time ago now, marooned islands in the stream of his life...only now, it seemed, the ribbon of time was unravelling, revealing the invisible fingerprints marked on his soul.

After placing the candlestick to one side, he moved to the curtained-off alcove by the bulkhead. Pulling the curtain aside, he removed the tarpaulin covering a set of sturdy sea kists and peered into the shadowy recesses. Behind them was a battered tin trunk, much smaller than the others.

Moving the larger trunks aside, he braced himself for what would come next. He lifted it out and put it on the floor. Brushing away a layer of cobwebs, he stared down at the small sea chest. Its dark blue paintwork was faded, chipped and rusted in patches. No wonder, considering its history, he thought. That it was still fairly watertight after being half-buried in a mangrove swamp for almost two years said a lot about the skill of the manufacturers.

Printed on the lid in his father's neat hand was his name, the lettering cracked and yellowed by salt water and tropical sun, but still legible:

C.R. MACLEAN
FRASERBURGH, SCOTLAND

He'd been just six months short of his tenth birthday when his father had brought the sea chest home from the Aberdeen ships' chandlers in preparation for his first voyage as an officer apprentice.

A rush of emotion hit him. The hand that had wielded the paintbrush with such skill was now stilled forever. His father, Captain Francis Maclean, had died the year before, mortally stricken by the loss of his youngest son, Henry, a few months earlier.

For a brief moment, Maclean saw the twinkle in his father's eye as he'd stood back to survey his handiwork, wiping his hands on a rag smelling of turpentine.

'Just in case you mislay it, Charlie,' he'd said, teasing him. 'One way or other, it'll find its way back to the Broch – whether you're with it or no'.'

The lid was stiff from disuse. As he prised it open in a creak of rusty metal, a whiff of herbs, dried grass and the acrid fragrance of wood smoke drifted out. Laying aside several layers of garments spotted with mould, Maclean's fingers came in contact with the hard edge of a wooden box.

Carefully he lifted it out, then stepped back and stared long and hard at it, conscious of the erratic beating of his heart.

About three feet long by a foot wide, and the same in depth, the box had been carved from solid ebony. The dark wood glowed with the warmth of the rich soil, summer suns and long seasons of rain that had nurtured the living tree. Though the delicate brass hinges, lock and key intimated the Arab influence of Dar es Salaam or Zanzibar, the ebony held the earthy essence of Africa itself, age-old and mysterious.

Maclean's forefinger traced the smooth curves created by the skilful fingers of the unknown carver. The man had been no follower of the Prophet, for the rounded bellies, full breasts and voluptuous curves of the human figures scorned the restrictions of Islam.

No need for him to wonder how long it had been since he'd last opened the box. He wasn't likely to forget finding it lying on his bunk the day before sailing out of the bay of eThekwini for the last time. By then, Shaka had been dead for almost three months. And Dingane, his stepbrother, one of his killers, was now the ruler of Zululand.

The sight and touch of the box brought a host of memories flooding back. 'Oh, God,' he muttered. 'And here's me thinking it'd all been stowed away for good.'

Reaching into one of the drawers in his desk, Maclean took out a bunch of keys and sorted through them until he found the one he wanted. Slipping it off the main ring, he regarded it with mixed emotions.

On either side of the small gilt key, six brightly coloured beads had been knotted into the thin strip of plaited rhino hide to keep it in place. Red, green and yellow – the colours of the royal house of Zulu, Shaka's colours.

Rachel, only Rachel would have been so thoughtful... Maclean felt the sudden sting of unshed tears, the memory of the former slave's kindness and work-worn hands suddenly overwhelming.

After discovering what was in the box, he'd run blindly halfway round the bay to reach the only place he felt safe – with Rachel. It was only afterwards he found that he still had the small key clutched in his sweaty hand.

Once again, the shadows in the corner leaped and flickered, changing shape. Suddenly, the cabin seemed small and stifling. Maclean felt it begin to dip and sway around him. *Too close – too many ghosts.*

Flinging open the cabin door, he stepped out on to the deck and drew in deep breaths of salty night air. Aware of the tremors running like a fever through him, all he could do was bow his head in silent resignation.

It was almost ten years since he'd last set eyes on what was inside the box. A little longer would make no difference.

WOULD YOU LIKE TO RECEIVE PRIOR NOTICE OF THE BOOK'S PUBLICATION AND FIND OUT HOW YOU CAN GET A FREE ADVANCE COPY?

TO LEARN MORE
www.stravaig-books.com

Before you go, don't forget to LEAVE A REVIEW for this book on Amazon. Thank you!

Made in the USA
Lexington, KY
23 May 2018